Dauntless

YVONNE M THOMPSON

Cover design: Sleepy Fox Studio

Editing: Storycentric Editing

Map created using Inkarnate
with elements from FantasyMapSymbols

Author photograph: Irena Vlach

ISBN 978-1-7773190-1-4

For my parents, who taught me to believe in my dreams.

Table of Contents

Dauntless

The King is Dead

King Roland staggered backward, his hands fumbling to stem the tide of blood. His mind reeled as shock set in and he turned to his beloved wife and queen.

"Ceci?"

The word shattered into silence.

Cecilia lay upon the floor, motionless, raven locks spread around her. For a brief moment, he thought she was still alive, until he saw the red dyeing her collar of pearls, crimson beads like rubies dripping from her slender throat.

It had been quick and painless at least, her expression serene and beautiful, as if she were merely having a sweet dream.

He reached for her, but his knees buckled beneath him and he slid to the floor.

Roland's thoughts strayed to his daughter. Their darling Caro. All their plans... What did they count for anymore? Now misery and sorrow awaited their only child, who would inherit his heavy crown and the burden of his sins.

The final slow beats of Roland's heart pumped weakly in his chest.

"Why?" he whispered, gazing up at his murderer, who stared back impassively. The dagger was held loosely at his side, droplets of blood staining the once-pristine white carpet.

The man's lips moved, and Roland struggled to make out his words, at first unintelligible, then: "...become the sacrifice."

Long Live the Queen

"The King is dead. Long live the Queen."

The formal words fell upon Caro's ears, and she struggled to register them. She looked up and met the sorrowful gaze of the messenger, who was both her tutor and the court physician.

"Gaius..." she whispered, forgetting decorum in the shock of the moment. "Is it true?"

He nodded at the question in her pleading eyes. "I'm sorry, Your Highness... Your Majesty," he corrected himself somberly and bowed low, his long blond hair drifting over his shoulders.

"How?" The word stuck in her throat, but she forced it out, her voice hoarse.

"They were murdered," he replied in the calm, even tone of a medical professional. "The king's chamberlain discovered them and summoned me at once. I examined them myself," he added, as if that fact would offer her some manner of comfort.

"I want to see them," Caro tried, but Gaius shook his head, handsome features drawn with worry.

"I would not advise it, Your Majesty. It would be better to remember them as they were."

A cavernous hole swallowed her heart, and she gave a slight nod. "I will defer to your judgment, Physician."

Gaius breathed a small sigh of relief.

"Do you have any suspects?" Caro addressed her question to the senior military officer who accompanied Gaius.

"None, Your Majesty," General Luther replied. "But rest assured, we shall not let their killer remain at large. I have ordered security within the palace tightened for your safety."

He wore a jacket in the deep green livery of the royal army, with a badge displaying the royal crest upon his left breast and epaulets upon his shoulders from which draped lengths of braided gold cord. With short, bristly auburn hair and sincere gray-blue eyes, he had been her father's most loyal servant.

"Thank you, General," Caro said, her voice quavering only slightly. "If you will excuse me."

Caro rose with a grace she fought to maintain. They all bowed as she swept out of the room, followed hurriedly by her bodyguard, Stelian.

"Your Highness—er, Majesty..." he stammered, stumbling over her new title.

She gritted her teeth, knowing it would be a common scenario in the coming days. *Your Majesty.* That title belonged to her father and mother, not to *her*.

She clenched her fist as she continued to her bedchamber, barely acknowledging those who bowed in the hall. By now, everyone knew, though Gaius had been quick to deliver the news himself, and glances of pity and trepidation preceded the tipped heads.

What now? It was the question running through all their minds, and Caro couldn't blame them. But she couldn't stop to reassure her subjects. Not yet.

She blinked away tears and quickened her pace as her door came into view. Stelian rushed ahead to open it for her.

"I do not wish to be disturbed," she said in a clipped tone.

The door shut behind her, followed by the shuffling of Stelian's feet as he dutifully positioned himself in the hall as a barrier to any intrusion. Finally alone, she froze. Her breath was the only sound in the silence of her room.

A tear splashed upon the marble floor, and then another.

The grief she had repressed with the distinguished pride of her rank came pouring out, and she couldn't hold it in any longer. Her knees felt weak and she stumbled to her vanity, leaning heavily upon it, her arms shaking.

She wanted nothing more than to tear apart her room, to smash the delicate glass vials of perfume, to rip her clothes out of her closet and wrap herself in a cocoon of silken fabric, to scream with the sheer unfairness of it all. Anything to give voice to the torment raging in her heart.

A week previous, she had celebrated her seventeenth birthday. She recalled the light of joy on her parents' faces as they raised a toast, the pride of her tutor Gaius, the adoration of her aunt Ezalia. A towering pile of presents: gowns, jewelry, wall hangings.

Now her parents' joy was frozen in the cold stillness of death, and only sorrow lined Gaius's face. The presents were hollow and empty.

She spotted her mother's shawl draped over the dressing screen. Caro had admired it since she was little, its thinly spun maroon fabric with black embroidered roses and beaded trim, and had been delighted beyond words when her mother gifted it to her. Her hands shook as she reached for the garment.

"Why..?" she whispered, her throat aching. "Why did you have to leave me alone? Papa, Mama...?"

Caro drew in a raspy breath as she collapsed against the wall and sank to the floor, burying her face in the soft material to muffle her sobs.

"Caro? May I come in?"

She lifted her head at a soft knock on the door. She'd instructed she wasn't to be disturbed, but Stelian would never try to stand up to her formidable aunt.

Caro sniffed. "Sure, Aunt Ez."

She rose, rubbing her face with her sleeve as Ezalia slipped through the door carrying a hinged box, which she placed on the bed.

While Caro's mother Cecilia had possessed sculpted brows, an upturned nose, and a small jaw, her Aunt Ezalia's features were more aquiline, giving her a mature, refined appearance, with blue eyes rather than green. She was also witty and charming, the most fashionable woman of court known for holding popular salons and gatherings, and Caro had always adored her.

Ezalia's forehead creased, then she smiled. "The Accession ceremony is coming up. Can't have you looking all puffy-eyed."

Caro nodded as Ezalia cradled her cheek.

"Oh, my sweet girl... Whatever happens, you know we're here for you."

Tears burst through the banks once more, and Ezalia dabbed them away. "Now, let's get you all tidied up. Everyone will be expecting their queen to look her best."

Caro could tell Ezalia had been crying too, faint traces of concealer visible around the corners of her eyes. Cecilia had been her younger sister, and they had been close since they were children. The loss must be hard for Ezalia, but she was putting on a brave face for her niece. The least Caro could do was the same for her people. While her own grief was personal, filled with memories of happy times long past, theirs was naturally filled with apprehension for the future.

"We're going to have to commission an entirely new wardrobe," Ezalia was muttering to herself as she examined each one of the gowns in Caro's wardrobe in an attempt to find one suitable for the Accession. Every noble of name would be in attendance, and the thought gave Caro jitters.

"Ah! This one will work, I think, with a few adjustments," Ezalia declared triumphantly, sweeping a gown off the hook.

It was one of Caro's least favorite dresses, a dark teal with gold lace and far too much adornment for her taste. Of course, Ezalia was right—it was perfect to portray her new formality as queen, as well as the sobriety of the occasion.

Caro peeled off her day dress as Ezalia laced her into the gown. This was the duty of a maidservant, but it felt somehow comforting to have her aunt attend to her in such an intimate way.

Ezalia rummaged through the jewelry box she'd brought along. She found a necklace of gems the same bluish-green shade as the dress and fastened it around Caro's neck. She then snipped off the large, tacky ribbon at the center of the bodice and replaced it with a matching brooch. Finally, Ezalia withdrew a gold tiara inlaid with pearls, affixing it into Caro's upswept curls. Though Caro had effectively become queen the moment the previous king had died, she would not wear the royal crown until her official coronation. Ezalia had anticipated this, and provided for it.

Caro examined herself in the mirror as Ezalia closed the box with a satisfied click. Tiers of ivory lace cascaded to her wrists, and the layered satin skirt swished with her every step. The gown was heavier than she was used to, as was the diadem on her head, subtly reminding her of the weight of her new responsibilities.

She tried not to feel crushed by it.

Ezalia was touching up Caro's makeup when there was another knock.

"Lord Gaius, you can't just—" Stelian protested as Gaius poked his head around the door.

"It's okay, Stelian," Caro said sympathetically, and her bodyguard gave a helpless sigh as he returned to his post outside.

"How are you?" Gaius inquired.

"I've been better," Caro admitted.

"You handled the news well. I'm proud of you. I'm just sorry I was the one who had to deliver it."

"I'm glad it was you, Gaius," she said sincerely.

"All gussied up for the Accession ceremony, I see," he noted as Ezalia liberally applied rouge to Caro's cheeks and lips.

She twisted her hands in her lap at the thought of all the nobles staring up at her.

"I can give you something for your nerves," Gaius offered.

She shook her head. "I'll be fine."

He massaged her neck with steady rhythmic motions, and her tense shoulders loosened. "It can't be all bad, though. Maybe you'll meet a young man who catches your interest?"

"Gaius, that's hardly appropriate," Ezalia chided, and Gaius shrugged, winking.

"Sorry, I couldn't resist. I'll make some tea to settle you before the ceremony."

Despite Ezalia's remonstration, Gaius's grin was infectious, and Caro felt herself relax. He had been so solemn before. It was a relief to have her easygoing tutor back.

He vanished, then returned a moment later with a steaming cup of mint tea. It was just the thing she needed to perk her up, and had the added benefit of settling the nausea fluttering in her stomach.

"Your Majesty," Stelian ventured. "They're ready."

Ezalia squeezed Caro's hands, then she and Gaius departed.

Caro shifted her feet and fussed with her gown. "How do I look?"

Stelian was three years older than Caro, a lieutenant in the army. He had hazel eyes and brown hair, a little more reddish than her own, shorn close at the back with short bangs. He had been her bodyguard since she was fourteen, as well as her sparring partner and confidante. He was brusque but quiet, with a serious disposition, and she always felt she could rely on him.

Stelian bowed low. "Like a queen, Your Majesty."

The words had filled her with intense discomfort before, but somehow she felt reassured. Stelian always knew the right thing to say.

As Caro strode down the hall with Stelian a half step behind, she pensively stroked the king's signet ring, the royal seal raised beneath her fingertips: two winged lions bearing a crown. It had been hurriedly resized so it didn't slip off her finger, and would be altered more permanently later.

Faced with the impending proceedings, she couldn't help a flicker of unease. She was still so young. Could she possibly lead her country? The answer, of course, was that she had no choice. If she didn't present a strong front, the other nobles might doubt her abilities and quarrel among themselves, or perhaps elect one of her uncles to take command instead.

Although the throne automatically passed to Caro as Roland's child, it didn't mean there couldn't be an argument made for one of them to rule as regent, at least until she was of age. In some ways, that might be wise, but she somehow felt like she would be shirking her duties and disappointing her father, who had held such hopes for her. The last thing this kingdom needed was internal strife, not when there was already so much uncertainty.

Caro paused outside the door and took a deep breath before entering the room where the Accession ceremony had been convened. One day at a time. She could do this.

The majestic throne room was the center of the royal palace, and it never failed to take Caro's breath away. There were three entrances which adjoined the room: one for the king's use, one for the courtiers, and a set of double doors used for official audiences, where a visitor would have to walk the full length of the hall to reach the throne.

The room was built entirely of white marble, the polished walls decorated with elaborate sculptural detailing painted with gold leaf, reflecting the wealth and opulence of the kingdom. Great candelabras lined the hall while crystal chandeliers hung from above, bathing the space in sparkling luminescence. The floor was inlaid with patterns of shimmering hue on a gold background, the moulded ceilings painted with murals so beautiful the eye could not help but be drawn to them. One wall had floor-to-ceiling windows leading to a balcony that overlooked the courtyard while the other was lined with mirrors, creating the illusion of scattered light.

Unlike a coronation, which would be full of pomp and celebration, this ceremony was more somber, and Caro was keenly aware of all eyes on her as she made her way to the throne. Due to Luther's increased security, soldiers stood at regular intervals and saluted as she passed. She kept her gaze facing forward, her expression neutral but serene; she'd spent hours rehearsing in front of the mirror to get her look of "regal indifference" just right.

It was an exceptionally rare occasion for the nearly two hundred nobles of the country to gather at once, and they were all packed together like herring. Of course, there were those whose properties were simply too far to travel on such short notice, but all of them would be making their way to the capital in the following week to attend her parents' funeral, and they would swear their fealty in private then.

She demurely lifted the hem of her dress so as not to trip, which would be a terrible first impression, and mounted the steps to the dais. She turned, sweeping her skirt aside with what she hoped was a graceful flick of her wrist.

Caro fixed her eyes upon a small spot on the opposite wall above the heads of those gathered. "Your Royal Highnesses, Lords and Ladies," she began. "Due to the sudden death of my dear father, I am called to assume the duties and responsibilities of the sovereignty. My constant endeavor will be to walk in his footsteps in undertaking the burden that now passes to me, and to work for the good and prosperity of my people.

"At this time of deep sorrow, it is a profound consolation to me to be assured of the loyalty and affection you have all shown as I accept this difficult task. I trust you to support me in the days to come as we all heal from the grief of this most lamentable loss, and in the years to follow as I devote myself to this kingdom. May I be a worthy successor to the great monarchs who have preceded me."

Caro finished her heartfelt speech and took her seat. It was strange sitting in her father's throne, and she felt like she was going to be swallowed up by it. It was stately and gold with deep green velvet upholstery and a high curved back, framed by two winged lions standing proudly, their sculpted feathers forming the sides. A cushion had been placed behind her to keep her from slouching, and she concentrated on maintaining the proper posture. Another cushion served as a boost so she could place her elbows comfortably upon the armrests.

A guard knelt and set down a pillow for her feet. She was quite a bit shorter than her father had been, and didn't wish to leave her legs dangling like a toddler in her high chair.

Caro, now settled, gave a short nod to the moderator. He stepped forward with a scroll of parchment, which he handed to her.

She unrolled it and read aloud. "I, Queen Caro Amarynth of Artemisia, according to the enactments which govern my realm, do solemnly swear to uphold and maintain those enactments to the best of my powers according to law."

The moderator held the scroll open upon a silver plate and handed Caro a pen, with which she wrote her practiced, stately signature. He then lifted a melting spoon and dripped violet wax upon the parchment. Caro reverently removed the signet ring and pressed the seal into the surface.

The Accession Declaration made and signed, the time had come for each of the nobles to swear their fealty to her as their new monarch.

Caro surveyed the faces in the room, each arranged in order of their status. There were many she didn't recognize, but others were familiar, and her heart swelled to see them standing before her. One by one, they approached the dais, and she nodded to each as they spoke the customary oath.

Her grandfather Ezekiel was the first to approach, as the highest ranked noble below the reigning monarch. His estate at Agassey was at least two weeks' journey by horse, and it had been coincidence he was in the city seeing to some business when he received the terrible news. His face was lined and weary with the all-consuming grief Caro shared, but he held himself with a stoic bearing. While he was sometimes gruff, he had always been kind.

His knees creaked as he knelt at her feet, leaning upon his ram-headed cane for support. "With the gracious permission of Her Divine Majesty, Queen Caro Amarynth of Artemisia, I, Grand Duke Ezekiel Garsiv, swear to be faithful and true, without deceit, for as long as I shall live," he said in his deep, resounding voice.

"I grant and behold it," Caro replied, and held out her hand for him to kiss her ring.

Next came Duke Vittorius, Caro's uncle. As her father Roland's younger brother, he more appropriately bore the rank of second prince; however, he had adopted the position of the Minister of Trade and the title of duke which came with it, superseding his own—though he had no patronym appended to his name, his lineage was inviolable. He had always been responsible and diligent, serving his brother the king with both duty and affection, though their relationship was strained at times.

After Vittorius was Prince Arvind. Unlike his brothers, Arvind was known for whiling away his time in idle delights, and Roland had never approved of his indolent ways. Arvind had doted on Caro when she was young, but a rift had developed between the brothers, and after that Caro rarely saw him except for formal occasions.

The Duchess Ezalia Mavella was next, and she sent Caro a secret smile. Cecilia, though a loving and affectionate mother, had rather enjoyed the privileges that came with being queen and spent most of her days hobnobbing with diplomats and hosting parties and galas. Caro detested superficial social gatherings and did not share her enthusiasm. Ezalia had filled the void, raising Caro through many of her formative years. She was like a second mother, and Caro loved her aunt dearly.

Countess Andrine Iduna was Vittorius's daughter, five years older than Caro. Her mother had died when she was young, and with Vittorius often away on business trips, the two had grown up in the palace much like sisters.

Her husband Earl Malcolm Dahl followed, the lone remaining member of the immediate royal family. He was a loving husband and father, and Caro had been overjoyed to see her cousin so deliriously happy when she had attended their wedding. Of course, their four-year-old twins were exempt from this ceremony, and were being entertained by a nanny somewhere they wouldn't disturb the proceedings.

The rest of the nobles and sitting lords, Gaius included, followed suit, and Caro wracked her brain to recall their names. Many of them lived at their residences outside the palace, and Caro had met them once or twice at most. Now she was expected to remember each and every one's title and rank. Luckily, she was good at memorizing lists, and so while she could not identify them by face, she knew exactly where they fell in the queue.

After what seemed like hours, Caro lost track of how many nobles had recited the oath. Her throat was parched from all of the replies she had recited. Still, according to the tally she was keeping in her head, she was nearing the end... which was a good thing, because she was starting to feel a little woozy.

"Divine Majesty," a smooth voice said, snapping her attention back to the present.

Lord Zhelyas Ralston was a minor noble and, as per the rankings of court, one of the last to approach the throne. He rarely attended soirées, and Caro tried to place where she had seen him before. He was handsome, with a sharp jawline and a slight smile tugging at his lips. Dark bangs drifted over his eyes, and the look he gave her was filled with an emotion she could not quite place.

Gaius's jibing words wafted across her brain and she mentally shooed them away, giving Zhelyas a regal nod as he rose. As soon as he turned away, she gulped down a goblet of water as modestly as she could.

After the formalities were concluded, the nobles trickled out of the throne room into the grand hall, chatting with old acquaintances or taking in the sights.

A magnificent set of staircases branched out from one level to the next, creating a dynamic, airy space, the play of light accentuating its vastness. High above stood statues of the historic predecessors of the royal family. Malianme, the first Queen of Artemisia, stood in the center, outfitted in draping robes with a resplendent crown upon her head. To her left was Guillam, her eldest son, who had only reigned for a short while, standing courageous and proud. His sister Guinevre stood to the right, holding the star of virtue. She had inherited the throne after her brother's untimely death, and issued the royal line from which Caro was descended.

A hundred years of royal lineage, ending with her. Caro avoided looking into their eyes as she passed beneath; she felt like they were watching her with their unblinking stone gaze.

At the base of each staircase sat a pair of winged lions, echoing the royal crest. They were magical beasts said to have been tamed by Aryama, the hero of lore. The legend was as old as the country itself: Aryama had once been mortal, a hero by any definition of the word, and he had loved the beautiful goddess Mahira. Her father Garjan, the fierce god of storms, disapproved of their match and set a number of trials for

Aryama in order to prove his worth, but he triumphed over each task, finally winning the hand of fair Mahira and a place among the gods themselves. Aryama had become quite a beloved figure, and the legend of his famous tasks was a common motif in both art and literature. As to how the lions became the crest of Artemisia, no records remained, but they were easily the most recognizable symbol in the country.

Located on the second floor was a theater where stage plays and operas were often performed, second only to the magnificent opera house at Agassey. *Gisela and Darim, Aryama and Mahira, Lady Butterfly, The Lament of Lucia*, and *The Golden Ring* were a few of the performances which Caro had adored as a child, watching the stage with rapt attention as the actors poured their hearts out in poetry and song. Love stories and adventures like that would stir the imagination of any restless girl.

The third floor was reserved for royalty and the upper echelon resident nobles, as well as their attendants and bodyguards. Caro's own quarters and those of her parents were located there, along with a private library, sitting rooms, banquet halls, and offices.

Caro's rooms overlooked the garden, and she loved taking in the view as patrons meandered along the pathways, many of them couples admiring the beautiful flowers or those looking for a little solitude from the hustle and bustle of castle life.

All these diversions and more would keep Caro's visitors entertained, and though it was quite the onslaught, the castle was large enough to easily house the newly-arrived contingent of nobility which had descended en masse upon the grounds.

Not all of them were planning to stay, however, and Vittorius approached Caro. Though younger than her father had been, Vittorius's short hair and close-shaven beard were already peppered with gray. His features were more stern and chiseled than Roland's, and his gaze was as keen as an eagle's.

"Apologies, Your Majesty, but I should return to my estate. As Minister, I must be prepared to address the unease of our trading partners during this uncertain time."

"Don't let us keep you," Gaius said tartly, and Caro sent him a quelling glance. The two men famously did not get along.

"Of course, Uncle," Caro replied with fondness. "I will be relying upon you, as my father did."

"Don't worry, I'll take care of her," Arvind added, and squeezed Caro's shoulders.

The youngest of the brothers, Arvind was clean-shaven with a sculpted jawline, coppery hair, and silver-blue eyes. Heavy brows and a hint of a smirk reinforced his playboy reputation.

Caro's skin crawled and she shrugged away from his touch, stepping aside under the pretense of chatting with Ezalia.

Vittorius frowned sternly at the gesture, which was far too casual toward a queen. "I'm sure Her Majesty will be depending on you as well to take over some of the duties of the palace. That is, if you can tear yourself from your leisurely pursuits."

Arvind scowled at his censure, then smirked. "Of course, Vito. I wouldn't have it any other way." He gave a flourishing bow and sauntered off.

"Honestly, that man," Ezalia huffed.

Vittorius watched his brother leave, then turned back to Caro. "Forgive me. Arvind and Roland had a falling out, but he is still my little brother. I can't help but be worried for him."

Caro smiled. "If I had an older brother, Uncle, I'd want him to be just like you."

He appeared somewhat flustered by her praise and cleared his throat. "Be that as it may, please do not hesitate to come to me if you need anything, Your Majesty."

As per tradition, the funeral was held nine days after the death of the reigning monarch. Caro gazed out the window into the gloomy sky. The sun was hiding behind a veil of shadow, as if it were afraid to show its face on such a sorrowful day.

She had cried for a full hour that morning until she couldn't cry anymore in an attempt to keep her composure during the ceremony. Her throat was sore and she was exhausted from the effort, but she felt somehow lightened. Her own grief spent for the moment, she could now face her people and share in theirs.

Caro descended the castle steps to the carriage, all in black with a collar of black pearls around her neck. A veil of scalloped black lace draped down her hair and shoulders, affixed by a tiara. She carried a bouquet of purple flowers known as promethia, which symbolized fidelity and devotion. Caro had admired the delicate blossoms before, but never understood their meaning as acutely as she did now.

The citizens of the capital, as well as many from bordering lands, had journeyed to pay their respects. They lined the streets to mourn and watched in silence as the king and queen's bodies were taken to their final resting place in the royal crypt. The procession was long and slow, the coffins shrouded in black cloth carried by an open carriage for all to see.

It was mid-autumn, and there was a chill in the air. The vibrant foliage of the maple trees blanketed the roadways, forming a carpet of orange and red beneath the carriage wheels.

Caro kept her gaze focused ahead, staring at a small flaw in the upholstery. During the coronation, she would wave and share in her people's joy, but the moment called for her to be stoic, a face of strength and courage for them. Ezalia squeezed her hand secretly, and Caro drew comfort from the warmth of her aunt's love through the lace gloves she wore.

The funeral traditions were old and established, but it was an added sorrow that both rulers had passed together. The king had been several years the queen's senior, and she had been expected to live on after his death. Ezalia, as the queen's elder sister, fulfilled the role that would have been expected of the king's dowager, offering Caro silent support as their carriage followed the cortège.

Throughout the service, Caro could sense all eyes on her. The heads of state from her own country and neighboring nations were in attendance, and she could feel the weight of their expectations.

As she stood before them all to deliver the eulogy, Caro clasped her hands to keep them from shaking. "When the death of the king and queen was announced to me, a great and overwhelming sorrow filled my heart, one which I believe all my people share, as do those who knew them. They were loved and respected, both as rulers and as people, far beyond this fair country over which they reigned. The dignity of their lives, their virtue, their sense of duty, but also their charm and their joy—all these won them admiration, from those who line the streets outside to those whose gaze I meet here now. They were wise and shrewd, but also kind to those with title and those without, a generosity beyond compare. They were my parents, and I daresay your companions. Dear to my heart and yours, their acclaim will live on even in their absence. May Aryama grant me the strength to bear my sorrow, to mourn with my people, and then take up the crown with dignity and live up to the example they have shown."

A small trace of Caro's overwhelming grief broke through her walls, and a single tear trickled down her cheek, dampening the black lace collar of her mourning gown. Her speech concluded, she approached the coffin.

After the ceremony, it would be taken to a sepulcher which would be Roland and Cecilia's final resting place among their forebears, but for now the polished marble box, carved with a relief of the royal crest and draped with a garland of fragrant eucalyptus, was in full display of the mourners. The garland represented the journey to the afterlife and the wish of the deceased to heal the regrets and worries of those left behind.

Kneeling, Caro placed the bouquet of promethia reverently before the coffin. "I swear I will avenge your deaths," she vowed, so quietly no one else could hear. "No matter the cost, I will have my retribution."

She rose, and the sacristan signaled to the bell-ringer. The tolling of the dolorous funerary bells rang in Caro's heart, echoing throughout all the land of Artemisia.

Sea Change

After the funeral, things in the palace returned to normal and plans were made for the coronation. The nobility shed their mourning attire, Caro last of all, and as the months passed, a sense of cheer and optimism for the future emerged. After all, a new queen was to be crowned—it was a time to set aside the tragedy of the past and rejoice.

"No, not those garish orange flowers! The new queen isn't an old maid, she's a young woman. We must emphasize her innocence and purity!"

The Countess Radella Alvara was around Ezalia's age, with a beaming smile, brown eyes, and dark blond hair which she wore up in an elegant roll, tousled curls draping across her forehead. Radella was a proud, diligent woman and Vittorius's assistant in his work as Minister of Trade. In addition to her political duties, she had taken it upon herself to serve as the coordinator for the momentous day.

Three months had gone by since the funeral, and it was now midwinter, not the most auspicious time for a coronation. The actual event would take months to plan and would likely be held in the spring.

Innocence and purity weren't exactly the highest traits on Caro's list—she'd prefer to be known for her acumen and fortitude—but Radella knew what she was doing. At least, Caro hoped she did. Cecilia had delighted in planning parties and galas, but Caro was less enthused with the prospect. Still, she had selected color palettes from among those suggested, and they had discussed decor, lighting, and the overall aesthetic.

Radella was also a keen woman, and while the floral choice was of apparent significance, Caro more highly valued her sagacity. Besides the logistics regarding the organization of the event, she had also compiled the seating plan for the meal to follow and miraculously managed to situate everyone so that they were offended neither by their placement in relation to their rank, nor their dinner partners—a feat unto itself. She also handled the task of commissioning the invitations, which Caro personally signed and stamped until her wrist was sore.

"Honestly, does nobody read my instructions?" Radella huffed, then realized Caro was watching and bowed low. "Your Majesty."

"Countess, is there anything the matter?"

"Of course not, my queen," Radella replied.

"Please let me know if there is any assistance you require."

Radella seized upon her offer. "Well, we do have a new set of swatches for the table linens."

Caro sighed inwardly as she handed over the fistful of fabric. Peach seemed to be the dominant color scheme, though Radella had managed to somehow incorporate the soothing pale green which was Caro's preferred hue. The resulting combination was unexpectedly attractive. Caro peered at the swatches in varying shades of cream and picked one that seemed appealing.

"Thank you, Your Majesty. I will not trouble you further," Radella said, evidently eager to return to her task.

Caro gave a regal nod and swept off before she was consulted for her opinion on dishware or some such thing.

As she strode down the hall, she passed two women who were holding a book between them and giggling. The brunette pointed to a particular passage, and the one with copper-blond hair blushed.

"Your Majesty," the two ladies said in unison and bowed.

She gave them a polite nod, sneaking a peek at what they were reading. She glimpsed the title emblazoned on the orange cover: *The Desert Prince*.

"You are far too young to be reading that," Ezalia chided, hooking her arm and dragging her off.

The two noblewomen glanced at each other and dissolved once more into giggles.

Caro sighed, allowing herself to be steered away. "But why, Aunt Ez? It's the most popular book at court. Isn't it my responsibility as queen to know how my subjects are entertaining themselves?"

Ezalia gave her a sideways look, and Caro winked. "I had to try."

"Don't be in a hurry to grow up too fast," Ezalia said fondly, stroking her cheek. "You'll find out about romance soon enough, but from the heart of someone who loves you, not some silly book."

Caro smiled, touched. "Okay, Auntie," she said, then gave a puckish grin. "But after I experience love, I'm definitely reading it!"

"You're incorrigible!" Ezalia laughed, hugging her close.

Caro's neck prickled and she glanced over her shoulder to see a familiar face watching her, dark eyes staring from beneath unruly bangs.

Their eyes met for a brief moment, then he bowed, returning to his conversation with her uncle Arvind across the hall.

"Auntie, who is that man?"

"Hmm?" Ezalia followed her gaze. "Lord Zhelyas Ralston, I believe. Let's see. He's from Rivellia, a country to the north of Drusus on our western border. His father is a peer there, the Marquis Ralston Cartoras, equivalent to our title of margrave. However, where it was once a powerful rank in Rivellia, his influence has waned, leaving Zhelyas among one of the lesser nobles in the Artemisian court."

Caro nodded. That explained his position during the ceremony.

"Why do you ask?" Ezalia inquired. "Has he spoken to you?"

"Not in so many words."

A slight frown traced Ezalia's lips. "He may be handsome, but rather too old for you. And as a queen, he is far beneath your station."

Caro blushed and waved her hands. "I'm not attracted to him," she said, trying to explain her impression. "It's just, the Accession ceremony was the first time I recall meeting him. He stared at me so intently, I almost forgot what I was meant to be saying, and now I keep seeing him everywhere. It's mildly unsettling."

"Do you feel threatened?" Ezalia's disapproval had morphed into motherly concern, like a lioness protecting her cub.

Caro smiled to allay her fears. "It's nothing like that. I'm sure I'm imagining things."

"Well, you are queen now, so it's natural the nobles will be drawn to you to curry favor, even if they are not permitted to approach you directly." Ezalia's lip curled slightly. "And he appears to be an associate of Prince Arvind, whose own presence has increased in court. Inform me immediately if Zhelyas breaks protocol and tries to speak with you. Otherwise, try to push it to the back of your mind."

Caro gave a slight nod.

"Besides," her aunt added slyly, "I can introduce you to a number of men who would be much more appropriate to your exalted birth. You're an attractive young woman, and I know many who would be interested in courting you."

She grinned, and Caro flushed to the tips of her toes. "Auntie!"

"I'm teasing you, dear, but you should at least consider it. Taking a consort would strengthen your political situation, especially if you consider the suit of princes and highborn lords from our allying countries."

Caro sighed. She didn't think she could handle any romantic entanglements right now. "While that may be true, I would like to focus my attention on my people for the time being. After my coronation, my queenship will be established for the world to see. I might entertain thoughts of a husband then."

Ezalia smiled and gave a bow. "You are very wise, Your Majesty."

Caro was relieved the conversation was over, but she couldn't help but wonder what Zhelyas's intentions were.

The general unease in the castle was lifting, and even Caro was buoyed by the impending celebration, although a weight still hung in her heart. They had not yet caught the assassin, and the military remained on high alert, patrolling the palace grounds day and night.

"I don't understand why this is taking so long," Caro said, trying not to snap at General Luther despite the frustration bubbling inside her.

Luther bowed. "I'm sorry, Your Majesty. I feel responsible. The matter with your parents hasn't been resolved, and I regret it deeply."

"It's been nearly three months. Are you telling me you have nothing to show for it?"

"Forgive me," Luther said, and hung his head.

Caro turned away to hide her irritation and pinched the bridge of her nose, trying to keep calm. "What progress *have* you made?" she tried, deciding it was a less confrontational question.

The heels of Luther's boots clicked together as he stood at attention. "After the discovery of the crime, interrogations were conducted immediately. First, the guards, nobles, servants, and staff were questioned; then checkpoints were set up throughout the city, followed by interviews with citizens on the streets. We also followed up on all the tips which were submitted, but none provided any useful information."

"So my parents' murderer is going to escape?" she demanded, spinning to face him, unable to hold back her fury anymore. "How is that justice?"

"We may have to conclude that their deaths were the result of an assassination ordered by a rival king or disgruntled trading partner," Luther said slowly, quailing beneath her livid glare. "The security restrictions are in place to protect you, should this be the case."

"For how long?" she countered. "Am I to be looking over my shoulder my entire life?"

Luther had no reply.

Caro dug her nails into her palms and took a steadying breath. "I don't care how long it takes, General. You will re-examine every last shred of evidence you have gathered. Do I make myself clear?"

Luther looked up as Stelian entered the barracks.

He lifted an eyebrow. It was unusual to see the boy anywhere other than by the queen's side since he had been appointed her bodyguard three years prior. King Roland had asked Luther to nominate his most stalwart and skilled soldier for the task, and he could think of none better.

"What can I do for you, Lieutenant?" he asked politely. Although Luther was Stelian's superior, logic dictated he was on the queen's business.

"Her Majesty wished for me to assist with the investigation, General," he replied.

"Much appreciated."

"You mentioned during the briefing that you had collected a rather unwieldy amount of testimony in the hours following the murders."

Luther shrugged. "Perhaps you may be able to shed more light upon it," he said, gesturing vaguely to a desk with overflowing boxes of scrolls and more on the shelves nearby.

Stelian rolled up his sleeves and set to work, sifting through the documents and arranging them in neat little piles. "Did the palace staff provide any useful intelligence?"

Luther shook his head. "There were no suspicious persons within the castle at the time, and the guards on duty saw nobody lingering in the halls. The night watchmen reported nothing untoward on the grounds either."

Stelian nodded to himself. "How exactly did the events of that night play out?"

"From the physical signs interpreted by Lord Gaius, the queen was attacked first. The royal couple had returned to their rooms and were in the process of readying themselves for bed, as evidenced by the fact she was in her nightdress but had not yet removed her jewelry. It appears she was preparing to do so when the killer approached from behind, slitting her throat before she could scream."

"I see," Stelian murmured, sounding slightly unnerved. "Go on."

"The door to the balcony was open, suggesting the king might have been distracted. He didn't call for his guards but instead picked up a candlestick to brandish as a weapon. His effort was futile; the killer easily overwhelmed him, and he was stabbed in the stomach by a thin blade, a lethal wound. It would have taken mere minutes for him to bleed out." Luther's voice cracked as he related the cold facts.

"King Roland was not a feeble man. Anyone who could match his prowess would have to be fit and strong."

"I concur," Luther agreed.

"The ball started just after the evening meal," Stelian mused after letting Luther's words sink in. "And a majority of the nobles were in attendance; I was present with Queen Caro, who excused herself early. The assassin must have made his move sometime after the king and queen returned to their quarters, approximately an hour after midnight."

Stelian indicated the scrolls he had been sorting. "I've organized the interviews by time and location taken. We should re-examine them in case anything was glossed over. Even the smallest detail could make a difference."

He turned to Luther, who gave a slow nod.

"Seems as good a start as any," he said thoughtfully. "Let's begin while there is still some daylight left."

Stelian sat down at a desk with a stack of scrolls, while Luther ordered supper to be delivered. It was going to be a long night.

Luther rubbed his bleary eyes and glanced at the candle, which had dwindled to a mere stub.

Across the room, Stelian appeared to be trying hard not to nod off, his chin resting in the palm of his hand in an effort to stay awake.

"Did you find anything?" Luther inquired, rousing him.

"Nothing of note," he admitted, yawning. "This testimony is interesting, though. If only I could make some sense of it..." He stifled another yawn.

"Go to bed. We can resume in the morning."

Stelian opened his mouth to object, but Luther held up his hand.

"Neither of us will be any good to the investigation if we miss some crucial detail. That's an order, Lieutenant."

Stelian pursed his lips at Luther pulling rank but nodded meekly. "Yes, General. You're right." He rose, tidying the scrolls.

"I'll do that. Go."

Stelian bowed, then shuffled out of the office.

Luther let out a long sigh, resigning himself to bed as well. He gathered up the pile of scrolls Stelian had read through, placing them in one box while the remaining unread documents sat in another.

A scroll lay in the center of the desk, propped open by weights, presumably the one Stelian had been reviewing in his drowsy state.

Luther darted his gaze over the document. He hesitated, then dangled it over the candle, watching with morbid fascination as the flames licked the parchment, reducing it to cinders.

Stelian scratched his head, stymied. He stooped, peering under the desk to see if the scroll had rolled off the surface.

"General, did you see a document here when you were tidying up last night?"

"None but the ones in those boxes. Why?"

"I could swear I was reading something, but I seem to have misplaced it." He had been so tired the night before, he could hardly keep his eyes open. He wasn't even sure how he'd stumbled to his guardsman's quarters in the palace. It was all a blur. "Maybe I was mistaken."

"Must have been," Luther said offhandedly. "Are you ready to continue?"

Stelian nodded, taking his seat at the desk and resuming his inquiry. As he scanned yet another scroll, he couldn't shake the feeling he'd come across something pertinent the night before. If only he could remember what it was.

Caro swished her sword and shuffled forward, jabbing at an invisible opponent. Her breath misted in the winter air. She had stripped off her royal gown and traded it in for a tunic and trousers. Her schedule was clear for a while, and she always felt like she could best work through her frustrations by practicing with the sword.

Roland had been a doting father and rather lenient with his daughter, who eschewed dancing and embroidery in favor of more practical hobbies. Of course, he was strict when it came to her royal duties—she was the crown princess, after all, and required to uphold a certain dignity and presence—but otherwise, he had often yielded to her whims.

Luckily, her tutor Gaius also supported her, and when Caro had expressed a desire to learn swordplay, he had convinced Roland it was a healthy pursuit. Roland recruited his most skilled warrior to serve as her instructor, and for years they practiced together whenever their duties allowed. Luther was both a friend and teacher, and had taught her everything she knew.

"Your Majesty?"

She turned to see Luther watching her from across the courtyard. He approached hesitantly at her nod, and she lowered the blade.

"How may I serve you, Your Majesty?" He shifted uncomfortably, which was understandable given the circumstances; she wasn't a willful princess anymore but his reigning queen.

Caro sighed and ran her fingers through her damp hair. "I'm sorry for yelling at you, Luther. I'm just so frustrated. How can I move forward when I have so much uncertainty holding me back?"

As with Gaius and Ezalia, Caro dropped the royal protocol in private with those she cared for. She saw titles as merely impediments that reminded the other person of how inferior their station was, and she never wanted her friends to feel less than worthy. It was her prerogative as royalty, even though Luther was far too upright to do the same.

"Please do not apologize, Your Majesty. It's my fault for not having made the connections sooner," Luther replied, sounding pained. "The lieutenant has been a great help in that regard, and I'm confident we'll unravel the truth soon."

She smiled, encouraged by his newfound optimism.

"However, I must inquire as to your reason for being outside on such a chilly afternoon."

"I needed to let off steam," Caro admitted with a shrug.

He rubbed his chin. "Your stance is weak," he noted, "if it's not too bold of me to say."

"You wouldn't mind sparring with me?"

He drew his sword, then bowed. "Any time, Your Majesty."

Caro smiled as she resumed her stance. "It's been a while since we've practiced together. I've missed this."

"As have I, Your Majesty."

Calm before the Storm

"I don't think I can go through with it," Luther ventured uncertainly.

Night had fallen, when all those with dark intentions stepped out of the shadows, shedding their disguises.

Zhelyas had agreed to this clandestine meeting, and he wore an expression somewhere between disappointment and irritation. "You got what you wanted. Now it's time for you to keep up your end of the bargain."

"But Queen Caro—"

"She's a child," Zhelyas purred. "You've already seen it. She's suffering from the burden placed upon her frail shoulders. This kingdom needs a strong hand to guide it, or it will be led to ruin. Will the other realms respect a ruler who is only seventeen years old, still in the blush of youth? You know this is for the best."

His honeyed words wore down the last remnant of Luther's resolve.

Zhelyas moved past him, then paused, leaning close to his ear. "You wouldn't be thinking of betraying me, would you?"

Luther hesitated. "No."

"Just do as you're told, and I promise no harm will come to the pretty little queen."

Wolf in Sheep's Clothing

"Queen Caro. Your Majesty, wake up!"

It took her a moment to realize Stelian was the one shaking her.

"Mm... What's going on?"

She knuckled her eyes and blinked in the darkness. Her vision adjusted, and Stelian's face became clearer. His intense expression, fear and concern in equal measure, swept away any lingering cobwebs of sleep.

"Stelian?" she whispered, now fully awake.

"There's no time to explain. Lord Zhelyas Ralston has staged a coup, and the castle is in chaos. I barely managed to make it past the soldiers swarming the halls."

"Zhelyas?" Caro repeated, bewildered.

Stelian looked ready to jump out of his skin, so Caro pulled on her slippers.

"What about my aunt and the others?" she inquired as she followed Stelian outside to the balcony, shivering.

He unwound a rope with a grappling hook on one end and secured it to the railing. "The Lady Ezalia is waiting for us, as is Lord Gaius. They managed to get out of the palace before the doors were barred."

Caro could now hear the cries of alarm and confusion. The amber light of torches gleamed in the windows as soldiers barged through doors and wrested sleepers from their beds.

She peered over the edge doubtfully. They were three floors up, and she'd never rappelled before. "Um, Stelian?"

"You'll be fine, just don't look down."

Caro took a deep breath and swung her leg over the railing, gripping the rope and planting her feet against the walls. Her satin slippers didn't offer much traction upon the smooth limestone, and her perspiring palms were slick upon the rope, but she managed to lower herself to the ground.

The moon cast their side of the building in shadow, and she could barely make out Stelian's figure as he shimmied down the rope with ease. He had scarcely touched down when there was a pounding at the door, followed by the splintering sound of it being torn off its hinges.

Stelian flicked the rope, dislodging the grapple, and caught it before it fell.

"Where is the queen?"

Luther?

"She must have escaped."

The second voice she didn't recognize, low and solemn.

"Hurry," Stelian urged, guiding her along the base of the wall.

She bunched her nightdress around her knees. This far south, there wasn't any snow and the weather was quite pleasant during the day, but a thin layer of frost blanketed the ground and her toes were freezing in her thin slippers.

"Where are we going?"

"We can slip out along the barracks," he suggested, but she shook her head.

"I have a better idea. We'll cut through the garden."

Stelian's brow furrowed in confusion, but he nodded.

Her bedroom faced the back of the palace, and they crept along the decorative bushes which lined the walkways. The foliage didn't provide much cover, but because their absence had just been discovered, Luther might not have had the chance to dispatch a full search party yet.

Luther.

Caro couldn't believe it. Her most stalwart general, and her father's before her. Had he truly betrayed her? It seemed inconceivable, and yet the matter of the investigation bothered her. If the lack of result had been due to him concealing evidence and deliberately stalling the progress of the inquiry, it would make sense. But why?

She shook her head to clear it; there would be time to worry about him later.

They skirted the fountain which stood at the center of the garden and made their way toward the far leftmost corner. Caro's breath caught in her throat as the glow of a torch lit the night. Stelian pulled her behind an azalea bush, the leaves kissed with silver. The sentry scanned the area, then moved on.

"This way," she murmured.

He nodded, and they darted across a patch of manicured lawn, then ducked into the shadow of a statue of a winged lion wrestling with a snake.

"Where are we?" Stelian asked as she reached through the brambles, numb fingers feeling the wall.

"Father told me the royal family has escape routes built into the grounds and made sure I knew where they were. This is the closest one I could think of," she explained. "It leads to the merchant quarter. Nobody's used it in decades."

Thick hawthorn hedges lined the limestone walls of the garden. They were covered with pink flowers in spring, but aside from trimming to keep their shape, they were left mostly alone—and for good reason. Caro was grateful for her long sleeves, which offered a little protection from the finger-length thorns which pricked at her skin.

She winced and bit her lip to keep from making a sound as Stelian nervously kept watch. Then her fingertips brushed against the spot she was looking for.

"Here," she said. "The hedges conceal a small gap in the wall. It's a bit of a tight squeeze."

Stelian lifted an eyebrow. "A secret passage?"

She stood aside as he chopped at the hedge with his sword, careful not to let the blade reflect the moonlight and give away their position. The brambles tore at her nightdress, but she managed to wiggle her way through the hole Stelian had made.

They emerged on the other side through a patch of thick evergreen vines. Caro was weary, cold, and exhausted. She leaned against the limestone, rubbing her arms. It seemed they were out of danger, but for how long?

"Lady Ezalia and Lord Gaius aren't far, Your Majesty," Stelian said, repositioning the vines to cover the evidence of their escape.

Caro nodded. "Then let's go meet them."

Morfran's gaze swept the room. It was immediately apparent they were too late by mere moments. He could still feel the anxiety and fear lingering in the air.

Luther's expression shifted from one of surprise to frustration.

"Damn!" he cursed, and stabbed a pillow with his sword. Downy feathers burst forth and floated across the room, draping the bed in white. "Order a search party to locate the queen immediately!"

A soldier in the hallway saluted and rushed off.

No doubt they were as confused as everyone else by the strange goings-on they had been party to, but they served under Luther with absolute loyalty. If he told them the queen had committed treason, then they would obey his orders, no matter their own personal feelings—a lie which was more convenient than the truth.

Morfran lifted an eyebrow at his compatriot's tantrum, though his expression was hidden behind the silver mask he wore. He flicked a stray feather off his black armor and glanced out the window, keen eyes scanning the impenetrable night. He saw a flicker of movement and spotted two shadows fleeing in the dark.

Morfran smiled grimly to himself. "Let's go deliver the distressing news."

"I see," Zhelyas said lazily, lounging in the throne. His untamed black hair swung in front of his eyes, his displeasure unmistakable despite his easy words.

"Forgive us," Luther groveled.

Morfran remained silent.

"Any idea?" Zhelyas inquired.

"Her retainers acted quickly," Morfran replied. "They must have been warned and aided her escape."

"Are any left in the building?"

Morfran shook his head. "I do not believe so."

"Then that just leaves them." Zhelyas cocked his head, indicating the nobles who had been herded into the throne room like frightened sheep.

"Lord Zhelyas Ralston?" one whispered, laying eyes upon the traitor for the first time.

Luther and Morfran stepped aside as Zhelyas rose.

"Your Highness, what's happening?" another fearfully asked Arvind, who took his place at the front of the queue, their representative and protector.

Arvind faced Zhelyas. He pushed back his shoulders and lifted his head, but then—he gave a deep bow. "My king."

A flurry of whispers rose up like an anxious tide. "Your Highness, why would you bow to this—this usurper?"

"The prince merely knows when it is in his best interest to yield," Zhelyas said, his voice laced with menace. "You would be wise to follow suit. Kneel."

Stunned, the nobles shared apprehensive glances. They imitated the prince, each bowing in turn, then sinking to their knees on the cold marble floor.

"The servants will do their duty, no doubt. They know the consequences should they defy their king. But you, I am less sure of."

He glanced over the crowd of stricken faces. "I see several of your company are missing, Lady Ezalia and Lord Gaius among them. Pity, I could have used their clout. However, they are now fugitives of the state and will be arrested on sight." He paused. "What of you? Will you swear your fealty to me?"

"Never!" a noble cried out rashly.

Zhelyas turned to him, an evil glint in his eyes. In a flash faster than the man could blink, Zhelyas drew a sword and ran him through the heart. His eyes bulged as he knelt there, his impaled lungs filling with blood as he gurgled, unable to form coherent words.

With a wet splurch, Zhelyas withdrew his blade, the unfortunate man's blood spraying in a red arc. "Anyone else want to test my temper?"

"I—I swear my fealty to King Zhelyas," a noble nearby stammered, his face dotted with his ill-fated neighbor's blood.

The rest murmured the same.

Zhelyas nodded and sank once more languidly onto the throne, the menacing bloodstained sword balanced across his knees. "Return these good nobles to their quarters, where they shall remain until I establish order in this castle. Prince Arvind, I am leaving them in your charge."

"Of course, sire."

Arvind bobbed his head, and the rest shuffled out, studiously avoiding looking at the body still oozing blood onto the floor.

"Morfran, prepare a notice declaring a curfew. The city is in a state of martial law. Anyone can be stopped and questioned without warning or cause. Those caught out after hours are to be taken into custody and interrogated."

"Yes, sire," Morfran replied.

"And get someone to clean this filth up."

After Zhelyas's display of dominance, the nobles were escorted by armed guard back to their quarters.

"Earl Dahl, I wish to speak with you a moment," Arvind declared.

Malcolm was quite bewildered by this turn of events, as well as Arvind's apparent shift in loyalties. However, he couldn't refuse, and meekly followed the prince.

Arvind closed the door to his office, then sat behind his desk.

"How can you be part of this treason?" Malcolm blurted, unable to keep quiet any longer. The prince had been indolent and less than diligent about his duties, but he had always seemed loyal to the Crown.

Arvind leaned his elbows on the desk. "Zhelyas has promised to give me what I most desire. What that is, is no concern of yours."

Malcolm frowned, furrowing his brow.

"The nobles will not easily submit to an upstart king, even after tonight's demonstration," Arvind continued. "You will help me keep them in line."

"And if I don't?" Malcolm countered, sounding rather more brave than he felt.

"Then I'm afraid I will be the one to express my regrets to your lovely wife... at your unfortunate demise."

Malcolm's face went white at the not-so-subtle threat.

"I have influence with our tempestuous new liege, but I can only help those who help themselves." Arvind turned his steely gray eyes to meet Malcolm's. "I'm sure you understand me, Earl. Keep your head down, ensure the others do the same, and this transition will be as painless as possible."

Malcolm shifted his feet, but he had no other recourse but to comply. "Yes, Your Highness."

"That's a good boy," Arvind said snidely. "And don't attempt to besmirch my name, or you will discover how terrible my own displeasure can be."

"Caro!" Ezalia exclaimed as she and Stelian entered the hideout.

Caro's silk nightdress was ripped to shreds, her slippers stained with mud, and she was certain her hair was like a rats' nest. Stelian had fared a little better, his leathers more suited to tromping through muck and underbrush.

She melted into Ezalia's embrace. Her aunt was composed as ever, a rock in the stormy sea.

"You must be freezing." Gaius offered her a welcoming smile and wrapped a blanket around her shivering shoulders, his expression one of obvious relief.

"That can wait," Caro said, trying to keep her teeth from chattering. "I need to know what's going on."

Gaius nodded, and Stelian perked up; apparently, he knew only a few of the facts himself.

"I don't know how much they planned or how much was coincidence," Gaius began, "but as you know, after the murder of the king and queen, the castle was put on high alert. Luther and his men tightened security, increasing their presence within its walls."

"And I placed Luther in charge of the investigation," Caro seethed. She clenched her fists, fingernails digging into her palms. "Zhelyas must have killed them and conspired with Luther to take my throne in the ensuing chaos."

Ezalia sighed. "That's how it seems. Gaius became aware of the disturbance and woke me."

Both of them were in their dressing gowns, having fled the palace before it was locked up tight.

"We knew that after you, Ezalia and I would be hunted down as your staunchest supporters. Stelian was heading for your room when he spotted us, and I informed him of this place. It will be safe enough for a short while," Gaius elaborated. "However, our provisions are limited, and I would not recommend an extended stay. We should depart after you rest."

Caro opened her mouth to protest, but Gaius held up his hand.

"Please, no arguments. From this night forward, we are fugitives, and we will need our strength for the trials ahead."

With another comforting hug from her aunt, Caro shuffled obediently into the small bedroom, the weariness of the evening's events catching up with her.

She was still in her tattered nightdress, but she slipped off her muddy slippers and climbed under the sheets. They were rough and itched at her skin, and she longed for the smooth silk bedding in the comfort of her own room, the familiar warmth which had been ripped away from her in the middle of the night.

She curled into a ball and pressed her cheek into the pillow. What else could she have done? How could she have foreseen this? Zhelyas was an enigma to her, but Luther's betrayal stung. He had always been faithful and kind. What could possibly have made him turn on her? Was she so naive and blind she couldn't see what was happening right in front of her?

She screwed her eyes shut, choking back the tears.

Finally, emotionally and physically exhausted, her body shut down and she sank into the oblivion of sleep.

Darkest Hour

The room was dim. Caro blinked, trying to focus.

"Stelian?" she called into the dark. "Ezalia?"

A spark flickered, then another. Before her eyes, a hundred candles burst alight, glowing in the chandeliers swaying from the gilded ceiling.

Momentarily blinded, she could barely make out two figures dancing, illuminated by the soft glow, casting twisted shadows across the floor of the grand ballroom.

"Mama? Papa?"

Again and again, her parents twirled in time to silent music. They were wearing their finest attire: Roland with his ruby-studded crown and military uniform, white with gold piping and badges adorning the breast; Cecilia in a violet gown that shimmered with blue highlights as she spun, raven hair upswept in a gleaming sapphire tiara. A circle of figures applauded, but their faces were shadowed and empty.

Roland and Cecilia stopped dancing, as if the unheard music had ceased. They turned toward her, reaching out their hands.

"Caro," Cecilia said gently.

"Little chickpea," Roland added, using his fond nickname for her.

Tears stung Caro's eyes. She tried to run to them, but her legs wouldn't move the way she wanted. She seemed to be a toddler again, and she tripped, her ungainly feet caught on the hem of her dress. She landed in something wet.

When she looked up, her parents were gone. The entire ballroom was a sea of red, thick viscous liquid dripping down the walls and from the chandeliers above.

She looked at her hands, and they were soaked with blood.

Caro awoke with a start, choking back a scream. She sat up in bed and took steadying breaths to calm her pounding heart. *So much blood.*

The horrific vision was still fresh in her mind, and the shadows which crept across the room filled her with renewed terror. However, they soon faded in the soft light of the morning. Sunshine was streaming through the window, small bits of dust dancing among the beams.

She rose, pulling back a corner of the flimsy curtain. The sky looked like that of a painting, pale blue scumbled with gray and streaks of pink applied as if by an artist's brush. It had a strangely surreal effect, and for a moment Caro wondered if she was still dreaming.

She went to the basin and splashed her face with water. Her head felt clearer.

On the chair was a set of leggings, boots, a blouse, and a deep green leather lace-up vest, as well as a belt and sheath with a dagger. She slipped off her nightdress and changed, grateful for the warmth in the crisp air of the winter morning.

Caro straightened after fastening the boots and stared at herself in the mirror. She'd turned seventeen mere weeks before her parents' murders. Roland had possessed an understated dignity and charm, with his thick, tawny hair and beard, strong jaw, and kind brown eyes. Cecilia had been a classic raven-haired beauty with the elegance and charisma born of fashionable society.

Caro herself had a small, pointed chin that made her look somehow immature and serious eyes that always seemed to gaze at the world critically. She was not particularly buxom and, rather than Ezalia's well-endowed figure, had her mother's more subtle curves. Like other royal ladies of rank, her long brown hair was brushed with sweet-scented oils and draped over her shoulders, softening the sharp angles of her face.

She balanced the knife in her hand, then gripped it with purpose, hesitating only a moment.

The three companions looked up as the door opened, then Stelian gasped.

"Your Majesty, what did you do to your hair?"

She had chopped off her long tresses, leaving only a bob that barely reached her shoulders. Caro shyly twirled what remained of a curl around the tip of her finger.

"Does it look bad?"

"It looks lovely," Ezalia said kindly, sending Stelian a withering glare. "But what possessed you to cut it?"

"They're looking for a queen in royal silks with long hair. I thought this would help me disguise myself."

Gaius let out a hum as he leaned back in his chair. "What now?" he inquired to dispel the tension.

Caro steepled her fingers. She'd had some time to gather her thoughts, and now believed she could approach their situation rationally. "Our first order of business must be to draw

47

up a list of nobles not among those arrested at the palace, then decide which would be most likely to cast in their lot with us."

"Yes, I believe that is a wise course of action," Ezalia agreed. "There are surely those who will remain loyal to the true sovereign."

Like Caro, Ezalia and the others were dressed in outfits that would help them travel unnoticed. In doing so, Ezalia had discarded most of her many hair accessories, her long raven locks wound up with only a single two-pronged comb. She was wearing a short, blue shift dress and leggings, very different from her usual elaborate court attire.

Stelian wore clothing that would help him blend in, a dark red tunic over black leather pants, but his broad shoulders were evidence of the light armor beneath his cloak.

Gaius never changed. He looked dapper in a tawny, knee-length suede coat and trousers, his sleek gold hair pulled over his shoulder with a simple black ribbon. Caro envied his unruffled manner, the traces of anxiety from the night before now erased from his easygoing expression.

Caro noted he had a sword with an elegant hilt belted around his waist, while Stelian's trusty blade was at his side. Of Ezalia's prowess with weaponry, Caro wasn't sure, but she wouldn't underestimate her; her aunt always had a trick up her sleeve.

"Ezalia. Gaius. Stelian. I can't imagine what I would do without you here. There is nobody I would wish more to be by my side in this time of strife. Thank you."

Stelian kept watch while Ezalia and Gaius drew up a document listing all the members of the extended noble families, as well as past benefactors and known supporters of the Crown.

"Earl Malcolm Dahl," Ezalia mused. "He was visiting the palace, so he's likely under house arrest with the others, including Prince Arvind."

"What about Uyria?" Gaius inquired.

"She returned to her estate, but it's halfway to Agassey."

"True."

It was bittersweet for Caro, seeing her parents' names upon the paper. She recalled a similar exercise during one of Gaius's lessons in recent months, a tapestry which had depicted her royal ancestry leading back to Malianme, and she had joked about there being no more room at the bottom. It didn't seem so funny anymore.

"So it looks like our first stop should be Duke Vittorius," Gaius declared, scratching his head. "He's closest to our present location, and would be a most powerful ally since he's your father's younger brother."

Caro nodded. "I agree Uncle Vito is a good first choice. He has many connections, and it would be a boon if he pledged himself to my cause." She chewed on a nail. "He can be tricky to deal with, however. Living in the king's shadow for so many years has made him somewhat recalcitrant. He did swear his support to me after the Accession and bade me come to him if there was anything I needed, but I don't know how far that extends. We may need to tread carefully."

Ezalia gave a cunning smile. "Or perhaps we should do the exact opposite and catch him off guard. Then we will know where his true loyalties lie."

It was a gamble, but one that might pay off.

"So how do we go about contacting my uncle?" Caro inquired. "It's not like we can just waltz into his estate."

"Of all of us, Stelian is the least suspicious. Perhaps we should send him ahead with a message," Gaius suggested.

"That's risky," Ezalia said, shaking her head. "I have a better idea."

Two to Tango

Morfran let out a barely perceptible sigh as Luther paced. They were waiting to deliver the day's report to the new king, and the news was not good.

Running a hand through his bristly hair, Luther paused and scratched the stubble on his chin.

"Well?"

The general jumped as Zhelyas strode into the room, stealthy as a wildcat.

"Have you found her?"

"N-not yet, sire," Luther stammered.

Morfran decided he might as well rescue his compatriot. "A company of four were reported in the merchant quarter," he stated with precise care. "However, the informant lost sight of them."

"I see," Zhelyas said, frowning at their lack of progress. "Follow up on this tip. Even if it comes to nothing, I won't stand by idle."

Morfran and Luther bowed, then departed, the skittish general with rather more haste.

Zhelyas waited until they were gone, then gazed out the window across the rooftops of the capital city.

His city.

He knew he should be satisfied with his conquest. The queen he had deposed was out there, a thorn in his side, but he was confident he would not be overthrown. Still, he couldn't quite silence the persistent doubt gnawing at him. So far, the efforts of the military had been woefully inadequate, and Luther seemed unable to track her down.

Then there was Morfran. Even Zhelyas was unaware of the true identity of the man behind the mask. It was frustrating, and he was beginning to suspect Morfran's allegiance was wavering, whatever of it he held. Zhelyas clenched his fists, wanting to strangle someone.

A cool hand reached from behind and stroked his chest. "You stress yourself out too much, my liege."

"Veena," he murmured, turning to face the sorceress.

She was as beautiful as the first time he had laid eyes on her, with dusky skin and long flaxen hair that caressed the curves beneath her satin indigo gown. A crystal like a star hung around her throat, nestled among deep blue lapis lazuli stones.

She stared up at him with eyes like the burning heart of a fire, and he felt himself engulfed in their flames. He disentangled himself from her embrace, resisting her sultry charms.

"Have I not been by your side since the beginning?" she asked, her voice enticing.

Veena's smile was slightly patronizing, and Zhelyas seized her arms.

"Don't play games with me."

"I wouldn't dream of it." She smirked and disappeared in a puff of blue smoke, leaving him clutching at thin air.

Zhelyas let out a sharp sigh. Veena was an infuriating woman, but without her—and Morfran as well—he wouldn't be where he was now.

When he had first arrived in Aurinesse, Zhelyas had been bored by the company of the other nobles at the palace— blithering idiots, the lot of them—and sought distraction elsewhere.

The Nocturne Carnival had come to Aurinesse, and he donned his most unobtrusive attire to blend in with the various citizens milling about the square. There were fantastic beasts in cages: a satyr, a harpy, a manticore, and even a unicorn— although its provenance, like the rest, was questionable. Illusions, conjurings. None of it was real.

"I don't know why I even bothered," Zhelyas scoffed.

A variety of smells assaulted his senses, and he scrunched his nose with distaste, resolving to leave the putrid place.

Then there it was. In between the salty tang of the popped corn and the overwhelming sweetness of the sugar floss, an enticing scent wafted through the air, herbal and spicy. He was drawn to the source.

Zhelyas found himself before a violet tent erected near the edge of the carnival, in the middle of the hustle and bustle and yet simultaneously far away from it. Gold tassels dangled from each corner, from which a banner was suspended: "Have your future read by the diviner Veena Fortuna."

He pulled aside the flap, and a chime tinkled, heralding his arrival.

A woman gazed back up at him. She wore a backless dress of pomegranate red, tied at the waist with a silk scarf matching the tent's purple hue. Her skin was the color of caramel, unlike anyone Zhelyas had ever seen, and her eyes were like garnets.

Pale ivory hair hung past her waist, and coins strung upon her belt jingled as she shifted in her seat.

"Are you Veena Fortuna?" Zhelyas asked, cursing his feeble-sounding voice.

She smiled, and his heart skipped a beat. "I am. I have been expecting you." She gestured to the seat across the table.

Intoxicated by her presence, Zhelyas's mind took a moment to register her words. "You said you were expecting me?" he said, sitting as bidden.

"Yes. Show me your hand."

He had anticipated a crystal ball, or perhaps some cards with esoteric images, and was startled when she turned his hand over, resting it in her own. Her skin was soft and pliable, the envy of every noblewoman who bathed in milk and slathered themselves with beauty creams.

Veena traced a line on his palm with her finger. "You are a nobleman of some repute, born from a long line, but you have found little fulfillment in the court despite your father's expectations. And you yearn for something you cannot express."

She looked up, and he nodded.

"Tell me more."

"Are you sure you want to know? The future can be an unpredictable thing."

"I do," Zhelyas said.

She traced another line, all the way up his center finger, lingering upon it. "There are secrets in your past from long ago. But nothing stays hidden forever. The truth will be revealed one day."

She rose and reached into a pouch on her belt. "Take this. Find me when you decide."

Zhelyas stared at the card she'd handed him. "Embers and Ashes," it read, with an address in a less-than-reputable area of the city.

He opened his mouth, then closed it again, unable to formulate his thoughts into words. "How much do I owe you for the reading?" he asked instead.

Veena gave a mysterious smile. "It's on the house. It was a pleasure to meet you, Lord Zhelyas Ralston."

Unnerved by her intensity and the fact that she knew his name, he gave a short nod and backed out of the tent.

As he hurried back to the palace, he almost tore the card in two. Then he tucked it in his pocket. What had she meant? When he decided what?

As much as he tried to distract himself with idle courtly pursuits, still he could not shake the strange encounter from his mind. It was six months later that the inevitable spiral of circumstance began, and soon he sought out Veena's establishment.

Zhelyas paced anxiously in the fortune teller's shop. It smelled of sagebrush and incense, and it made him a little dizzy.

"What am I going to do? Knowing the truth, how can I simply sit by and let things stand as they are? You told me I should decide, but what does that even mean?"

"Calm yourself," Veena soothed, stroking his gloved hand. Her silver bracelets jangled, the only sound other than his pounding heart. "What do *you* want to do?"

He turned to her, puzzled.

"I am no mere fortune teller, Lord Zhelyas. I have the power to get you everything you wish."

"And what would I have to give you in return?"

"Nothing I can't take for myself," she assured him with a sly smile.

Her words were vague and the sweet-scented smoke muddled his senses, but her offer was a tantalizing one.

"If I can take the throne," Zhelyas said, grasping at straws, "then no one could deny me what is rightfully mine."

"Is that what you truly desire?" Veena purred.

Zhelyas's mind railed against him, but logic meant nothing compared to his obsession. "But it's impossible..."

Veena placed her cool hand on his cheek. "Nothing is impossible as long as you have the right tools for the job. I happen to know someone perfect for your purposes. All you have to do is seize what is yours for the taking."

Her words were like honey, and the notion, born of desperation, began to take shape in his mind.

When Veena returned, a man in black accompanied her. He wore a silver mask that concealed his face, and Zhelyas could not even guess at his identity, nor why he would want to take part in their treason.

"Why do you wear that mask?" Zhelyas asked.

The man seemed entirely unperturbed by the question. "An injury I sustained in the past, my lord. I do not wish to be reminded of it, yet it is ever present, so I use it to my advantage."

When the man turned his head, Zhelyas glimpsed the edge of a scar. It could have been his weakness, but he had turned it into his greatest strength, for one look at him would certainly strike fear into the most courageous heart.

"Morfran is an unparalleled fighter and a skilled strategist. With him on your side, you are sure to succeed," Veena assured him.

Events were set in motion with the murder of the king and queen in the dead of night, and their blood was on Zhelyas's hands—he could see it red as crimson, fulfilling all his desires.

At that moment, he knew his heart was blackened, his fate cursed. The words had burned his tongue as he swore loyalty to the pithy princess-turned-queen, but he knew her day would come.

Now, Zhelyas leaned back in the throne, staring at the ceiling. It was painted with a mural of astonishing skill, scenes pulled from mythology and lore. He had never been fond of history. It was over and done with, which made it even more ironic that the current situation had been dictated by the actions of his ancestor long ago.

He finally had the throne, but at what cost? Luther was weak-willed and easy to sway, but Morfran was another matter. Zhelyas was fairly certain the masked man was serving his own interests. And what of Veena? Her own motives were equally as nebulous. She had said she wanted nothing from their coup other than "what she could take for herself," whatever that meant. He didn't trust her in the slightest, but he didn't know what would happen if she left him.

An uncomfortable sensation bubbled up in his stomach, and Zhelyas rose, the long fur-trimmed robes pooling behind him as he gazed into one of the mirrors which lined the room.

"Yet what other choice did I have?" he asked his reflection staring back at him. "Once I discovered the truth... I knew the throne had to be mine. And now I have it, I'll kill anyone who tries to take it away from me."

Morfran returned to report that Luther had gone on ahead but hung back outside the door. Zhelyas's ramblings made little sense, but they piqued his curiosity.

"Who's there?" Zhelyas demanded, spinning to the door.

Morfran stepped out of the shadows and bowed. "Forgive me, sire. Luther's forces are patrolling the city. I shall depart shortly to investigate the tip we received, as per your orders."

"Very well, get on with it," Zhelyas said curtly, and Morfran had the impression he'd seen the true face behind the merciless usurper: that of a sniveling coward.

Skin Deep

"Milord, you have a visitor... of sorts."

The inflection in the voice of his normally stoic butler made Vittorius look up from his papers. "Who is it?"

"A 'Lady Darda,' milord."

Vittorius frowned. He didn't remember anyone by that name. "Very well, I shall greet her," he said, rising.

Other servants and members of his household paused in their work and gathered in the hall to await the mysterious guest, unable to contain their curiosity.

"Lady Darda," the butler announced.

Vittorius blinked a few times, unsure of what he was seeing. Standing before him was a person of a most peculiar nature, wearing a dress of luxurious blue silk. They had long, flowing golden hair and feminine features enhanced by lip and eye paint, but it all seemed overdone somehow.

"Lady... Darda, was it?" Vittorius began. "You must forgive me, but I do not recall making your acquaintance."

A second person accompanied Darda, their identity obscured by a dark hood. Slightly behind stood another two smaller cloaked figures.

"I must insist your companions show their faces."

"Pardon me, Lord Vittorius," a delicate voice said, "but the deception was necessary."

Vittorius stared at the raven-haired beauty before him as she threw back her hood. "Lady Ezalia?" he gasped. "I heard you were on the run from the palace with Lord Gaius..."

He leaned forward, scrutinizing the blond visitor. "Don't tell me..."

Gaius made a kissy face. "Got you good, didn't I? Have to admit, I make a fine-looking woman."

Vittorius pursed his lips as Gaius posed in what he thought was an alluring manner in Ezalia's dressing gown.

She rolled her eyes at his antics. "Gaius, would you behave? This isn't what we came for."

"True," Gaius admitted, chastised.

"Enough!" Vittorius snapped. "What is the meaning of this charade?"

Gaius moved aside as a third figure stepped forward, smaller and more petite with short, cropped hair.

"A pageboy?"

Ezalia smirked. "Your Lordship, may I present Her Majesty, Queen Caro."

Vittorius nearly fainted.

Gaius and Ezalia bowed as Caro came into full view. The fourth figure hung back, who Vittorius realized must be Stelian, her ever-present bodyguard. He struggled to reconcile the image of the trouser-clad youth with his recollection of his niece: dressed in fine gowns of silk and lace, hair long and flowing. He had to admit it was a clever disguise.

Vittorius's servants and staff were already on their knees. Recovering his sense of propriety, he bowed. "Your Majesty, I am relieved to see you well. Forgive my rudeness, but your arrival caught me by surprise."

"I took great risk in coming here. Zhelyas and his minions no doubt are hunting me doggedly."

"I assure you, my household will not breathe a word of this. You are safe within these walls. Please, come in and rest. You must be weary."

Caro faced him, green eyes unblinking. "I will be blunt, Duke Vittorius. I require resources to reclaim my throne, and I call upon the oath you swore after my father's death. Will you uphold it?"

Vittorius was unaccustomed to being challenged in his own house. He genuflected, his hand on his heart. "Without reservation, Your Majesty. My loyalty is with you, as it was with my brother."

Caro stared down at Vittorius. So far, everything was going according to plan. She could tell he was offended, and it was admittedly difficult to keep up her act of imperious indifference. She hated to test his loyalty in such a callous manner, but it would be worth it in the end.

Perhaps sensing Caro's wavering emotions, Ezalia smoothly stepped in. "Her Majesty is fatigued from her long journey."

"Of course," Vittorius said, rising. "I shall have rooms prepared immediately. And wipe that ridiculous junk off your face," he added to Gaius, who gave a coquettish wink.

"Was it too much?" Caro whispered to Gaius as he waved at the maids, who stared at him in bewilderment.

"Nah, you were perfect. Now we see how Vittorius reacts to having his entire household turned upside down."

"Your quarters, Your Majesty. Milord. Milady. Sir," the butler said, sounding like he was reading off a laundry list of noble personages.

A maid stood nearby holding a basin of water and a towel, and Gaius whisked it out of her hands, rubbing his face.

"Hey, Ezalia," he said, peering at the towel, which didn't have a trace of makeup on it. "How do you get this stuff off?"

"Oh, let me do that."

Ezalia took the towel and wrung out the water, then scrubbed his face vigorously while he yelped. Caro chuckled as Ezalia finished her work and tossed the towel back in the basin.

"Done."

"Thanks... I think." Gaius winced, touching his red face gingerly.

"His Lordship has eaten, but if Her Majesty wishes, I shall have dinner sent to your rooms," the butler said, ignoring their childish behavior.

The only food in Gaius's hideout had been stale biscuits, and Caro was starving. She nodded regally. "That would be much appreciated." She might be testing her uncle's loyalty, but that was no excuse to be rude to the servants.

The butler bowed again and swept off, black coattails flapping behind him.

Devil's Advocate

"I don't have to look over my shoulder, do I?" Zhelyas inquired.

He poured a glass of wine for Arvind, then one for Veena, who cast a glance at her co-conspirator. She had to admit she was curious as well. Arvind had been recruited to their cause by Zhelyas himself after he had discovered the prince's secret, but what that secret was, Veena had no clue. She couldn't read into his heart like she could Zhelyas's, and it unnerved her.

"What do you mean?" Arvind replied, taking the proffered goblet.

"You've endorsed me all along, but you have a legitimate claim to the throne."

Arvind gave a lazy shrug. "Roland was groomed to be king, and Vittorius couldn't sit still; he always had to have his fingers in some pie or other. I was sickly as a child, so I managed to avoid any sort of responsibility—and I would like to keep it that way. I have no interest whatsoever in the Crown and the tedious rigors of duty that come with it."

Veena didn't miss the note of bitterness in Arvind's tone when he spoke of his brothers' laurels.

"Is that really true?" Zhelyas asked, sounding doubtful.

Arvind bowed, grinning. "You know what I want, sire. As long as I get that, you have my full support."

Zhelyas raised his eyebrows at that, then turned his attention to Veena. "And you have what I asked for?"

"Yes, sire," she replied. "I will be able to track the queen and her entourage once the moon reaches its zenith."

"Excellent."

Arvind leaned close, inhaling Veena's perfume, and she scowled at his audacity. Keeping Zhelyas charmed and under her sway was one thing, but Arvind filled her with disgust.

"I would take care if I were you, Prince," she warned through gritted teeth.

"You're not really my type," he purred, ignoring her, and stroked her arm with an indolent finger. "But I wouldn't mind a little distraction."

Veena let loose a spark of blue flame, and he withdrew his hand quickly.

"Not if you were the last man in the world," she hissed.

Arvind shrugged and wiggled his singed fingers. "Your loss."

"Sire, Earl Malcolm Dahl has arrived."

"If you would excuse me," Zhelyas said, dismissing Arvind and Veena, who pushed past the prince, still incensed by his indecent proposal.

Once they were gone, he settled himself comfortably on the throne. "Send him in."

Malcolm entered and bowed low. "You called for me, sire?" He shifted his feet, a little nervous, as he should be. The last time he had been in the throne room, one of his peers had died.

The earl was still a young man. He had short black hair with slightly tousled bangs which seemed to resist any attempt to tame them, soft brown eyes, and an honest face. He was wearing a white shirt, dapper blue waistcoat, and matching jacket in a slightly darker hue.

Zhelyas had observed that Arvind had taken Malcolm aside, entrusting him with oversight of the nobles. With no dukes currently residing in the palace, the earl held the highest ranked title. Countess Alvara was equally as powerful, though Arvind had issues dealing with women, so naturally he would gravitate to the earl instead. The two had been overheard arguing on more than one occasion, though it was usually resolved by a swift word from Arvind. Clearly, the earl was a man who wasn't afraid to speak his mind but knew when it was better to desist. Zhelyas had enough lackeys who meekly obeyed his every order; to run the country, he would need someone with a little more spine.

"I understand you have been granted a certain amount of trust by Prince Arvind."

"I am grateful to His Highness," Malcolm replied.

A careful man, indeed.

"Earl Dahl, with the lack of a resident duke, you are among the highest ranking nobles in the palace. As such, I wish for you to serve as their representative before the throne. I intend to resume court as soon as things settle down, and I nominate you Royal Officer."

Malcolm looked a little taken aback, and Zhelyas waited for him to argue he was too young, or the countess was more suited to the position. However, he merely nodded. "Your Majesty graces me with your favor. I will do my utmost to serve you in this capacity."

He knelt before the throne, and Zhelyas handed him a small brooch bearing the royal crest, which Malcolm pinned to his cravat.

Malcolm left the throne room and slowly let out the breath he'd been holding. He ran his thumb over the smooth blue enamel of the crest pin marking his new role.

Royal Officer. As if he needed more responsibilities. Trying to keep out of Arvind's way was hard enough, but now he had to avoid saying something that could get him executed by the usurper king as well.

Silence is Golden

Malcolm shuffled into the throne room along with the rest of his fellow nobles, feeling a distinct sense of trepidation.

"With the palace returning to normal, King Zhelyas has decided to hold court," Arvind declared. "Don't disappoint me."

Arvind glanced significantly at Malcolm, and he swallowed. The first day of his new duties; he prayed he wouldn't let everyone down.

The hum of discontent was silenced as Zhelyas entered, sweeping across the floor in royal robes. He had evidently raided Roland's wardrobe, and the effect was striking. His jet-black hair matched the collar of a long, crimson jacket embroidered with gold thread, worn over a rust-red damask waistcoat with gilded buttons. Across his shoulders draped a heavy chain of office with the royal crest upon a medallion: gold inlaid with pearls and rubies that matched the resplendent crown upon his head. Even the royal signet ring gleamed upon his finger.

He paused, casting a stern glance upon each of them, then flicked aside his fur-trimmed black cloak and took the throne. "Welcome, Lords and Ladies. I hope you have enjoyed your respite, however the time has come to resume your duties. Now that my claim to the throne is unassailable, I wish to return to the business of running this kingdom, and I require your cooperation in doing so. I'm sure I won't encounter any more opposition."

The words hung in the air ominously, and there was a flurry of bows.

"Good. First on the agenda: I understand the population of the capital has greatly diminished."

The silence was thick in the air and Malcolm, as Royal Officer, took a deep breath and stepped forward. "Yes, Your Majesty." The words still felt bitter upon his tongue, but he swallowed his distaste. "During the"—he wavered, trying to think of a suitable word that wouldn't get him killed— "uncertainty, many of the citizens of Aurinesse fled the city. King Farangis of Drusus, our closest neighbor, welcomed them and established a refugee camp across the border."

"For which I am immensely grateful, of course," Zhelyas said silkily. "However, the time has come for my people to return home where they belong."

"King Farangis will no doubt ask for a gesture of good faith."

Zhelyas cocked his head, and Malcolm very much wished to sink into the floor. "Is that so? And what do you suppose that will be?"

"I'm afraid we cannot possibly guess what he will demand, but a guarantee of reparations in the amount of what has been spent on his part to house our citizens, as well as an additional thirty percent, would be a suitable token to open discussions."

Zhelyas leaned back in the throne, looking thoughtful. Or murderous. It was rather difficult to tell between the two.

"Very well, Earl Dahl, I accept your recommendation. Countess Alvara, as Duke Vittorius has been branded a traitor, the duties of Minister of Trade now fall to you. Draw up an offer stipulating what has been discussed, and I will send Prince Arvind as my envoy."

Malcolm's heart sank. He had been hoping Zhelyas would send him. He would be of better use to his fellow nobles with more freedom to wander, but of course the king was not such a fool as to trust someone he didn't utterly control with such a vital mission.

"At once, Your Majesty," Radella said.

"If I may, sire, there is one more matter to consider."

Malcolm blinked at the woman who had spoken, oblivious to the glare Zhelyas turned upon her. Takaria was the widow of the former Minister of Finance and well respected at court. She was also General Luther's mother.

"Duchess Takaria Ruxa," Zhelyas said, acknowledging her. "Of what do you speak?"

"King Farangis's younger brother was kidnapped on his return from a diplomatic trip to Artemisia when he was but a child, and Farangis has never forgiven us. Our kingdoms still have a trade agreement, but relations are frosty between the two royal families. Prince Arvind should take care when dealing with the king, lest he think we are taking advantage of his generosity. It would not do to make him an enemy."

Zhelyas considered her words. "I am sure the prince will exercise caution, and not do anything to endanger his mission."

He shot a glance at Arvind, who gave a curt bow.

"In that case, I believe this meeting is adjourned," Zhelyas declared, and waved his hand imperiously.

"Lady Takaria, I appreciate your candor," Zhelyas added as Malcolm trudged out of the hall with the rest. "It is a rare quality in times like these."

"Of course, sire," she replied, genuflecting. "I wish for nothing more than to see peace restored to this court, whatever manner it may take. Though I am surprised you would place such faith in my son. He is nothing but a fool."

"General Luther has been loyal, Lady Takaria. I owe him much."

"I will have to take your word for it, Your Majesty," she scoffed. "He has shown no such redeeming qualities to me."

"Your Highness," Malcolm said, appearing at the door of the prince's office.

Arvind was packing, muttering to himself as he stuffed scrolls of questionable relevance into a satchel, and he swore as he caught the latch of a trunk on his thumb.

"Why in the world would he send me? I'm a prince, not meant to be traipsing through the filthy wilderness."

Malcolm cleared his throat, drawing Arvind's irked gaze.

"Yes, what is it?"

"Pardon me, but Countess Alvara finished writing up the document, and the king has reviewed it."

"Let me see that," Arvind snapped, and snatched it from Malcolm's outstretched hand. He frowned, examining the scroll with a careful eye, ostensibly for tampering, but the royal seal stood clearly upon the wax binding the ribbon.

"Fine," he grumbled, tucking it into the satchel with the other scrolls.

"If you would excuse me..." Malcolm ventured, and took a step back toward the door.

Arvind's eyebrows shot up. "Don't think because I'm gone that you can try anything and I won't know about it. Our agreement still stands, Earl. Behave yourself."

As a legitimate earl, Malcolm technically outranked the widower duchess, but he always felt like he was an insect in her imposing presence. Even so, after the advice she had given Zhelyas about dealing with the king of Drusus, he felt it was worth approaching her. She clearly had the interests of the refugees, and the people of Artemisia as a whole, at heart.

Takaria had dark hair, which she always wore braided behind her head in an austere style, and smoky gold eyes. Though in her fifties, her skin retained a luminescent quality to it, smooth and unblemished, with sculpted features and a penetrating gaze; she must have been a stunning beauty when she was young. She was wearing a saffron and black gown accented with ivory lace, a string of golden pearls around her neck. Her maid Senna hovered nearby, wearing a striped mauve uniform and white apron.

"What brings you here, Earl Dahl?" Takaria inquired pleasantly. "I take it the prince has departed to negotiate with King Farangis?"

"Yes, I delivered the signed requisition myself."

Takaria took a sip of tea. "It seems King Zhelyas has decided to get on with the business of running the country, at least."

She held up her teacup, and Senna refilled it obligingly. Takaria lifted an eyebrow, and Malcolm shook his head, politely refusing.

"It is for that reason I've come to see you, Duchess," Malcolm elaborated. "With the prince gone, there is an opportunity to perhaps do some good for the people who are being treated unjustly. However, while I have the framework of a plan, I have neither the means nor the acumen to see it through. I could use your advice."

She leaned back in her vermilion upholstered chair, fixing him with her eagle gaze. "My husband had many resources, and I would see them contributed to such a worthy cause. I assume Lady Radella is involved in this enterprise as well?"

"Of course. You may approach either of us as you see fit."

Takaria inclined her head. "You have my attention."

Malcolm was suddenly wishing he had accepted the tea; his mouth felt dry. Anticipating his discomfort, Takaria gave a slight nod to her maid, who poured him a fresh cup.

"Have you heard of the term 'disapprobation'?"

Takaria frowned. "Not, I think, in the context you are referring to."

"It's one of the new policies Zhelyas has put into place in order to control the populace and censure those who would defy his new regime."

"I see," Takaria murmured, setting her teacup aside and crossing her hands in her lap.

"There have been numerous uprisings resulting in widespread arrests. Some have been significant, organized by a group of instigators who have the military grinding their teeth in frustration, but others are minor, merely a misplaced word or offhand comment. These people are arrested and interrogated at length for any connection with the rebel faction, and many are eventually released—but that is not the end of it. Disapprobation is put into effect: their businesses are boarded up, and they and their families are branded as malcontents. Few are willing to give them aid of any sort, even sell them food or supplies, for fear of being arrested as sympathizers themselves. It is a cruel sentence. Essentially, they have been made pariahs with no refuge or resort, and these are the people I would endeavor to save."

Takaria's brow furrowed as he related these unsavory facts. "This is indeed disturbing. I had heard of the measures Zhelyas was taking to stem the tide of people fleeing the city, but I was not aware things were so dire."

"If they attempt to depart without papers giving them leave to do so, they will be turned away by the soldiers at the city gates. These papers will need to be forged, or the guards bribed to look the other way and let them pass. Better both, in case something goes awry."

"I agree," Takaria said, nodding. "I know someone who can take care of the papers. Meanwhile, diverting funds to the accounts of the soldiers should be an easy task since I was married to the Minister of Finance, a glorified banker," she added with a sardonic smile. "Senna should be able to collect the duty roster. The soldiers find her quite charming."

Senna's lips twitched with amusement, and it seemed she was eager to go along with her mistress's wishes.

"It will be up to you and your associates to carry out the extractions. Trust only the nobles under your sway. No third parties should be hired; the fewer people involved, the better. I would also advise you to come up with a method to ensure complete anonymity in case one of you is caught."

"Don't worry," Malcolm assured her. "Radella and I have been talking it over, and we think we have a plan."

"I will leave the rest up to you, Earl," Takaria declared, nodding approvingly. "You may use Senna to communicate discreetly if needed, and I know a way out of the palace by which you will be able to come and go without detection."

"Thank you, Duchess," Malcolm said, rising and bowing.

"May the blessings of Aryama be upon you."

Senna escorted him to the door.

"Are you sure you want to be part of this?" he asked, having the slightest doubt at her level of devotion.

The maid looked mildly affronted, but she nodded. "Yes, Your Lordship," she replied. "My mistress treats me more like a daughter than a servant. I owe her everything."

Malcolm was stunned at the depth of her conviction. "I will send word soon."

After discussing the proposition at length, Malcolm was starting to feel more confident in his abilities to put it into practice. They would, of course, still need to be wary, but with Arvind not looming over his shoulder at every turn and Morfran and Luther out hunting the queen, attention had been turned away from the capital for a while, and he could breathe easy.

Insult to Injury

"Duchess," Luther said with forced politeness, and flinched inwardly as Takaria turned her scathing gaze upon him.

"General Luther," she replied in an icy voice. "What precisely can I do for you?"

Propriety was ingrained in the nobility, and none adhered to it more strictly than his mother, but every word cut like a knife.

Lord Luther Lasca. That was who he had been before he joined the army. His father hadn't cared since his elder brother Lars had inherited the barony, but Takaria had been devastated.

"How dare you?" she had spat when he told her about his decision. "You are the son of a proud and noble line, and you would turn your back on that to—what? Play soldier?"

"That's not my intent," Luther tried to explain. "I'm hopeless with finances and managing a business. Lars is a much better choice. I want to serve the kingdom as you and Father do, but the only way I can do that is as a soldier. I'll uphold our family's honor, and I'll be a general one day. I promise I'll make you proud."

Takaria glared at him, smoky gold eyes remorseless. "I will *never* be proud of you. You do this, and I will no longer acknowledge you as my son."

The words stung him, as she knew they would. Perhaps she thought her threat would be enough to dissuade him, but he had made up his mind.

"I'm sorry, Mother. I hope one day you understand."

She was a formidable woman, and they had rarely spoken since. Their interactions had been reduced to those dictated by duty, with little trace of familial affection. They had once been close, which made his perceived betrayal that much more bitter—and their strained relationship that much more painful.

Luther wanted to apologize, to try and clear the air between them, but every time he opened his mouth to speak, the disappointment in her eyes rendered him mute. "Forgive me for the imposition, Duchess, but the king requests your presence."

She pressed her lips together, and he wondered if the same scene had been flitting through her memory as well.

"Of course, General. I am at his command."

There it was again. "General." She hadn't called him by his name even once in the intervening years, and he had only called her "Duchess" in return. It maintained the cold formality between them.

"One question, though," Takaria said, interrupting his gloomy thoughts. "Why did you come yourself? The king could have easily sent a messenger."

"Because I have a matter to discuss with you as well."

Takaria appeared both mildly annoyed and intrigued. "Very well, General, I will hear you out. Please sit."

The request was polite, though curt, and Luther sat down gratefully in the chair opposite his mother. His knees felt like jelly. He wasn't a little boy anymore, but she was still the same beautiful, strong, sophisticated woman he had always adored.

"With the prince gone, I expect the nobility must be anxious, given recent events." Luther winced at his poor choice of words.

"So this is not an official inquisition?" Takaria let out a sharp sigh. "You may set your mind at ease, General. We won't do anything to try the patience of King Zhelyas. It is true, however, that we're all on edge. Court is a careful dance of politics and decorum at the best of times. You know that well enough."

Luther frowned at her reproach. "Indeed. I'm content with your assurances, Duchess. I will trouble you no further."

Takaria set down her teacup and rose, smoothing out her dress. "Just stick to the business your new master has for you, and leave us to ours."

She made him sound like a dog called to fetch and heel, and he supposed she was right. For a moment, it had seemed as if they'd be able to have a civil conversation, but he should have known it would be short-lived.

Zhelyas looked up as Luther entered the dining room, followed by Takaria, who swept in with her usual dignified hauteur.

"Duchess Takaria Ruxa," he greeted.

"You called for me, sire?" she replied, curtsying regally.

"Yes. Join me, won't you?"

He gestured to an empty seat, and Luther pulled the chair out for her. It was a strangely intimate moment between a mother and son who were otherwise estranged.

"That will be all, General," Zhelyas said curtly.

Once Luther had gone, he turned to his austere guest.

"I was impressed with your honesty during court earlier."

"As I said before, Your Majesty, I wish only for peace to be restored to this castle."

Zhelyas gave her an assessing look. "Perhaps I should nominate you to be Royal Officer instead of Earl Dahl," he suggested, but she shook her head.

"With respect, sire, the earl is far more suited to the position. I am a jaded old woman, and I do not see as clearly as I once did. I wish only to live out the remainder of my lonely life. I am your servant, but I humbly request you reconsider." She tipped her chin in deference.

"Very well, Duchess, I will not compel you. However, I expect you to show the same candor in the future."

"Of course, Your Majesty."

A slight smile traced her lips, and he had the impression that extracting an opinion from the assertive noblewoman would not be difficult.

They lapsed into silence, feasting upon steamed clams served with garlic wine cream sauce: a meal fit for a king.

"Thank you for your hospitality, sire," Takaria said, once she had finished the last morsel and wiped her lips with her napkin.

Zhelyas gave a short nod and she rose, bowing.

"One more thing, Duchess."

She glanced up.

"What is the reason for the enmity between you and your son? Luther is my general, so I insist on knowing."

A dark shadow passed across Takaria's face. "His service to Your Majesty notwithstanding, I did not approve of his decision to join the military," she said evenly. "I felt he was betraying his family. Is that all?"

"I am satisfied, Duchess. You may go."

She bowed again, then swept out of the room, her skirts rustling with her vexation.

Takaria stood outside on the balcony and wrapped her arms around herself, seized by a sudden chill.

"Milady?"

"I'm fine, Senna," she replied, shrugging into the shawl her maid wrapped around her shoulders.

"Is there anything I can do?"

"You've always been so good to me. I hardly deserve it. You should leave, find a better life for yourself and start a family, not dote on a bitter old woman like me."

Senna drew in a short breath, as if wanting to say something but unwilling to contradict her. "I can never repay your kindness, Mistress. You took me as your handmaiden, not a girl from a well-to-do family, but the daughter of a philandering steward. You promised to teach me to read and write, even instruct me in social graces so I might find a suitable match someday, but I am no longer tempted by the promise of a wealthy husband. I wish only to remain by your side."

Takaria's shell collapsed, and her shoulders began to tremble. "Forgive me, Senna. I just... Seeing my son, it makes me hate myself. I had such high hopes. I saw a future with him leading the family, not his brother. When he left, I was so angry, and my foolish pride made me say those heartless words. Now I can't take them back, and every time I see him I'm reminded of that day, and how I failed."

Senna adjusted the shawl. "Come inside, and I'll make you some tea."

Takaria gave in to her tender care. Of course Senna didn't have an answer; how could she? Still, her mild presence was a comfort Takaria desperately needed.

Rock the Boat

Vittorius's estate in the merchant quarter was built on a small plot of land set back from the thoroughfare, which afforded him some privacy yet allowed him to remain near his line of work. It was an elegant building with a green exterior, the front entrance shielded by a portico with attractive white posts and applique mouldings which reflected his refined tastes.

Since her arrival, Caro had taken up residence in Vittorius's study, claiming it for her use. The furnishings were understated yet attractive, with olive velvet-upholstered chairs and couches, paneled walls, and silk curtains in a saffron shade. What was especially fascinating were the small trinkets her uncle had picked up during his career as Minister of Trade. Many of the pieces were of a similar style: a large brass disc with complex knotwork figures; a miniature barge, complete with cloth sail; and an artfully engraved helmet. Others were quite exotic: a proudly sitting black cat with pointed ears, a miniature tree with jade leaves, and even a delicate porcelain unicorn. Caro recalled the beautiful creature was the symbol of the neighboring country of Drusus, just as the winged lions were the symbol of Artemisia.

She sat behind her uncle's oak desk and sank into the chair, feeling rather small. The sophisticated piece of furniture was made of sleek wood, with four drawers on either side. The legs resembled the clawed feet of lions, the edging and wood face trim ornately carved. It was a twin to the one in the royal office at the palace, two of a kind shared by two brothers. Once again, Caro felt a twinge of guilt and rose.

"Where is Uncle Vito?" she inquired of Stelian.

"He has moved his documents to a temporary office."

"I want you to inform him I wish to speak to him," Caro said. "Press the issue if you must. You are acting on my authority."

Ezalia and Gaius had made themselves scarce, so Stelian was on his own as he mounted the steps to the second floor. The door to the makeshift office was open, and he rapped upon the wood as he stepped across the threshold.

"Your Grace," Stelian began, "Her Majesty has summoned you to the study."

Vittorius stood at a table poring over old maps, every surface overflowing with parchment and documents in the cramped space.

"I will see her when I am done here."

"My lord, I must insist—"

"You *insist*?" he replied sharply. "I will not be dictated to in my own house!"

Stelian stood his ground. "I did not intend to undermine you, Your Grace, only to fulfill my queen's wishes."

As the queen's messenger, he spoke on her behalf, and Vittorius's glare simmered to mere embers. "I will attend upon her presently. She requested information, and I am gathering it for her."

Stelian bowed, then returned to the study to await Vittorius, who descended a few minutes later. He opened the door for the duke, who swept past and bowed to the queen, his arms overflowing with scrolls.

"Your Majesty."

There was a moment of uncomfortable silence as a maid set a tea tray down with a small clunk, then left.

"My queen, I regret that I spoke with anger to your bodyguard. He was merely acting on your orders."

"You should apologize to Stelian, then," Caro said pointedly.

Vittorius frowned, then turned and dipped his head. "My apologies, Lieutenant."

Stelian gave an awkward nod.

Apparently satisfied, Vittorius turned back to Caro. "The maps you asked for. They will require more analysis, but I believe they should provide the information you seek."

Stelian took the opportunity to slip out of the room, and Caro waited until he was gone.

"I'm sorry to have been such an imposition," she said, keeping up the charade.

"You are certainly not that, Your Majesty," Vittorius replied, denying her words with a pained look. "I will do whatever I can to help, you have my word. However, you have not made things easy by arriving without notice and questioning me at every turn. My entire house is in a state of disarray."

She lifted an eyebrow. "Am I obliged to do otherwise, Duke?"

Vittorius bowed his head. "Of course not, Your Majesty. Forgive my impertinence. I just wish you trusted me..."

"I do," she said, and Vittorius looked up, his expression of shame dissolving into confusion.

"Pardon?"

Caro felt a swell of affection for her uncle, whom she had abused rather mightily. "I'm sorry for intruding upon you like this and taking advantage of your hospitality," she said kindly. "But I had to know that even if my demands seemed unreasonable, you would stand by my side, loyal to the Crown rather than a fair weather ally ready to turn your back on me at a moment's notice. I am now convinced and offer my sincerest apologies for deceiving you."

"I admit, I am relieved to hear it, niece. I had hoped our relationship was more affectionate. I reaffirm my pledge: I am at your service."

Caro smiled and gestured to the couches. "Would you care to discuss this over tea?"

Vittorius nodded and stared at her as she lifted the stately silver teapot and poured the tea first for him, then herself. It was something a servant would do, but the gesture felt intimate and comforting as the cobwebs of deceit and cold detachment were swept away.

Caro stirred a spoonful of honey into her cup as Vittorius laid the scrolls on the table between them.

"Here is what I have gathered so far."

At some point during their discussions, Ezalia and Gaius ambled into the room through the door adjoining the terrace.

Vittorius looked up and lifted an eyebrow. For a moment, Caro worried he would berate them for entering unannounced, but he merely shrugged.

"This look is much better for you, Lord Gaius. I'm relieved to see my beloved niece is not, in fact, in the company of a madman."

"We wouldn't want you thinking that, Your Grace," Gaius replied glibly.

"I suppose that little farce was your idea, Lady Ezalia?"

Ezalia gave him an innocent look. "I couldn't help it. He's just so *pretty*."

Caro snorted into her teacup.

"It's nice to see you've made up, however," Ezalia added.

"Was that your idea, too?" Vittorius asked pointedly.

Ezalia and Gaius exchanged a nervous glance. "Yes, we did counsel Her Majesty to use some underhanded tactics to gauge your intentions."

"But all's forgiven now, right?" Gaius interjected hopefully.

Vittorius sighed. "I recognize the necessity of your ploy. I may not be pleased, but that is due to my own failings more than any design of yours. Let us say no more of it. I will do whatever is in my power to achieve success for my queen."

Ezalia poured a cup of tepid lemon tea and stared at it dubiously.

As if on cue, there was a rap on the door and Stelian poked his head through. "Is there anything else I can get for you...? Oh, Lord Gaius is here, and Lady Ezalia."

"Perfect timing. More tea please!"

"And then you can join us," Gaius added, glancing at Vittorius. "He is no mere attendant, but the queen's bodyguard and a member of our company. He should be included."

Vittorius gave a short nod. The tea was refreshed and doled out to all gathered, and they once more turned their attention to the maps.

"If you would, Uncle," Caro said, "please elaborate on what you were saying before, for the benefit of those who have just joined us."

Vittorius cleared his throat. "Artemisia is a large country. Zhelyas may find it more challenging to control than he thinks. The capital is at the southernmost edge, backing onto the Veggur Mountains abutting the sea, but it stretches north by quite a ways. Even if one raced at full tilt on horseback all the way, it would still take over a week to traverse the distance. Putting down any sort of rebellion would be difficult. With so far to travel, he would have to spread his forces thin.

"The terrain is unpredictable as well. Many of the noble estates are erected upon fertile grassland suitable for farming, but to the east lies a forbidding desert, with a dense forest below that, and treacherous swamplands rumored to be inhabited by a witch. As one grows closer to the northern border, the weather grows colder, and the prairies devolve into hills and rocky outcroppings sparse with vegetation.

"As Zhelyas focuses his attention upon keeping the capital region under his sway, I fear outside influences may see this as an opportunity to strike while the iron is hot, or the nobles already ensconced upon their properties may make a bid to expand their own influence. Additionally, many have private armies of their own, so they could easily amass a force to challenge an incursion upon their lands."

To be honest, Caro had never left the capital, except to venture into the mountains with Stelian to learn some survival skills which Gaius had insisted were necessary. With the balance of power ordinarily maintained by the nobility and their respect for the king's authority, she had taken the internal peace of her kingdom for granted. She was just now realizing how delicate a balance it was.

"Zhelyas already has a stranglehold on the city, courtesy of his new sycophants, Luther and a man named Morfran," Vittorius was continuing.

"Morfran?" His might have been the second voice Caro had heard coming from her bedroom. "What do you know about him?"

"Scant little, I'm afraid," Vittorius said, shaking his head. "Luther, as you know, has been a servant to the king for decades, so his betrayal is difficult to swallow. As for Morfran... While his name is not unknown in the lower circles, his origins are shrouded in mystery. I hear he even wears a mask so as to conceal his identity."

"A mask?" Caro repeated.

"Yes. They say he will kill anyone who sees his face."

"That's interesting," Ezalia murmured.

"Our first mission must be to get Your Majesty out of the city."

"What are our options?" Caro inquired.

Vittorius plucked a small paring knife from between Gaius's fingers.

"Hey, I was using that," Gaius said indignantly, then bit into his half-peeled apple.

Vittorius wiped the knife on a napkin, then laid it upon the map as a pointer. "East is the country of Effrenia, but the political situation is tenuous and crime runs rampant there. The former king did little to help the situation, and now his son is desperately trying to put an end to the corruption, but he has enough problems within his own borders. Above that is Salissard, a mountainous region with a harsh, bitter climate. Artemisia has a standing trade agreement with them, but they will lend no military aid."

Caro recalled as much from the reports of her ministers. She wondered how many of them were still alive, then pushed those thoughts to the back of her mind.

Vittorius turned the blade in the opposite direction. "West is Drusus, a kingdom who was our ally in the past, but after the tragedy involving their own royal family, they have been distant. Their official stance is that they are staying out of this dispute. However, they are accepting refugees, and displaced citizens are being welcomed and provided for in a camp set up across the border. Since he established his conquest, Zhelyas has attempted to stem the tide of fleeing citizens, with mixed success. I believe there is an underground effort to help those who have been unjustly arrested and their families escape the city."

That was intriguing, and Caro wondered who could be responsible for initiating such an enterprise. "Noted."

She nodded, and Vittorius turned the knife northward.

"The Grand Duke Ezekiel Garsiv, the late queen's father and your grandfather, has an estate at Agassey. If Zhelyas was involved in the murder of his daughter, he will be enraged and already preparing his forces. He has always been staunchly devoted to the throne," he added as Ezalia frowned at the mild slight to her father.

"Agassey is over two weeks' ride with a good horse," Gaius pointed out, waving the apple core around.

Vittorius held up a plate and lifted an eyebrow for Gaius to discard the core before any of the juice dripped upon his precious maps.

"Lord Gaius is correct," Vittorius admitted with a touch of reluctance in his voice, "but there are others along the way. Baron Oswin Odric is the nearest at Tamford, a half day's journey from the capital. Then there's Count Thoril Viehr, who oversees a mill outside Sharnwick, and Countess Uyria Ilyana of Dalry—"

"However," Caro interrupted, turning the paring knife northeast. "I think we should first visit the Margrave Alenard Giness at Biding. He has a sizable private army, and I doubt Zhelyas would risk sending his forces so far out to subdue the march."

"But that road is nearly as long as to Agassey."

"Not if we take a more direct route."

Gaius leaned forward, peering with new interest at the map while Vittorius stared at Caro.

"But that would mean crossing the Esaphis Desert, a treacherous, lawless wasteland filled with brigands and thieves. Such a journey should not be undertaken lightly."

"But it's unlikely Zhelyas will anticipate this course of action, isn't that right?"

Vittorius nodded reluctantly. "True. If that is what you wish, I have contacts to whom I can reach out while I await your return."

"What contacts?"

"My late wife's family in Salissard."

Caro had forgotten Iduna had been Salissardian, although that explained the common theme in the study's decor. Vittorius had met her during a trade excursion and returned with her as his bride, a fierce beauty with long red hair and eyes like a winter lake. She was a kind woman, with a generous heart and a temper which could match his own. She had taken ill when their daughter Andrine was still young, so Caro only had vague memories of her, though she remembered Iduna singing of her mountain home and the magnificent drakes which dwelled there, soaring across the skies. They were the smaller kin to dragons, and there were even rumors of tribes in those mountains who had befriended the creatures and lived alongside them.

"I will see if they will assist me in hiring some mercenaries," Vittorius elaborated.

Caro cocked her head. "Mercenaries?"

He nodded patiently. "Yes, Your Majesty. Rather than putting out a call to arms to recruit from among civilians, it is much more efficient to contract mercenaries who are skilled and battle-hardened. They are expensive, and my resources—as well as those of any allies you can convince to donate along the way—will be drained since Zhelyas controls the royal coffers within the palace. Therefore, the more contributions you can muster, the more forces will be at your disposal."

Caro pressed her lips together. "Does that mean Zhelyas has hired mercenaries as well? Could that be who this Morfran is?"

"I cannot say," Vittorius said, shaking his head. "Because he did not have access to the Crown's assets until recently, Zhelyas would have had to do so with his own personal capital. If we are lucky, he will consider his strength unassailable now that he controls the full might of the royal army. However, we must consider all possible likelihoods. The fact remains, he now possesses all the funds he needs to add to his ranks, which is why we must hurry."

"Then it's decided," Caro declared. "We will first visit the house of Baron Oswin Odric, then veer east through the Esaphis and make for Biding." She drew the point of the knife along her proposed path. "From there, it will be an easy journey to the grand duke at Agassey."

She waited for them to nod, then rose. "If we are all in agreement, we shall leave at dusk."

Live by the Sword

The first thing Malcolm noticed was the strange arrangement of lights. The room was dark. Thick curtains had been pulled across the windows, snuffing out all trace of the sun outside, bathing the black-clad figure in shadow.

"Sit," the figure said, and something in Malcolm's mind echoed that command.

A single chair had been placed at the center of the room, upon which three lamps shone. There wasn't another trace of light, and Malcolm swallowed, feeling much as if three glowing eyes were fixed upon him in addition to those of the masked man.

Commander Morfran.

Before that fateful night, nobody had heard his name. Since then he was like a ghost, flitting to and fro to fulfill his master's orders, yet he did not quail before the new king. There were whispers he was an assassin, and though Zhelyas had taken it upon himself to mete out discipline to assert his own authority, Malcolm had no trouble believing the rumors.

"Earl Malcolm Dahl, is it?" Morfran began, his voice like velvet.

"Yes, Commander."

Malcolm's lips felt dry, and he licked them nervously. He could barely see Morfran, merely an outline illuminated by the lights shining in his eyes.

"From where do you hail?"

"I... uh... My father is from Drusus, and my mother is Artemisian," Malcolm replied.

"And you are married to the daughter of Duke Vittorius?"

Malcolm nodded, visions of his wife and family bubbling into his consciousness. "Yes, my wife is the Countess Andrine Iduna."

Morfran made an indistinct sound in his throat. "Children?"

"Two. Twins, age four."

"I see," Morfran murmured, and began to pace slowly.

Malcolm wasn't entirely sure why he was being so forthcoming. It wasn't that he feared the commander so much that he felt compelled to answer.

"How long did you court your wife?" Morfran continued. Again, that strange intensity.

"Andrine and I have been friends since we were children."

"You must be quite familiar with the royal family, then."

Malcolm's palms were sweating. "I grew up in the palace, yes."

"Then perhaps you may recall that eight years ago, there was a ball. It was the princess's birthday."

Malcolm swallowed and nodded. Andrine, fourteen at the time, had been radiant, wearing a gown of shimmering gold. He'd been fifteen, and it would be four more years until they married, but he'd been completely smitten.

He realized from the uncomfortable silence that he'd missed Morfran's next question. "P-pardon?" Malcolm ventured, hoping to soothe the commander's palpable displeasure.

"Something was taken from me that night," Morfran repeated, his voice low. "Copper hair, ice-blue eyes. Do you remember anyone like that?"

Malcolm tried to cast his mind back, but all his memories that night were of Andrine. "Eight years is a long time—" he began, and Morfran leaned forward and pinned his wrists against the arms of the chair.

Malcolm recoiled, bracing his feet against the floor at the unexpected invasion of his space. The lamps above refracted off the silver mask and he blinked rapidly, small points of light dotting his vision.

"Are you certain?"

The soft words were laced with a suppressed fury that made Malcolm numb, and he bobbed his head, his heart pounding in his chest. For a moment, Malcolm feared the man would lash out, and he held his breath.

Finally, Morfran straightened, releasing him, and retreated once more into the darkness. "Very well, you may go, Earl."

Malcolm rose, his knees quaking.

"Tell no one of this," Morfran added, and Malcolm gave a hurried bow.

"Y-yes, Commander."

He opened the door and staggered from the room into the brightly lit hallway, feeling lightheaded. What had all that been about? Why had he asked those questions?

Wait. "He" who?

Malcolm shook his head to clear it, but it was like cobwebs muddled his thoughts.

Morfran sighed as he straightened the chair, which had been knocked askew.

The earl would remember nothing of their conversation— none of them would. Morfran had his own methods of interrogation, and as much as it frustrated him, it was better if his inquiries left no trace behind. This ensured that at least there was no way for the nobles to come up with a cover story together or obscure their testimonies.

It was an efficient method that seemed almost mystical in nature, but no magic was involved. The three lights tricked the brain, inducing a susceptible hypnotic state. Once the "trigger" was removed upon exiting the room, all memories of what the person had said under its influence trickled away. There would be a gap in their perception of time, but that too would fade within a few hours.

It was hardly a perfect approach, but Morfran had little other choice. Unless he intended to cut a great swath through the court—something he doubted Zhelyas would approve of— he had to utilize what tactics he had at his disposal. Unfortunately, it required him to be quite precise in his questioning, focusing the subject's mind on a certain subset of memories, and so far that had yielded few useful results.

He'd almost worked his way through the denizens of the palace, but the face he had seen that day, the one clue as to the traitor in his past, was seemingly invisible. Veena knew something—she was the one who'd enticed him into joining this little insurrection with the promise of discovering the truth, but these methods wouldn't work on her even if he tried. He had already established that Zhelyas hadn't yet arrived at court at that time, Arvind was currently away on a mission from the king, and Luther was as clueless as the rest.

Morfran growled with vexation and clenched his fist, the wood splintering beneath his fingers. Eight years. The truth was almost within his grasp. He would be patient a little longer.

Morfran's thoughts drifted back to the day when he had been roped into this conspiracy.

A figure in a deep blue cloak drifted through the night and slipped into the tent of the assassin.

He looked up as a sweet scent in the air heralded the approach of a strange presence. In the blink of an eye, his dagger was at her throat. "Can I help you?"

"You're as good as they say." She glanced at him out of the corner of her eye with a patronizing smile. Then she vanished into a puff of blue smoke, which wafted across the room before she rematerialized.

"Cute trick." Morfran's voice was light, but he tightened his grip on the dagger. He hated sorcerers. They were unpredictable and cagey, and had an annoying habit of speaking in half-truths. "I'll ask again: who are you, and what is it you want?"

"My name is Veena, and it's not what you can do for me— but what I can do for you."

"I highly doubt that," Morfran scoffed, but he was intrigued.

Veena's long finger traced the scrolls on his desk, lingering upon a list of names, all crossed out with angry strokes.

Morfran strode to the desk and stabbed the dagger into the parchment, a hair's breadth from her fingers. "You are trying my patience."

"I know who you are, Morfran. I know the darkness in your heart, and what it craves."

"And what is that?"

"Revenge. I can get it for you."

He narrowed his eyes at her. "The knowledge you have is very dangerous, sorceress. I have killed men for less."

She blinked up at him in mock surprise. "Oh, I have no doubt. But I'm serious."

He pursed his lips. "Go on."

"There is a client of mine who has designs upon the Artemisian throne. Aid him in his goals, and you will attain your desires as well," she said tantalizingly. "Everybody wins."

Half-truths. But still... if she was sincere, it might be worth the risk. Years of fruitless research had yielded nothing—the impaled scroll proved as much.

Morfran's cheek began to itch beneath the mask, and he resisted the urge to scratch it. "And what would I have to do?"

She reached up and stroked the silver metal which obscured his scarred features. "Only what you do best."

Pearls before Swine

It was with mixed feelings that Caro left Aurinesse.

She glanced back at the castle upon the hill, its walls of ivory stone gleaming rose and lavender in the glow of the setting sun. Banners waved from the parapets, emerald against the crimson sky. The crest of the Artemisian royal family was emblazoned above the gates, twin golden winged lions bearing a crown, and the shafts of light streaming through the clouds made them seem almost alive, growling and beating their wings against the injustice of their rightful queen forced to escape into the night.

It wasn't only the capital of Artemisia, it was her home. She silently vowed to return once more as its queen.

"Caro?" Ezalia ventured.

"I'm ready," Caro replied.

With a heavy heart, she turned her gaze from her beloved city and focused on the road ahead.

As they traipsed toward Oswin's estate, the discussion of donation came up.

The currency of the land consisted of three types of coins: rukmas, made of gold; chandras, silver; and kamsyas, bronze.

The ratio of each amounted to 1:20:40. Only those of wealth and stature used rukmas in their general dealings, while chandras and kamsyas were far more common. For instance, two chandras was the standard weekly rent for a small room, while a kamsya could purchase a bag of apples or a bucket of coal. A person could comfortably get by on twenty rukmas a year, forty if they had a family. Those more well-off earned one to five hundred rukmas, while the truly rich enjoyed an annual salary of one thousand. To wealthy lords and land barons like Oswin, that was a drop in the bucket.

"His holdings are prodigious, so we could ask for quite a bit," Ezalia mused.

"I'm not sure that's the right tactic, however," Gaius said, and Caro cocked her head.

"Why is that?"

He gave a wry grin. "A question for Lady Ezalia. If there is something you want, but you're not certain your suitor will provide it, do you ask for it directly?"

"Of course not. You make it seem like it's their idea," she replied, her lips turned up with amusement.

"Precisely. I would suggest asking for a sum of five hundred rukmas."

"Five hundred?" Stelian repeated, evidently puzzled. "That's not much."

"Oh, don't worry," Gaius assured him. "We'll get more. With the right persuasion, I've no doubt he'll play right into our hands."

The sun was high in the sky when they reached Oswin's manor. Caro wasn't sure what to expect, but the tall, blocky house painted a murky shade of blue, with fringed brown awnings and oddly-placed gold accents, was not it.

Not wishing to attract any more attention than necessary, she sent Stelian ahead to inform Oswin of their arrival. It was apparent he took the news of their impending visit with a certain panic, and the house was in a state of utter bedlam when they arrived.

"My Lord Baron Oswin Odric," Stelian began once they were inside, "may I present Her Majesty, Queen Caro."

He stepped out of the way, and Oswin gave a flourishing bow.

"My dear queen!" he exclaimed. "It is a pleasure—nay, an honor—nay, a delight—to have you visit my humble home!"

Caro sighed inwardly. Oswin was not known for his subtlety—or his discretion.

He was a fleshy, stout man with a girth that suggested a lifetime of indulgence in food and wine. He had a round head with a thatch of brown hair brushed over a visible bald spot, prominent sideburns, a bulbous nose, and watery blue eyes that peered out from beneath bushy eyebrows.

"I am pleased, Lord Oswin," she said. "However, I do not want to put you to too much trouble. After all, I am traveling in *secret*."

She stressed the word, and Oswin deflated somewhat.

Then he perked right back up again. "Nonsense, my queen! It is no trouble!"

Caro would have to ask her uncle about his questionable recommendation another time. Still, as loud and boisterous as Oswin was, he had a great deal of wealth which she could use for her purposes. All she had to do was butter him up, and that didn't seem a difficult task. Oswin was already barking orders for "the finest rooms and food to be prepared for their delectation at once!" An odd choice of words: how could a room be "delectable"?

Caro smiled her most endearing, benevolent smile. "I am grateful for your hospitality, Lord Oswin. My feet are tired. May I come in and rest?"

"Right this way! Only the finest chair for my most esteemed guest!"

The inside of Oswin's home was even more disconcerting than the outside, if that was possible. The floor was covered in a patterned orange carpet so ornate and garish it made Caro's head spin. The wood accents were an oppressively dark mahogany, while the upholstery and even the walls were an unnerving shade of red. Whoever had come up with the decor must have been spiteful or had zero taste, and glancing at the noisy baron, she suspected it was the latter.

Oswin paid Gaius and Ezalia similar, though lesser, courtesy, while servants, even those of a queen, seemed to be beneath his notice. Caro sent Stelian a sympathetic look.

"My Lord Oswin, I'm sure you are aware of what has transpired in the capital," she began, turning to her host, who had knocked Gaius out of the way to take the seat closest to hers.

"Yes, such a terrible business," Oswin said. "My loyalty lies squarely with you, Your Majesty!" he added in a high-pitched voice that made her ears ache.

"Naturally, I do not doubt your fidelity," Caro purred. "In fact, that is why I have come. You see, I am in a most wretched situation. The traitor Zhelyas has seized control of all the castle assets, and my own funds are too meager to furnish my rebellion. I would be in your debt if you could lend me some aid."

Oswin had fallen silent, perhaps expecting she was going to ask him to serve as a combatant in her army—heaven forbid.

"Of course, in doing so, you would share in the glory," she added coyly.

"Your Majesty!" Oswin exclaimed, the words reverberating off the walls and rattling around in Caro's skull. "All that I have is yours! Why, I would drain my coffers to serve you!"

"That won't be necessary," Caro said. "Five hundred gold rukmas will do."

"Five hundred?" Oswin gasped, rising in a dramatic fashion. "I would never dream of it. You must have five *thousand* rukmas at the very least!"

Stelian's mouth fell open, and he quickly closed it.

"You are so generous, I can't even express my gratitude," Caro gushed as Gaius tapped the baron's shoulder with a feather pen.

A bank writ appeared on the table as if by magic, and Oswin signed it for the declared sum.

"There is no need, Your Gracious Majesty," Oswin said once the writ was signed and tucked into Gaius's pocket. "I ask only that you honor me with your presence for a while longer."

"Alas, my good sir," Caro said regretfully, "we must move on."

"But you must at least stay for the banquet!"

Caro blinked. "Banquet?"

Caro sat in the dining parlor at the head of the table at Oswin's urging, his usual place which he had given up for her use. Though she would have preferred a quiet dinner with her companions, considering the amount of money he had contributed, it would be rude to refuse.

The kitchen served no less than nine courses, and Caro ate a polite portion of each, knowing there was more to come. First was a potato soup served in a silver tureen, then a salad of shredded greens and sausage, followed by salted fish, fried pork with clams, and lamb with mint sauce. A delicate sorbet cleansed the palate before a meaty roast beef marinated in wine and garlic.

The penultimate course was sweets, a variety of regional custards, puddings, and pastries arrayed before her on Oswin's gaudy orange china. Lastly, fruit and cheese was served in the drawing room along with liqueurs, and it appeared Oswin liked to indulge.

Caro sat by the fireplace while Oswin and the members of his household attempted to entertain her with salacious gossip and the occasional lewd joke. They were all quite drunk, and she very much wished to leave.

After a while, Oswin began to prowl around the room like a hungry dog, and Caro watched him warily as she sipped her tea.

"You there, boy!" he snapped, and Stelian jumped.

"Yes, my lord?" he replied, bowing.

"Who are you, eh?"

"I am Lieutenant Stelian, Your Lordship. I am Miss Caro's bodyguard—" He realized his mistake the moment the words fell from his lips. "I mean, Her Majesty's," he said, backtracking, but it was too late.

Oswin's face turned an ugly shade of puce, his eyes bulging. "How *dare* you speak so casually of your sovereign, whelp? I should have you whipped for your insolence!" Oswin's shadow loomed over Stelian as he lifted his arm to strike.

There was a blur of white as a teacup sailed across the room, passing a hair's breadth from Oswin's pudgy nose before it smashed into the wall.

He froze, his arm dangling in midair as Caro stood and made her way across the room, which had been stilled into silence.

"A slip of the tongue, my lord," she said calmly. "You must forgive my bodyguard. He forgot himself."

"My apologies," Stelian said, bobbing his head to placate their angry host.

However, it seemed Caro's timing was impeccable, and Oswin sobered up instantly.

"Pardon me, Lord Oswin. I saw a spider," she added, indicating the teacup, which had been reduced to smithereens.

"Th-that's quite all right, Your Majesty," he replied, stammering as he mopped sweat and tea droplets off his face with a handkerchief.

"In that case, I wish to retire for the night."

"Yes, Your Majesty!" he exclaimed, recovering, and the occupants of the room bowed low. "Your quarters are prepared, as are those of your companions—"

"I shall not require a room, my lord. A blanket will suffice," Stelian interjected.

Oswin frowned. "That simply will not do."

Caro glanced over her shoulder and smiled sweetly. "Where else should my bodyguard be but by my side?"

Gaius and Ezalia made a discreet exit as well.

"Nice to see your dart practice hasn't gone to waste," Gaius quipped.

Caro chuckled. "You never know when it'll come in handy."

A maid around Caro's own age waited by the door of her room, dressed in a prim uniform with a black dress and a white apron. She had a sweet round face, golden curls beneath a frilled cap, and shy blue eyes.

"I have filled the warming pan with embers to heat the bed and brought sir's blanket as requested," she said, curtsying. "Does Your Majesty need any help undressing?"

"What is your name?" Caro inquired, taken with the angelic maid.

"Lottie, Your Majesty."

"Thank you, Lottie, but I will manage."

The girl flushed at her name being spoken by a royal personage. She curtsied again, then handed the blanket to Stelian, who wrapped it around his shoulders and positioned himself cross-legged outside the door, his sword at the ready.

.

Upset the Applecart

Veena crouched, drawing a circle on the floor of the throne room in blue chalk. Zhelyas stared down from his throne, his chin resting on his hand. Morfran stood off to the side, silent as a ghost.

"Will this work?" Luther asked doubtfully, lips creased in a frown. Of them all, he was the one who put the least stock in magic.

"If you quit interrupting me," Veena replied tersely, not looking up from her work.

Inside the circle, she drew a complex series of triangles, forming a thirteen-pointed star, then placed a clear crystal at each of the cardinal directions. Finally, she drew a spiral rune at the center, standing before it with a handful of feathers clutched in her hand.

Varisha
God of air and sky
Lord of winds which ceaseless blow
Heed my call and to me fly
Arise as I beckon and follow

She sprinkled the feathers, and a breeze rose up in the room, swaying the chandeliers and rustling the curtains. Luther took a step back, visibly nervous.

The feathers swirled around Veena's body, never leaving the circle.

Along the pathway be my guide
Seek the traces left behind
Which from my sight may try to hide
And whisper what I wish to find

Veena finished chanting the invocation, and the maelstrom died down. She swept her hair out of her eyes, turning to her expectant audience.

"The queen and her retinue have left the capital and are journeying along the road to Ock. They have stopped at the house of a nobleman in Tamford," she said.

"Baron Oswin Odric, I'd reckon," Luther murmured, running a hand over his unshaven jaw.

Zhelyas rose. "Investigate this immediately," he commanded, cutting the air with his hand. "I want Caro found!"

Luther obeyed.

Veena waved her hand, and the chalk circle upon the throne room floor dissolved, every trace wiped away. The feathers also vanished, and she stooped to pick up the crystals which had served as a focus for the spell.

"That was rather impressive," Zhelyas said as she rose to her feet.

"Thank you, sire," Veena replied wearily. She knew she should respond with more sweetness to his compliments, but she didn't have the energy for it. "If you will excuse me, I am quite spent."

Caro didn't sleep a wink that night. They had planned to slip out before dawn, so she was already dressed and wide awake, counting the speckles on the ceiling, when she heard a scuffle in the hall.

"Stelian, what's going on?" she inquired, peering out her door.

"This maid insists on speaking with you, Your Majesty," he replied, trying to dissuade a girl who appeared very determined.

"Lottie, isn't it?" Caro said kindly, recognizing her.

"Milady, you have to get out of here. You're in danger," she said breathlessly. "General Luther's on his way. If he finds you..."

Gaius had also apparently been lured by the commotion, and he poked his head into the hall. "Should've known. Did Oswin tell him?"

"No, milord, the master is still sleeping—I checked. I was taking the slop to the pigs when I overheard a couple of the farmers saying they saw Luther and his men coming down the road."

Caro exchanged a glance with Gaius. They had expected something like this to happen. Oswin hadn't been even remotely discreet, but she had thought they'd have a little more time.

"Gaius, get Ezalia," she instructed, and her aunt appeared.

"I heard everything. So we're leaving then, I gather?"

There was a thumping sound, then a pounding on the front door.

"I think we know who *that* is," Gaius quipped.

"Is there any other way out of here?" Caro asked, eyeing the window in her room, though they were two stories up.

Lottie nodded. "The servants' stairs."

The pounding grew louder.

"Lord Oswin Odric, open the door!" a voice bellowed, unmistakably that of Luther.

"Hurry!" Lottie bounced on her toes as she urged them down the hallway.

There was a door at the far end of the corridor that looked like an innocuous broom closet, but Lottie opened it to reveal a spiral staircase leading to the floor below.

"When you get to the bottom, the exit before you will take you outside by the guardhouse. The one to the left leads to the scullery."

Caro nodded at Lottie's hushed instructions. "What about you?"

"I'll be fine, Your Majesty. Please go!"

Oswin could be heard muttering from downstairs, apparently awakened from his stupor.

Caro gave the girl a quick nod, and they all slipped through just as Luther kicked in the front entrance.

"What is the meaning of this?" Oswin demanded as Luther stormed through the door, followed by a dozen soldiers.

"King Zhelyas received intelligence that the criminal Queen Caro was seen in this vicinity and may be harbored by one of the nobility. That person would be a traitor to the Crown for doing so."

"I don't know what you mean, General," Oswin blubbered. "No queen here!"

The baron was a wreck, wearing a robe tied over his portly belly and only one slipper. He hovered on the staircase, trying not to look nervous, which only served to make Luther more suspicious.

"Search the manor!" Luther ordered. "You don't object, do you, Baron?"

"Of course not, General. Feel free. My home is your home!" Oswin said, laughing hysterically and mopping his brow.

Luther scowled at his levity and pushed past him, heavy boots sending shudders up the side of the house with every thudding step up the stairs.

He kicked open a door, eliciting screams from a man and woman who had been interrupted *in flagrante delicto*, as it were.

The soldiers opened the doors to the other two rooms.

"Find anything?" Luther asked.

"No, sir. Looks like the beds were slept in, but they're empty." He held up a wrinkled sheet as proof.

"Same with these," said another guard.

"Unhand me, you ruffians!"

Two of the soldiers had grabbed a maid standing nearby, and Luther glared down at their wriggling captive.

"You know anything about this?" he demanded, shaking the sheet in her face, and she paled.

"I—I'm not sure what you mean..." She darted a glance at Oswin.

"You," Luther called gruffly. "Get up here."

"Yes?" Oswin said in an innocent voice.

"Looks like you had quite the party last night." He glanced around at the rest of the staff, who had gathered in the hall in their nightclothes, bedraggled and obviously intoxicated.

Oswin gave a shrill laugh. "With my cousins, wouldn't you know? But they left at cock-crow, wanted to miss that early morning traffic to Ockbridge."

Luther turned his attention back to the maid, nodding to the soldiers to release her. "Is this true?"

She bobbed her head. "Y-yes, General. The master's guests left a little while ago. I was coming to clean their rooms..."

"Silly little wench, don't pay her any attention," Oswin interrupted with an oily smile.

He took the sheet from Luther and thrust it into her arms. "I'll deal with you later," he hissed, then waved his hand briskly, shooing her away. She scurried down the hall and out of sight.

Oswin turned his attention back to Luther, a cheerful grin plastered on his face, and guided him back down the stairs. "My good general, while you're here, why don't you sample some of the fine Tamford wine we're so famous for? I don't want to boast, but the palace wineries can't hold a candle to my own personal store..."

Luther grabbed him by the collar, pressing him into the wall, his sword at the man's fleshy neck. "Did you think I would be dissuaded so easily?"

Stelian had already packed their bags with provisions and loaded them onto a wagon he had liberated from the shed, and Caro could barely see the outline of where it had been stashed in the woods at the edge of the lord's demesne.

Gaius flapped his hand, and they crouched, backs against the wall as they rounded the manor and shuffled under the large foyer window.

One of the soldiers opened the sash and peered out into the dark.

"What is it?"

"I thought I heard something."

Caro pressed her hand to mouth, praying he couldn't hear the thumping of her heart.

"Must've been the wind."

The group let out their collective breaths as the sash snapped shut above their heads. They crawled the rest of the way into the cover of the hedges bordering the prim lawn.

"Everything ready?" Caro inquired.

"Yes, miss," Stelian replied, patting the horses so they stayed quiet.

Ezalia looked a little rumpled from their abrupt flight, but otherwise nobody was the worse for wear.

"Then let's get going. I don't want to linger any longer than necessary."

"I agree," Gaius said, glancing back the way they had come. "I have an ill feeling."

Caro shivered at his foreboding words.

"If you would permit me?" Stelian offered. At Caro's nod, he placed his hands on her hips and lifted her into the wagon.

"Milady?" Gaius said with a wry smile, and Ezalia glared at him halfheartedly.

"Oh, very well," she said with a sigh, and allowed him to do the same.

There was a yelp and a cry of indignation from the manor, and Caro looked up.

"Lottie?"

"We have to go, Caro," Ezalia said rationally.

Caro bit her lip, then glanced down at Stelian.

He nodded, perceiving her intentions. "I'll see to it."

Gaius took the reins, and the wagon set off.

Lottie bundled the sheets into her trembling arms and hauled them down the servants' staircase to be washed.

She'd done her duty as a loyal citizen of the Crown, just as her pappy had taught her, but the look on her master's face had chilled her to the bone. She had no doubt Oswin was planning to turn the queen in himself to get the reward money and weasel his way into the usurper's good graces, and she had denied him that. The least she could expect was a whipping. The worst...

Lottie's throat went dry as she considered the implications. Still, she refused to regret her actions, rash as they were. If someone as insignificant as her could make a difference, then it was worth whatever befell her.

As she started to open the door to the scullery, a hand covered her mouth, muffling her cry.

"Shh, don't scream."

"You were with the queen," Lottie whispered, recalling the man's reddish hair and rugged good looks.

"Lieutenant Stelian," he replied.

"What are you doing here? It's not safe!" Lottie's frantic gaze flitted back up the stairs, where raised voices could be heard.

"Did you think Her Majesty was going to abandon her rescuer?" Stelian inquired with a wry smile at her shock.

"But I—"

"I won't force you to come, but the baron knows what you've done, doesn't he? Will he punish you?"

Lottie looked away and nodded.

"Then it's too dangerous for you to remain here at the manor." Stelian held out his hand. "Come with us, and we'll keep you safe."

"I'm going to give you one last chance, Baron," Luther growled.

Oswin's lip trembled, then he cracked. "Oh, forgive me, General, I was deceived! The queen came and threatened me, extorted money out of me!"

111

Luther leaned close. "And? Where is she now?"

"The wench helped her escape!" Oswin snapped, jutting his chin in the air.

"The maid?"

Oswin bobbed his head.

Luther stepped back, the blade still extended. "Find the girl. We'll see what King Zhelyas has to say about this."

There was a half-empty bottle on the table, and Luther took a swig. He should have just gotten drunk and avoided this whole rotten mess.

"General!"

"What is it? Where's the maid?"

"She's not in the house, sir."

"Wonderful," Luther grumbled. He turned to Oswin. "Well, it seems you have nobody to blame but yourself, Baron."

Luther passed by Morfran, who was waiting with his squadron at the edge of the capital.

"You smell like spirits," Morfran said, wrinkling his nose.

"The baron had quite the party last night, so it was only right of him to share with us hard-working lads."

Morfran sighed at his compatriot's glibness, then frowned. "A party? For whom?"

Luther ran a hand over his face. "Claimed it was some cousins of his, but with a little convincing, he finally confessed it was the wayward queen and her entourage. I'm taking him to the capital to see the king."

"I see. And the queen?"

"Off to Ockbridge, I'd wager. From there, though, who knows."

Morfran pursed his lips. "I suppose we keep looking, then. I'll leave the miscreant to you, while I set up patrols along the bridge."

The door to the throne room flew open and a portly man stood there, looking as if the sky had fallen on his head. Luther hauled him forward and pushed him to his knees before Zhelyas, who leaned over, scrutinizing his prisoner.

"My liege!" the man cried in a shrill voice, panic in his tone and the way he wrung his perspiring hands.

So this was Baron Oswin Odric.

"Well?" Zhelyas inquired without preamble. "I hear you gave sanctuary to the queen after she fled the city, and even handed over quite a large sum of money. Then, when Luther arrived, you lied to him to save your miserable skin. What do you have to say for yourself?"

"I crave your forgiveness, sire! Good, merciful, beneficent king." Adjectives tumbled from Oswin's mouth like a sumptuous buffet.

Zhelyas found him intolerable yet amusing, like a jester. Perhaps he might even spare the halfwit's life.

"Come now, surely you do not think me such a fool," Zhelyas scoffed, and Oswin shook his head like a toy on a string.

"Her behavior was deplorable, my liege! Her servants were rude, and she even broke one of my favorite teacups," he sniveled. "I reluctantly allowed her to stay the night, but she snuck out before your man arrived, or I would have turned her into the proper authorities!"

Zhelyas scowled down at his blubbering form. "Why didn't you say anything to Luther?"

"I was ashamed I had committed such a grievous and unpardonable crime! Oh please, my liege, spare me!"

Zhelyas smiled as Oswin cringed. He enjoyed seeing the man squirm.

"Perhaps I will forgive you," he said silkily, and Oswin's face lit up with hope. "In time. A visit to my dungeon should be an enlightening experience. Meanwhile, your estate shall be repossessed as an army base, so you'll be serving me even in your absence."

Oswin moaned incoherently as he was led away.

"Station soldiers at Tamford to await further orders," Zhelyas instructed.

"Yes, sire," Luther replied.

"And when you're done, go check up on Morfran."

Luther passed the art gallery after leaving Oswin to his miserable fate in the dungeon. There were a dozen such galleries in the palace, each with a different theme: royal portraits, seasonal landscapes, and depictions of notable historical events, among others.

Radella was staring pensively at a portrait of Queen Guinevre. The deceased monarch was depicted with upswept dark copper hair and blue eyes, wearing a white dress with floral accents and a violet shawl. Many of Guinevre's surviving portraits had the same wistful expression, and Radella often said she wondered if the queen was thinking of a lost love.

He cleared his throat so as not to startle her.

"General," she greeted with a smile, turning to him. "I haven't seen you around in a while. The new king having you run errands?"

Her slightly derisive tone could be seen as treasonous, but Luther knew Radella too well for that.

"So it seems," he replied glibly.

"You've been drinking again," she noted with no trace of accusation in her voice. "I worry about you."

Luther furrowed his brow. "You don't blame me for what I've done?"

"I can't even fathom what could have made you turn on the royal family, but I know you must have had a good reason. I only wish you would confide in me like you used to." She took his hand. "I'm always here for you, I hope you know that."

He forced a smile, swallowing the guilt. "Please don't worry about me, Radella. I made peace with my choices long ago."

"And now?" she pressed.

"Now... now there's nothing more to say." Luther met her pleading gaze. "If you will excuse me, Countess, I must return to my duties."

Radella's shoulders slumped, deflated by his evasion, and he felt a pang of regret at the sadness which flickered across her lovely face.

Love and War

Zhelyas stormed down the hall. Yet another annoyance to deal with. Would it never end? If it wasn't army inspections or signing a thousand requisitions, it was consultations with financial advisers and stuffy politicians.

A woman stepped out of one of the rooms and failed to notice him approach; he didn't have a chance to slow his pace and crashed into her, knocking her off balance. Zhelyas reached out to keep her from falling.

"Y-Your Majesty!" she stammered, her cheeks flushed.

She was petite, with copper-blond hair pulled back from her face by a flamboyant ribbon, revealing attractive features. Her wide chestnut eyes stared up at him beneath arched eyebrows, her ruby lips parted in surprise.

"Forgive me, Lady Diascia Anthusa. I didn't see you," Zhelyas said.

Diascia and Lobelia, her elder sister, were the nieces of the former king of Effrenia. King Roland had been reluctant to have any dealings with Effrenia due to its unstable political climate, but had agreed to let the sisters remain at court. Lobelia was haughty and prideful, and had always looked down on Zhelyas with disdain for his low status. Still, Diascia was mild and comparatively shy. They were hardly ever apart, and seemed inordinately obsessed with their appearance, so Zhelyas generally avoided them, but he found himself attracted to the younger sister without the elder one around to sour his impression.

He steadied her on her feet, and she curtsied, her hair ribbon fluttering.

"I won't keep you any longer, sire. I'm sure you are busy."

Zhelyas thought about it a moment. Why ruin his good mood by dealing with pesky nuisances? He was the king; he could do as he liked.

"On the contrary, Lady Diascia, I was going to take a stroll around the grounds. Would you care to accompany me?"

She gave a dimpled smile and another curtsy as he held out his arm.

"I always love going to the garden," Diascia sighed. "Effrenia was so glum and gloomy, but here everything is bright, so many flowers. My name is a type of flower, did you know?"

"Oh?" Zhelyas murmured, feigning interest. Diascia liked to chat, it seemed, but she wasn't nearly so boring as the ministers who droned on and on in their monotonous voices.

"That one, right over there," she said, pointing to a pot with a frothy cluster of small, apricot-colored blossoms. "It's sometimes called 'twinspur.'"

Somehow, the showy yet delicate flower fit Diascia's temperament.

"Over there is lobelia," she added, indicating a bush covered with tiny sapphire flowers that seemed contradictory to its namesake. He recalled it was also used to induce vomiting, and he smirked to himself. "And lisianthus, after which my mother Anthusa was named." She gestured to a cool purple flower resembling both a tulip and a rose.

"I'm only now realizing how many women's names are related to flowers," Zhelyas mused.

Diascia chuckled. "Of course, because we're beautiful and desirable. Men are sometimes named after trees for their strength and steadfastness."

She winked up at him, pulling him a little closer. "Let's see..." She rattled off a number of tree names that sounded vaguely masculine, but Zhelyas wasn't paying attention. Diascia was not the most clever woman, but she was rather sparkling company. She was effervescent and laughed at his jokes, smiling adoringly up at him, quickening his pulse.

Was she cozying up to him because of his position? Probably. Did he care? Not in the slightest.

Zhelyas had been attracted to Veena—what man wouldn't be? She was a temptress and beautiful as sin, but he also knew better than to trust her. She was wily, and lately their relationship had been increasingly strained. He owed Veena everything, and he couldn't help but resent her for it. After their stifling, brusque conversations, Diascia was a breath of fresh air.

Diascia returned to the quarters she shared with her sister, humming a little ditty.

Lobelia was lounging on the bed, painting her fingernails, and looked up.

"I hear you were entertaining the king," she commented offhandedly.

"Why shouldn't I?" Diascia replied tartly. She sat at the vanity and began to dab her cheeks with rouge.

Lobelia frowned, then hastily readjusted her expression. "No, this is good," she said, rising to fiddle with her sister's ribbon. "If you're charming the king, he'll never suspect."

"I'm not sure..." Diascia murmured.

Lobelia came around beside her and placed a finger to her lips. "You trust me, don't you, Dia?"

"Lebby..."

"It's always been you and me. Our father was as corrupt as all the other nobles in Effrenia, but Mother was frail and couldn't handle the strain, so we were left to defend ourselves." Lobelia stroked her cheek. "And I always protected you, didn't I?"

Diascia nodded.

"Our uncle, the king... All he cared about was wine, women, and gambling. Then he decided to reach out to the king of Artemisia and send us as 'gifts' to ply his good will. King Roland took pity on us and allowed us to stay—but we were never welcome here. All we have is each other, and nothing will come between us."

Lobelia squeezed Diascia's hands. "Everything will work out in the end, you'll see. Once Zhelyas is defeated, the queen will reward me with the crown of Effrenia instead of our imbecile of a cousin, and you will have everything you've ever desired. Men will be falling at your feet, and we'll finally have the respect we deserve."

Out of the Frying Pan

Caro had been sitting in the wagon for two days, and her rear was sore from the bumpy ride.

"When I take back my throne, the first thing I'm going to do is re-pave the roadways," she grumbled as she worked a crick out of her neck.

"I hope Oswin's generous check doesn't bounce," Gaius mused. "We'd better cash it in as soon as we get the chance."

"So what are we going to do about her?" Ezalia inquired, glancing at Lottie, who had fallen asleep in the back. She pulled a knitted blanket over the girl's shoulders.

Caro sighed. "I couldn't just leave her behind knowing she was going to be beaten—or worse—for aiding in our escape."

"Not a nice way to repay someone for saving our lives, true," Gaius agreed, and that seemed to end the discussion.

In actuality, Ockbridge was two towns, Ock and Frok, connected by an aptly-named bridge spanning across a wide canal. Before the canal had been built, the land had been the demesne of a baron who owned a mill on the land. After the canal was completed and the two settlements sprang up on either side of the bridge, the mill was leased to the newly-established township and the baron and his vassals resettled elsewhere.

A few years ago, there had been a devastating fire at the mill. The powder-fine flour had caught alight, setting the entire place ablaze in a moment. It had taken hours to put out the flames, and Caro recalled her father contributing a sum of money as royal charity to help the reparation effort. The mill had been rebuilt, but the loss of life was no doubt still fresh in the minds of those who lived there.

"I think it would be better if we scoped out the bridge first," Gaius suggested. "I'll remain with the wagon and take care of our little Lottie."

"Perhaps the ladies should stay as well?" Stelian added, but Ezalia shook her head.

"It will be less suspicious for a man to be traveling with women. Caro and I can pretend to be shopping."

Ock was a quaint little town. Cozy, narrow cobblestone streets bordered buildings in brick and tawny clay, with high peaked roofs and colorful painted shutters. Vines of ivy climbed overhead, sweet-scented jasmine blossoms mixing with the smells of the market. The people all wore clothes in muted yet cheery shades, projecting a sense of gaiety. It was a picturesque scene, but there was a noticeable chill in the air—one not caused by the weather but the cloying uncertainty of the townsfolk whose peaceful lives had been upended by the armored men who stalked the streets.

"What pretty earrings, Esca," Ezalia said, attracting Caro's attention to a stall as one of them strode in their direction.

"Ah, yes. Very," Caro agreed. She held up the silver chandelier earrings and pretended to admire herself in a mirror, glancing surreptitiously at the reflection of the soldier behind her.

"They look lovely," Ezalia gushed, trying to keep the shopkeeper quiet. "Should we buy them?"

"Yes please, Auntie... Elandra, that would be wonderful."

Caro mentally kicked herself, but it was the best she could come up with on the spur of the moment. They should plan their pseudonyms in advance next time so she didn't sound like a complete ninny.

Ezalia paid for the earrings, and Caro tucked them in her bag. They were quite flashy and unlike anything she would normally wear, but she supposed they might come in handy.

While the ladies were browsing, Stelian returned his focus to perusing the charcuterie. He was chatting with the butcher at the best angle to observe the bridge, as well as the checkpoint which had been erected.

"I'll get some of this cured sausage," he said, nodding to himself.

"With sweet or spicy seasoning?"

"Sweet, please. That'll be less harsh on a lady's tongue."

"Ain't that the truth! My missus can't stand my peppers!" The butcher laughed jovially as he wrapped the meat in white oiled paper. "How about cheese? My missus makes a great chasi spread, and just down the street is the baker, my brother. Can't forget bread, too!"

"Naturally," Stelian said, wary of drawing too much attention, and paid the man.

The soldier at the guard post glanced in his direction, and Stelian gathered his purchases, heading back the way he had come. As he did, he passed a sign nailed to a door:

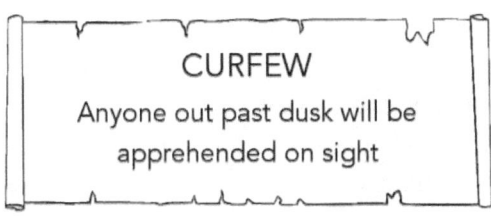

CURFEW
Anyone out past dusk will be
apprehended on sight

"Great," he muttered. "That's all we need."

They were all once more gathered at the edge of Ock, sitting by the wagon which Gaius had stowed behind a copse of trees.

Stelian unpacked his wares and sliced up the charcuterie while Gaius handed out napkins. Caro's mouth was watering; they had skipped breakfast due to their abrupt flight from the baron's manor. She tore off a piece of the soft baked bread and spread it liberally with creamy cheese.

"So it looks like Ockbridge will be a challenge," Stelian ventured.

Gaius nodded. "But there isn't another bridge for miles."

"Going around would send us heading due north, which is what Zhelyas is expecting," Caro added between bites. "That's precisely what I was hoping to avoid."

"What else can we do?" Stelian asked.

Ezalia pondered, glancing at the wagon, then stared at Gaius, whose expression turned from one of puzzlement to abject horror.

"No, you can't be thinking... Not again!"

"It worked once," she said sweetly.

Caro snorted as Gaius wilted.

"Okay, fine. So what is your grand plan?"

"I think we should split up," Ezalia said, her tone once more serious. She turned to Caro. "I hate to do that, but at least if we're found out, you'll be safe."

Caro nodded glumly.

"Using my 'magic,' Gaius and I can pass through the checkpoint with the cart, then you can follow closer to dark when the guardsman is getting sleepy."

"Stop!" the soldier said, holding up his hand and striding briskly to the front of the wagon.

"What's the problem, Officer?" Gaius inquired in a voice a few octaves above his usual pitch.

"Who are you, and where are you going?" The soldier peered into the back.

"Oh, me? I'm Darda. I'm taking my poor old mum to Flossholme for treatment. Bunions," Gaius added in a whisper. "I sell goods at market to pay for her salves. They're not cheap, you know."

"Show me your face," the soldier commanded, and lifted his sword to pull aside the veil Ezalia was holding.

He recoiled. Her wrinkled skin was dotted with pockmarks and warts. A particularly large one perched at the end of her hooked nose, and there were more beneath her chin. She grinned, and her teeth were blackened and rotten.

The soldier shuddered. "Go ahead," he said, shaking his head to banish the nightmarish image. "Move along."

Gaius batted his eyelashes for good measure before snapping the reins and urging the horses across the bridge.

Once they were safely out of Frok, Gaius turned to Ezalia. "You should be on the stage, woman. You frightened *me* to death with that getup. That poor soldier won't sleep for a week!"

Ezalia smirked, the expression making her theatrical cosmetics appear even more hideous.

"Neither will I," Gaius added, grimacing. "Can I get this stuff off now? My face is itching. I swear it's worse than torture."

Ezalia rolled her eyes at his whining and rubbed the charcoal off her teeth. "Men just can't handle what women suffer for their beauty."

Into the Fire

Dusk had fallen, and everything was bathed in hazy light. The autumn mist gathered like a sparkling cloak. It was a dreamy scene, and the soldier yawned. His shift was nearing its end, and he was ready to take off and drown himself in a vat of cider to scrub away the memory of that nightmarish woman's face. He shivered at the thought.

There was a shuffling of feet, and two figures stumbled out of the fog.

"One more drink, babe," the man said thickly, his arm curled around the woman's shoulder.

"We have spirits at home, and besides, I made a nice stew today. I'd hate for it to go to waste," she replied, pouting.

"Tell me you weren't out picking mushrooms again, Lola. Do you want to kill us?"

"It can't be any worse than *your* horrendous cooking, Stan!"

The two appeared to be quite inebriated as they tottered down the street, arm in arm. The woman was comely and well endowed, with blond curls and heavy makeup, wearing a revealing dress and a pair of shiny silver earrings.

"And what do you do with my hard-earned money? You buy trinkets! Or did some other lover give those to you?"

"You're a brute!" she huffed, pushing him away. "Maybe I should find myself a new man since you obviously don't appreciate me."

She spotted the guard, and her lips curled up into a smile. "Now here's a man who knows how to treat a woman, isn't that right, honey?"

The soldier rebuffed her advances. "You two aren't allowed to be out after curfew, you know that," he said sternly.

"Hey, you, don't touch my woman!" Stan snapped.

"Aw, we just wanted to have a little fun," Lola said sweetly, tapping the guard's nose. "How about a kiss and we call it even, eh?"

The sweet scent of her perfume was intoxicating, and he closed his eyes as she wrapped her arms around his neck, leaning in for a kiss.

The guard spluttered as his mouth was muffled with a cloth containing a mild soporific.

"Gaius's special concoction," Caro whispered with a wink, having snuck up from behind while he was distracted.

"Stan" propped him up against the wall so it looked like he was still awake, arms crossed around his spear for stability.

"Sweet dreams," "Lola" said, and kissed him on the cheek.

The three of them hurried to the other side of the bridge and into the welcoming darkness.

Caro sighed. "Now we just have to make it out of town."

"It would be best to keep to the back streets, out of sight of the patrols," Stelian suggested.

They made it about halfway through without being spotted. Caro was trying hard not to jump at shadows as they passed through the dark, misty alleys. Stelian peered around the next corner, then beckoned Lottie forward first.

"They're around here somewhere!" a voice cried.

It sounded like the guard wasn't napping anymore, and was now accompanied by a couple of friends.

"What do we do?" Lottie asked.

Stelian turned to Caro.

"Get out of here and find Gaius and Ezalia as planned," she replied in a hushed voice. "I'll meet up with you there."

He nodded. "We'll lead them away. Come on, Lottie."

Stelian grabbed her hand, and then they darted out of the alley, drawing the attention of the soldiers.

Caro ducked behind a stack of crates as the pursuers thundered past. She counted to ten under her breath, then emerged, heading in the opposite direction. She crept along the alley, keeping low until she got to the road.

"You there!" a gruff voice said, and Caro's heart sank.

A lantern swung in her direction, bathing her in light. No escape now. She took a deep breath and held up her hands.

"I'm sorry, mister. I got turned around when I was heading home," she said in her most innocent voice, facing them.

A senior officer of captain's rank stood there looking decidedly displeased, with four other soldiers at his back, one holding the lantern.

"It's so dark, and all the streets look the same in the fog. I didn't mean to miss curfew." She gazed up at him, making her eyes wide like a lost puppy.

The crease between his brows softened, but his frown remained. "I'm afraid the law is the law," he said. "You're coming with us."

The detachment escorted Caro to an army camp erected outside of town, and she stood before the captain in an orange tent, the flap pulled closed for privacy.

"What's your name?" he asked.

"Esca, sir," Caro replied obediently, using the moniker Ezalia had dubbed her with.

"And you were returning home? From where?"

"My uncle works at the mill. I delivered his dinner and was heading back to my aunt's house."

That sounded plausible. Night shift laborers would be exempt from the curfew as long as they didn't leave their place of work.

"What happened to your parents?"

Caro clenched her fists and hung her head. "They were killed." The best lies came from the truth. That was what Gaius had always taught her.

"How?"

"In the fire. Papa and Mama both worked at the mill."

"I remember," the captain said, his tone turning to one of pity.

"When the rubble was cleared away, nothing was left." The sorrow in Caro's voice wasn't entirely an act, and she fought to keep her composure. "So my aunt and uncle took me in."

"That was good of them."

Caro gave an imperceptible sigh. He seemed convinced, at least.

"We'll have to hold you overnight, but you should be able to go home in the morning."

The captain nodded to his subordinate, who unlocked her shackles and led her out of the tent to an empty billet.

Caro nodded her thanks, but she knew she wouldn't sleep a wink. The garrison was too well manned to slip away unnoticed. The best thing to do was to sit tight and wait.

Ezalia knew something was amiss as soon as Stelian and Lottie skulked out of town to the arranged meeting place.

"Caro?"

Stelian shook his head, his expression a conflation of failure and defeat. "We got past the guard, but the next shift must have arrived and roused him. The three of us split up to try and lead them away, but another officer caught Caro and arrested her for breaking curfew. There wasn't anything we could do. Forgive me, Duchess," Stelian said miserably.

Ezalia sent him a gentle smile, soothing Lottie, who had started to cry.

"When we realized what had happened, Lottie and I followed at a discreet distance. Caro was detained at the garrison on the other side of the mill, but it is well guarded, and we couldn't go any farther or risk being captured ourselves. I chatted up some of the soldiers who were coming off shift, and she should be released in the morning."

"Caro won't take unnecessary risks. Have faith in her."

Stelian gave a slight nod.

"Where is Luther right now?" Gaius inquired.

"Still back at Tamford," Stelian replied.

"And Morfran?"

Stelian shook his head. "No word on his whereabouts. The man's like a ghost. Not even his own troops know where he is."

"At least we're safe from Luther for the moment," Gaius said.

Ezalia sighed. "I just hope Caro doesn't run into this mysterious man Morfran. Who knows what would happen?"

Despite her earlier assertion, Caro managed to doze off, and she awoke when the billet door creaked open.

"Can I go now?" she asked, rubbing her eyes.

"Not yet."

It was the same soldier from the night before, but he seemed more jittery.

Caro swallowed. "Is there a problem?

"I don't know the details, miss," he said in a clipped tone, herding her down the line of tents.

They entered a building with a taupe exterior and navy roof tiles, which likely had been the baron's house but was now derelict. Many of the windowpanes were cracked and the brickwork was in need of repair.

"Excuse me, Commander," the soldier said, interrupting her musings. "I have brought the girl as you ordered."

"Very good. You may go."

He clicked his heels and gave Caro an impatient shove, knocking her off balance. She stumbled into the room, tumbling to her knees on the hard floor as the door slammed shut.

"Hello, Queen Caro."

Caro froze. That same low, solemn voice. She lifted her head and looked up into the face of the masked man.

"Morfran..."

Thin Ice

The commander sat upon a straight-backed chair as confidently as if it were a throne. His armor was entirely black, as was the lank hair which framed his silver mask, gleaming in the lamplight and casting his eyes in shadow.

He leaned forward, resting an elbow on his knee, and stared at her intently. "Isn't this a surprise? I thought it might be you from the captain's stirring description, but never in my wildest dreams did I imagine it to be true." The mask concealed much, but his mocking smile was painfully evident.

"But where are my manners? You must be parched." His black cloak rustled across the floor as he stood and crossed to a dining table with a decanter upon it. "Wine?"

"No thank you," Caro replied tersely, but she rose to her feet so she was on equal terms with him—figuratively, at least. He was a head taller, and it irked her that she needed to crane her neck to look up at him.

Morfran shrugged and drained the goblet. "Now, what am I to do with you?"

Caro bristled. "I'm not afraid of you."

"Oh? You may have noticed—despite having confirmed my suspicions regarding your identity—the room is not swarming with soldiers. Nor have I informed my liege Zhelyas I have located you. Why do you think that is?"

Caro frowned, but she didn't have an answer. It went against everything she'd heard about the elusive man. "Enlighten me," she said coldly.

He reached out and grasped her chin, forcing her gaze to meet his. "Because, my dear little queen, I have other plans for you. For the moment, it will be amusing to see you cater to my every whim."

Caro gritted her teeth and stepped back, jerking her jaw out of his grasp. "I am a queen. I do not take orders."

Morfran's smile lost some of its charm. "You are mistaken. You are a prisoner, and you will obey your captors or else face the consequences."

The underlying menace in his voice sent a shiver down her spine.

"Don't get me wrong. I have no intention of holding you hostage any longer than necessary. When the opportunity presents itself, I will help you escape. Deal?"

She hesitated, weighing her options. In many ways, this was the best outcome given her current predicament—albeit unlikely. Morfran's intensity unnerved her, and he ostensibly served Zhelyas, who was both a usurper and murderer. The thought that Morfran might have had a part in the plot made her blood boil, but she was decidedly at a disadvantage. She was convinced his generous offer was not all it seemed. Still, it appeared her only recourse was to play along.

"Very well," Caro said. "However, bowing to soldiers who are oblivious is one thing. My honor will not allow me to kneel before one who knows my true authority."

Morfran's smile turned sinister. "Then I shall give you no other choice."

He uncoiled the whip at his waist and cracked it sharply, the lash ricocheting upon the floor with a snap that made her flinch.

Even under threat, a queen could not yield; a lowly peasant girl, on the other hand...

She forced her protesting knees to submit, lowering her gaze to the floor. "Your servant, Esca, obeys."

Morfran raised his eyebrows at the use of her pseudonym. "Rise," he commanded, and Caro did so quickly.

He rewound the whip, hooking it on his belt, then retrieved a small silver bell from his tunic. It made a delicate, tinny sound. A moment later, a woman appeared at the door. Her hair and eyes were the color of pale honey, and she faced them with serenity.

"Ines, this is Esca. Please find her an appropriate uniform to wear."

Caro glanced at her leggings and vest, apparently deemed not fitting for an officer's servant.

"Yes, Commander," Ines replied. "This way, Esca."

Ines led Caro down the hall. At one time, the house would have been richly furnished and decorated, but most of the trappings had been removed, leaving the corridors stripped bare, as befitted a military command center.

There was a small dresser in one corner of the room, and Ines crouched, rummaging through the bottom drawer. Caro observed her. Something about Ines's behavior seemed out of place.

"You're blind, aren't you?"

"I am," Ines replied, as if it were the most obvious thing in the world. "Try these."

She held out a fistful of clothes, and Caro slipped out of her outfit.

There was a cracked mirror against the wall, and Caro looked at her distorted reflection. She was wearing a long-sleeved, muted green chemise under a linen dress that laced up at the sides and soft kid slippers. While Ines's draped elegantly, Caro felt as if she were wearing a potato sack.

"Do they fit?"

"Ah, yes. But how did you know?"

Ines chuckled at the innocent question. "Surely you have heard that those deprived of one sense develop a stronger affinity for the others. I guessed your height since you didn't have to stoop to avoid the lantern outside the door. The rest was conjecture, so I chose a uniform that would be a little roomier. If it's too large, please say so."

"No, it fits well enough. Thank you."

Ines smiled and stood, then sat on the bed, patting the covers beside her. Caro joined her, and Ines began to brush her hair, detangling the curls with the tips of her fingers.

"Your hair is soft, but recently cut it seems, and not with much patience," she said, touching the uneven edges where Caro had sawed it off with the dagger. "It must have been lovely when it was long."

Caro shrugged. Like most noblewomen, her hair was a source of pride, but she had cast away her sense of self. "I prefer it this way," she admitted.

"Is that so?"

"Tell me, Ines," Caro ventured. "Why do you serve Morfran?"

"The commander saved my life. I was being tormented by brigands, unable to defend myself from my oppressors, and I was frightened. Then they fell silent, and a gloved hand helped me to my feet."

She smiled at the memory. "I have been with him ever since. I have never laid eyes on his face, for that were impossible, yet I know the anguish in his soul better than anyone. He is truly kind."

Caro stared at her. Kind? Morfran—that cold, conniving man—was the sort who would rescue a blind woman? She could hardly reconcile the two images in her head.

Ines finished brushing Caro's hair and rose. "We should present you to your master."

Morfran acknowledged Ines's soft knock. "Come."

"I have prepared Esca," she declared, and nudged Caro forward.

"Commander," Caro said with a little curtsy. It was his rank, after all, and grated less than "master."

Morfran gave an approving nod. "Thank you, Ines. That will do."

"Very good, sir," Ines replied, and padded out of the room.

Caro stood stiff as a statue while Morfran examined her like a vulture circling its prey.

"You look quite fetching," he commented, and Caro scowled at him.

"Watch your tongue."

Morfran was no longer smiling, and he lifted a warning finger. "Take care. Such words may be tolerated in private, but you are meant to be my servant, and I am not known for my mercy."

"I'll be sure to be appropriately obedient," Caro replied, scorn lacing her voice. "Just tell me one thing: why did you save Ines? She told me about your past."

"That's a rather impertinent question."

"Indulge me."

Morfran gestured dismissively. "I couldn't stand by and watch someone be abused when they were helpless to fight back."

He seemed like he wanted to say something else, so Caro waited.

"Besides," Morfran continued in a low voice, "when she turned to me, she did not recoil in fear."

"You spared her because she couldn't see your face?"

Morfran shook his head. "Perhaps in her sightless eyes, I saw myself for the first time."

Caro had the impression Morfran had revealed something of his shadowed history. Was he once helpless, abused as Ines was? Perhaps she had glimpsed past the façade to the tormented soul beneath the mask.

"So how long did you get your wages docked for falling asleep at your post?" a soldier asked, sitting across from his fellow in the mess hall.

"Three weeks," he replied, grumbling. It was the same one who had been manning the bridge the night before. "But I swear it wasn't my fault! This woman with golden hair—"

"Yeah, yeah," his friend jeered. "But nobody else saw this phantom couple of yours, did they? And you know, the commander doesn't like excuses."

Morfran paused as he strode across the mezzanine above their heads, and they returned to their meals in awkward silence.

"I suppose that was your doing?" he mused, resuming his brisk pace. Caro had to nearly jog to keep up.

He glanced over his shoulder, and she shrugged.

"We had to do something to get past the checkpoint. It almost worked."

"The next guard on shift arrived early, otherwise it might have. But then we wouldn't be here."

Caro averted her gaze, refusing to rise to his bait.

"Oh, Miss Esca. You decided to stay?"

Caro's head snapped up at the sound of the captain's voice. Morfran sent her a warning look, which she ignored.

"When the commander offered me a position on his staff, I could hardly refuse," Caro said sweetly.

"I'm sure your aunt and uncle are pleased with your good fortune. Coming to the briefing?" he inquired of Morfran.

"I'll be right there."

The captain whistled as he strode off, and Morfran turned to Caro, the corner of his lips turned up with amusement.

"What?"

"You were surprisingly docile."

"Do not mistake my compliance for meekness, Commander. I am merely playing a part," Caro retorted under her breath. "I realize the danger, and I agree it is better to keep a low profile."

Morfran stared at her a moment, then gave a slight nod.

"So what now?" she asked.

"Now you do your chores." He thrust a pair of filthy boots into her hands. "You'll find shoe polish in the storehouse. I want to see my face in them when you're done."

Caro scowled up at him.

"You *are* my servant, aren't you?" he inquired in a low voice, and her lip twitched at the evident entertainment he was getting from this.

"Of *course*, Commander."

After scrubbing the muddy boots until they shone—Caro was going to make Morfran swallow his smug words—Ines suggested she had better get a good night's sleep. Caro apparently had the dubious honor of delivering Morfran's breakfast in the morning, followed by her first real chore: laundry.

Ezalia was waiting on tenterhooks for Stelian, apprehension and hope lining her beautiful face. "What's the news?"

After Caro had not returned the next morning as promised, her companions had grown antsy. Stelian, the least suspicious of them, had left to survey the camp and find out why.

Lottie handed him a towel, and he took it gratefully, wiping his face.

Gaius nodded. "Yes, tell us everything."

Stelian plopped onto the ground, rubbing his ear with the towel. "From what I can gather, the girl apprehended a few nights ago, 'Esca,' was to be released after her interrogation. However..."

"However?" Ezalia prompted.

"Morfran arrived at the camp under cover of darkness and asked that she be brought to him."

Ezalia groaned. "I was afraid of that."

"Strangely, though, instead of imprisoning her, he offered her a position on his staff. She's free to wander about, though undoubtedly under close watch. None of the other soldiers are aware of her true identity, either. It seems he's keeping that tidbit of information to himself."

Gaius held up a hand. "Wait. If he recognized her, why hasn't Zhelyas come swooping in to take her into custody?"

"I must admit, that puzzles me also," Ezalia mused. "And if he doesn't plan on turning her in... What does this Morfran have planned for Caro?"

"Either way, we may not have much longer to wait," Stelian interjected.

Gaius frowned. "Why's that?"

"I heard through the grapevine that Zhelyas has ordered Luther to check up on Morfran, and he'll be arriving within a week."

Ezalia shared a grim look with Gaius. "Then there isn't much time."

"Are we going to rescue the queen?" This from Lottie.

"It looks that way," Gaius said. "Now we need to come up with a plan."

All eyes turned to Ezalia.

"Honestly!" she huffed. "What would you do without me?"

Stelian laughed, then winced at a sharp pain in his arm.

"You're hurt!" Lottie exclaimed.

"Sorry. I got in a tussle with one of the soldiers in the tavern."

"Lottie, please bring me my bag," Gaius said, examining the wound.

"What am I, your nurse?" she replied crossly.

"If you like," he said offhandedly, not paying attention.

"Do you mean it?"

Gaius looked confused as he pieced together the fragments of their conversation. "Sure, why not?"

Lottie twisted at her apron. "I mean, cleaning and mending are the only things I'm good at."

Stelian thought that was rather unfair. She'd shown as much spunk and courage as ten men put together.

"You're already more qualified than most nurses I've met," Gaius said with a lopsided smile. "Get my things, and I'll show you how to stitch up this wound."

She leaped up and returned a moment later with the leather bag, from which Gaius withdrew the necessary materials.

"Wash the injury thoroughly. We don't want it to get infected," he instructed, and Lottie followed his directions diligently. "You seem to be more comfortable with this than I would expect," he mused. "Most people are rather put off by blood and bodily fluids."

Lottie shrugged, squeezing out the dirty cloth. "I worked on a pig farm before I started serving at the manor. Not to mention the kinds of things one had to clean up after the master overindulged."

Stelian wrinkled his nose at the revolting thought.

Gaius let out a little hum. "All right, it looks like the wound is clean enough, so it's time to stitch it up."

Stelian twitched his arm, earning a stern admonishment from Gaius.

"Stay still, would you? Or would you prefer an ugly scar?"

"I hear ladies like scars," he quipped with a wink for Lottie.

Gaius pricked Stelian with the needle, and he yelped.

"Honestly," Gaius huffed. "Lottie, would you like to give it a try?"

"Are you sure?"

"Your hands are steadier than mine—and your eyesight is better too," he added, awkwardly adjusting his spectacles.

She nodded and took the curved suture needle, threaded with strong silk filament. "We used ones a bit like this to repair upholstery."

"In that case, it's not much different from mending torn seams on a sofa," Gaius explained, apparently relieved to have a shared point of reference. "Gently pinch the edges of the skin together, keeping them as even as possible to reduce scarring.

When you run the thread back toward the other side, I'll snip it and tie it off. Ready?"

Lottie pressed her lips together and gave a determined nod. She concentrated intently, suturing the wound with neat little stitches.

"How did I do?"

Gaius washed his hands, then ruffled her blond curls. "You did great."

"So you're gonna be a nurse now, Lottie?" Stelian asked, flexing his hand. He'd had his share of nicks and cuts but had rarely been attended to by someone with such a delicate touch.

She giggled, beaming. "It's funny how things work out, isn't it?"

Caro slipped on her shoes and made her way to the kitchen at the crack of dawn, covering a yawn.

Sun streamed through a small window with faded yellow curtains. A hutch stood against the back wall to store the dishes, while shelves held various metal tins. On a counter was a coffee grinder, which she recognized as similar to the one Gaius used, as well as a device that looked like it might be used for chopping meat. In the corner was a rusty iron stove with wood burning in the firebox, and in the center of the room a large wooden table, the beams slightly warped.

"You, eat this," the cook said tersely, thrusting a bowl of porridge in her face.

She sat down at the table, still dusty with flour from that morning's baking, and began to eat. The porridge was rather tasteless, but it was warm and filled her up. She hadn't realized how hungry she was, and she devoured the modest meal. She licked the last traces from the spoon as the cook finished preparing.

"Take this tray to the commander," he ordered, placing a lid over the pewter plate to keep it warm. "And don't dawdle!"

"Yes, sir," Caro said hurriedly, wondering if the cook in her castle was this impatient.

She returned to Morfran's quarters and stood in the hall, summoning all her courage. Balancing the tray with one hand, she gave a soft knock.

"Come." Morfran looked up as she entered.

The commander's quarters were large but sparsely furnished. To the left was a bed, dresser, and washstand. The window, covered by curtains that were thick but threadbare in places, opened onto a balcony overlooking the land which had been converted into the army garrison. To the right was an ebony desk and beside it a bookcase, the bottom two shelves concealed by locked cabinet doors.

Morfran was sitting in a chair upholstered in gray with faded blue stripes, legs crossed, reading over some papers. Beside him was a matching chaise and a low glass table with pewter legs. He appeared to have just risen and was only half dressed, his tunic loose over his pants, his feet bare. Without his customary armor and cloak, he could almost pass for an ordinary man, except for the curtain of black hair draped over his ever-present silver mask.

"Your breakfast, Commander," Caro announced without preamble, and set it on the table, rattling the dishes.

He pulled off the lid, and the salty aroma of freshly cooked ham wafted from the plate. Nestled between the slices were two boiled eggs and a small salad of sliced tomatoes. Caro's mouth watered.

Morfran noticed her watching and cocked his head. "Do you want some?" he asked in an apparent attempt to entice her.

"No thank you," she replied haughtily, but it wasn't a lie. The porridge, though plain, had been surprisingly filling, and she felt like she had enough energy to face the day.

Caro set about gathering the clothes from the hamper to be washed, then turned to the door.

"You really should ask permission from your master before leaving."

Caro frowned, then turned to Morfran and gave a little curtsy, her arms overflowing with laundry. "If you would excuse me, *sir*."

He smirked and gave a slight nod.

Caro winced, rolling her shoulder. It had been hours, and her arm ached more than if she'd been swinging a sword all day. She had filled the giant metal tub with hot water and imitated Ines as she rubbed a shirt against the ribbed washboard. The fabric had been coated in soap, and the suds made the water filmy and filled with bubbles. Now her knuckles were bruised and sore from scraping them against the washboard repeatedly, and her fingers were pruney.

"Are you all right, Esca?" Ines inquired in her patient way. "I can finish up if you need to rest."

"I'm fine," Caro said, resuming her chore with renewed vigor. It wasn't that she enjoyed it, but she couldn't leave a job half done. That wouldn't be fair to Ines.

Finally, all the laundry was washed, and they clipped the garments and linens to a long clothesline.

"What now?" a breathless Caro inquired of Ines, who looked as if she was perfectly capable of handling it all herself.

"Have you returned the breakfast dishes to the kitchen?"

Caro blinked. She had forgotten about that. "Er, no."

Ines sighed. "You should do so. The cook won't be pleased if you leave it too late. The commander usually takes his midday and evening meals with the officers," she added. "Have something to eat, and by then the laundry should be dry."

Caro returned to Morfran's quarters and knocked. No answer. She saw the dishes on the table where he had left them and whisked them back to the kitchen.

"I know you're new here, girl, but are you completely inept?" the cook raged. He shook a wooden stirring spoon in her face, and it sprayed her with small droplets of soup.

She shook her head, trying not to rile him up.

"You return the dishes before you start any other chores, got it?"

"Yes, sir."

It didn't grate on her too much to be respectful; he was like the king of his own little kingdom. She had come to realize a household ran smoothly only if everybody knew their place, and she didn't want to get in the way of that, even if it hurt her pride.

"Eat," the cook said, apparently satisfied with her contrition, and gestured to a plate. Caro nodded gratefully and cut herself a slice of bread with some thinly-spread butter and a piece of cheese.

By the time she returned to the yard, the washing was dry, as Ines had predicted. Caro helped take the laundry down from the pegs, and she was careful not to let them fall on the ground lest they would need to be washed again. Ines draped a sheet over her arm until it was a neat little square, which she set on the pile. Caro couldn't help wondering how she managed all of this on her own.

"I'll put the sheets away in the linen closet," Ines said. "Will you be able to fold the commander's shirts?"

"Of course," Caro said, and hefted the basket.

Again there was no answer when she knocked, and she set the basket on the bed. Despite her confidence, she had never actually folded a shirt before. She laid the tunic out and frowned, then pulled across one arm, then the other, trying to recall how she had seen her nightdress folded in her drawer.

"Like... this?" she muttered to herself.

Caro was so intently focused she didn't notice Morfran enter the room.

"What are you doing?" he asked, peering over her shoulder and making her jump.

"Folding clothes," she replied evenly. "What does it look like?"

He crossed his arms, observing the scene the way one might an act by a street performer. "You've never folded clothes before, have you?"

She flushed at the cynicism in his tone. "If I'm doing something incorrectly, Commander, by all means tell me how it should be done," she said, her voice sugary sweet.

Morfran made an indistinct sound. "Carry on. But I don't want my shirts wrinkled."

"I wouldn't dream of it, Commander."

Of course, Caro was far too much of a stickler to mess up on purpose despite his goading, so Morfran returned later to find his shirts neatly folded on the bed.

Dinner that night was a cream soup with vegetables and a stock bone left over in the pot from the officer's stew, as well as a cup of mild tea. Before Caro was a queen seeing to matters of state and meeting with politicians, she had been a princess whiling away her days in leisure and study except for the odd sparring match with Luther or excursion with Stelian. She had never worked so hard in her life, and she was more exhausted than she thought a person could be and still function.

She climbed under the covers, not bothering to get undressed, and tried to find a comfortable position on the lumpy mattress. She had a new respect for Lottie, and made a mental note to tell her if she ever got out of this place.

Caro wondered what the others were up to. She was relieved to know Stelian and Lottie had escaped, but what now? Were they planning some sort of rescue? With just the four of them, it would be dangerous, and she still didn't understand what Morfran had planned for her.

Her worries niggled at her even as she fell asleep.

The same routine followed the next morning, but this time Caro tidied the bed and drew back the curtains while Morfran ate his breakfast so she could take the dishes down to the kitchen once he was finished. The cook gave her a short nod of approval before hurrying her out to do that day's chores.

Ines brought her to the storeroom and handed her a broom and dustpan. "You need to clean out the fireplace in the commander's quarters. You'll find the shovel on the hearth. Scoop out the ashes onto a sheet and bring them to the garden to be added to the compost. Then shake out the rugs and sweep the floor."

The fireplace was made of black stone with floral detailing along the mantle, a brick interior, and a decorative grate for the embers. Caro shifted the heavy grate, then began to shovel out the ashes. She sneezed, rubbing her nose with the back of her hand.

Cleaning out the fireplace was a strenuous task, and Caro soon found herself covered head to toe in soot and ash. Every inch of her from her fingernails to her hair was dirty. Trying not to cough, she tied up the sheet and lugged it to the greenhouse.

"Over there," a man said, gesturing from where he was tending to the vegetables, and she heaved the bundle into the corner.

The garden was situated behind a small storage shed presumably containing all the gardening implements. It was a rectangular plot of soil, and Caro recognized vines with beans and tomatoes, as well as cabbage, cauliflower, and tufts of what could be carrots or radishes sticking out of the ground in neat rows. In a basket nearby were freshly picked onions and beets with deep red stalks.

She stretched, cracking her back, then went to get the rugs. On her way, she scoped out the garrison. She didn't trust Morfran to fulfill his end of their bargain, such as it was; she needed an alternative. She would be in trouble if she left the grounds, but the manor had been built on the crest of a hill, and she could see enough to make a strategic judgment.

There was only one way in and one way out: through a guard post manned at all times. A wire fence had been erected around the camp, and soldiers were stationed on watch at regular intervals. Trying to slip through would be extremely risky since there would be no cover, even at night. If she tried to take the direct route to the gate, she would have to pass through the lines of tents erected for the personnel stationed at the garrison, including the one in which she had been interrogated when she first arrived.

Finally, there was the baron's former manor, which served as the residence for the senior officers. Soldiers patrolled the grounds surrounding the manor, as well as the woods at the rear. That might be her one option, if somehow she could find her way back to her friends.

Then there was Commander Morfran. He had been cordial so far, but if she defied him and tried to run, he could easily lock her up, and then she'd have no chance of escape whatsoever. It wasn't worth the risk. For now, she would have to bide her time and wait for an opening.

"I hope you're not going to be cleaning with those grubby hands," a snide voice said behind her, and Caro turned.

It wasn't Morfran, however, and she hurriedly replaced her look of scorn with something more demure, hoping the man hadn't noticed.

"Pardon, sir?" she replied, playing her part.

"You're filthy!" he snapped, and grabbed her wrist, twisting her arm to indicate the soot that stained her fingers and smeared her skin.

Caro trembled from the pain and indignity.

"Unhand my servant, Sergeant."

The officer, obviously Morfran's junior, paled slightly and tossed Caro aside like a rag doll.

"Apologies, Commander," he said bitterly, standing to attention.

"Dismissed," Morfran ordered, and the sergeant slunk off.

"I told you to keep your head down," he growled, and Caro shifted her feet. He had rescued her from a rather unsavory situation, so she owed him some courtesy at least.

Morfran scrutinized Caro's appearance. "You are indeed quite a sight. I'll be dining in my room tonight. Have Ines give you a bath before you bring dinner. You can finish up the rest tomorrow."

Deciding discretion was the better part of valor for the moment, she nodded.

Caro shivered as she slid into the washtub, previously used for that day's laundry by the maids who took care of the other officers. The once-hot water was cold, and the leftover soapy sludge felt slimy against her skin. She mercilessly scrubbed her nails with a bristle brush, trying to get every trace of the offensive stuff off.

"I can't imagine how you must look to ask a blind woman to wash you down," Ines said with a chuckle as she sponged off Caro's back.

Caro rubbed her nose, and her hand came back dirty. She must seem like a complete fool.

"I'm pretty useless, aren't I?" Caro whispered. "I can't do something as simple as wash clothes or clean out a fireplace without making a huge mess of it."

"I don't think you're useless," Ines said gently, "just inexperienced. I can tell from your frustration you've never done any of these things before, yet you try so hard. There's beauty in that."

She made her way around the front of the tub, tousling the ash out of Caro's hair with a damp towel. "You try to act mature, but you're still so young. You're allowed to make mistakes."

"What if those mistakes hurt other people? How do I live with myself?"

Of course she sounded childish—how could messing up at cleaning or washing hurt anyone?—but Ines gave a patient smile, seemingly reading the depth of her words.

"You acknowledge your mistake, make amends, and know better next time."

Caro blinked away tears, glad Ines couldn't see her cry.

"There, you should be clean now. I brought you a fresh uniform."

"Thanks, Ines," Caro said, and touched her hand to convey her gratitude. She wiped away her tears and dressed before making her way to the kitchen.

The cook already had the tray prepared, so Caro ate a quick meal of white fish and greens, then made her way to Morfran's quarters.

"Enter," he said at her knock.

He was sitting at the desk, and he turned as she set the tray on a spot clear of papers. Caro stood awkwardly as he appraised her.

"Much better. Can't have my servant looking like a little soot girl."

His chiding words filled Caro with anger and shame. "Enjoy your dinner," she said, trying to maintain a modicum of civility.

She gave a curt bow, then spun away, busying herself about the room while she waited for him to finish eating.

The silence was thick in the air, and finally Morfran sighed. "Do you play chess?"

She looked up, surprised by the question. "Yes," she replied warily.

"There are still a few hours left in the evening, and I'm bored."

Caro blinked at him.

"Unless you'd rather do some more cleaning?"

She was exhausted at the thought. "If those are my two options, chess it is."

He rose and went to the bookcase, withdrawing a chess set from one of the cabinets.

Morfran gestured to the chaise, and she sat down as he set the board upon the table between them, maneuvering his chair. The chess set was constructed of high quality marble, the pieces and alternating squares in white and crimson.

He turned the white pieces to Caro's side, giving her the handicap, while he took the red ones. Caro made the traditional first move, and Morfran followed up. They played for a while in silence.

"You're quite good," Morfran quipped as she took another of his pawns.

"I learned from my father," Caro replied, her thoughts drifting. Roland had been more down to earth than Cecilia, so while she was flitting around hosting parties and entertaining diplomats, he set aside time to spend with his daughter, instilling in Caro many of the views which were ingrained so deeply in her. "He taught me chess in order to appreciate the give and take of politics, as well as the need to plan ten steps ahead during negotiations. Gaius would play me whenever I needed to work through something, and Stelian was usually up for a game, though he always lost."

She pushed back the pain which clenched her heart each time she remembered her parents, and shook her head. "I'm meant to be on a mission, but instead I'm stuck here playing maid."

"I told you it wouldn't be forever."

"All I have is your word," she said, frustrated. "It's too dangerous for me to try and escape on my own—I'd be discovered for certain, and then everything would be for naught." She laughed shortly. "Maybe that's why Stelian always loses at chess: he's so impulsive, while I have to weigh the consequences of every action."

"You don't follow your heart?" Morfran inquired, sounding curious.

"I try," Caro replied with a shrug at the odd question. "But it's hard when your head intervenes."

She cocked her head at him. "Do *you* follow your heart, Commander?"

"Perhaps more than I should."

She hadn't expected him to answer, and the tender reply caught her off guard; he had never shown even a modicum of vulnerability before. He fixed her with his gaze behind the silver mask, and Caro was startled by his intensity.

"It seems you have me in check," Morfran said finally, returning his attention to the game. He flicked the red king with a gloved finger, and it tipped onto the board, admitting defeat.

Caro rose. "Then with your permission, Commander, I will turn in."

He gave a brief nod, still staring at the board as she slipped out of the room.

Morfran leaned back in his chair and held his conquered king up to the light, rolling the smooth marble piece between his fingers.

The white queen stood upon the board, shining with triumph.

Walls have Ears

Malcolm swallowed his trepidation as Zhelyas sat on the throne, glaring at the two men who were forced to their knees before him, their chains clanging against the marble floor. One was the royal treasurer; the other, bookkeeper Viscount Arcus Casus.

Arcus was a noble with a minor title and an unpretentious, affable disposition. He had brown hair falling to his shoulders and a full beard trimmed close to his face. His features were slightly craggy, but he was popular among the ladies for his rugged good looks. He was a little older than Malcolm, and a valued mentor as well as a close friend.

Zhelyas crooked his finger. "Earl Dahl, come here."

Malcolm stepped forward, bowing. "Your Majesty."

"Here we have two criminals. One is an embezzler who stole from the Crown's accounts, while the other failed to execute my orders when I commanded him to deliver evidence of the fraud," Zhelyas began, steepling his fingers. "One I will welcome as a guest of my dungeon; the other will be granted clemency. Which shall it be?"

"Uh..." Malcolm said, words failing him. "You want *me* to decide, Your Majesty?"

"You are my adviser, are you not? Advise me."

Malcolm's palms felt sweaty. The easiest choice would be to defer to the king, avoiding the matter entirely, but then it was likely both men would suffer. He clasped his hands behind his back to stop from fidgeting.

"The treasurer showed blatant disregard for your authority and has proven he has no fear of you or reprisal for his actions. If given the chance, he would likely repeat his crime without remorse."

"And you believe the viscount committed a lesser offense?" Zhelyas inquired, lifting an eyebrow.

"No, sire," Malcolm replied, choosing his words carefully. "Rather, he has been a loyal servant until now. I would recommend he be placed in the vacant position of treasurer. He will be motivated to prove himself worthy of your grace and not make the same mistake as his predecessor."

Zhelyas leaned back, tapping the arms of the throne, and the corners of his lips curled. Malcolm's breath caught in his throat, and he wondered if he had stepped too far.

"Very well. I accept your ruling, Earl." He waved his hand. "Release the viscount."

The guards unshackled Arcus, and he rose shakily to his feet.

"Viscount Arcus Casus, you are now the Keeper of the Keys of the Treasury. Fulfill your duties and do not defy me again." He narrowed his gaze, his tone laced with warning.

Arcus wrung his hands and bowed low. "You have my word, Your Majesty. I won't disappoint you."

Zhelyas dismissed court for the day, and Malcolm let out a weary sigh.

"Malcolm," Arcus ventured as they left the throne room. He now wore the ring of gold keys on a belt around his waist, and they jangled softly as he walked.

"Please don't," Malcolm replied, shaking his head. "I would have made the same decision if the situation had been reversed."

"I know. You're a good man."

Somehow, that didn't make Malcolm feel better. "I'm not so sure."

Arcus squeezed his shoulder. "I am. And I'm honored to have such a friend."

"Even though I could have sentenced you to prison instead?"

"Yes. Because you would have made the right decision, regardless."

Malcolm smiled, reassured despite himself. "Why did you disobey the king anyway? That's the one part I don't understand. He already suspected the former treasurer of stealing from him."

Arcus sighed.

"I didn't want to be the one to add another weight to the scale. If the king was determined to find him guilty, he would, with or without my help. I wasn't going to betray a colleague, even if he deserved it."

That sounded like Arcus. He had been arrested before Malcolm could try to recruit him into his coalition, but given the man's unassuming demeanor and strong principles, he was the perfect candidate. His bookkeeping skills would be useful in covering up the bribes as well.

"Actually, there is something I wanted to ask you," Malcolm said, and steered him toward the balcony where they might speak with more privacy. "I don't want you to think you're obliged in any way. It's quite dangerous."

Arcus lifted an eyebrow with an amused smile. "Color me intrigued." He sobered when he realized Malcolm wasn't joking. "What is it?"

"A few of us are endeavoring to put together a venture of sorts, one that would enable us to aid the citizens who are being maltreated by the military. It's risky, but we feel it is our duty to do what we can."

Arcus nodded. "Whatever you need, Malcolm. I'd be glad to help."

Malcolm frowned. "Arcus..."

"I'm grateful for what you did for me, but I'm not agreeing out of gratitude. If you believe in it, so do I."

"Lady Takaria," Radella greeted from across the hall, and the older woman smiled. She had always liked the young countess, despite her naïveté. Radella was honest and forthright, and had difficulty believing others were anything else. Takaria knew better.

"Lady Radella, is everything running smoothly?" Takaria inquired, deliberately vague.

"Yes, Duchess. We couldn't have done any of this without your assistance."

"You flatter me. I can't imagine what you see in Luther. You would have been a much better match for Lars."

Radella gave a slight shrug. "I'm afraid I can't say, milady. The heart is unpredictable."

"I suppose it is." Takaria sighed.

"Will you ever make up with him? I know he has always regretted what happened between you."

"Perhaps one day, but recent events have not improved my opinion of his choices."

Radella looked thoughtful. "I can't condone his actions, but he fervently believes in something he can't explain. It haunts him. I have to believe his reasons were just."

Takaria frowned. "You have more faith in him than I do, Radella."

"How many is that now?" Malcolm inquired.

"Twenty-one," Radella replied under her breath, her gaze darting about nervously.

The coded messages had been Radella's suggestion, concealed within the text of an innocuous poetry book so anyone caught with it would be innocent of suspicion. It was very clever.

Twenty-one families had been safely escorted out of the city so far. It wasn't a lot, but it was all Malcolm could do with few resources from inside the palace.

"I'm still not comfortable doing this behind His Highness's back," Radella said. "Surely he would be sympathetic to their plight?" There was a small sound, and she cast a furtive glance down the corridor.

Radella hadn't seen that side of Arvind and still believed he had good intentions. Malcolm knew better. "You've seen the hold the king has on the prince. He can't be trusted."

She looked uncertain, but nodded and handed him the poetry book bound in periwinkle blue leather, *Reminiscence* by Mallory Blanc. The satin bookmark indicated the relevant passage.

In midnight
I see your eyes
A faded shade of blue
By dawn's light
The sun will rise
A face of vibrant hue

Midnight was the agreed meeting time, the secret carrier would be wearing a visible blue item, and they would be out of the city before dawn.

Malcolm tucked the book into his jacket. "I'll see to tonight's assignment."

"Well?" Zhelyas demanded.

Arvind had been summoned to the throne room the moment he returned from Drusus, and he was weary and worn. Zhelyas wore a smug expression, as if he couldn't help but feel a certain sinister amusement at the prince being reduced to a mere messenger.

Arvind sighed inwardly. "King Farangis has agreed to consider our terms, but he says he is still concerned for the welfare of the people should they be sent home. Word of the strict curfew and summary arrests has reached his ears, and we have no leverage with which to counter."

"And yet they keep slipping out of the city past the checkpoints!" Zhelyas seethed.

"I'm sure I have no idea how," Arvind said, shrugging. "In any case, unless we find a way to bargain with Farangis on equal terms, we won't be able to sway him."

Zhelyas pursed his lips with evident irritation. He was in no position to threaten a foreign king. "Lady Takaria mentioned something before you left, did she not? That Farangis hasn't forgiven Artemisia for the loss of his younger brother. What were the circumstances?"

"It was quite the scandal. The young prince attended my niece's ninth birthday celebration as an emissary from Drusus. As the prince was returning home, his carriage was accosted and he was kidnapped. His parents delivered a ransom, but their son was never found. The sorrow hit the Drusian royal family hard, and after years of ceaseless searching, the queen fell ill and died, followed shortly by the king. Prince Farangis, still a young man at the time, inherited the throne—as well as his parents' enmity."

Zhelyas stroked his chin. "Surely King Roland mounted an inquiry of his own. Was there no result?"

"None, sire. It was determined that the kidnapping had been committed by malefactors with a grievance against the prince's parents. My brother was frustrated by the lack of useful intelligence, but the randomness of the crime led to a dead end, and the investigation was all but dropped."

That was putting it mildly. Roland had been more than frustrated—he'd been furious, facing accusations on all sides of collusion, negligence, and even worse: a deliberate act to serve as a prelude to war.

"It took a lot of concessions on Artemisia's side to draw up a treaty with Drusus absolving us of all blame and maintaining our trade agreements. Thankfully, an all-out war that would have devastated both countries was averted, but while we ostensibly remain allies, relations have been strained ever since."

"I don't recall hearing about this before. Why was it not made public?"

"To save face, naturally," Arvind scoffed, unable to keep the disdain from his voice. "It was a matter of wounded pride for the monarchy. If anyone knew, it would tarnish the alliances we had with other countries; that was one of the terms Drusus was forced to agree to. The kingdom mourned their prince, but they could not speak of the circumstances of his disappearance, nor suggest who might have had a hand in it beyond the 'evil brigands' who stole him away in the night. The rest was swept under the rug, a shameful secret kept by silent tongues. Only those of Lady Takaria's ilk remember the details now."

"So do you," Zhelyas pointed out.

Arvind flicked a piece of lint from his jacket. "I was there. I had just turned twenty, and happened to have met the boy. He was pleasant, in a vapid sort of way."

Zhelyas sighed. "I suppose Farangis would see through any lie we could invent."

Arvind nodded. "Unfortunately, I suspect so. He seems difficult to deceive."

"Then it's up to *you* to think of something." Zhelyas waved his hand after this declaration. "Go now. We'll speak later."

Arvind bowed out of the room, hiding his livid expression, only looking up once the doors slammed shut. The nerve! To dictate to him, a prince! A lesser noble should know his place. But his agreement with Zhelyas was not one he would toss aside so easily, so he calmed himself with thoughts of the prize that awaited him for siding with the usurper.

His anger not yet spent, he searched for Malcolm in order to learn what had transpired in his absence and vent his temper. But the earl was nowhere to be found. A guard reported seeing him heading to the west corridor.

"Odd," Arvind murmured to himself. "What business would he have there?"

Arvind donned his cloak and resolved to follow Malcolm. Although he was exhausted from his journey, he was determined to find out what the troublesome earl was up to.

Malcolm shifted his feet, blowing on his hands to warm them. Between him, Radella, Arcus, and the dozen other nobles he'd recruited, they'd executed many similar missions, but this situation still made him nervous. Takaria had acquired the falsified departure papers through her own means, so all Malcolm had to do was wait for his charges at the agreed meeting point and execute the hand-off—a dangerous job in and of itself.

Midnight was upon them, and he glanced down the street. He wore a blue ribbon affixed to his lapel, identifying him as the secret carrier as the poem implied.

A small family huddled in the shadows, and he stepped into the light so they could see him and the ribbon.

The father nodded, urging his wife and children forward, a boy and a girl. "By dawn's light, the sun will rise," the man said in a hushed voice.

"A face of vibrant hue," Malcolm replied.

"My name is Eloso. This is my wife Kiala and our children."

Eloso was a simple man, a baker who had been arrested for an offhand comment against the king. He was later released after hours of questioning, but his family were afraid for their lives and their livelihood, particularly since his bakery had been shut down under the law of disapprobation.

The woman held her children close, eyes darting fearfully. They couldn't have been much older than Malcolm's own twins, and his heart went out to them.

"This way, hurry," Malcolm urged.

They followed him down the back streets until they reached the crossroads leading to the city entrance, where a checkpoint had been erected.

"Here are your papers. Show them to the guard. He has been bribed, so he'll let you through."

Eloso nodded, taking the documents with shaking hands.

"Once out, head west to the Drusian border. There, you will be welcomed as refugees," Malcolm continued. "I only wish we could do more."

"You've already done more than enough," Eloso said warmly, and his wife nodded with a slight smile. "Thanks to you, my family won't starve."

Malcolm nodded, and the small group departed. The light of dawn was just kissing the horizon when they reached the checkpoint. The guard looked at them, then the papers, with a frown on his face, and Malcolm's heart stopped. Was he going to arrest them? Perhaps the duty shift had been changed unexpectedly? Or maybe Eloso had decided to seek a reprieve by turning in his benefactor?

The soldier was eyeing them suspiciously when another strode up. There was a rapid-fire discussion while the family huddled together, frozen with fear.

Malcolm couldn't hear what was said, but after a tense minute, the first guard nodded and removed the barricade, allowing them to pass. They didn't look back as they scurried out of the city toward the promised asylum.

Malcolm ran his hand through his hair, damp with sweat. That had been a close one.

He pulled out the poetry book and moved the satin bookmark to the next page, then made his way back to the palace.

"So that's what you've been up to while I've been gone," Arvind hissed to himself.

He should have known Malcolm would come up with some kind of stunt, he simply hadn't thought the earl would be so brazen as to do it right under Zhelyas's nose.

He leaned against the wall, swathed in his cloak, and tapped his chin. Therein lay the quandary. If Arvind revealed the plot, Zhelyas might well blame him for failing to keep a tight rein on the nobles under his charge.

"Even though he was the one who sent me on that foolish jaunt to Drusus in the first place," he grumbled bitterly. "Of course Farangis was going to refuse."

But what now? He had to admit some admiration for such a clever, yet subtle form of rebellion, though Malcolm couldn't have done it on his own, that was for certain. Countess Alvara was likely involved, and any number of others might have been recruited as well. He would have to carefully observe their movements from now on and determine who was part of this clandestine charade. With a little patience, he could even make it work to his benefit.

He wouldn't confront the earl about it yet. He'd let it play out a little longer, and if the king did find out, he could always claim ignorance.

A smile slithered across Arvind's face at his willful deception. After all, he'd been out of town. How could he possibly have known?

Desperate Measures

After the chess match, peace seemed to be restored between Caro and Morfran, but she was getting antsy. With each day spent in this place, her mission was falling further and further behind, and she grew increasingly worried her companions were going to try something rash. She needed to make a move, and soon.

Every day after breakfast, Morfran attended a strategy session with the other senior officers. Caro had an inkling what they were discussing, but she needed to hear it for herself.

They said their usual greetings, bemoaning the weather and such, then sat down for business. As one of the soldiers went to close the door, she slipped past, carrying a decanter of wine.

"Ah, perfect. Just the thing to pick me up," the captain said, and Caro obligingly poured a glass for him, glancing surreptitiously at a map on the table.

Morfran's lips curled in a frown, but he said nothing to berate her.

Her infiltration successful, Caro stood off to one side, holding tight to the decanter in her hands. None of the other officers paid her any mind, and they launched right into their discussion. Caro listened as they debated troop movements and updates to the curfew.

Morfran stroked his chin and peered at the plans. "So, gentlemen, it seems the hunt for Queen Caro continues."

Irony struck Caro as he spoke those words with her right in the room—yet unseen by all but him.

"It's a pity our blockade didn't catch her at Ock. She must have evaded it somehow," the captain said. "Do you think she continued north, as King Zhelyas predicted, or crossed into Frok and eluded us there?"

"Neither is a pleasant alternative." Morfran's expression was grim, but Caro had the impression he was holding back a smile at his own private joke.

"Perhaps we should take more drastic measures?" the sergeant suggested.

"Such as?"

"Why don't we burn one of the outlying villages and set an example for anyone who would dare defy the king's edict?"

"That does sound like something King Zhelyas would approve of," Morfran replied lazily.

The decanter slipped from Caro's trembling hands and crashed to the floor. It exploded in a rain of glass, deafening in the silence. All eyes turned to her, and she was acutely aware they were seeing her for the first time.

Morfran growled deep in his throat and seized her arm, dragging her from the assembly.

"You little fool!" Morfran snapped, throwing Caro into an empty room and locking them both in.

"You can't let them—!"

"What I can and cannot do is none of your concern!" He took a deep breath. "I hope you enjoyed your little peek behind the curtain. Was it worth it?"

Caro furrowed her brow. "You're not angry?"

"About that? No. I was expecting you to do something eventually. However, you have made a nuisance of yourself, a situation which I must now rectify."

He paced the room like a vexed wildcat, then stripped off his armor. First his breastplate and pauldrons, then bracers and wrist guards.

Caro stared at him warily.

"As I told you before—I am not known for my mercy. They will expect me to punish you severely for such an infraction."

"And Ines?"

Morfran seemed startled by the scathing retort. "I have never struck Ines, and I don't intend to hurt you either." He sighed, drawing his sword and discarding the sheath. "As we have an accord, I can't very well beat you, but it must appear as if I had. So we will spar."

He tossed her a dagger, small but well balanced, the leather-wrapped handle somewhat bulky for its size.

"It's the best solution I can come up with. Any blows I land against you will be seen as proof of my cruelty, while any you deliver in return I can conceal under my armor so no one will suspect the duplicity."

Caro was genuinely surprised by the scheme. Not only was he sparing her, but he was not glib in the slightest about her chances of holding her own in this mock battle.

"All right," she agreed.

The match was arduous, and anyone who overheard them would conclude he was indeed giving her quite a thrashing.

Caro's heart beat rapidly in her chest, her lungs burning as she struggled to maintain her stamina. Meanwhile, Morfran had barely broken a sweat. He was well versed in the ways of battle, that much was apparent, and Caro bore several cuts and bruises from where his attacks had broken through her feeble defenses.

Still, it was as much of a fair fight as it could be. Morfran was stronger and more skilled than the rebellious princess who'd taken up sword fighting as a hobby, but he was less nimble, and she was able to dart out of his way.

She slipped beneath his blade as it arced above her head, then curved the dagger upward and flicked her wrist, catching the fleshy part of his arm. Morfran gnashed his teeth, suppressing a cry.

Caro retreated out of reach and darted her gaze to the door, wondering if she could take advantage of his momentary lapse to escape. However, Morfran was not as distracted as she'd hoped. He looked up, his eyes glittering with warning behind the mask.

"Enough," he declared, and held out his hand for the dagger, which Caro returned reluctantly.

He tucked it back into his belt, then took her arm and pushed up the sleeve. "Yes, this will do." True to his word, the lacerations were superficial.

Morfran began to put his armor back on, grimacing as he wound a strip of cloth around his forearm before sliding the bracer over it. It was a more grievous injury than she had intended, but he deserved it for keeping her captive and forcing her to take part in this ridiculous farce.

"Return to your quarters for now," he instructed. "I've just given you a merciless beating, so remember to behave accordingly."

"Of course, Commander," Caro replied with a disdainful bow.

She headed straight for her room and flopped onto the bed, burying her face in the pillow. She wasn't sure how much longer she could go on like this.

Ines came in a short while later and didn't say a single word, but left a change of clothes and a small tray of bread and cheese. Caro was grateful for her thoughtfulness, although it did little to soothe the hopelessness which weighed upon her heart.

"Luther's on his way," Stelian said grimly.

"What?" Gaius gasped. "This isn't good. Even if Caro's somehow managed to go incognito in the camp, he'll recognize her for sure."

"I have an idea," Lottie ventured, summoning her courage.

They all looked at her.

"I'm the same age as the queen. Lady Ezalia, do you still have a court dress with you?"

Ezalia frowned. "Yes, but why...?"

"Few of the soldiers would have seen Her Majesty except for those who worked in the palace, right?"

"That's true," Gaius mused.

"I can pretend to be her. If I get captured by the general, I can delay him long enough for you to communicate a signal."

Stelian frowned. "But that's too dangerous."

"It could work," Gaius pointed out, exchanging a look with Ezalia, who sighed.

"If you're determined, I can make a few adjustments, and I think I have something with which to darken your hair."

Lottie stood still while Ezalia pinned up the hem of the dress.

"Are you scared?" Ezalia inquired.

"Of course I'm scared," Lottie murmured back, "but we don't have any other options."

"This will be twice you've risked your life."

Lottie thought hard about that. "I don't think the general will hurt me."

Ezalia cocked her head. "Why?"

"I believe he's a good man. Even when he was interrogating me back at the manor, he never hit me. The baron wouldn't have hesitated."

Ezalia tutted sympathetically as she tucked the last pin into place. "All right, it's as good as it's going to get. What do you think?"

The men had wandered off to give the ladies some privacy, but now they turned around.

Gaius nodded. "Not bad. Luther will see through the deception right away, though, you do realize that?"

Lottie nodded. Her hands started to shake, and Stelian clasped them in his.

"After we send the message to the queen, I'm coming back for you, Lottie. I promise."

Luther arrived at the garrison a few days earlier than expected. He had yet to meet up with Morfran, preferring to indulge in a little libation in the local pub before facing his compatriot.

He took another gulp of ale, draining his flagon, and slammed it upon the table. "Another."

The barkeep himself came over and swept the empty cup away, replacing it with a full one. His wife and daughter tended to other things in back, evidently trying to keep their heads down. Smart people.

"General, sir."

Luther looked up, annoyed his peaceful drink had been interrupted. "What is it?" he grumbled.

The messenger appeared at a loss for words.

"Out with it, man!"

"Um, we've captured one of the interlopers, sir."

This was welcome news, and Luther's head started to clear. "Who? Lady Ezalia? Lord Gaius?"

"It's... uh..." Luther strained to hear as the soldier leaned down and whispered in his ear.

"What?"

Luther rose, toppling his chair, and grabbed his coat, the half-drunk flagon of ale forgotten on the table.

The army had appropriated the constable's station for their use, though prisoners were usually brought back to the camp for interrogation. However, in a situation such as this, Luther thought the less who knew about it, the better.

"Where did you find her?"

"In the cellar of an abandoned restaurant, sir, amongst the vegetable crates and jars of preserves," the messenger replied, hurrying at his heels. "A few of their patrons were arrested for being out after curfew, and the place was shut down by official mandate."

"I see."

His heart was in his throat, his entire body tense with anticipation. Had he finally fulfilled his mission from his new king? And if so, what then? He shook his head, banishing those thoughts. What mattered now was less than ten feet away.

Luther stormed into the station, and the soldiers hauled their prisoner to her feet, looking somewhat apprehensive. Apparently, not all of Luther's forces were convinced of the queen's supposed treason, but he nodded to himself.

"You should be careful who you trust, Your Majesty," he said glibly.

The teenage girl in their grasp was wearing a courtly gown, with long brown curls tumbling over her shoulders—but Luther instantly knew something was amiss.

He crossed the space between them in two steps and jerked up her chin. The timid gaze which met his was not vibrant green, but sky blue.

"You—!" he hissed.

It was the maid from Oswin's manor, the one who had eluded his forces after Oswin had confessed his own part in harboring the queen. He noticed the dress she wore did not fit properly in places, and her blond curls had been hastily colored with some sort of brown dye. She flinched as he gestured angrily.

"You fools, this isn't the queen!" he snapped, and the soldiers paled, exchanging nervous glances.

Luther stormed over to the corner and picked up a bucket of water, then threw it in her face, drenching her.

"Wash that stuff out immediately," he ordered, tossing her a rag.

The soldiers released her arms, and she began to tousle her hair. The dye wasn't permanent, and it stained her dress, leaving her blond tresses faintly tinted. Her hands were trembling, and Luther pushed away feelings of pity for the girl.

"What's your name?"

"L-Lottie."

"Tell me, Lottie, what exactly did you hope to accomplish?" She evaded his gaze.

"Where is the queen?" Luther demanded, his anger rising, and he ripped the cloth from her hands.

"Her Majesty's long gone by now," Lottie replied brazenly. "You won't find her."

He let out a low growl, the throbbing in his head colliding with his hangover, then dragged her to a cell and slammed the door.

"Wake up, Esca."

Caro roused to Ines shaking her.

"It's morning. Commander Morfran is calling for you."

She blinked an eye open, and the events of the previous day flooded back to her. She swung her legs over the side of the bed and drew in a sharp breath. Every inch of her body ached from her head to the tips of her toes. The smarting blows aside, it had been a long time since Caro had fought with such intensity.

Morfran cocked his head from the high-backed chair as she shuffled into the room. "Are you unwell?"

"I'm fine, Commander," Caro replied a trifle brusquely.

He lifted a goblet of wine to his lips and winced, clutching his arm. He hadn't yet put on his bracers, and the wrapping was visible beneath the sleeve of his tunic.

Caro felt an unexpected sense of guilt. "I didn't mean to cut you that deep," she confessed, and Morfran scowled.

"I'll live."

"Let me clean it at least."

He met her insistent gaze and sighed. "The box of bandages is on the washstand."

Caro pulled the chaise closer. She opened the box and withdrew a length of gauze and some clean cloths. He rolled up his sleeve, and Caro unwound the bandage, setting it aside. She then dipped a cloth in the basin and began to wash the wound.

Morfran sucked a sharp breath through his teeth. She turned the cloth over and dabbed away the excess before applying the fresh bandage.

"How did you learn to do this, anyway?" Morfran inquired after a long moment of silence.

"I was a precocious princess," Caro replied without looking up at him. "I insisted on learning how to fight, so my tutor made sure I knew how to tend to my own injuries. He said I couldn't have one without the other."

It seemed strange for her to be tending to him, but he had made every effort not to injure her, while she had done the opposite. Her heightened emotions had returned to normal, and she felt somehow as if it were a betrayal. He could have whipped or beaten her for her transgression and she would have been helpless to stand against him, but he hadn't done either.

She was conflicted. At first, she had hated him for holding her against her will, forcing her to do demeaning chores and taunting her every chance he got, but she'd been grateful when he saved her from the sergeant's wrath. Now she respected him for his restraint, perhaps even trusted him—to an extent. His actions so far had been devoid of logic, and she wondered if perhaps there was more to the man than she thought.

"There," she declared finally, pinning the bandage in place.

Morfran gave a slight nod and flexed his hand, tensing the muscles in his forearm.

"... reputation well deserved."

"... wouldn't want to test his temper."

"... keeping a wide berth."

Hushed whispers and half-spoken warnings followed Caro and Morfran down the hall. It seemed their little deception had the desired effect.

"See to your chores," Morfran instructed, then lowered his voice, his expression unchanged. "I will update you if there is anything relevant."

To anyone watching, it looked like he was giving her a stern reprimand, and Caro gave a submissive bow. Inwardly, she was relieved he was going to confide in her despite her blunder, if that was indeed his intent.

"As for the tactic proposed yesterday, I believe we should consider such an extreme action only if there is no other recourse. Naturally, it would also require the direct approval of the king," Morfran began once the officers were all settled.

None of them, not even the sergeant, seemed keen to approach Zhelyas.

"I propose we concentrate our efforts along the northern route," he continued. "In the unlikely event the queen slipped through the blockade, she would need to pass through Flossholme to bypass the Esaphis Desert. We should place sentries there."

There was a series of nods.

"Apparently, General Luther arrived early for his scheduled check-in," the captain noted, speaking up.

Morfran's shoulders tensed beneath his armor. If Luther was at the garrison, he would recognize the queen for sure, and that would ruin everything.

"However, he was waylaid in town when a peasant reported the queen hiding out in an abandoned building."

Whispers flurried around the table, and Morfran felt a flicker of confusion. "Is that so?" he inquired, his voice carefully neutral.

"Seems it was a false alarm, though," the captain added, shrugging.

Morfran wondered if it was a ruse by one of Caro's companions or another benefactor, though that was unlikely. There were some rabble-rousers who had been stirring up trouble in the town, but they weren't very organized. Of more immediate concern was what Morfran was going to do about this situation.

Lottie's cell was the only one occupied. It was small and didn't even have a cot, only a threadbare mattress on the ground. She shifted uncomfortably, shivering. Her hair was still wet, and the cold floor offered little comfort.

Because Lottie had been deemed unimportant compared to her would-be persona, there was only one soldier on guard duty, and he was moodily flicking wads of paper at the wall. The door opened, and the man rose as Luther entered.

"Corporal, step outside."

The guard bowed and departed as fast as his legs could carry him, leaving the two alone. Luther shut the door.

Lottie cast a furtive glance up at him. She tried to be brave, but deceiving the general twice was more imminently dangerous than whatever the usurper king might do to her.

Luther was silent a long moment, and Lottie could barely hear his footsteps over the pounding of her own heart as he paced the room.

"Do you regret it?" He paused in his pacing and stared down at Lottie.

She blinked at the solemn question and shook her head. "Even if you beat me for it—I don't."

"I suppose I must commend your courage, misplaced as it is. I prefer it to the baron's sniveling cowardice." He pursed his lips. "Tell me, why did you help the queen escape? Even now, impersonating her like this?"

"Because I have faith in her. I believe she can make it right." Luther's forehead creased.

"Why did *you* betray her?" Lottie countered, and he frowned.

"I'm afraid I don't share your conviction," he said, a hard edge to his voice, and Lottie dared not press the matter.

She hugged her knees against the chill in her heart. "Are you going to keep me in here?" she asked tremulously.

"Until I figure out what to do with you."

"You—you're not going to give me to the king?"

"I haven't decided yet," he replied, and it was clear the conversation was over.

That night, Morfran ordered dinner served in his quarters, avoiding the officer's mess. Caro delivered a tray of roasted quail and rosemary potatoes prepared by the kitchen. He gestured to the table, and she could feel his eyes on her as she crossed the room.

"It seems our time together is nearing its end."

She looked up sharply at his melancholy tone.

"Luther arrived early, and though he was delayed in town by a ruse I can only imagine was conceived by your people, I can't risk tarrying any longer." He pursed his lips at her suspicious frown. "You didn't think I would hand you over to him?"

"I had my doubts."

177

"Be assured, I have no intention of doing so."

Before she could reply, there was the sound of a small explosion. Caro raced to the window, peering into the darkness. Down below, a small group had gathered, marveling at the display.

"Fireworks?" one of them inquired.

"Maybe those dissidents are causing a ruckus again?" another one replied.

There was a second rain of sparks, and Caro counted under her breath. "One, two, three..."

A third firework exploded, this one blue.

Three miles east. It was the signal she and Stelian had used whenever they'd been traveling in the woods and happened to become separated. Of course, he'd used flares which were less disruptive, but they fulfilled their purpose. The first was to get her attention, the second to set a baseline, the space between measured the distance, while the color of the third indicated direction: blue was east; red, north; green, south; yellow, west.

"I presume that was meant for you?" Morfran inquired, coming to stand beside her. He sounded equal parts annoyed and impressed.

"They've made their camp three miles east of here."

"It seems I'd better get you out of the garrison before they try something even more foolish."

Caro narrowed her eyes up at him. She still had her doubts as to whether he truly intended to fulfill his end of the bargain. "Tell me the truth. If you aren't devoted to Zhelyas's cause, why serve him?"

Morfran stared back at her. "For revenge," he replied. "There is someone I wish to see utterly destroyed. When I accomplish that, I will have no further need for the usurper."

"And then?"

"Then it won't matter."

Caro was taken aback by his blasé demeanor, but she identified with the feeling. "I suppose I can't blame you."

Morfran cocked his head at her words.

"I too desire revenge for the murder of my parents," she said, voicing the emotions which she had bottled up for so long, and clenched her fists to still the raging fire in her heart. "When I have Zhelyas at my feet, I will show him the same mercy he showed them."

She wasn't sure why she was confiding in him. Perhaps because he didn't expect her to be above such things, and wouldn't be disappointed.

Morfran remained silent, and Caro scowled.

"And what was the point of all this in the end?"

"That is a conversation for another time, little queen," he said, and smiled at her vexation. "Your plucky friends have communicated their location, so I won't be abandoning you to the wolves... although that would be a more pleasant fate than the one you will suffer should you find yourself in Zhelyas's grasp."

Despite his young age, Stelian was a distinguished soldier, and ranked higher than any of the men Luther had on duty. The signal sent, it was little trouble to evade the patrols as he made his way back through town to rescue Lottie.

He crept up on the guard, who had stepped outside for a breath of fresh air. While the man was distracted, Stelian wrapped an arm around his throat, pressing one hand against the back of the guard's neck and the other against his windpipe, preventing him from making a sound as he struggled to breathe. A moment later, he fell limp in Stelian's arms.

Stelian dragged him into the shadows and listened at the door, but didn't hear any other sounds inside. Taking a deep breath, he crossed the threshold.

"Lottie!" he gasped, spotting her in the cramped cell. Her hair was limp, almost washed back to blond, and she shifted to her knees, gripping the bars.

"You came for me?"

"Of course. I promised I would."

"How touching."

The door creaked open and Luther stood there, his gaze narrowed, his sword drawn.

Stelian turned, conflicting feelings warring inside him. Luther had been his commanding officer, his mentor. He had nominated Stelian to become Princess Caro's bodyguard when King Roland had asked for a recommendation. He owed the man everything, but now fate had made them enemies.

"General," Stelian ventured, drawing his own sword. "I don't want to fight you."

"You think you have a chance against me, boy?" Luther taunted, but his eyes flickered with emotion.

"Even if you take me hostage too, I won't let you capture the queen."

Stelian positioned himself in front of the cell. He didn't want to believe Luther would use Lottie's life against him, but he wasn't sure anymore.

Luther attacked first, rushing forward, and Stelian skidded backward across the stone floor at the force of the blow.

He planted his feet and pushed forward. Luther might be bigger physically, but Stelian was lithe and strong, and he wasn't about to back down from this fight.

Luther smirked as Stelian pressed his advantage, countering his next strike. "I'm pleased not all of your training was a waste, Lieutenant."

"None of it was, I assure you," Stelian replied, keeping his focus.

Another frenzied parry, and they both parted, their breathing heavy.

"You're here for the girl, I assume?" Luther said.

Stelian nodded.

"Take her, then. She is of no consequence to me, and the king has already vented his frustrations upon the baron for his part in the deception."

Luther flung him the keys, and Stelian eyed him warily. After a moment, the general sheathed his sword. Stelian unlocked the cell, helping Lottie to her feet. Her legs were shaky after kneeling on the hard floor for so long, but she managed to stand, leaning against him.

"I won't forget this," Stelian said as he and Lottie edged toward the door.

"Nor will I." Luther turned his gaze to Lottie. "Perhaps I may also be convinced one day of the faith you have in the queen."

"I hope so," Lottie replied quietly.

After confirming the coast was clear, Stelian took Lottie's hand and they raced down the street.

"Is he going to follow?" Lottie inquired breathlessly.

"Undoubtedly," he replied, taking a sharp detour. "But I anticipated that."

He tugged Lottie around a corner as Luther's boots could be heard thumping down the cobblestones behind them.

"Which way did they go?" he bellowed.

Stelian pulled a small ball out of his pocket. "Hold your breath," he whispered, and Lottie covered her mouth, nodding.

He peered out from his hiding place, then lit the fuse and rolled the object into the street. It wobbled around on the ground for a moment before erupting into billowing bluish-purple smoke. A present from Gaius: saltpeter, sugar, sawdust, and powdered indigo dye.

"Go!" Stelian cried over the indignant shouts of Luther and his men.

Lottie grasped his hand as they fled the opposite way, their passage obscured by the smoke. They made it into a side alley which led out of town and to the safety of the woods.

"What now?" Gaius asked, once the two wayward members of their party had returned unscathed.

"Now we wait," Ezalia replied.

"That's it?" Lottie said, once more in her maid's uniform and snuggled beneath a warm blanket in the wagon.

Stelian nodded. "I'm afraid so. The fireworks will have told Caro our location. We have to give her some time to escape and find us here."

"I don't like it any more than you, but we have to be patient a little longer." Ezalia sighed. "While she's in the camp, there's not much we can do but keep an eye on her. Hopefully, Luther was delayed by the ruse long enough for her to slip away with no one the wiser."

"But we know Morfran has probably figured out her identity," Gaius interjected.

Ezalia bit a nail, betraying her nervousness. "That bothers me as well, but we don't know his motives. In any case, if either of them plan on turning her in, she'll have to be transported to the capital, and we can make a plan to intercept. Until then..."

She didn't have to finish her thought, and they all shared grim glances.

"What if we fail, Ezalia?" Gaius said, frustration creeping into his voice. "What do we do then?"

"We continue the mission as Caro would have wished. Our fates will be no different if we're captured," Ezalia added. "We recruit Alenard if we can and visit my father, then return to Duke Vittorius. If Caro is imprisoned within the palace, we can attempt to mount a rescue. If not..." She shook her head, her face lined with sorrow at the thought. "Then we do our duty and support the remaining heir to the throne."

Stelian hung his head, and Lottie huddled beneath her blanket, her eyes glistening with tears.

"Let's get some sleep for now," Gaius declared finally. "I'll take first watch."

Caro and Morfran departed the camp in the dead of night. He had not left his mount stabled, but tied to his own private hitching post behind the manor. It was a massive stallion, taller than any horse Caro had seen before, with powerful muscles and a gleaming black coat without a single flash of white. He stamped his feet and snorted as they drew near but made no other sound.

Morfran prepared the saddle, then lifted Caro up, her legs dangling over one side. He climbed behind her and shrouded her with his cloak; she nearly vanished beneath the thick, draping fabric.

"Keep quiet," he urged, and Caro nodded even though the warning was unnecessary. None of Morfran's crafty dissembling would get them out of this mess if they were discovered.

They skulked through the shadows and emerged in the darkness of the woods. Little was visible in the gloom, but horse and rider seemed to find their way well enough, as if accustomed to night and shadow.

They traveled for a while in silence. Finally, Morfran slowed his horse, tugging on the reins.

"Your people are over that ridge," he said. "It won't be long now."

Morfran had done everything he'd promised, but Caro was still wary. As much as she longed to see her companions, she also wanted to avoid a confrontation, one she could not predict. She was done with going along meekly with his plans; she needed to regain control of the situation.

Caro nodded, then threw her head back, knocking him in the jaw. He reeled, and she spun in the saddle, then rammed her heel into his gut.

Morfran's armor protected him from the blow, but he was caught off guard and toppled over the back end of his horse. By the time he righted himself from his inelegant fall, Caro had gripped the reins, planted both feet against the horse's flank—her legs were too short for Morfran's stirrups—and was away like a shot.

Caro raced through the woods and crested the hill, where she spied the faint outline of a wagon in the distance. "Ezalia!"

The small group looked up at her voice.

"Caro?" Ezalia gasped and stood so fast she tripped over her feet.

Caro pulled the horse to a stop, and he heeded her command without protest. Since the stallion was so tall, she swung her legs over the side and pushed herself off, supported by Stelian, who eased her to the ground.

"I—I can't believe it," Gaius said, bewildered. "We were hoping you had received our message, but we honestly weren't sure."

"So I gathered," Caro chuckled.

Ezalia embraced her. "You must tell us everything."

Stelian jumped back as the horse nipped at him. "Is this Morfran's?" he inquired.

Caro smiled and stroked the stallion's muzzle. "He's a good boy. Thank you for being so obliging. Return to your master now."

He nuzzled her hair, then turned and galloped off the way they had come.

Stelian breathed a sigh. "You have impeccable timing. Luther was on his way to the garrison tonight."

"I know. That's why Morfran helped me escape."

Gaius was sipping a cup of water, and he coughed, snorting half of it up his nose. "The commander *helped* you? Whatever for?" he asked, recovering and dabbing at his wet shirt.

Caro shrugged. She didn't have a good answer.

"Whatever the case, I'm glad you're safe," Ezalia said, hugging her close.

"Do you still intend to cross the Esaphis Desert and head for Lord Alenard's?" Stelian inquired.

Caro nodded. "Yes. Morfran convinced the other officers I could not have snuck past the checkpoint, and that in the unlikely event I did, I would bypass the desert."

There was another round of disbelieving looks, and Gaius scratched his head. "In that case, let's get out of here before daybreak. I'm tired of this town and its ruddy bridge."

Morfran picked himself off the ground, rubbing his jaw as Caro disappeared into the trees. He hadn't expected her to fight and was rather embarrassed he'd fallen off his horse.

"Good thing nobody was watching. I would never live it down," he grumbled, shaking detritus out of his cloak.

Just as he was wondering how to make up some believable story, the stallion came trotting down the path toward him.

"Traitor," Morfran quipped, and the horse whinnied as if laughing with amusement at his predicament. He patted his mount and swung onto his back, tugging the reins toward camp.

"I suppose she's back with her people now," he mused, and glanced over his shoulder. "Farewell, little queen. We'll soon meet again."

Luther arrived a scant few hours later, and Morfran greeted him. "General."

"Commander," Luther replied. "I have been sent by His Majesty, King Zhelyas, to see about the progress of your efforts."

He didn't sound like he was thrilled with the task, and would much rather be conning nobles out of their wine. Morfran handed him a goblet as a peace offering.

"I heard rumors from the soldiers that they arrested a girl wandering around at night, and then she became your servant?" Luther lifted an eyebrow, and Morfran shrugged. "So where is she now?"

"She proved to be an inconvenience, so I sent her on her way."

"Pity."

"It sounds like you had a troublesome encounter of your own."

Luther drained the cup. "Much the same, I'm afraid," he sighed. "Things aren't going well in the city, so Zhelyas has sent me to call you back to the palace to ferret out dissent there."

"What sort of dissent?" Morfran inquired.

"Even after the harsh measures Zhelyas put in place to subdue the populace, there are still small pockets of rebellion which have popped up. We've been confronting them on the streets and raiding their hideouts, but they're like voles: we catch one, then trip over a dozen more."

Luther lowered his voice, as if he was afraid of unwelcome ears. "It's getting increasingly difficult to tell an ordinary citizen from a rebel sympathizer, and there have been numerous incidents resulting in wrongful arrests. As if that wasn't bad enough, somehow those unjustly accused have been able to slip out of the city with their families in tow when released after lengthy interrogations. Zhelyas suspects treason, the guards accepting bribes for looking the other way, but there's no proof. Needless to say, the king is not pleased."

Luther grimaced in such a way that implied he'd been on the receiving end of Zhelyas's tirades more than once since Morfran's departure.

"So I'm to bring it to a swift resolution," Morfran concluded. He shrugged, pouring them both another glass of wine. He was content with his role as a thug, as long as it got him what he wanted.

"Anything else to report?" Luther inquired.

Morfran shook his head, suppressing a smirk. "Not a thing. It's been entirely uneventful."

Devil's Due

Malcolm had a bad feeling about this. He was carrying the yellow ribbon which would identify him to his charges, but they were nowhere in sight. Had they been spooked? He peered around the corner, straining to see into the darkness.

A small glow appeared at the end of the street, then another, until twenty or so torches came into view, hoisted in the air by men and women wearing black armbands bearing the royal crest emblazoned in red.

The civilian insurgents. RAZ, the "Resistance Against Zhelyas." Malcolm had heard of them through the whispers of the guards at the palace, but this was the first time he had seen them in person. In a way, he admired their courage, fierce eyes blazing with righteous anger at the audacity of the usurper king, the murderer of their beloved former rulers and persecutor of the young queen who was the rightful heir to the throne.

They strode down the street, torches held aloft, calling for revolution. But Malcolm had seen what happened to those who defied Zhelyas's will. Soldiers gathered, summoned by their rallying cries.

"Down with the usurper!" the leader shouted, a man called Gerrin according to the rumors. "Down with the pretender to the throne!"

The soldiers appeared overwhelmed by the crowd, perhaps feeling twinges of sympathy themselves. Not all were convinced by Luther's claims of Queen Caro's treason, but to say so would land them in jail alongside the rebels. They began to retreat, and Malcolm watched in amazement.

One of the rebels, emboldened by their success, threw his torch. It landed in the street, scattering the soldiers. The crowd rose up in a triumphant cry, which was drowned out by the sharp sound of hooves upon the stone.

A black-clad man sat upon a horse as dark as night, silver mask gleaming in the torchlight. "All of you, desist," he commanded. "I shall give you this one chance: disperse immediately!"

"Morfran?" Malcolm gasped, ducking behind a shed. What was he doing here?

"We won't be dictated to by a hoodlum!" Gerrin shouted, and the others uttered their assent.

"So be it. You are under arrest for willful disobedience against the king. Take them into custody," Morfran ordered.

The soldiers immediately fell in line. A man stabbed a guard with a dagger hidden in his boot and broke free, racing headlong toward Morfran.

"Yanric, no!" Gerrin cried.

Deftly holding the reins of his horse, the commander drew his sword and turned to face the rebel. Yanric bobbed and weaved, leaping to strike at the horse's unprotected flank, but Morfran's mount was responsive to even the smallest command and sidestepped out of the way as a low hiss escaped his lips.

Morfran swung his sword in an arc and swept the man's blade out of his hand, slicing him across the palm. Malcolm couldn't believe anyone was capable of such a precise strike. Yanric staunched the bleeding with his handkerchief as he was hauled away.

"I will not repeat myself again," Morfran bellowed, turning his horse toward the rebels, who had now been corralled. "You are in defiance of King Zhelyas's edict. Surrender and you may be spared, or else face the consequences."

His merciless words sent a shiver skittering through the crowd, and Malcolm trembled where he hid, unable to do anything to help. Gerrin, apparently realizing the danger, urged his followers to comply and offered no further resistance.

Once the unfortunate citizens had been hauled off, Malcolm slunk back to the castle, his heart weary.

"Earl Dahl."

Malcolm jumped at the voice and turned to see Morfran staring at him. The masked man's expression, as always, was unreadable, though his lips were curved into a frown.

"Yes, Commander?" he replied, trying to sound innocent.

"I trust you and the other nobles have had no part in encouraging the people of Aurinesse to risk their lives and defy the king's will."

"I assure you, we have done nothing of the sort. We wish only for the citizens to be able to live out their lives, free from tyranny and suffering." That much he could say honestly, at least.

"Unfortunate, then, that they seem determined to bring it upon themselves," Morfran said coldly.

Malcolm shivered. "Yes, very regrettable," he managed, wondering just how much Morfran knew.

As long as Morfran was in the capital, they would have to be extra cautious—the man was cunning and far too clever for Malcolm's comfort.

Fancy-free

Evading the throng of ministers and nobles who sought a royal audience, Zhelyas stole out of the throne room for an amorous encounter with Diascia.

He met her in the library, surrounded by walls of musty books, and they huddled behind the curtains like youths fumbling in the dark for their first time.

Diascia's hair was up as usual, exposing her perfect skin. Zhelyas bent down and nibbled her neck, eliciting a gasp of delight. She bit her lip in a seductive way.

"Tonight, my room," he whispered, tracing her collarbone.

She gripped a handful of her skirt, sighing with anticipation. "I'll be there, Your Majesty," she said breathlessly.

Diascia glanced at the door to see Veena wander in, looking unimpressed at their frivolity. She gave a hurried curtsy and a kittenish giggle before departing.

"Pardon me, it seems as if I interrupted something," Veena said dryly, eyeing the door which Diascia had fluttered through.

"You sound like you disapprove."

"Is that simpering woman really your lover?"

Zhelyas smirked. "Why not? She's rather attractive."

"But not very bright."

"Are you jealous?" Zhelyas jeered, and he grinned to see Veena's blood boil at his scorn.

"Hardly," she replied icily.

"Well, you'll have to put up with her. I don't need an intelligent woman by my side, just an amusing plaything."

"Make sure you keep an eye on her. I wouldn't want her to wander into my tower and find herself turned into a toad."

Zhelyas lifted an eyebrow. "By accident, of course."

"Naturally," Veena purred, flicking her hair over her shoulder.

Zhelyas let out a derisive snort, then swept past her, eager to find a more discreet location in which to continue his illicit rendezvous.

Zhelyas stretched out on the lounge, one arm draped over the edge. He was naked but for a robe which was loosely tied, and he lolled his head to the side as he watched Diascia undress. She pulled the ribbon from her hair, and long copper locks tumbled free, caressing her flawless skin.

He rose, sauntering over to her.

"Your Majesty..." she murmured with an amused lilt as he came up behind her, running his hands over her body. She responded to his touch.

"You smell good," he said, inhaling her floral perfume as he peeled away the remaining layers of her clothing.

A sigh escaped her lips as he kissed her shoulder. Then he stroked the nape of her neck, and she drew in a gasp. He cupped her chin, tracing her lips with the tip of his finger.

"Who am I?"

"You're the king."

"Say it again," he whispered, his passion aroused.

Diascia turned to face him and wove her slender fingers through his thick black hair. He kissed her, fire spreading through his veins.

"You are my lord and master, sire," she replied, smiling enticingly up at him. "And all of me is yours."

Zhelyas gripped her long, silky tresses and kissed her again. Her arms wrapped around him, fingernails clawing at his back as his kisses grew more fervent, and she trembled as her desire rose to meet his own.

With a coy glance, Diascia took his hand and lead him to the bed, shuffling backward playfully upon the covers as he crawled after in amorous pursuit. With little effort, he pushed her down, her hair strewn across the pillow, and she writhed in pleasure as he began to explore her body.

Smoke and Mirrors

Diascia preened in front of the mirror, wearing only her lingerie. It was very sensual, and Zhelyas wanted to pull her beneath the bed covers once more.

She was delightfully unspoiled, but not virginal; wise in the ways of physical pleasure, but not wanton. Diascia was everything he could ever want in a lover.

"You know what I've been missing?" she asked.

"What is that?" he replied, distracted by the sloping curve of her breasts.

"A soirée."

He frowned. "A soirée? Whatever for?"

Diascia turned to him, her copper-blond hair partially unpinned, her chestnut eyes gleaming. "Oh, you know! Dancing, music, gossip. A chance to let loose and drink your cares away."

Zhelyas had never been fond of parties. The other nobles were far too pompous for his taste, and the only women interested in dancing with him were dull. The rest were looking for bigger fish than him in their search for a prospective husband. It was ironic that Diascia suggested one, since he believed he had even asked her once and been refused. Still, in the afterglow of their intimacy, he felt like giving her anything she wanted.

"Very well then, you shall have your soirée."

"Really?"

She leaped up and threw herself onto the bed, wrapping him once more in her lean body and intoxicating perfume.

"A soirée? Dia, what were you thinking?" Lobelia sighed as Diascia tore through the closet, discarded dresses flying across the room to land haphazardly on the bed.

"Come on, Lebby, it'll be fun! Besides, everybody will see that I'm with the king now. I'll be the talk of the court!"

She twirled, holding a shimmering gold dress to her bosom, and swayed the skirts in front of the mirror as she hummed to herself, apparently imagining dancing with Zhelyas.

Lobelia tapped a long fingernail. She couldn't imagine what her sister saw in the surly brute, but their dalliance was proving to be the distraction she needed. And since all the court would be in attendance, it might be the chance she was waiting for to make her move.

"Oh, Lebby, you should definitely wear this one."

She looked up to see Diascia indicating a deep green velvet dress. Not as flashy as Diascia's gown, but it would do. Besides, Lobelia wanted all eyes on her sister, and only two men looking at her: her own lover, and the person whom she intended to convince of her sincerity.

"Welcome, everyone," Zhelyas said, his voice carrying across the hall as the idle chatter dissolved into silence. "Let us toast the future of our kingdom and the prosperity of this fine court."

The nobles all lifted their glasses, looking somewhat nervous.

Diascia was radiant in a golden dress with ruby jewelry that highlighted her ivory skin. Her copper hair was upswept in a froth of curls crowned with a diamond tiara instead of her usual ribbon, making her look refined and elegant. A long train trailed behind her as she strode with Zhelyas down the queue, her satin-gloved hand wrapped around his arm.

She appeared rather pleased at all the attention, and Zhelyas realized this was as much a power play to solidify her public position as his lover as it was a diversion. She was more clever than he'd given her credit for. Perhaps she even thought she would be his consort someday.

He hadn't thought of her as anything other than a plaything, but he supposed it wasn't out of the realm of possibility. He admired her tenacity and her willingness to do whatever it took to get what she wanted—rather like him, actually. She might make a suitable partner, though the thought of having Lobelia as a sister-in-law made his toes curl.

Still, he had agreed to her request, so he decided he might as well let her have her way. It would make their other pursuits even more stimulating.

Zhelyas lounged on the throne, and she sat beside him in a smaller chair set aside for her use. The musicians, who had ceased playing at his entrance, struck up again at a wave of his hand, and the nobles hesitantly began to mingle.

Servants milled about the hall, carrying trays with wine, liqueur, and hors d'oeuvres. The abundance of alcohol flowing seemed to break down some of the tension, and soon Zhelyas's guests were chatting amongst themselves. He had to admit it was a more pleasant atmosphere than when they were all in terror for their lives. Maybe a party had been a good idea after all, something to restore a sense of normalcy to the court.

Zhelyas noticed Diascia looked bored, and recalled she had mentioned dancing. "Would you care to dance?" he inquired, and her face lit up.

"It would be my pleasure, sire."

He took her hand and led her to the center of the ballroom, the crowd parting at their approach.

With a flourish, Diascia swept up her skirt train, and he wrapped his arm around her back. Her satin dress felt smooth beneath his fingers, caressing her curves. She beamed with pleasure as they moved slowly in time with the music, all eyes in the room on them.

After the song was over, Zhelyas took a step back and Diascia gave a deep curtsy before they made their way back to their seats.

Zhelyas plucked a quail egg tart from a passing servant while Diascia bit into a fig stuffed with crumbled cheese and drizzled with honey. She licked the honey from her fingers, and his pulse began to race.

He couldn't wait for this tedious soirée to be over.

Radella and Malcolm were conversing in the corner when a dark-haired woman sidled over. She was wearing a clinging green dress with a capelet of sleek black feathers that reflected the flickering candlelight.

"May I speak with you a moment, Earl?" she inquired in a low, sultry voice, carrying two glasses of wine, one apparently intended for Malcolm.

Radella gave her a sideways look. "I'll leave you two alone, then."

Malcolm stared at her helplessly as she walked away, then he turned his attention back to Lobelia.

"What can I do for you, Lady Anthusa?" he inquired politely, a little flustered at being approached in such a manner. Noblewomen were known to be tenacious, but it was common knowledge he was happily married, and that usually dissuaded them.

"I hear you've been doing some good work for the people of this city," she said in a conspiratorial whisper. "I know I don't have a title behind my name, but I want to help however I can."

She sounded so earnest, and the pool of potential allies was a small one. However, she was known to be having an affair with Sejic, a major in the army, and that gave him pause. Trusting someone so intimately involved with the military wasn't something he was keen to do.

"I'm not sure what you are referring to, Lady Anthusa," Malcolm said evasively.

"There's no need to be coy, Earl," she chided, then glanced over her shoulder and flashed a smile at Sejic, who stood guard at the far end of the room, on duty for the soirée. "The major suspected something was amiss when his soldiers started receiving unexpected windfalls. He confided in me, and I pieced it together, so you have nothing to be concerned about. Besides, Sejic is willing to offer his help as well by giving the men under his command a little extra incentive to look the other way. He can also modify the duty roster, making it simpler for everyone involved. No more guesswork."

Malcolm couldn't help but be tempted by her offer. There was a chance she could be lying, but it might be worth the risk. There had been a few close calls lately.

He darted a glance across the room, where Radella was now in conversation with Takaria, and met the duchess's gaze.

Takaria appeared to gauge the situation and gave a slight nod of approval.

"All right," Malcolm agreed. "Meet me at midnight by the back staircase, and I'll outline our plans."

That night, Lobelia arrived at the appointed place. Malcolm had half-expected her not to show, which would have left him looking silly standing all alone in a dimly lit corridor twiddling his thumbs.

She sauntered down the hall toward him in a black silk robe with a plunging neckline that looked more like a negligee than a dressing gown, long dark hair flowing free to her waist. The only woman Malcolm would ever love was Andrine, but he couldn't help blinking at the alluring vision.

"This entrance isn't used often, so we should be safe, but we have to watch out for the guards doing their rounds," he said, focusing on his task with some difficulty. "I'd say we have twenty minutes."

Malcolm glanced down the corridor, realizing how incriminating it would look in other ways. Especially to his wife.

Lobelia smiled. "Don't worry, if someone sees us, Major Sejic will corroborate our story."

Malcolm cleared his throat. "In that case, to the business at hand."

He explained the details of their enterprise, Lobelia nodding all the while.

"Do you think you can do this?" Malcolm inquired once he was finished. "If it's too intimidating, I understand. Nobody wants to get on the bad side of the king."

"We have a duty to the people, isn't that right?" Lobelia replied, and he felt oddly as if he were listening to himself.

"I'd like to think so."

"Then I am fully committed." Lobelia squeezed his arm. "You won't regret it, Earl, I promise."

"I think you might be a better fighter than I am," Sejic quipped as Lobelia dodged his strike, tapping his ribs lightly with the edge of her sword.

One side of her dress was pulled up and tied in a knot to give her greater ease of movement. Strands of hair drifted free of their pins.

"I should be," she retorted, tasting bitterness in her voice. "As a woman in Effrenia, I had to protect myself and my sister. No one else was going to." She turned on her heel and swished her sword. "Dia isn't nearly ruthless enough, so I was the one who faced down every man who sought to assert himself against us. Coming to Artemisia, we faced challenges of a different sort, but at least we had the protection of the king, as opposed to our indolent lout of an uncle."

She resumed her stance. "I admit I've let my skills grow dull in the intervening years, so I'm grateful to you for helping me sharpen them again."

Their swords met with a fierce clang, faces barely inches apart.

"Anytime, vixen," he replied, using his pet name for her. "I just wish you'd let me win sometimes."

He twisted his sword, disarming her, then spun her around and trapped her arms. His lips traced her collarbone, and she arched her neck in delight.

"Now, what fun would that be?"

She went limp, slipping out of his grasp, and swept his feet from under him.

Sejic landed flat on his back, winded by the impact, and Lobelia straddled him, pinning his wrists to the ground. Her dark hair drifted across his chest like tendrils of fine-spun silk as she leaned close, drinking in his scent.

"See? Isn't this more fun?" she inquired with a lascivious grin.

She dipped her chin, meeting his lips in a kiss that left them both breathless, then pulled away. "As much as I would love to play some more, darling, I have work to do."

She rolled to her feet, undid the knot in her skirt, and smoothed out the fabric. "You know the plan?" she asked, tucking her errant locks back into place.

He nodded, then rose and retrieved their swords. "Everything's set. After tonight, the earl will have no reason to believe you are anything other than completely devoted to his cause."

"Excellent."

She fluffed out her skirt and turned to leave, then paused. "Oh, by the way, thanks for changing the duty roster the other night. That little scare was precisely what the earl needed to convince him."

"You know what you have to do?" Malcolm asked, sounding slightly doubtful as he handed Lobelia the poetry book.

Her glance darted across the page, the stanzas confirming his instructions. "Of course," she replied with a disarming smile. "Everything is well in hand. I won't let you down."

His brow creased in mild uncertainty, but he nodded. "You realize if anything goes wrong, we can't help you."

"No need to worry about me. I'll be fine."

An hour later, Lobelia stood in the scattered light of the falling dusk, awaiting her charge. The poem was cryptic like all the rest, and far too mushy for her taste. She wanted Sejic to tie her to the bed, not tickle her feet with roses. Though upon second thought, it might be an intriguing sensation. She'd have to suggest it to him later.

She turned her thoughts back to the present, peering at the poem once again.

Those hot days
When we would lie on the grass
The wind tugging at our clothes
The sun would kiss our bodies
And I would kiss your lips
Tickling your feet
With the sweetness of a rose

Lobelia peered around the corner, a pink rose held in her hand, marking her as the "secret carrier"—an ostentatious name, but an obscure one in case anyone overheard it come up in conversation.

This was it. If she could pull this off, she would have Malcolm and his fellow conspirators right where she wanted them. She was well aware Malcolm had followed her; she had expected him to. Unlike the others he was personally acquainted with, he had no reason to trust her, and Takaria, ever-cautious, would have insisted upon it.

She plastered a benevolent smile on her face and pulled off her hood, holding up the rose.

"Tickling your feet," the man said.

"With the sweetness of a rose," Lobelia replied, utterly nauseated.

"My name is Jon, and this is Jayla." He was apparently a widower and had only a little girl with him.

Lobelia crouched at her level, offering the rose. "Here you go, sweetie. We'll make it out safely tonight, don't you worry." Lobelia despised children, but she knew it painted a pretty picture for the one observing her from the shadows.

She led them through the narrow streets, wary of any unseen spies. There had been a uptick in people who had been previously censured by the military attempting to regain their standing by reporting their neighbors for any impropriety. Fear had a strange effect on people, even making them do things they would never have considered before—she knew that well enough.

They were nearing their destination when there was a shuffling sound in the darkness. Jon looked around nervously, holding his daughter close.

"Don't show any alarm," Lobelia said in a low, even tone. "Just keep walking."

There was another scuffling sound, and Jon twitched. "What if—?"

She faced him, still smiling, an expression that didn't reach her cold eyes. "We're almost there."

They turned the corner. A man lumbered out of the dark, pointing an accusing finger at Jon.

"I knew it!" he hissed. "I'm going to call for the guard!"

A hand wrapped around his mouth from behind and his eyes rolled back in his head as a thin blade was slipped between his ribs.

"Oh, hun. They already know."

Lobelia glanced at Jon, who'd turned white as a sheet. "The checkpoint is over there. Here are your papers. Take your daughter and go." She leaned close, as if to give him an encouraging kiss on the cheek. "Speak of what you saw here tonight, and I'll kill you, understand?"

He bobbed his head, steering the girl toward the gate with shaking hands. Lobelia watched as the soldier gave the papers a once-over, then nodded, ushering them through. She let out a satisfied sigh.

"You did well," Malcolm said once she'd returned to the palace. "I was watching."

Lobelia feigned surprise. "You don't trust me?"

"I do now," he replied, shaking his head. "I'm sorry for doubting you. You were very good with the child, by the way. Thank you for everything. And thank Major Sejic, too."

"Oh, I will," Lobelia assured him with a sly smile, then sauntered off toward Sejic's quarters, snatching a crimson rose from a vase along the way.

All that Glitters

After days of traveling the placid countryside, lush green grasses growing more sparse and feeble as they drew closer to the desert, the town of Kego was a welcome change. It was brimming with an excitement that was contagious.

People danced on street corners in bright costumes with jangling belts and veils, accompanied by a variety of musical instruments: pipes, drums, and tambourines. Colorful silks hung in windows, waving in the hot breeze, while the owners of shops and stalls lined the streets hawking their wares, savory aromas filling the air.

Caro was entranced. She felt as if she had stepped into another world.

"That will be far too hot for a trip through the desert," Stelian observed, noting the servant's outfit Caro still wore. "You'll melt in those layers, and sandals will suit you better for walking in the sand."

To Caro, the desert had always been a featureless yellow blemish on an otherwise green map, and it surprised her how bright it was. She shielded her eyes as she peered into the cloudless sky.

"Better get used to it. The sun's an almost constant fixture around here," Gaius said. "You should go with Ezalia to pick out some new clothes, or she'll leave you behind."

"I'll come too," Lottie offered, but he shook his head.

"I don't think that's a good idea. You're so fair-skinned, you'll burn in the blink of an eye, and the desert is a harsh place for even the most seasoned traveler."

"Gaius is right," Caro said gently. "You've been brave, and we couldn't have made it this far without you, but it will be treacherous in the desert, and I don't want to put you in any more danger."

Lottie sighed. "Then where should I go?"

"Take the road around the periphery of the desert to Agassey. There, you will find the Grand Duke Ezekiel Garsiv, and you can alert him of our intentions," Caro said. "You'll be fine. Besides, Gaius will be with you."

"He will?"

Gaius blinked. "I will?" he repeated, sounding like a parrot.

Caro gave him a mildly remonstrating look. "If anyone will burn to a crisp in the desert, it will be you."

"You sound like Ezalia, you know that?"

Caro smiled. "Then it's settled. We'll send word to the grand duke once we reach Biding and communicate Alenard's response to our petition."

"As you wish. Take care, my queen," Gaius added, using her title for the first time since their departure.

"You as well, My Lord Physician."

Lottie appeared puzzled by the exchange, and Gaius nodded once more before steering her away.

Caro turned to Ezalia, who was watching from across the street.

"We've still got a strapping young man with us, so I don't think we have much to worry about." Ezalia winked over her shoulder at Stelian, who was munching on a spiky fruit.

Caro ate a quick lunch of cucumber mixed with tangy yogurt, then changed into the clothes Ezalia had procured for her.

"That's better," Ezalia said, appraising Caro's new attire.

She had traded the blouse and linen dress for a belted, mossy green robe and lightweight pants bound at the ankles, and the kid slippers for sandals as Stelian had suggested.

Ezalia wrapped a woven teal shawl around Caro's shoulders, draping it over her head. "The sun's hotter than you're used to. I don't want you to faint."

It was as far from a royal Artemisian gown as anything Caro had worn. Ezalia's own attire was similar, dusky blue with a maroon scarf. Stelian looked perfectly comfortable in his desert clothes, shedding his leather outfit for an embroidered tan shirt and pants with a draping mantle in a sandy saffron, though he carried his armor in his pack. It would be more difficult to replace on the other side than the rest of their things.

Because the wagon would be unwieldy in the sand, they packed their remaining provisions into knapsacks, purchased additional water skins, then traded the wagon to a merchant for a large tent and camels which were better suited for the desert than horses.

Caro had only seen camels in books, with their thin, gangly legs, wide feet, and long necks. Lidded eyes and large lips made them appear as if they were smiling contentedly, unbothered by the world around them, and Caro thought they were adorable. In person, however, she was surprised by the pungent odor. She supposed she wouldn't smell like a bed of roses either if she never bathed. It wasn't unpleasant for long, and she soon grew accustomed to it.

She watched as Stelian demonstrated how to mount a camel while it was sitting.

"Hold on tight."

"Whoa!" She gasped and leaned back to keep her balance as it rolled onto its feet, lifting her high above the ground. She felt a little unsteady, and gripped the rope for dear life.

"You okay, Caro?" Ezalia inquired, looking rather at ease as she gracefully mounted her own.

Caro nodded, relaxing into its ambling gait. "I didn't expect it to be so... big."

Stelian chuckled, riding with the ease of a seasoned traveler. "You're doing fine."

The desert was even more desolate than the yellow blotch on the map had suggested. Caro was astonished by how vast it was. After little more than an hour, she couldn't see the border town any longer, nor perceive the edge of the desert in any direction. One might think it was endless.

"If we get separated, be careful not to veer too far off course," Stelian cautioned. "It's easy to get lost out here, but you can always find your way by following the stars."

He gestured to the sky, as if the shining points of light were already visible and not the ball of blinding fire that was the sun.

Caro had almost forgotten what a cloud looked like. "Is it always so hot?"

"I'm afraid so," he replied, shielding his eyes as he peered out into the distance. "It's because of the sun reflecting off the sand and a lack of foliage or water to disperse the heat, but it gets extremely cold at night. Once the sun goes down, it will be like an icebox, so we'll want to pitch the tent and keep ourselves warm until morning."

She nodded.

"In the desert, it's easy to lose your bearing because there are no landmarks to speak of, just one wide expanse of sand. People have gone mad wandering in circles. Only the lucky have made it through, usually by stumbling upon nomads who can point them on the right course. And you definitely don't want to get lost. There are more than sand crawlers out there."

"Like what?" Caro asked, curious.

"As Duke Vittorius said, the Esaphis is a dangerous place, filled with brigands and thieves. It's so desolate that the amount of uninhabited space far exceeds the number of inhabitants. Many small clans and tribes struggle to eke out a living, and it's difficult to keep any sort of order in such conditions. However, the four largest tribes form a sort of coalition, though they have been known to quarrel over land and resources from time to time. They are known as the Omaira, the Sufra, the Khadra, and the Zarqa. All four chieftains share a common ancestry, which is why they have maintained a tenuous peace over the centuries."

He lowered his voice. "There is, however, a fifth clan: the Sharir."

"Sharir?" Caro repeated.

Stelian nodded, looking like he was speaking of something taboo. "If you're going to be traveling in the desert, you should know about them. They are a clan of assassins whose very name strikes fear into those who live in the Esaphis. The Sharir leader, *La Firar*, is the law of the desert, and he maintains the balance between the tribes and the various merchant and trading guilds. Even the security forces in the border towns are hesitant to cross them."

Caro gaped at him, stunned. "Have you met them before?" she asked, and Stelian shook his head.

"No, and I am glad of it. Drawing the attention of the Sharir is like finding yourself in the midst of a pride of sleeping lions: it's far better not to be noticed."

"You seem comfortable in the desert," she observed, having noted his ease with the camel and his knowledge about the supplies they would require for their journey.

"Actually, my mother was from here. My father, a servant of the Royal House, met her when he was on a mission much like this. They fell in love, and she returned with him to the capital, but she was a free-spirited woman. The city couldn't contain her."

Stelian smiled at the memories. "I traveled with her often to visit her family, and she taught me everything she knew. The Esaphis is my second home."

Until today, Caro hadn't known a place existed that was both so magnificent and merciless, but it had its own beauty, she supposed. Rolling hills of windswept golden sand shifted and gleamed in the sun like a kingdom's worth of treasure.

"But that was before I became your bodyguard. I haven't been to the desert in quite a while."

"Do you miss it?"

"You might think it strange, but I do."

"I don't think it's strange at all," Caro said, shaking her head, and she was reminded of her own beloved castle back in Aurinesse.

"Milady..."

She shook her head to allay his guilt. "'Home is where the heart is,' isn't that how the saying goes?"

"There is a similar proverb in the desert. 'If there is paradise in this world, it is my abode.'"

She smiled. "I like that."

Caro woke in the middle of the night. The wind whistling outside invaded her dreams, and for a moment it seemed as if someone was calling for her.

She rubbed her eyes and tiptoed out of the tent, wrapping the blanket around herself like a shroud.

The night was silent and peaceful, and the cool sand felt nice between her toes. The dunes, blazing gold during the day, were now tinted violet and silver, a haze of purple in the distance. It was like she had strayed into a fairytale landscape.

Stelian was lying on the ground, his fingers laced behind his head for a pillow. "Can't sleep?" he asked, propping himself up on his elbows.

She shook her head and sat beside him, careful not to get any of the grit into her clothes. She wrapped her arms around her knees and stared up at the sky. "I've never seen the stars so bright."

"There isn't enough moisture to form clouds, so the sky is as clear as a reflection in a pool."

"Gaius taught me the constellations, but the only time I spent out of the castle at night was in the woods when you took me camping. I never really got to appreciate them."

"In the desert, you can try to follow the sun, but after a while it messes with your sense of perception. If we're separated, your best bet is to navigate by the stars," Stelian explained. "Let's see how much you remember."

Caro wiggled herself into a more comfortable reclining position.

"Let's see... To the north?"

"Ari, the Eagle," Caro replied. That was an easy one.

Stelian traced a pattern resembling a bird in the air. "Correct. A guide for all lost souls, its outstretched wings and plumed tail are recognizable in the sky."

Caro followed his finger as he drew invisible lines connecting the stars.

"To the west?"

"Is Eik, the Great Tree."

Stelian nodded. "A symbol of perseverance and growth in the harsh, unyielding desert landscape."

Caro could almost see its crooked trunk and the leaves fluttering at the ends of its boughs.

"To the south?"

Caro wracked her brain. "Um, an insect of some sort?"

"Orm, the Scorpion," Stelian corrected, "with its barbed tail like a hook and pincer claws. It is a deadly creature, but also a potent symbol of protection and survival."

Caro had never seen a scorpion before, but its tail did look a bit like a fish hook dangling its body in the sky.

"And finally, to the east?"

"Ros, the Flower," Caro said. "It's my favorite."

Stelian nodded again with a slight smile at her enthusiasm. "Beauty and hope in a desolate landscape. But this rose has its thorns, for nothing that grows in the desert is without its defenses. Even if it looks harmless, one must always be cautious."

He traced the outline of the stem and angular petals. "As long as you always know where these four constellations are, you will never be lost."

Caro stared up at the starry canopy, perceiving the patterns hidden within, and her thoughts drifted to the past. "My father used to tell me a fable about those four," she mused, and Stelian cocked his head. She had rarely spoken about her personal life since the tragic events, but she didn't feel the same pain anymore—or rather she had buried it deep inside.

He met her gaze with interest. "What sort of fable?"

Caro cast her mind back to those happier times. "One day, an eagle found himself lost in the desert. He was hot and weary, and weak from lack of food. For hours, he searched for a meal, until he spotted a scorpion scuttling across the sand. He scooped it up in his talons before it could escape and flew to a tall tree, pinning it against the branches.

"The scorpion tried to sting the eagle, but the poison did not pierce his thick skin.

"'Oh please, spare me!' the scorpion begged. 'I would not make a good meal, for my shell is hard and difficult to crack.'

"'Not for my beak,' replied the eagle.

"'My flesh is bitter.'

"'I am too hungry to care. Now be quiet and accept your fate.'

"'What if I could give you something even more enticing, oh great eagle?' the scorpion offered.

"'Is it tasty?'

"'It will not fill your belly, but it will fill your soul.'

"The eagle was intrigued, and nodded his feathered head. 'Very well, but if you are tricking me, you shall become my dinner. I haven't decided to spare you yet.'

"Once again in the grasp of his predator, the scorpion guided the eagle to a hollow where the sand graduated into arid soil and sharp, eroded spires of stone. Before the eagle's eyes spread a blanket of the most astonishing purple blossoms. He descended, expecting them to be a mirage, but was amazed to find they were real.

"Something bubbled up within him, and the helplessness and sorrow melted, filling him with renewed hope and courage in the face of such perseverant beauty.

"The eagle released the scorpion, who scurried out of reach.

"'Why did you free me?' the scorpion asked. 'You could have had both the flowers and a meal.'

"The eagle shook his magnificent head. 'You traded your life for these blossoms. To take it now would make me unworthy of the pleasure they have brought. I would rather be hungry and full of hope than full and contemptible to myself. One should always fulfill their promises to deserve what has been granted them.'

"With that, the scorpion watched as the eagle plucked a flower from the dry earth, then flew away."

Stelian listened with rapt attention to her tale. "I never imagined they had such an eloquent and poignant narrative."

"Legend says the eagle is a metaphor for the god Aryama, when he was but a mortal man. He planted the first of those flowers in the capital, the vibrant purple blossoming promethia, a symbol of promises kept and oaths honored. He then placed the constellations of the eagle, scorpion, tree, and flower in the sky to guide other travelers like himself, who had lost their way."

Caro smiled, leaning back on her hands. "This is the first time I have seen the constellations so brilliantly, however. I appreciate the tale in a whole new light."

"There are a few hours yet until daybreak, so try to get some rest," Stelian said as Caro covered a yawn.

She nodded, creeping back into the tent and crawling into her bedroll.

Caro felt like she'd been asleep for mere minutes before Stelian's cheerful voice invaded her unconscious mind.

"Rise and shine!"

She pressed her face back into her blanket. He had always been a morning person, and she most definitely was not. She could already feel the pervasive heat of the desert send beads of sweat trickling down her skin. Her first night's sleep had been less than ideal, and though her conversation with Stelian had been enlightening, she felt dead on her feet.

She stumbled out of the tent, wincing at the sun's unrepentant glare.

Stelian passed her a handful of dates. "These will boost your energy for the day ahead. It wouldn't do to topple off your camel."

Caro chuckled and nibbled on the sweet, fleshy fruit.

Curiosity Killed the Cat

Morfran stalked the castle like an oversized bat. No one could see his glare behind the ever-present silver mask, but the frown which twisted his features made servants and noblemen alike scurry out of his path.

Zhelyas was not pleased with the lack of progress in finding Caro and had delegated the task to Luther alone, recalling Morfran to the capital to ensure minor eruptions of dissent were snuffed out without mercy.

Morfran did so obediently, slaking the wrath of the irate king, but all the while his own anger simmered beneath the surface. Veena had promised he would find the object of his vengeance if he aided Zhelyas's coup, but so far his efforts had been fruitless.

"You look irritated."

Morfran spun to face the voice, but to his surprise it was not Zhelyas who had spoken. "Prince Arvind," he replied, lacing his voice with respect.

The prince had only recently been on a mission to Drusus, and Morfran had not seen him since his return.

"Perhaps if I knew what was causing you such consternation, I might assist?"

Morfran wanted to tell him to jump off the castle parapets but thought better of it. He was loath to confide in Arvind. A traitor could hardly be trusted, but his investigations had yielded few results, and he doubted he could lure the prince to his interrogation room as he had the others.

He drew in a slow breath. "Eight years ago, there was a gala staged at the palace. Dignitaries and military leaders were in attendance."

"I remember. It was my lovely niece's ninth birthday celebration."

"Perhaps," Morfran replied, his voice carefully neutral. "I was fulfilling a contract that day and, while my target did not elude me, an item of mine was stolen by an attendee of that gala. I would very much like to retrieve it."

"Hmm, tricky. Do you remember what he looked like?"

Morfran had replayed that night over and over in his mind until he recalled it with perfect clarity. "The last I saw, he had long copper-brown hair in tight curls and stormy blue eyes."

"I think I know who you mean," Arvind mused, and Morfran's breath caught in his throat. "Count Thoril Viehr. He resides in the castle but was called away on business prior to the coup. I believe he oversees a mill in Sharnwick. You should find him there."

"Thank you, Your Highness," Morfran said tonelessly. He'd been waiting for this day for eight years; he couldn't back down now.

Arvind sauntered off with a wave over his shoulder. "I hope you find what you're looking for."

"Are you sure you trust him?" Veena purred, sidling up to Morfran as he digested this new clue.

"More than I trust you," he retorted.

"Oh, don't be like that. I brought you into this collusion. Be a little grateful."

"I'll be grateful when you make due on your promise."

Veena chuckled. "You may find that to be unwise, dear Morfran."

Morfran dismissed her warning and went to the throne room to request Zhelyas's permission to leave Aurinesse.

"You say you've heard rumors the queen may have stopped by Sharnwick rather than passing through Ock?" the king asked.

"Yes, sire. I thought I would go to determine their veracity."

Zhelyas pursed his lips. "Very well. Meet up with Luther upon your return."

Morfran bowed, hiding the frenzied excitement which bubbled up inside him. After eight years, he would finally have his revenge.

Morfran pulled down the cowl and fabric mask to hide his face, formless black robes blending in with the darkness as he scaled the manor walls. He crept through the window, his footsteps silent upon the plush carpet as he approached his target.

There was a reason Morfran was renowned as an assassin: his victims never saw him coming, and he never left a trace—but tonight, he had questions.

Morfran pressed his palm to the unfortunate man's mouth, muffling his cries, and forced him into a corner. "I want information, and your fate this night depends on your answers. Clear?"

Thoril nodded, pinned against the wall, Morfran's dagger at his throat.

Count Thoril Viehr was as Arvind had described, perfectly matching the physical description in Morfran's memory. His mane of copper hair was just as curly, the wide, fearful eyes that stared up at him a stormy blue. But the moment Morfran had the man within his grasp, he knew something was amiss.

"Eight years ago, there was a gala at the palace. Do you remember? It was the young princess's birthday, and she was given a rare white Drusian pony."

Morfran lifted his hand from Thoril's mouth, allowing him to speak.

"I—I was never at that gala!" he whimpered. "My father was sick, and I had to stay and tend to him."

"Do you swear?" Morfran leaned close, the dagger's blade glinting in the candlelight, and Thoril bobbed his head.

"On my life!"

Morfran pursed his lips. He considered disregarding the man's plea as a blatant lie, but then a horrible thought occurred to him. He clenched his fist until his nails dug into his palm through the glove.

If it hadn't been Thoril at the gala, that left only one possibility...

"This never happened," he hissed, and the man nodded, his lip trembling.

Morfran believed the fear in Thoril's eyes and released him, giving him one last menacing glance before vanishing out the window.

Zhelyas had ordered Morfran to meet with Luther, so he rode for the garrison as bidden.

"I could relieve you," Luther offered, and Morfran shook his head. "Normally, you would jump at the chance to get out of the palace."

"Not this time. There's something I need to do, and I don't care if Zhelyas reprimands me."

Luther rubbed his chin. "You never told me what you want out of all this."

Morfran glanced sideways at his compatriot. "I was wronged, and I wish revenge on my wrongdoer. That's all there is."

"I see," Luther murmured. "What we spoke about, the night I..." He trailed off, and Morfran poured him another goblet of wine.

"I swore I would keep your secret. But what happens if the queen retakes her crown?"

"Then it won't matter, I suppose," he said with a sigh. "I'll either live as a traitor, or be executed as one. I never intended for any of this to happen. I only wanted to protect her."

He shrugged, draining his goblet, and his cheeks grew flushed. "But sorry holds little weight in matters like these. I betrayed her and sided with a usurper. There's nothing else for it. I'll live with that regret for the rest of my life—however long it may be." Luther gave a sardonic laugh, then fell silent, morosely staring at his wine.

The general was an odd character, so fiercely loyal that what he had discovered had shaken him to the core. His entire life had been built upon a foundation of fidelity and trust, so much that he had become estranged from his family to become a soldier. When that faith was broken, his world shattered around him, leaving him ripe for the picking by Zhelyas, who needed a man inside, a man who had no principles left to hold onto.

A man like Morfran. Despite Luther's flaws, he was almost what Morfran could call a friend. He sympathized with the general's motives, and he wondered if he too would feel empty after having attained his revenge. With nothing left to live for—what would he do?

"You look miles away, Commander," Luther said wryly, holding the near-empty decanter. "So what now?"

"Now I return to the palace and face my fate."

Luther rose. "Then I won't delay you any longer. But put in a good word for me with the king if you get the chance. I would like to get out of this backwater hellhole one day."

Morfran shook his outstretched hand. "I'll see what I can do."

Shifting Sands

On the third night, as they were erecting the tents once more, Stelian looked up.

"What is it?" Ezalia inquired, noting his tension.

He narrowed his gaze, and Caro followed his finger as he pointed to a puff of sand on the horizon.

"A sandstorm?"

"No," he said, shaking his head gravely, and reached for his sword. "Raiders."

Caro had been relieved of her dagger at the garrison, so Gaius had given her his own rapier before they parted ways. Ezalia removed the comb she wore in her hair, and her curls fell loose about her shoulders. What appeared to be a decorative hairpiece had razor-sharp prongs that glinted in the piercing light.

Caro poised defensively, the others shielding her from the spray of sand as the riders thundered toward them.

"There must be a camp nearby," Stelian whispered. "Horses are no good for long distances in the desert."

The raiders broke into two lines, approaching from both sides. With a sweep of his long sword, Stelian brought the first rider off his horse. Two more leaped off their mounts and advanced at a run.

With the deadly grace of a dancer, Ezalia spun and sliced with her comb at anything within range. Caro and Stelian had sparred together often, and worked in tandem to dispatch their attackers.

"Enough!" a voice called above the tumult.

The remaining riders formed a circle around the small group, then parted for the young man who had spoken. He looked to be around Caro's age, with wavy, dark brown hair and gold eyes that glowed in the sunset. Over the dusky skin of a desert dweller, he wore a sandy robe, while a menacing curved sword hung from a crimson sash at his waist.

"I am Khalil of the Omaira. My mother Hadiya wishes to meet with you."

Caro recognized the name from Stelian's lecture about the most powerful tribes.

Stelian glanced over his shoulder, and Caro gave a slight nod. "Very well, we shall attend upon your grace," he said respectfully.

As they trudged behind their new hosts, Caro noticed a distinct flash of crimson on the raiders' outfits, matching that of Khalil's sash.

"Omaira means 'red' in the local dialect," Stelian informed Caro in a whisper, seemingly reading her mind. He indicated the dyed pennants waving in the distance.

"I can't help but be a little puzzled about their methods," she murmured.

"Mettle is the only currency in the desert. If a person does not have strength and resilience, they are not worthy of respect." Stelian's voice held a certain regard for their captors, and she hoped it would be repaid in kind.

Khalil led them to the far tent, larger and more luxurious than the others, trimmed in red silk. He swept aside the flaps and bade them enter with a curt wave.

Inside was a woven carpet which served as a floor, and propped upon cushions sat a woman who could only be the Omaira's leader. She was middle-aged, with long dark hair covered by a patterned scarf. She was wearing a taupe dress and an embroidered, red wool robe with long sleeves— evidently identifying her as the chieftess of the Omaira tribe. Her amber eyes surveyed them with interest.

"*Sayyida*," Khalil greeted. "I have brought the strangers."

"Welcome," she said graciously. "I am Hadiya. You have already met my son and heir, Khalil."

"We are..." Stelian trailed off, casting an uncertain glance at Caro.

"I know who you are: Duchess Ezalia, Lieutenant Stelian, and of course... Queen Caro of Artemisia."

She inclined her head as she spoke the royal title, and Caro returned the gesture.

"May I ask how you know? We have endeavored to keep our identities secret."

"Please sit," Hadiya said invitingly, gesturing to the carpet and cushions arrayed before her.

Caro did so, and the others followed suit.

"You must try some honey mead. I promise it isn't poisoned. Fatima, if you would."

A woman with titian hair poured a cup and set it before Caro. She felt it would be rude to have one of the others taste it first and so, despite Stelian's nervous look, she took a sip of the clear golden drink. It was smooth and sweet but crisp, with a fruity aftertaste.

She nodded to her host. "It's delicious, thank you."

"You have shown courage, fortitude, and conviction, all qualities necessary for a ruler."

Caro dipped her head again in acknowledgment of the compliment.

"But as to your question, I am what my people call *kahina*, a priestess, and it was the desert that whispered of your arrival. It informed me I should seek you out, for you are looking to cement an alliance. Is that not so?"

Caro hadn't thought of it that way. "Since you know our identities, you must also be aware of the circumstances which have brought us here. I seek assistance in reclaiming my rightful crown, but until now it has been in the form of benefactions from my subjects or the use of their own private forces. I had not considered seeking other avenues of patronage."

She cocked her head at Hadiya. "What do you propose?"

"If you were to marry my son, I would pledge my entire tribe to fight by your side. The Omaira are the largest clan in the Esaphis. We number two thousand strong, and every man, woman, and child is trained from birth to survive in this harsh climate."

That was a decent number of potential warriors for her cause. Caro did a quick mental calculation of population statistics and came up with at least five hundred, give or take.

"If he were to become my consort, who would inherit your role as chief of the Omaira?" Caro countered strategically. "However, I promise to consider him. When I once more sit upon the throne, we may revisit the matter of my marriage."

"I believe I can take you at your word," Hadiya said. "However, such a promise is nebulous. I require something more tangible than a vague prospect to pledge my forces to your aid."

Caro glanced at her traveling companions. "What you see is all we have, except for some meager rations."

She hated to admit weakness in such a delicate discussion, but honesty seemed like the best policy with Hadiya, especially if she truly had some sort of precognitive power as she claimed. The usual political dance of give and take had no meaning here.

"I can't guarantee anything other than my friendship until I reclaim my kingdom. Once I do, if I do not take Khalil to husband, I would be willing to furnish provisions, both foodstuffs and wares, in the amount of three gold rukmas per soldier you contribute to my cause."

Stelian's eyes widened a little. Oswin, with his prodigious wealth, had donated five thousand in an effort to win her favor; the average soldier's monthly stipend didn't even come close.

"And if you do not win your battle?" Hadiya inquired, lifting an eyebrow.

Caro swallowed. So far, she'd avoided thinking about that particular scenario. "I will ensure my subordinates are aware of our agreement so they may fulfill it in my place should they succeed where I do not. If I fail with no hope of recourse, yet somehow escape alive, then I will make due on my debt however I am able."

Hadiya let out a small hum. "Then I shall be satisfied with that. However, when you leave this place, I insist that my son accompany you."

"As you can see, I have quite a few traveling companions—" Caro began, but Hadiya held up her hand.

"This point is non-negotiable. Perhaps you will even grow to like each other," she suggested with a sly chuckle.

Caro glanced at Khalil, who appeared nonplussed by his mother's proposal on his behalf. He seemed to be a capable young man and carried himself like a warrior, respected by his clan. She could use another fighter for the journey ahead, though she couldn't help wondering how he would fare once they left the desert.

"Very well, I agree to your terms."

Hadiya clapped her hands. "Excellent! To celebrate this new alliance, we shall have a grand feast!"

Caro was frankly tired of grand feasts since the debacle at Oswin's, but was pleasantly surprised by the array of exotic dishes. Communally, they tore pieces of thin, griddle-baked flatbread and dipped them into hearty slowcooked stews seasoned with aromatic spices, alongside golden yellow rice baked into small cakes as they sipped sweetened mint tea.

"Chieftess Hadiya."

"Lady Ezalia," she replied with a nod. The others had been shown to their lodgings and were settling down for the night.

"Thank you for your gracious hospitality."

"I notice you did not speak, nor did your other young companion."

Ezalia shrugged. "Stelian defers to his queen in all matters, and his duty is to stay by her side, whether or not he is acknowledged."

"Admirable," Hadiya murmured. "And you?"

"I trust my niece. It is her choice how to proceed regardless of how we may advise her. Under the circumstances, I felt no need to do so."

"The queen would be quite at home here in the desert. She has the strength of will to survive in the harshest of conditions—yet I suppose that has been the case all along. I can only imagine the ignominy and suffering she has endured. But surely you did not come to hear me flatter her?"

"True," Ezalia said, nodding. She leaned against a pole jutting out of the sand, arms crossed, the red pennants flapping about her shoulders in the wind. "I just don't want you to get the wrong idea about her."

"Oh?"

"Your offer of support was one she could not resist in this time of crisis. Yet, no matter how well suited she may be to this life, her duty will always call her back to the capital."

Hadiya gazed across the desert sands of her domain. "Forgive me for my presumptuousness, Lady Ezalia. I made that comment to gauge her reaction and did not mean to offend. I hope one day my son finds love, and I wish for his happiness, but I also want him to accompany your party so he may learn a little of what it means to be a ruler. Your niece is already capable at such a young age, and he is still a child in many ways. If they fall into a romantic liaison, then we shall cross that dune should we come to it. Regardless, he will have gained an appreciation for the duties and responsibilities that await him when I pass on."

She turned and faced Ezalia. "I assure you, I have no untoward intentions. The desert is a land devoid of time, with few comforts, and even those are hard won. I respect Caro for the strength she has shown and believe she can accomplish what she has set out to do. My help is not contingent upon any factor other than those stipulated in our agreement, not even the affections of my son."

Ezalia smiled. "Thank you, Hadiya. That puts my mind at ease."

"One more thing," Hadiya added, her voice low. "If you happen to meet a woman named Veena, be wary. She is a desert nomad, but a pariah among our people, and I fear she may have a hand in the plot by the upstart king who opposes you."

"How do you know this?" Ezalia inquired, furrowing her brow at this unexpected revelation.

"The same way I knew you were venturing across the sands," Hadiya said mysteriously. "The desert told me."

An Eye for an Eye

"It was you, wasn't it?" Morfran's voice was quiet and sharp as a razor.

Arvind turned and smiled innocently. "I don't know what you mean."

"Eight years ago. After that gala, you engineered my kidnapping and sold me into slavery. I was only thirteen!" Morfran spat.

He had been waiting so long to say those words that they tumbled out of him. He remembered his training, and took a deep breath to regain his composure.

"Did you kill Thoril?" Arvind inquired, unperturbed, then sighed. "Pity. I was hoping to buy up the mill."

"Is that why you set him up?"

Arvind gave Morfran a patronizing look. "It was amusing, watching you chase your tail." He smirked. "Thoril and I were childhood friends. We looked so much alike, people often thought we were twins. But I was sickly, and so while he has retained his youthful good looks, I, alas, have not been so lucky."

Morfran could see it now, and wondered how he could have missed something so obvious. Arvind's copper hair had lightened to a dull brown and his blue eyes had turned silvery-gray, but it was the same cruel look in his gaze.

"Don't you have any conscience?"

"That's not what you want to ask, is it? You want to know *why*."

Arvind leaned against the wall, facing Morfran, whose eyes were mere slits behind the mask. "It was nothing personal. You had your eye on something that was mine, and I couldn't let you have it. Besides, I never liked those simpering parents of yours. It was fun seeing them squirm, and in the end they never knew what happened to you. They must have died with such heavy sorrow in their hearts, to lose their precious son."

Morfran's eyes blazed with fury, and he advanced upon the cruel nobleman, his dagger drawn.

"That's it. That look," Arvind said, baring his teeth. "Give me the pleasure of seeing your face. It just isn't the same with the mask."

Morfran paused, then slid the strap over his head, revealing his gruesome deformity.

"You should thank me. You were somewhat handsome as a youth, but unremarkable. Now, you are a name feared in all the lower circles."

Morfran's scowl deepened as Arvind's sneer grew wider. "Make your peace with your gods," he hissed.

"But can you really kill me?" Arvind was pinned against the wall, the dagger mere inches from his chest, and still his expression was as smug as ever. "She'll hate you, you know. Is that what you want?"

Morfran smiled, and Arvind blinked at the unnerving change in his manner. "She will hate me anyway when this is all over. Adding you to the list is a minor offense when tallied against the rest."

He leaned close enough that his cold breath fell upon Arvind's ear. Gray eyes widened in horror, then grew lifeless and dull as tarnished silver.

Morfran withdrew the blade and watched as Arvind's body slid down the wall, collapsing in a heap upon the floor like a marionette whose strings had been cut.

He was not quite dead yet. It would take a few minutes for him to bleed out, but the deed was done.

"And so you have your revenge," Veena said from the doorway. "Is it everything you've ever dreamed?"

Morfran stooped to wipe the bloody dagger on Arvind's silk coat, then slid it back into its sheath. Eight years of imagining this moment. Did it fulfill him? Damn right it did.

But while it was a means, it was not the end. His vengeance sated, another feeling replaced the rage which had ebbed out of him.

"What now?" Veena inquired, apparently irked by his silence. "You're not about to do something reckless, are you?"

Morfran smiled. "You already know the answer to that, Veena Fortuna."

"Where is Morfran?" Zhelyas demanded, arriving moments later.

Veena gestured over her shoulder. "You just missed him."

"He hasn't given me his report yet..." Zhelyas trailed off upon seeing Arvind's still-warm corpse slumped against the wall, a large pool of blood at his feet. "Did he do this?"

She cocked her head. "Oh yes, that's Morfran's handiwork."

"Is he still alive?"

Veena lifted an eyebrow, glancing at the flaccid heap on the ground. "Barely."

"Heal him."

"Do I have to?"

"Now!" Zhelyas growled, and stormed down the hall after Morfran.

Veena ambled over to Arvind. She glared down at him, then plunged two fingers into the wound Morfran had inflicted. Sorcerous fire cauterized it from the inside, her magic repairing the damaged tissue beneath.

This spell is cast between the worlds
Beyond the bounds of space and time
Zamana, keeper of what unfolds
Seize from the brink essence sublime

With her fingernail, she carved the rune of an hourglass upon the prince's heart, and it started to beat again weakly in his chest.

"Guess you have to save my life," Arvind chuckled, coughing up red foam, roused to consciousness by the pain spreading like white-hot fire through his veins.

She slapped him, snapping his head to the side, where it flopped on his shoulder. "Maybe so," she hissed. "But I can still make you suffer."

Arvind grinned, bloodstained lips curled in triumph. "My dear Veena, it sounds like you've gotten soft."

Her eyes blazed at his scorn and she dug her fingers in deeper, his anguished screams reverberating off the tower walls.

The black-clad commander swept past Malcolm as he stalked down the hall out of the palace. Moments went by, and when Malcolm strained his ear to listen, he could make out the sounds of screaming.

Malcolm waited out of sight until the sorceress had finished her task. He took a deep breath, knowing it would be better if he didn't investigate further, but he had to know.

He found Arvind slumped against the wall, a grievous wound glowing and pulsing as it was repaired by sorcery. Malcolm pressed his hand to his mouth, retching from the horrid sight.

The prince realized he was being watched and lifted a finger to his bloodstained lips, his face white with agony.

Malcolm bobbed his head and hurriedly departed, leaving the prince to his fate.

The sounds of Arvind's cries followed Zhelyas down the hall, growing fainter as he reached the courtyard—though he was certain the man was still screaming.

Zhelyas spotted Morfran at the foot of the palace steps, adjusting the saddle on his horse. "You *dare?*"

He drew his sword and lunged down the stairs. Morfran's blade met his with a clang.

"You killed Arvind, and now you flee? I did not take you to be such a coward!" Zhelyas lashed out with his sword, jabbing savagely.

Morfran's gaze glittered behind the mask. "Trust me when I say Arvind deserved to die," he replied, evading Zhelyas's strike. "His depravity and cruelty knew no bounds."

"Then why are you running? I might have accepted your actions if you had explained yourself."

Morfran sighed. "I am afraid things are not so simple."

Zhelyas frowned at his oblique response. "I cannot let you go."

"And I won't let you stop me."

Zhelyas tightened his grip and raced forward, blade parallel to the ground. Morfran stood still as a statue, then held up his hand and countered the attack with dazzling violet light.

When Zhelyas's vision cleared, Morfran was upon his horse. None of the soldiers loitering about dared confront the commander as he rode out of the courtyard unchallenged. Zhelyas beheaded one on the spot.

"Send a message to General Luther. Morfran is now an enemy of the Crown and is to be killed on sight!"

"Morfran? A traitor?" Luther said, reading the missive with incredulity. "I don't believe it."

But he recalled their last conversation. Morfran had been in an unusual hurry to return to the palace. If he had achieved revenge on his wrongdoer, perhaps he no longer had a need for Zhelyas and his schemes.

Luther felt oddly abandoned. He would miss their conversations and shared trials serving their volatile new king. Still, it didn't seem as if Morfran would have acted so rashly, even for revenge. The thought niggled at Luther as much as he tried to disregard it.

He scratched his stubble. "I hope I don't meet him on the battlefield one day."

Needs Must

"You wished to see me, sire?" Veena asked, sidling into the room.

Zhelyas turned to her, tapping his finger upon the back of the throne. "How is Arvind?"

"He'll recover," she replied tersely. "Is that all?"

"I want you to teach me magic."

Veena blinked at him. "Pardon?"

"Magic, Veena," Zhelyas repeated. "You're a sorceress, aren't you? That confrontation with Morfran was *humiliating*!" He dug his nails into the gold plating, seething.

Veena chewed a lip, considering her options. She needed Zhelyas, but he was unpredictable. It might be better to cater to his whims... though magic was no mere whim.

"Very well, sire, I will try. However, not everyone has the capacity to wield magic. If that turns out to be the case, I need your word you won't hold me culpable."

Zhelyas gave a curt nod.

"If you're intent upon this, come to the tower tonight. I will prepare some materials."

Later that evening, Veena paced her sanctum and rubbed her temples. What had she been thinking? She'd studied for years to learn sorcery. What could she teach the petulant king? Magic was complex, and Zhelyas wasn't exactly a master of subtlety.

Elemental gods, spellcasting, magic circles, runes. Where should she start?

She paused, her fingers lingering upon her spellbook. The pages were of parchment, bound with twine and encased in dark violet velvet. Veena stroked the textured softness and reverently lifted the cover.

To the one who desires what is contained within, both great power and danger awaits.

The spellbook had been written by a sorcerer named Avtandil, and Veena had discovered it in an old trunk belonging to her father, hidden in a pile of worthless junk. In the privacy of the desert before dawn, she had applied herself to her study of the arcane. The concepts were straightforward, and after a few sessions, she was able to make a spark of blue light dance upon her fingertips. The power was intoxicating, and soon she had desired more—but maybe that would be enough for Zhelyas.

"Veena."

She sighed inwardly at the voice which came from the door, intruding upon her solitude. "Sire," she replied, bowing.

Zhelyas lifted an eyebrow as he surveyed the scrolls, potions, and other paraphernalia scattered across the tables. "So where do we start?"

"Come stand over here in the light," Veena instructed.

He obeyed, looking irked.

Veena steepled her fingers together, summoning all her composure. "Magic is based on three fundamental principles. One, it is a mirror of what is inside us, therefore our intentions are reflected in our use of it. Two, every cause has an effect, every spell has a consequence, and the strength of that consequence depends on the power of the spell. Three, everything flows. There is a constant cycle to existence, and magic follows that flow."

Zhelyas gave a curt nod.

"In order to summon magic, you must visualize it as an extension of yourself."

"I've watched you draw runes and chant mumbo jumbo. This seems less than constructive," Zhelyas grumbled.

"That's for more specialized spellcasting," Veena explained with forced patience. "When performing a particularly complicated spell, an elemental god must be invoked. However, reflexive magic does not require spoken incantations. Close your eyes and hold up your hand."

Zhelyas's eye twitched at her instruction, but he did as he was told.

"Moonlight is a powerful conduit. Let it flow over you and envision it seeping into your skin. Feel it coursing through your veins, pulsing in time with your heartbeat." Veena's voice was low and resonant. "Now, call it forth."

His brow furrowed in concentration, and she held her breath. *Moment of truth.*

A flicker of red, then another, like the embers of a blazing fire.

He opened his eyes and rotated his hand, gazing wonderingly at the power which was now his to control.

"Magic," he said breathlessly.

Veena crossed her arms, not sure whether she should be proud or uneasy. "So it seems you have the aptitude after all."

Zhelyas clenched his fist, snuffing out the flames, and he stared at her with hunger in his eyes. "Show me more."

Once Zhelyas was gone, Veena sank into a chair and stared at the curtains of gold damask fabric. She hated the color, and would never wear it. It reminded her too much of her painful past.

Like red for the Omaira, gold was the color of the Sufra tribe into which she had been born as the daughter of the chief's vizier. It sounded like a lofty position, filled with wealth and riches; in actuality, it was anything but. The Sufra were not as progressive as the Omaira, mostly due to Hadiya's influence, and so Veena was good to her father only as a bride to be bartered for marriage.

Veena had met Khalil at the gatherings of the tribal chiefs and envied him for his princely affluence and lifestyle of ease and comfort, while she was relegated to the role of a lowly servant. Years passed, and his obliviousness only made her resent him more.

Finally, after a particular incident in which a potential groom of her father's choosing tried to lay his hands on her, Veena vowed she would obtain the power necessary to make her own destiny and force others to respect her. She had already been secretly practicing magic through the spellbook she had found, and she paid for passage on a merchant caravan heading north to the Barren Lands to locate the book's creator.

Avtandil, his name was, a sorcerer of no small skill, and he took her as his apprentice. While under his tutelage, Veena devoured his lessons, obsessed with mastering magic. She even modified his spells into ones only she could use, invoking not the elemental gods of his sect, but those of the desert instead.

After a while, however, she began to feel he wasn't teaching her everything, that he was suppressing her potential like everyone else had done. Dissatisfied with her teacher, she defied Avtandil and snuck into his private study, searching for something that could make her even more powerful.

Veena hesitated outside the door, listening for any sound. Avtandil had departed for a consultation with one of his clients, but he was cagey, and it would not do to confront her teacher even as she was disobeying his edict.

She held her breath as his tiger familiar padded down the adjacent hall, its striped orange tail swinging lazily. Avtandil had placed magical seals around his study, but she'd been practicing, and with the correct combination of symbols was able to break them easily. Veena smirked. He obviously underestimated her.

Once inside, she propped the door slightly ajar in case it sealed itself again, locking her in. She turned, surveying the sorcerer's private room.

Avtandil was a tidy man, if a little eccentric, with everything in its proper place. Bookshelves lined the walls between tall torchères, and she lit them with a wave of her hand. The floor was of a caramel-colored wood while red carpet softened her footsteps. Firelight reflected upon a window at the far end, crafted of violet and ruby glass, depicting the phases of the moon. A display case stood in one corner, filled with a myriad of odd items: a gold coronet perched upon a skull; an open box with a pale green gemstone suspended upon a chain; even some sort of dead eel, immaculately preserved.

Upon his desk was a pile of scrolls and a variety of paraphernalia: a scale and weights, a pestle and mortar, and a stand with vials of vibrantly hued substances, along with a book of maps. Apparently, Avtandil had been in the midst of an experiment and was sourcing the locations for the ingredients he needed.

A glass sphere rested upon a pedestal, yellow and green fire swirling hypnotically beneath the surface. Veena reached out, compelled to touch it, but before she could, her gaze was drawn to a tome on a nearby bookshelf.

Pulling herself from the sphere, she made her way to the book and took it down. It was surprisingly light. It had no title, but emblazoned upon its faded green cover was a hand with a spark upon the finger's outstretched tip. Above it was a symbol like a mystical sun, rays radiating out from a central point: two interlocked circles forming the handle of a key. The key to magic? She was intrigued.

Veena paused to listen and, satisfied with the silence, sat down to read. The book was centuries old, the pages yellowed and brittle, and she turned them with extreme care, trying to make out the faded words. In some places, the ink had disappeared entirely, its secrets lost forever to the ravages of time.

She had an idea. It was risky, but it might work.

Zamana,
Goddess of time, that sea with no shore
What once was lost, let now be restored

She pricked her finger with a pin and drew a pictogram of an incomplete hourglass with her blood upon the book. Zamana was an elusive goddess but a powerful one, and demanded specific tokens for her favor. In order to reverse time, she required a symbol of life's impermanence. A single drop was enough for something like this, but to turn back the hours over a larger area meant a much more potent sacrifice.

The hourglass glowed a deep purple, then vanished. Before Veena's eyes, the pages started to rewrite themselves, the ink growing clear and vivid against the paper, which was once more pristine and new.

Like most ancient tomes, there was a lot of flowery language and references to things both mystical and mundane that had no bearing on the current world, but Veena was able to glean information from some of the relevant passages.

The Temple of Aryama, the text read.

After his ascension to the heavenly plane, the hero Aryama, now revered as a god, decided to test the mettle of human courage and righteousness. He set upon the creation of a temple, hidden from mortal sight but in plain view of all who looked upon it. Those who entered would face trials to determine their merit, and if proven worthy, would be granted a boon by the god, to remake the world or even change the course of fate itself.

Veena's heart skipped a beat. This was what she had been searching for, she was sure of it.

Two crystal keys emit the sun's light from within. The largest shall be kept by those who worship the sun, while the other, a shard from the same raw material by which they were both fashioned, will be scattered across time.

A piece of parchment had apparently been torn out, perhaps depicting sketches of the crystals.

She frowned, scouring the page. That was all well and good, but where was the temple? Then her finger froze, and she traced the words again to make sure she had read them correctly.

At the base of the convex mountains, you will find the entrance, but only if you are wise. Between adulation and song, the solar gate will be revealed. The crystal will light your way.

Convex mountains... She rifled through the book of maps on Avtandil's desk. Hundreds of years after the book was written, maybe even thousands, the country of Artemisia had been settled and the capital established near the southernmost shore, nestled inside an unusual ring of mountains called the Ferilla Slopes, with the royal castle at its apex.

The temple would be found on the palace grounds.

Gaining entrance would be no mean feat, but she was too elated to worry about that now. Having deciphered the temple's approximate location—the book was annoyingly vague in that regard—the question of the crystals remained. The first was with "those who worshiped the sun." She recalled an ancient solar cult in the desert, though it had long since vanished into antiquity. Aryama remained a popular cultural figure, however, even after his adherents had gone. Perhaps by revisiting her people's legends, she might find the answer.

So what of the shard?

Her thoughts returned to the small green crystal in the display case, and she wandered over to it. The case was not locked, and she lifted the necklace from the velvet. It didn't shine as the book had said, but perhaps it was too dark in the dim room.

She drew the rune for light and held up the chain as a glowing ball bloomed in her hand. The light was immediately refracted through the facets of the crystal, bursting forth like the rays of the sun.

Avtandil had been no slouch. He had found one of the crystals spoken of in the book and kept it close. Perhaps he too was seeking the temple?

Veena draped the chain around her neck, feeling the crystal's warmth as it rested against her skin.

With her new mission, she fled Avtandil's keep and returned to the desert, flush with her triumph. Still, she could not quite shake the need to be accepted by her people, so she tried to win their favor with the sheer awe of her newfound magic, but Hadiya refused her.

Before she could approach the rest, the Sharir cast her out of the Esaphis, for they saw her practice of sorcery as heresy. What did they know? They were merely a clan of uncouth assassins, with no concept of the beauty and nuance of real magic.

Alone in the greenlands, with nothing to her name and no marketable skills besides her magic—she would never again abase herself as a servant—she was forced to resort to parlor tricks in order to make ends meet. Nobody wanted to see real sorcery, for it was looked upon with even more suspicion than in her homeland, so she disguised it as a gimmick, selling cheap incense and the illusion of wonder.

"Veena Fortuna," they called her. A ridiculous name, but few had ever seen an Esaphite outside of the desert, so she was able to make a decent living through her mystique and exotic looks alone. She settled in the capital, establishing a small shop of esoteric but harmless goods and occasionally telling fortunes at a traveling carnival.

That was where she had met Zhelyas.

She was what her people called a *kahina*, one who could see beyond, which aided greatly in her fortunes. Veena knew immediately who he was and sensed the discontent inside him, a tool she could cultivate for her use. That night he left her tent, she was certain he would return.

Eventually, Zhelyas sought her out again, and she carefully placed the suggestion in his mind. She needed free reign of the castle; he wanted to become king. She could accomplish both goals if she was clever enough.

Morfran was a man she had seen only in her dreams, a black shadow who walked the night, and she knew he would be perfect to suit her purposes. She also saw what he craved, and she used that to entice him to join their little conspiracy.

The third member of their crew landed practically on her doorstep, and she ensured she was there at the tavern when Luther was at his most vulnerable, easily swaying him to their side.

Arvind was an unexpected addition, and an unpleasant one, but she tolerated him as long as she needed Zhelyas to believe she was under his control, when really it had always been the other way around.

That Arvind had turned out to be the unknown target of Morfran's revenge had been a surprise, however, as had the masked man's abrupt departure. It complicated matters, but Veena would still have what she sought. She just had to be patient.

Fortune Favors

It took three more days and nights, but Caro and the others eventually crossed the Esaphis Desert. Khalil proved to be an invaluable guide, pointing out hidden dangers, as well as an oasis where they could refill their canteens.

Caro spotted tufts of grassland and rocky outcroppings with the promise of more fertile land beyond, and she urged her camel forward.

"What's her hurry?" she heard Khalil ask, struggling to keep pace.

"You have lived here all your life, but Caro is from the country," Ezalia replied. "Grasslands and flowers, paved streets—all these things you have never known are her comforts."

"Those bits of grass make her happy?" he said, sounding doubtful.

Ezalia chuckled. "We'll see how you feel after you've been in our world for a while, and maybe you'll be that excited to see a patch of sand."

Caro slowed her pace to let the others catch up. They crossed the last of the sand dunes into the outskirts of Veld, a town on the northern edge of the Esaphis.

"We'll rest here tonight, then make for Biding in the morning," Ezalia declared, dismounting her camel and stretching.

Caro inhaled deeply. The air smelled dry and dusty like the desert, but with the earthy, lush scent of soil and plants.

"We should exchange our attire again too," Ezalia added. She lifted a corner of Khalil's loose tan shirt. "You'll need a new wardrobe for traveling in Artemisia."

"Why? These are my best clothes."

"Trust me, Khalil," Caro assured him. "You'll be thankful. The weather is not at all what you're used to, and—if I may be so blunt—you will stand out somewhat like that."

He stared back at her blankly.

"We would prefer to avoid being arrested and meeting a sticky end from Zhelyas and his goons," she said emphatically.

"Whatever you wish, Caro. I am at your command."

Caro sighed. "You are my companion, Khalil, and my ally. I have no wish to command you, but please heed our advice from time to time."

"I can promise that much. All right, Ezalia, I surrender myself to your ministrations," Khalil declared cheerfully.

Khalil's new outfit buttoned up to the collar and was belted at the waist, with cotton pants and sturdy leather boots. He looked dashing and princely. He had trouble with the large curved sword, however, and settled for wearing an ankle-length duster to better conceal it.

"How odd, it doesn't itch," he murmured, stroking the silk tunic. "But what is this footwear?" he asked, grumbling. "Is this some new form of torture?"

"You've never worn boots before?" Stelian said, mildly incredulous, looking relieved to be back in his own clothes.

"My people wear light sandals or go barefoot in the desert. This is so strange. I am sure to get blisters!"

Caro couldn't help but feel sorry for him as he waddled about, much like a duck which had stepped out of the water onto land for the first time.

"Don't worry, you'll get used to them," she said, pulling on a pair of her own. She too was happy to be wearing familiar garments. She was certain she would never forget the uncomfortable grittiness of the sand between her toes, no matter how many times she scrubbed them. "The roads here are hard and rough, so without boots or at least thick-soled shoes, your feet would be cut up in no time."

Khalil practiced walking in the shop, pacing awkwardly back and forth. "In that case, I shall endure."

"So, Ezalia," Caro inquired, watching with amusement, "this Alenard... How much do you know about him?"

"Allen?" she replied, and Caro blinked at the fond nickname. "He's a fair man, stubborn but unyielding in his principles. He is a good choice for a potential ally." Ezalia smiled wistfully and stared at the blue sky. "He was also once a suitor of mine."

Caro gaped at her. "You never mentioned that! Why didn't you say something when his name came up at Vittorius's?"

"Because I didn't want to sway your decision, and I thought he deserved the chance to earn your favor through his own merit. Guess I've bungled that." She chuckled, and Caro shook her head.

"Not really. If you had said you despised him, maybe that might taint my impression, but you seem to speak of him rather fondly."

"Do I?" Ezalia murmured, her cheeks pinkening like the first blush of love.

Caro had always wondered why Ezalia wasn't married. She was in her late thirties, the older sister of Caro's mother Cecilia, and was well known in court for the men who swarmed around her like worker bees to their queen. She played coy, but never seemed to be attached to anyone in particular.

The most eligible lady of court. Perhaps something had happened between her and Alenard? Caro wanted to ask, but she felt it would be an invasion of her aunt's privacy.

They reached Biding a few hours later, while the sun was still high in the sky and the shopkeepers had begun to close up for the day.

A man dressed in an approximation of military garb approached them. Caro thought he must be a constable of some sort.

"Welcome to Biding. It's not often we get strangers in these parts," he said, doffing his cap. "What can I do for you?"

"We would like an audience with Margrave Alenard Giness."

"Do you have an appointment? His Lordship is a busy man."

Khalil frowned. "Do you know who you are speaking to? This is..." He trailed off with a pained look on his face as Ezalia pinched him.

The constable cocked his head in confusion.

"We're merely travelers," Caro said smoothly, reminding herself to once again explain the concept of going incognito to Khalil later. "Trust me, Lord Alenard will want to see us."

"Well..." the man said, scratching his thinning hair beneath his hat. "His Lordship lives on that yonder hill, but it's locked tight except after dusk when he takes a ride through town. Biding is in his purview, and he is magistrate and lord. He protects us without asking for anything in return."

Caro was getting a sense of the man and rather admired him.

"I suppose if yer to accompany me to headquarters, you could await him there."

"Thank you. That would suit us just fine."

"Nothing fancy. 'Tis a station house after all," the constable said, gesturing around the small room.

There was a desk at the front where a sleepy-looking official sat, and a small table at the back where a few officers were supping while playing cards. To the right, a couple of chairs rested beneath the windows by the door, while two cells jutted out from the opposite wall. They were secured by gates of sturdy iron bars, and each contained only a small cot and a latrine.

Two officers sat in the chairs, and they rose to make way for the ladies. One of them gave Khalil a suspicious look.

"We don't see many visitors here in Biding, and even fewer foreigners."

"He is from the Esaphis, which makes him a fellow Artemisian," Caro said, her calm voice easing the tension. "He is my companion."

"Begging your pardon," the officer replied, looking abashed at her mild censure. "Welcome to Biding, good sir."

Khalil looked like he was about to burst out laughing at the man's contrition, but he restrained himself.

The hours ticked by, and Caro had just dozed off when the door jangled open.

"Good evening, gentlemen," a refined voice said from the doorway, and boot heels clicked upon the floor as they crossed the threshold.

"Lord Alenard!" the constable exclaimed, and he and the other officers shot to their feet, bowing with respect.

"How fares the day? Nothing untoward, I hope."

"About that..." the constable began. "There's this group of strangers, see, and they said they wanted an audience with you."

"What strangers?" Alenard inquired.

"Hello, Allen."

Alenard's eyes landed upon the woman who had been playing cards with the officers in the corner. She rose from her chair and he stared, eyes wide.

"Ezalia?" He watched as she swept across the station.

"Long time, no see."

"I— What are you doing here?" Alenard, who Caro surmised was usually eloquent, seemed at a loss for words. "The last I heard was the attack on the capital. We feared for all within."

"I escaped, along with others of the queen's retinue."

"Thank all the stars for that! But then, that means..." His gaze raked the room, passing by Stelian and Khalil before settling upon the small girl seated to the right of where he stood.

It took a moment for him to process what he was seeing, then he nodded. "I see. Thank you, Constable, for taking care of them. I will escort them to my house for the night. Is there anything else I should know?"

"There have been some odd rumors of a shadowy figure lingering about, but none of them can be substantiated. I'm sure it's all balderdash, milord."

Alenard furrowed his brow, then nodded. "Be on your guard. I don't like unwelcome strangers in my town."

The officers bowed once more as Alenard departed along with his surprise guests.

The margrave's carriage rumbled up the cobblestones to the estate at the top of the hill. Surrounded by rolling fields, the expansive building gave an impression of relaxed affluence, with a creamy yellow exterior, white framing, and a slate-gray roof. Inside, the walls were ivory with elegant wood paneling and furnishings in an understated blue.

Alenard handed his coat to the steward, then dismissed the servants. He fell to one knee, resting his hand upon his heart. "Your Majesty, Queen Caro Amarynth. I bid you welcome to my house."

He had a youthful face with an easy smile, windswept sandy-blond hair, and honest hazel eyes.

"Thank you, Margrave," Caro replied.

"I was dismayed to hear of the events which transpired at the capital, and am relieved at Your Majesty's safety," he said somberly. "Be assured, my loyalty lies with you, not any pretender to the throne."

"I am pleased to hear that, Lord Alenard. I traveled here at great risk, hoping that was the case."

"My men and the resources at my disposal are at your command," Alenard assured her, rising. "You must have had a long, tiring journey. Please, rest yourselves."

Caro appreciated Alenard's mild manner and unassuming gentility, particularly compared to Oswin's cloying gaiety and wanton extravagance.

"We are obliged for your hospitality."

Ezalia strolled onto the balcony after settling Caro into bed. She was wearing a silk chemise, and it swished against her skin as she walked. Her hair was down, and the ebony curls fell loose about her shoulders.

Alenard was staring at the moon and did not hear her.

"May I join you?" she asked, holding two glasses of wine.

He turned, registering her presence, and straightened. "My apologies, Duchess."

"There's no need to be so formal, Allen. And, you'll find, not with Her Majesty either. She values integrity and dignity over stiff-backed decorum."

Alenard took the goblet Ezalia held out to him. "Time passes so quickly, doesn't it?" he mused.

Ezalia leaned against the balustrade beside him. "Just yesterday, we were children without a care in the world. Now we're facing an uncertain future and a kingdom in disarray, on the brink of war." She sighed, shaking her head. "I never thought I would see anything like this in my lifetime."

Alenard was silent a long moment. "Why did you come here?"

"To Biding? It's not what you think."

He frowned. "What do you mean?"

"It wasn't my idea but Caro's," she explained. "The first person we went to see following our flight from the palace was Caro's uncle, Duke Vittorius. They discussed the matter and both decided meeting up with my father, the grand duke, was the most prudent move, but they disagreed on the path to get there."

Ezalia paused. "Vittorius wanted us to go north, but Caro had other ideas. She recalled your sizable private army and your devotion to her father, and so determined we should seek your aid. We crossed the Esaphis Desert—where we added Khalil, a clan prince, to our entourage—and traveled to Biding."

"And you... didn't say anything about us?"

"I swear, I had nothing to do with it. I had faith you would not send us away, nor turn traitor."

"Certainly not," Alenard scoffed. "Still, Her Majesty seems different somehow."

"In what way?"

"How do I put this...? In the few times I saw her before her parents were killed, she was dutiful but carefree. Then, when I swore my loyalty during the Accession ceremony, she was weighed down by the burden which had been passed to her so suddenly. But now, it no longer seems to overwhelm her. I can see the light in her eyes, as if she is thriving rather than suffering in facing this adversity."

"Thank you for your kind words, Lord Alenard," Caro said from the door, and they both turned to her, Alenard nearly spilling what remained of his wine as he bowed.

"Your Majesty."

"I had hoped you would not think less of me."

"Of course not," he said. "You are my queen, but beyond that, I respect your strength and courage."

"Is something the matter, Caro?" Ezalia inquired in her motherly way.

"The rumor the constable mentioned of the man in black... It's been bothering me."

Alenard cocked his head at Caro, puzzled. "You have an idea of who he could be?"

"Perhaps, but I can't say for certain. I don't want to worry you until I'm sure. Is that acceptable?"

"I am your servant, Your Majesty."

Caro shook her head. "But I am your guest. You have your own way of doing things, and your house has its rules. I will abide by them unless I have a specific reason to do otherwise."

"Thank you, Your Majesty." Alenard nodded. "If you are troubled, I would feel much more at ease if we tightened security at the house and placed patrols around town." He paused. "If you concur?"

"Yes, I agree that is wise. Do as you see fit, Lord Alenard."

He bowed and left the room, issuing orders to his men. Stelian and Khalil entered a moment later, drawn by the commotion.

"You think it was Morfran?" Ezalia asked quietly.

Khalil frowned. "Who's Morfran?"

"A despicable cur!" Stelian snapped, clenching his fists.

Caro sighed. "Morfran is the commander of Zhelyas's army. I was sloppy and got arrested, but rather than turn me in, he kept my identity secret and helped me escape before I could be found out."

"Curious behavior," Khalil said, nodding. "And you think the phantom stranger was this fellow?"

"That's why I'm not sure. He usually wears a silver mask, which would have been a dead giveaway—"

Khalil slapped his palm, making Stelian jump. "A silver mask! Why didn't you say so? We Omaira know of him. We call him 'Mukhif.'"

Caro blinked. "Wait. You've heard of him, Khalil?"

"Sure. He's pretty famous. He was recruited by a tribe of deadly warriors, the Sharir, who trained him in their ways."

"The Sharir?" Caro repeated breathlessly, exchanging a startled glance with Stelian. She shivered. It explained a number of things, in particular how he seemed to be able to switch between being courteous and polite to menacing and ominous with no warning.

"If you think Mukhif is roaming about town, I would prefer if you were not unprotected tonight, Caro," Khalil added.

She nodded. "Stelian, please watch over Ezalia. I will stay with Khalil since he may be more familiar with Morfran's tactics."

One for Sorrow

Caro did not feel much like sleeping, so she pulled out a chess set instead. Her thoughts couldn't help drifting back to the match she had played with Morfran back at the garrison. If the mysterious person was him, why was he here?

"You don't speak Morfran's name... er, Mukhif's, with any anger. Why is that?"

Khalil sat across the table from her, peering at the unfamiliar game pieces. "The Sharir are a necessary evil, one which protects us from rival clans and those who would steal our resources, livestock, and families. Mukhif was known to be both merciless and honorable."

Caro shifted in her seat. "Would you say he was... kind?"

"Hmm," Khalil murmured, staring at the figure of the black knight as if recalling the horse Morfran rode. "A friend of mine, Fatima, told me she saw Mukhif once with a young boy. Fatima feared for him but dared not approach. As she was wrestling with her feelings, she was stunned to see Mukhif crouch to the boy's level and offer him a sweet so he would stop crying. She said it was the first time she had seen a Sharir smile."

Caro puzzled over this tale. She didn't understand Morfran at all—it was like he was two different people.

"So the guy with the funny pointed hat can only go diagonally; the castle goes straight; the horse kinda wobbles around like it's drunk; the queen has all the best moves; while the king is the weakest, but the game is lost if he's defeated?"

Caro chuckled at Khalil's rudimentary comprehension of the rules.

He leaned his elbow on the table and scratched his head. "Chess is weird."

She was wondering if perhaps they should try tackling a different game when her skin prickled at a gust of cold air. "Strange, I thought I closed the window."

Caro glanced up, and her heart caught in her throat. She rose, rattling the board and scattering the pieces, and glared at the figure who stepped out of the shadows. "Morfran."

"Mukhif..." Khalil whispered, moving to stand before her, his sword drawn.

The moniker seemed to catch Morfran off guard.

"You are keeping strange company, little queen, and I thought your former companions were a hodgepodge lot."

"Enough, Morfran," Caro snapped. "This is not the garrison, where you can do as you please and I will meekly go along for fear of being discovered. You are in my domain now, and you will address me with respect!"

"My sincerest apologies, Your Majesty." Morfran bowed his head and sank to one knee on the plush carpet.

Khalil went slack-jawed, while Caro narrowed her eyes down at Morfran with suspicion.

"What sort of trick is this?"

"No trick, I assure you," Morfran replied, the sarcasm melting from his voice.

"Why should I trust you after all you've done?"

He looked up at her, the line of his lips uncertain. "I told you once that I served Zhelyas because I wanted one thing."

"I remember: revenge," Caro said curtly.

"Now that I have attained that, there is nothing more I need from him." The expressionless silver mask reflected the light of the moon, casting his eyes in shadow. "I am, and always have been, your servant. That was why I could not lift my hand against you, not even to maintain your cover—and my own. For the harm I have caused, you may exact whatever penance you will."

Caro pursed her lips, conflicted. She glanced sideways at Khalil, who seemed somewhat bewildered by the turn of events, and recalled his story from before. "Tell me, is Ines with you?"

Morfran's shell of careful indifference faltered at the question. "I would never leave her behind."

Caro nodded, and he rose, snapping his gloved fingers softly. Khalil tensed, but only a delicate woman stepped from behind the curtain.

While Morfran looked the same as ever, clad head to toe in black armor, Ines had traded in her servant's garb for a long-sleeved peach dress, the bodice fastened with easy-to-manage buttons up the front.

"Esca, I thought I heard your voice."

"It's 'Caro,'" Morfran corrected, taking her hand to guide her. "Queen Caro of Artemisia."

"Is that so?" Ines mused. She gave an elegant curtsy.

Caro turned to Morfran, who awaited her response. "Very well, I believe you. However, others may not be so obliging. I hope you are prepared for that."

She lifted an eyebrow, and Morfran nodded obediently. "Of course, Your Majesty."

"Morfran?" Stelian gasped as Caro came downstairs with a sinister-looking masked man who couldn't be anyone else.

She had sent Khalil to gather her companions in the entrance hall, and she met their startled gazes.

"He's working for me now," Caro replied, and Morfran bowed low.

"I suppose you are the man in black who has been seen prowling around?" Alenard asked suspiciously.

"I apologize for the trouble, Lord Margrave."

Alenard gave a short nod. "If you vouch for this man, Your Majesty, then I will not pursue charges."

Caro turned to the rest of the stunned onlookers. "Everyone, this is Commander Morfran."

"Alas, I am not that anymore, Majesty," Morfran said. "Zhelyas has likely stripped me of my rank due to my defection."

"Then I restore it," Caro said imperiously.

Morfran gave a deep bow.

"You can't be serious!" Stelian protested. "This man—"

"The commander shall accompany us from now on," Caro continued, interrupting Stelian with a wave of her hand. "I understand this may be difficult to accept, but despite what may have transpired in the past—I trust him. I ask you to do the same or, at the very least, to be civil."

Her tone left no room for argument and there was a series of nods, some more reluctant than others.

"This is Ines, Morfran's acquaintance. She is to be treated with all due care and consideration."

Ezalia approached the blind woman and took her hand. "Don't worry, Commander. I'll take good care of her."

He bent his head, and she looked him up and down with a critical eye.

"I'll be watching you."

"I would expect no less, Duchess."

Ezalia turned away, her arm around Ines's shoulder.

"In that case, I suggest we all try to get some sleep," Caro declared, thoroughly exhausted. "Morfran, you will not object to rooming with Khalil for the night?"

"Is it true you used to work for Caro's enemies, Mukhif?"

Morfran paused as he removed his sword belt and nodded. He decided Khalil would not be shedding his old moniker anytime soon, and he might as well answer to it. "It is."

"Then I'm glad you did not hurt Caro, as she says."

Morfran cocked his head, wondering what Caro had told them about what had transpired at the garrison. "Why is that?" he asked instead.

"As her fiancé, I would have had to kill you."

Morfran nearly choked. "Her *what*?"

"A potential suitor, anyway," Khalil said with an embarrassed laugh. "I'm to accompany her, and she'll consider me for husband once she's queen again."

Morfran could see Hadiya making such a pact. She had been one of the four great chieftains when he was still with the Sharir, and she was a shrewd woman. No doubt it was the condition upon which she had pledged her warriors to Caro's cause.

He considered the boy. Though Khalil knew of Morfran's reputation in his homeland, he was unafraid and unbiased, both of which Morfran suspected would be rare among Caro's entourage.

"I see," Morfran said. "I suppose we're both lucky that scenario will never play out."

"My name is Ezalia. Yours is Ines?"

"Yes, that's right."

Ezalia led the soft-spoken woman up the stairs, noting she had no luggage or possessions with her, and watched in case she needed any help.

While Caro had mentioned she had not noticed Ines was blind until later, Ezalia could tell immediately by the delicate way she walked and how her gaze did not linger in one place too long. Morfran had apparently saved her life, which explained why she would remain by him.

However, Ezalia was less sure why a man like Morfran would keep someone like her at his side. Ezalia didn't trust the commander, not entirely, despite the faith Caro seemed to have in him. She'd related much of what had transpired during her captivity at the garrison, but Caro always had difficulty articulating her emotions, and the two of them had evidently formed a connection she couldn't quite express.

Ines had been a defining factor in those events as well, a voice of comfort in trying times, and Ezalia could see why. Still, she wasn't sure yet if the blind woman could be trusted either. Ezalia decided to let things play out for now. No sense kicking over a thorn bush and trampling the flowers instead.

Ines was quite capable and mounted the staircase without difficulty. By running her hand along the banister ahead, she could tell where the stairs ended, so she didn't overstep. Ezalia was fascinated by the significance of something she herself took for granted.

"My room is the first door on the left," she said experimentally.

Ines walked along, her hand lightly touching the wall. She stopped before the doorway, feeling the edge of the frame with the tips of her fingers.

"Your room is the next one," Ezalia added. "I thought since you have no bags, you might like a dress for sleeping in and a change of clothes. We should be about the same size."

"Yes, I believe so, though you are a little taller."

Ezalia was surprised. "Caro told me about your skill at perceiving your surroundings. May I ask how you know?"

Ines chuckled. "That's easy. When you took my hand and walked beside me, your shoulder brushed against mine."

"Now I feel rather foolish for asking," Ezalia admitted sheepishly.

"Please, don't be. I appreciate your concern, and that of the queen. Despite my independence, I struggle sometimes, especially in a place that is unfamiliar. I am not too proud to admit this, so I will not be offended if you ask me if I need help. If I don't, then I will say so."

"I will keep that in mind."

Ines cocked her head. "I must confess, you surprise me as well. I could feel you watching, yet you did not step in. I assume you would have if necessary?"

Ezalia was unsure of how to answer. "Let's sit. There is a chaise to the right."

Ines held out her hand, and Ezalia guided her to the settee, then sat down beside her.

"Caro, the queen, is my niece," she began. "In many ways, I have always felt like she was my own daughter, since I have no children of my own. This journey has only magnified that feeling. She is still young, only seventeen years old, and has undertaken a difficult quest to reclaim her throne and bring peace to her kingdom."

Ezalia sighed, leaning back and staring at the moulded panels of the coffered ceiling. "As both her aunt and her subject, I want nothing more than to protect her. But I also realize I have to step back and let her do things for herself, even make mistakes if need be. You are not a child, nor a relative of mine, yet the same applies. Is that strange?"

"Not at all," Ines said, smiling. "I appreciate it. Often people will either leave me to my own devices, or smother me with attention. It's nice to find someone who will let me stand on my own two feet, yet be there to catch me if I fall."

The gentle woman's assurances put Ezalia at ease, and she felt much as Caro must have.

"If you wouldn't mind waiting a moment, I will get you a few things," Ezalia said, then rose and went to the dresser. On the road, she would sleep in her clothes, but a nobleman's house always provided nightdresses and robes to visitors.

She found one that was a bit short on her and folded it on top of a spare outfit. "Here are leggings and a tunic. I don't have any extra boots, so we'll pick those up later if we're traveling a distance on foot. There's some sleepwear, too. Did you want me to accompany you to your room?"

"I'll be fine, thank you," Ines said as Ezalia placed the pile of clothes in her outstretched arms.

"If you need me, I'm here. We share a wall, so you can knock if anything happens in the night."

Ines dressed herself in the silk nightgown Ezalia had loaned her, so much softer and smoother than the ones in the army. It smelled faintly of lavender. She had never slept in a noble's house before, and felt both comfortable and nervous at the same time.

When Morfran had spoken with her at the garrison before he returned to the palace, he had apprised her of his intention to defect and suggested she make herself scarce. Nobody noticed her slip away or was even aware of her absence until Luther had received notice of Morfran's treason.

She had waited in the woods nearby, their agreed meeting place. Never once did she think Morfran would consider leaving her behind to face Zhelyas's wrath, but as she sat in the silence, doubts started to creep in. Would he be able to escape after all? If not, what would happen to her? Would she be hunted down by Luther and brought before the king as a prisoner?

Ines looked up at the sound of hooves upon the ground. It had drizzled, so the soil was damp, and the horse made soft splishing sounds in the muddy puddles as it approached. She was familiar with Morfran's stallion, Eclipse, a gentle beast she loved tending to.

"Morfran?" she called out into the darkness.

"I'm here," came his quiet reply.

She stepped out of the shadow of a tree.

"You're wet," he observed, apparently noting the droplets of moisture which clung to her hair and traveling dress.

"I'm fine," she replied, grateful for his concern.

He approached and bunched up his cape, tousling her long tresses. "That's better."

She heard the groan of the leather as he tightened the strap, adjusting the saddle to fit a second rider.

"We're leaving, then?" Ines inquired.

"Yes." He paused. "Do you trust me, Ines?"

"Always," she replied without hesitation. "I don't need to know our destination, only that you'll take me with you." Because she was blind, there were many fears she'd had to overcome, but the one she could not shake was her fear of abandonment, even after so many years.

The strap buckle clicked into place, and a gloved hand reached for her own. She approached the stallion, stroking his nose as he nuzzled her cheek, then Morfran placed his hands upon her waist, lifting her onto the horse. She gripped the stallion's mane as Morfran swung up behind her and pulled the reins taut.

"Hold on tight. We have a long way to go."

Ines huddled within the safety of his cloak as the night closed in around them, traveling along the path of shadows. She had never felt scared, not once, since he had saved her that fateful day, and she always trusted him.

The revelation Esca was the queen, however, was a shock, though everything fit into place. Her unfamiliarity with even basic chores, the tension and strained words between her and Morfran. Esca—Caro—was still just a young girl fighting for a future which seemed out of reach. And now Morfran was fighting by her side.

Ines closed her eyes, listening as the breeze from the window swirled through the room and ruffled the pages of an open book on the table, the hair on her arms tingling as it brushed against her skin.

Wherever Morfran went, she would follow. That was the choice she had made long ago. She had no regrets... save one. But perhaps that too was fate.

Balancing Act

Morfran stepped out early. Khalil was pleasant enough company, but he was also somewhat aggravating. He had a surprising lack of animosity, which was a relief, but Morfran had been preparing himself mentally for more enmity.

He turned the corner and met Stelian's gaze. *There it is.*

"Lieutenant," Morfran said, tipping his head to the younger man.

"Commander," Stelian replied evenly, his tone laced with ice.

"I want you to know—"

"No, I want *you* to know," he retorted. "The queen has suffered enough in these past months, and I won't let anyone else hurt her."

"I have no intention of hurting her." Morfran blinked as Stelian glared at him.

"I don't care what sort of promises you've made. You're going to have to do better than that."

He stepped aside as Stelian swept past without another word.

Morfran sighed. It might have been expected, but it was still discomfiting. He decided to get some air and encountered Alenard on the grounds, taking a morning stroll.

"Lord Margrave," Morfran said, bowing. "I wanted to apologize again for trespassing upon your property. I needed a discreet way to speak with the queen and still keep Ines close."

Alenard lifted an eyebrow. "The blind woman, is that right?"

Morfran nodded. "Ines and I... We met during a difficult time in my life. I feel responsible for her."

"I'm sure she'll be fine in Lady Ezalia's care."

"I'm certain, my lord," Morfran replied, vividly recalling their exchange the previous night. He took a steadying breath and shook out his cloak. "If there is anything I can do to make amends, please allow me to do so. I intend to serve Her Majesty, and would not wish my actions to tarnish that."

"Very well, Commander, I will give it some thought," Alenard said. "In the meantime, I would like to invite the queen to appraise my troops. Please inform her of this."

"Right away."

Caro sat upon the front stoop, dangling a piece of string for a kitten who had strayed out of its basket. The kitten was small enough to fit in the palm of her hand, white with mottled patches of orange and black, and it mewed as it batted at the string, leaping and tumbling on the step.

"Cats of that color are said to be lucky."

Caro looked up to see Morfran standing at the foot of the staircase. He knelt on the steps beneath her and held out a gloved finger, letting the kitten sniff it.

"I am sorry for startling you, Your Majesty."

"Commander..."

He shook his head somberly. "Please call me Morfran. Our roles have reversed; you are the master now."

The irony of their peculiar situation hadn't been lost on her. "Morfran, then."

"Lord Alenard wishes to know if you would like to appraise his troops." he added.

If it was a ploy, it was a complicated one, and Caro dismissed the notion. She rose, placing the mewling kitten back into the basket with its mother and siblings. Morfran stepped aside as she descended the stairs, a trace of his usual smirk playing about his lips as she waved off his aid.

"Lord Alenard," Caro greeted as she reached the barracks with Morfran in tow.

He had arranged his troops in lines, straightening a collar here and there, and bowed crisply to her, his hands clasped behind his back.

"Attention!" he ordered, and his men clicked their heels together, chests out, heads held high. "This is Queen Caro Amarynth, your rightful sovereign! You owe her all loyalty and duty!"

Morfran stood unobtrusively off to the side while Caro started at one end of the queue.

"I have heard of Lord Alenard's men," she began. "Loyal. Just. Reliable. Steadfast. You protect this land and its people with faithfulness and virtue, and I am honored to fight alongside you."

She nodded to each, then returned to stand beside Alenard. "What say you, men?"

"Yes, Your Majesty!"

Caro was sure the bellowing cry could be heard clear through to the town below, but she no longer cared about anonymity. Her heart swelled with hope as she faced these brave soldiers, honest and true, so dedicated to her cause. Mercenaries were one thing, but men who would fight with her for love of their queen and country were an irreplaceable gift.

Alenard beamed with pride. "Shall I show you around the encampment, Your Majesty?"

Caro nodded, and he gestured invitingly. Morfran followed at a watchful distance.

"These are our training grounds."

Two soldiers were in the middle of a match, attacking each other with skill and speed, swords clanging. A drill instructor observed their movements critically.

Further along, a logistics analyst was examining the cost balances and comparing them against the military budget as dictated by the margrave. He scribbled notes on a graph which seemed to suggest they were well within their financial means.

There were also storage sheds stacked with supplies and provisions. It had been some time since Alenard's private army was called upon to do anything other than police their locality or subdue the occasional tussle, but they were fully equipped. Caro nodded to the quartermaster, who was tallying the contents.

"This is the sparring circle, where warriors test each other's skills and their own," Alenard continued, leading them to an empty patch of field. "Perhaps your commander would like to challenge one of my men?"

A soldier with a scar over his left eye stood on the sidelines. He nodded to Alenard as they approached.

"Guard Captain Lance, this is Queen Caro," Alenard said, and Lance bowed crisply.

"Your Majesty." Then he lifted his gaze to Caro's shadow, who was a few steps behind. "You're the famous Commander

Morfran, eh? Come back when you're ready to fight a *real* man."

"Manners, Lance," Alenard chided, and Caro sensed a familiarity between them. She doubted his remonstrations for discourtesy were usually so mild.

The guard captain bowed. "Apologies, Majesty. I did not mean to be crass."

Caro peered over her shoulder at Morfran, whose expression was, as usual, impenetrable. She had learned to read his moods, however, and was surprised to find he did not seem offended but intrigued by the provocation.

"If Her Majesty approves, I would like to take the captain up on his offer."

Caro gave a slight nod of permission, admittedly curious. She hadn't seen Morfran fight other than their own bout, and that had not been a reliable indicator of his prowess.

Alenard looked a little nervous but also nodded. "Very well, I will referee."

The two men strode onto the field.

"Don't take it easy on me," Lance said. "I want to see the full extent of your skill. Besides, this is just a friendly match, isn't that right?"

He cocked his head, and Morfran nodded.

"Your master and my queen are allies. I would not want to hinder their efforts by harming their most distinguished guard captain."

Lance smirked at the jibe. "Likewise, Commander." He unsheathed his sword. "If you prefer, we can use practice weapons."

"This suits me just fine," Morfran replied, drawing his blade.

"If one of you draws blood or leaves the circle, the match is over," Alenard declared. "Ready? Bow."

They held up their swords in salute, then bent at the waist in a gesture of respect. The formalities observed, they began to circle the field.

Morfran placed one foot in front of the other, moving sideways, and Lance mirrored his movements. Neither knew what to expect, and so waited for the other to make the first move.

Lance attacked first. He lunged, and Morfran was surprised at his speed. The guard captain was a seasoned warrior. His moves were calculated and efficient, expending only as much effort as necessary. At the same time, he was gauging the measure of his opponent, so he was also wary.

Morfran applauded inwardly as he was forced to take a step back to counter the blow. Lance did not press his advantage, so Morfran took the offensive, forcing the guard captain to retreat.

The captain was nearing the edge of the circle when he planted his feet, then leaped sideways, dodging with impressive agility for a man his age. Morfran recovered, shifting direction and spinning his sword in an arc before Lance could take advantage of his exposed underarm.

Lance rolled to his feet and spun around, his sword meeting Morfran's as it followed his angle of ascent, but he did not have time to regain his equilibrium. His momentum drove him off balance as Morfran followed up with a flurried attack.

Lance fell to the ground, his hand twitching for his sword just out of reach, and looked up to see Morfran standing above him, the blade's tip at his heart.

Other soldiers had gathered to watch their guard captain take on the famous commander, and a hush fell over the circle as they held their collective breaths.

"Point!" Alenard declared.

Morfran stared down at Lance a moment, then lifted his sword and held out his hand. Lance took it, and Morfran pulled him to his feet.

"If I'd been your opponent for real, you would have killed me. I could see it in your face."

Morfran shrugged and stooped to retrieve Lance's sword. "That used to be how I made my living. Old habits die hard."

"But not anymore?" Lance inquired.

Morfran glanced at Caro, who was watching with Alenard on the sidelines. "My sword no longer belongs to me," he replied.

"In any case, I'm glad we're fighting for the same cause, Commander," Lance quipped as Morfran returned his blade. "I look forward to when we fight side by side in battle."

Among the Sharir, few could match Morfran's prowess, and even fewer he had fought since he left their ranks—but Lance came close.

"As do I, Guard Captain."

"In order to avoid drawing too much attention, I propose we split into two groups to make our way to Agassey," Caro said as they all sat in the foyer discussing their next plan. "Stelian, Morfran, and I will take the lower road. Alenard, Ezalia, Khalil, and Ines will take the higher one."

She waited for everyone's nods.

"Lucky you, Mukhif, traveling with Caro." Khalil pouted.

Morfran twitched one corner of his lip.

Khalil had welcomed Morfran as a comrade-in-arms, accepting his presence without question, and they seemed at ease. Stelian, meanwhile, was glaring daggers at the commander. Caro hoped they could mend their fences along the way, or at least come to some understanding.

"I can carry that," Ines said as Ezalia stooped to pick up a satchel.

"Oh, thank you," Ezalia replied cheerfully.

It seemed, despite Caro's earlier reservations, the two women were getting along quite well.

They all retired to their rooms, and Caro decided to check on Ines. She lifted her hand to knock, but Ines spoke before her knuckles touched the door.

"Come in, Your Majesty."

"I'm sorry to disturb you. I wanted to see how you were getting on. Morfran's been staying close to my side, and I don't want you to feel lonely."

Ines smiled, and Caro felt a trifle foolish.

"Thank you, but you needn't have worried. I am content by myself," Ines said with an elegant shrug. "I understand we are to be leaving soon. I hope you don't find me an inconvenience, my queen."

"Nothing of the sort, I promise," she assured Ines. "And Caro, please. I would like to think we are friends."

"And Morfran?"

The question caught Caro off guard. "He and I... It's complicated. I was his servant, and now he is mine. There is an unspoken formality between us of his own choosing, but it does not reflect the level of trust I have in him."

"Very well, Caro, I will do as you ask." Ines smiled and lifted a hand to tousle Caro's brown curls. "I am pleased to call you by your real name."

Caro flushed at the intimate gesture.

"It seems your hair has grown since I last brushed it. Would you like me to cut it for you?"

Caro nodded, the motion conveyed through Ines's caress, and sat at the vanity. It was an odd notion to have a blind woman cut one's hair; but her fingers seemed to remember the length Caro had worn it before, and she trimmed away the excess. It was comforting, sitting in silence, listening to the gentle *snip snip* of the silver scissors.

"Much better," Ines declared.

Caro turned to examine herself in the mirror, stroking the feathered ends, which were now soft and even. "Thank you, Ines."

Ines dusted off bits of hair that had fallen onto her dress, then bowed. "Whenever you depart, I'll be ready."

Morfran found Lance in the stables.

"Commander, what brings you here?"

"I came to check on my mount, Eclipse," Morfran replied.

"Oh, the gorgeous stallion over there, that's his name?" Lance said, and Morfran nodded.

Lance held out his hand with a cube of sugar. Eclipse snuffled it for a moment, then to Morfran's surprise, gobbled up the treat.

"He's not normally so friendly with strangers. You have a way with horses."

Lance patted Eclipse on the nose. "Always loved them since I was a boy. Before I became the guard captain, I spent most of my time in the stables." Lance chuckled, gesturing to the scar over his eye. "People think I got this wound from some great battle, but really I was a little too close to a foaling mare, and she caught me upside the head with the edge of her hoof. Still can't help loving these old horses of mine, eh, Patty?"

The nag in the stall beside Eclipse snorted.

"Lord Alenard was always getting into trouble when he was a lad, so I took him under my wing. See, the former Lord Margrave died when Lord Alenard was in his youth, an impressionable age, and a difficult one to take on such a heavy responsibility. Much like our young queen," he added, and Morfran knew that to be true. "I guess I was the closest thing to a father figure he had, and I raised him as best I could. I am honored to serve the man he has become."

In a way, Lance reminded Morfran of an old war horse, and the way he spoke, it seemed he greatly respected his master.

"On that note, I have a favor to ask of you," Morfran said.

"Oh?"

"I came to Biding on my steed, but I suspect we will travel the rest of the way on foot. Would you stable him for me? You can bring him along once your forces are called for battle."

Lance looked surprised by the request but nodded. "I'd be glad to, Commander Morfran."

Age of Miracles

Ezalia checked on Caro and Ines, of whom she had grown fond, then made her way to the library. It was quiet with no servants about and the raucous troop she had been traveling with all asleep for the night.

There was a chair near the center of the room, with a light stand and a small spindly table. Ezalia peered at the book which rested upon it and smiled. She liked libraries, always had. Her father had some of the rarest publications in the world in his collection, and she had inherited that passion. She traced the spines of the books on Alenard's shelves, inhaling the sweet, musky scent of the leather.

"Ezalia?"

She turned to see Alenard at the door.

"Can't sleep?" he asked.

"No. You?"

He shook his head. "I was about to have a nightcap. Want one?"

Ezalia nodded as he crossed the room to the cupboard and poured two glasses of brandy.

"Thank you," Ezalia said as he handed one to her. Their fingers brushed, and she smiled shyly, like a teenager again.

"I see you still like adventure novels." She gestured toward the table, and Alenard's eyebrows creased at her smirk.

"Historical exploits," he corrected, making the genre sound somewhat more mature.

Ezalia giggled at his chagrin. "I miss this. Why did we ever stop talking?"

"You know why," Alenard replied, and the words cut like a knife.

She nodded, the smile slipping from her lips. "Foolish words, spoken by a spoiled little girl." She turned away to hide the pain in her eyes. "I wish... I wish I had answered differently that day."

She waited for the inevitable "It hardly matters now," or "That's just the way it is."

"Do you, Ezalia?"

The response was unexpected—as was the emotion behind it—and she turned at his words. Where she had anticipated cold indifference or outright loathing, she saw only affection and hopefulness in his eyes.

"I..." she stammered, her tongue betraying her for the first time.

That day, so long ago, she had refused his proposal of marriage and broken his heart into a million pieces. Seeing him after all these years, she was amazed to find him not a shattered man, but one brimming with confidence and dignity. She had assumed he'd moved on.

Tears pooled in her eyes and fell as she tried to blink them away. "I thought you'd forgotten me. That you hated me for what I'd done. I was so cruel..."

"I could never hate you, Ezzy," he said, stepping closer and stroking away her tears. "I love you, and I always will. Even if you don't love me, that will never change."

"I do!" Ezalia interrupted, grasping his hand in her own, feeling her wet tears upon his fingers. "I love you."

The words came out in a hoarse whisper, and he pulled her into a tight embrace. The glass of brandy tumbled from her hand to the floor, gold liquid pooling upon the marble.

The two were cuddling on the couch, reminiscing about the happy days spent together in their youth, when Ezalia spotted a glimpse of orange in a stack of books on the table. She swiped the book up triumphantly.

"Hey!" Alenard protested, and she held it out of his reach, giggling.

"*The Desert Prince*," she said, reading the title aloud with a smirk. "Allen, I never took you for the type to read this sort of tawdry romance novel!"

The cover was plain orange with the title emblazoned upon it, along with the innocuous symbol of a rose and a crescent moon. However, turning to the second page revealed a risqué illustration of a roguishly handsome dark-haired man, the desert prince of the title, fondling a woman with flowing auburn locks wearing a revealing orange gown.

The author, writing under the pseudonym Luxura Scarlett, had apparently been inspired by the legend of Gisela and Darim, a popular love story about a princess fleeing an arranged marriage who ends up in the arms of a desert nomad, and had rewritten it to be amorous and passionate, with scandalously steamy love scenes. It had swept through the court like wildfire, and Ezalia had spent a certain amount of time trying to keep her curious niece from getting wind of it. She did, however, enjoy it very much herself. An opera had been based upon the same legend, and her own mother

Mavella had performed it so many times she could recall the plot by heart.

Princess Gisela, sister of King Gilbert, flees to the desert to escape her engagement to the nobleman Lord Tyrus Ruben and meets the handsome rogue Darim there. But the marriage she sought to escape was a political arrangement, and her brother orders her return. The rogue is not dissuaded and follows her, sneaking into the palace garden at night. The king's guards arrive and arrest the rogue, but the king, out of love for his sister, spares her lover—on the condition they never see each other again. That was how both the opera and the novel ended, with the princess bravely choosing duty over passion, though their parting in the book was sensual and dramatic.

"I wanted to see what all the fuss was about," Alenard replied, coughing and blushing at Ezalia's suggestive grin.

"Oh?" she teased.

"However, my interest was academic," he added, indicating the other books in the stack, which Ezalia realized were of a far more mundane nature. "Intrigued as to the story's origin, I did a little research. The legend is, in fact, loosely based upon a historical event."

"Really?"

"Yes. In actuality, Gisela was named Guinevre."

Ezalia blinked. "As in *Queen* Guinevre?"

"The very same," Alenard said with a nod. "Both Guinevre and her brother Guillam, known as Gilbert in the story, were the children of Malianme, the progenitor of the Artemisian royal line. Queen Caro is her direct descendant. Like Gisela, Guinevre ran away to escape from an arranged marriage, but what transpired afterward isn't clear, nor how she ascended the throne in place of her brother. I seem to recall reading about it a long time ago, but for the life of me I can't remember the details."

He frowned, and Ezalia snuggled closer, both impressed and attracted to him for his effort. Since Gisela was Guinevre, she wondered if Hadiya might know who Darim was, and if the same legend had somehow become a fixture for the desert people as well.

A story of unexpected, passionate love. She couldn't argue with that.

No Stone Unturned

"You must be careful, sire," Veena cautioned as Zhelyas grew more fervent in his use of magic.

Zhelyas glared at her. "Oh?"

"What was the second principle of magic I taught you?"

"Something about consequence," he replied dismissively.

"Spells have consequences, and the more magic you use, the more that will become apparent."

He lifted an eyebrow. "Such as?"

"Sire, have you not noticed yourself feeling... off?"

Zhelyas shrugged and flicked his fingers, causing sparks to fly. "Actually, I feel pretty good."

Veena frowned. Something was wrong, but she couldn't quite put her finger on it. He should feel weakened from his continued use of magic, if not completely drained as she often was.

"You were saying?" Zhelyas asked, his voice laced with irritation, and Veena shook her head.

"Nothing, sire. Pay me no heed."

Luther entered, saluting, and Zhelyas turned to him.

"Report."

Luther shifted his feet. "Before his defection, the commander suggested troops be placed at Flossholme, so we must assume the queen did not pass that way," he replied nervously. "There are countless roads and villages beyond, so it will take time to search them all. However, I will see it done."

Zhelyas turned to Veena. "Can't you perform another spell to locate them?" he asked tersely, and she let out a long sigh.

"Summoning incantations are far more taxing than regular sorcery. I depleted my reserves reviving Arvind, and I need time to rest."

She had been teaching him magic but kept her own use to a minimum. It wasn't entirely a lie, but it wasn't the whole truth either. Her investigations had taken a toll on her magical capacity, but she wasn't about to tell him that.

Zhelyas pursed his lips, irked. "I suppose I'll have to make do. Dispatch more men at once. The little queen won't elude me forever."

Luther clicked his heels together. He looked exhausted, with dark circles under his eyes, and Veena sent him an encouraging smile. He nodded in appreciation, then departed to resume his search.

"You might as well go yourself. Be sure to get some *rest*." Zhelyas gave Veena a disdainful look, then turned to the tower window, staring down into the courtyard below.

"I wonder what else magic can do?" he mused to himself, and Veena paused in the doorway. "For instance... can it raise the dead?"

A grin slithered across his face, and Veena shivered as though spiders were crawling across her skin.

As she returned to her quarters, Veena thought back to the conversation she'd had with Luther that first night. It had been difficult to make out much through the pervasive aura of self-pity and his slurring drunkenness, but she gathered he'd seen something so terrible he had lost all faith in the royal family. Of course, that was perfect for their purposes, so she had groomed him as one of the conspirators, but she had a much more personal interest. She recalled that during his ramblings the queen had come up more often than the king, as if Cecilia perhaps were the ringleader, or at least the impetus, behind whatever scheme he had observed. If so, she might hold the clues Veena was looking for.

She returned to the queen's chambers, which she had been given use of by Zhelyas, and flopped upon the bed. The royal couple shared a set of quarters, but the queen also had her own chambers for her private use. This was not to encourage indiscretion, supposedly, but rather to show sensitivity to both royal personages if one or the other was unwell. Additionally, should the king be away for any reason, the queen would retire to her own quarters rather than remain alone in the ones they shared.

The king's apartment was imposing but sparsely furnished with gold leaf wallpaper, slate tile flooring, and plush rugs. The canopy bed was gilded wood, quilted in ocher velvet and silk, golden winged lions supporting each of the tall posts. A covered desk stood at one side for private correspondences, near a large window with tasseled curtains.

The queen's quarters were more feminine, much better suited to Veena's own taste, with ivory detailing and lush violet tones. The quarters Caro had occupied before the coup were decorated in pale gold and green, and remained empty, left exactly as they had been that night, the broken door still dangling off its hinges. As per tradition, the queen wouldn't have moved into her new quarters until after her coronation and would have occupied the king's chambers as the reigning monarch, reserving the queen's rooms for her future consort.

As the third prince, Arvind was eligible for his own royal apartment, but he had apparently taken up residence near the far end of the palace since his falling out with his brother, so they did not have occasion to cross paths.

Veena stared up at the embossed ceiling. While Zhelyas's lofty tastes seemed in line with Roland's, Veena would much prefer desert scenes to the paintings of the pastoral rolling hills of the highlands where Cecilia had been born. Not that she cared anyway. She had no intention of becoming Zhelyas's consort, no matter what his own delusions might be.

For now, it was a place to sleep, and perhaps to uncover clues. Luther had implied the queen had discovered the very thing Veena was looking for, and she would search in every crevice to find evidence of it. So far, Cecilia had proven to be annoyingly clever at concealing the second crystal, but Veena was undaunted.

She swung her legs off the bed, her determination renewed. She chanted a spell under her breath, sealing the room from all intruders, then drew a looping symbol in the air, a rune to prevent eavesdropping.

Satisfied with her defenses, she unlatched the crystal necklace and held it above the ground by the ends of its long chain. Though she had obtained the shard years ago, she had never thought to use it for this purpose until now. She wasn't certain whether it would work or if the crystal was even attuned to her magical energy, but it was worth a try.

Veena closed her eyes and held her breath, holding her hand as still as possible. For a moment, nothing happened, then the crystal began to swing, at first imperceptibly, then with more force.

Dowsing was a tricky art that required more than mere magical skill, but it seemed her affinity with the natural currents was strong enough. Veena kept her eyes closed, visualizing her desire in her mind. She only had a vague idea of what it might look like, so the image was not as clear as it could be, but the crystal responded.

She opened her eyes to see the crystal swinging in a definite leftward motion, and she followed its cue, turning on the ball of her foot so as to not disturb its rhythm. It wasn't as precise as a location spell, but so far those had proven less than helpful. The shard was part of a larger whole, and she hoped it would resonate with its other half.

The crystal led her to the queen's washroom, which had a tub inset in marble with gold rosettes, and a white-and-peach mosaic floor. At the crystal's urging, Veena scraped at a tile in the far corner.

She broke a nail and cursed. Perhaps this had all been directed by her subconscious, and she was indulging some fantasy. Still, she prodded until she felt the tile shift.

Finally, she managed to work her fingers beneath the edge. There must be a mechanism somewhere in the room which would release it, but Veena didn't have the patience for that. With magic bolstering her strength, she pried it loose.

Beneath the tile was a hidden compartment, and in it, a mahogany box. Veena removed the container from its hiding place and returned to the bed, sitting cross-legged upon the duvet.

The box wasn't very ornate, which in itself was unusual for Cecilia, who seemed to have enjoyed the opulence of her position. Veena's fingers were tingling. Was this what she had been searching for all along? She reverently lifted the lid.

The interior was similarly unadorned, and it contained only two items: a small pink notebook bound with leather cord, and a black velvet drawstring pouch. Veena could barely contain her excitement, but she forced herself to open the book first. It was a journal, written in the former queen's own hand.

Following the traces, we have finally found it, the realization of all our dreams. Never did I imagine one of the crown jewels would be the key. We have left another in its place, enough to fool the treasurer, for he would not have recognized its true provenance. A gift from the gods.

She turned the page.

What could one do with limitless power? The possibilities swirl in my head, endless. Roland is still unsure, but he will come around.

She flipped to the end, the final entry. The letters were slightly shaky.

The time is almost upon us. I tremble with anticipation. We are so close...

Veena smiled. Along with the cryptic musings was an old piece of folded parchment, the same page which had been torn from Avtandil's book and had spurred the king and queen on their own quest. She had no way of knowing how the royal couple had come into possession of it, but it detailed exactly what she needed to know. Everything except the temple's exact location—that was kept deliberately vague. Still, it was more than Veena had hoped to find. She closed the journal and picked up the pouch, pulling back the drawstring and dumping the contents into her palm.

A crystal the size of a plum, pale green and magnificent, glittered in the candle's glow, casting a million points of viridian light across the walls so it looked like she was sitting in the midst of a field of stars. The parent of her own tiny crystal.

She had found the key. Now she had to find the door.

Knowledge is Power

The soldiers went about their usual daily regimen, trying hard to avoid Zhelyas's gaze as he paced the barracks, scrutinizing their training. Luther hovered nearby, apparently hesitant to disturb him.

Zhelyas had the entire complement of the royal forces, thousands of men at his command. What could one upstart queen do against him?

He strode over to the forge. A fire blazed in a stone furnace, and Zhelyas began to sweat from the sheer force of heat emanating from it, confined in the small room. On the wall hung every manner of instrument: mallets, tongs, swages, and farrier's tools.

An anvil stood to the side, upon which a blacksmith with thinning hair worked and shaped a piece of metal. He plunged it into a barrel of water to quench it, and the metal made a sharp hissing sound as it released a cloud of steam. He withdrew it and placed the new, long blade upon a table to cool before affixing the hilt, then turned to the hearth, pumping upon a pair of bellows to stoke the dwindling flames.

Zhelyas scoured the swords and spears upon the racks with a doubtful frown. "Isn't there anything more powerful than these?"

"There is one thing," the blacksmith ventured, shooting a nervous glance at Luther.

Zhelyas leaned close, and the man quailed beneath his glare. "Well?"

"We have the molds for a portable incendiary weapon, but King Roland forbade their use and had them all destroyed."

"What sort of weapon?" Zhelyas inquired, intrigued.

"It's called a 'dragon-breath,' sire," Luther explained, looking uncomfortable.

Zhelyas smiled. "I like the sound of these dragon-breaths. Resume manufacture of them at once."

Zhelyas returned to the palace, pleased with his new discovery. This would give him a distinct advantage over Caro and whatever paltry force she could muster. His magic was growing stronger, too. He usually practiced in the privacy of the tower, where no one could stumble upon him, but the throne room was deserted and he had commanded he was not to be disturbed.

He held up his hand and called upon the familiar feeling. A spark burst to light upon his finger, and he once again marveled at its beauty. Fire raced through his veins; like the effects of a drug, it was intoxicating.

Zhelyas wondered if it could take other forms, and envisioned a dagger. A moment later, he held a dagger in his hands, one created from magical energy, the blade wreathed in flame.

He threw it experimentally, and it embedded itself in one of the noble's benches, then dissolved. Zhelyas watched as the cushion smoldered, then waved his hand lazily, extinguishing the blaze.

He would have to be more careful from now on about where he practiced, lest he set his castle alight. Still, one more experiment couldn't hurt. Inspired by the dragon-breaths the blacksmith had told him about, Zhelyas summoned a stream of flame that coiled around his arms in the shape of a serpent with eyes like coals, hissing and slithering.

He could feel it: a vast reservoir of energy filling him, as though he could bend the whole world to his will.

There was a crashing of china outside the room, and he banished the snake, then strode to the doors, throwing them open. A maid was kneeling on the floor. She had apparently stumbled, dropping a tray. Her face was ashen, and she looked ready to faint.

"F-forgive me, sire," the maid said fearfully, and Zhelyas gave a curt nod.

He watched as she cleaned up the pieces and hurried off, teetering on her feet as if she had lost the strength to stand.

He grinned at the realization. Veena had said he should be cautious, and she had been drained by her own use of magic — while he only felt rejuvenated and brimming with limitless power.

Familiarity Breeds Contempt

Diascia sauntered into the king's private dining hall, and Zhelyas gave her a nod of appreciation. She appeared to have found one of the late queen's dresses in the wardrobe, and mulberry silk clung to her curves while a tiara of gold and garnets sparkled in her copper-blond hair. It suited her, appropriate for a noblewoman yet alluring. He enjoyed looking at her.

"Did you sleep well?"

"You quite exhausted me, sire," she replied impishly as she sank into the chair.

Zhelyas smirked, amused by her insinuation, and bit into a slice of bread topped with minced meat. Diascia surveyed the array of luxurious dishes, finally selecting a soft cheese pastry.

"What are your plans?" he inquired.

"Oh, the usual," she replied. "Lobelia and I often spend the day together."

Zhelyas managed to suppress a grimace. His growing fascination with Diascia was one thing, but her snobbish sister was quite another.

"I have to conduct a rather boring session of court, but after that, perhaps I might show you some of the pleasures of the palace?"

Diascia batted her eyes at him coquettishly and lifted her foot beneath the table, running her toes along his leg. "I would like that very much, Your Majesty."

Zhelyas had the servants place a smaller chair beside his throne, and Diascia seated herself with a confident swagger. He supposed it would be a good test of her suitability to be his consort. She had the attitude of a queen, and all that remained was to see if she had the temperament.

"What is on the agenda for today?" Zhelyas asked Malcolm, who stood to attention.

"There are a few matters to discuss," he began. "First, the foundry is requisitioning more material to make the weapons you requested."

"Granted."

Malcolm moved his finger down the list. "The steward has a list of requests, including but not limited to: new carpets for the entrance hall, draperies, light fixtures, replacement keys for the storeroom doors—"

"Yes, yes, get on with it," Zhelyas said irritably.

Malcolm cleared his throat. "Also, since our furbisher has been... otherwise detained, someone else needs to be appointed to the position."

In a particularly bad mood, Zhelyas had imprisoned the servant in charge of polishing the silverware upon noticing a cloudy spot.

Zhelyas waved his hand. "Have the steward handle it. That's servant's business and hardly the purview of a king."

"Of course, sire. My apologies."

"You're a monster!"

All eyes turned to the nobleman who had spoken. Malcolm blinked in evident surprise as the atmosphere in the room grew distinctly chilly.

"Lord Nefion Atef, that was uncalled for," Malcolm admonished. "Apologize at once."

"Say that again," Zhelyas hissed.

"You think you're so much better than all of us?" Nefion spat. "You're nothing but a tyrant."

Zhelyas approached him, and Malcolm took a step forward.

"Stand aside, Earl Dahl."

"Your Majesty—"

Zhelyas cast him a warning look. "I said—stand aside."

Malcolm hung his head and obeyed.

"Now, let's see what's to be done about a filthy dog who can't remember his place." He snapped his fingers, and a guard seized Nefion's arms, pinning them behind his back. "What is it they say? Don't bite the hand that feeds you."

Zhelyas gripped Nefion's head with both hands, clenching his teeth as he increased the pressure, squeezing and digging with his thumbs. Blood flowed from the suffering man's face and down Zhelyas's arms as he gouged out Nefion's eyes.

When he was done, Zhelyas released him, and he collapsed to the ground, drops of blood like tears dripping upon the floor. He was still alive, though it might have been kinder if he had died. But Zhelyas had no intention of being kind.

"Dismissed," he ordered, and another noble helped Nefion hobble out of the room, whimpering in anguish.

Malcolm looked like he was going to be sick, but he shuffled out with the rest.

Zhelyas turned to Diascia, who was staring at him in undisguised horror. His hands were dripping with blood, and he smiled with wicked pleasure.

She stumbled back as he approached, and he grasped the back of her neck, forcing her into a passionate kiss. Blood slicked her skin as he caressed her body, and she shuddered beneath his touch. She tried to pull away, but he held her firm, savoring the moment.

He licked his lips, tasting the sharp tang of blood. "You wished to be my consort," he chuckled darkly. "Do I excite you now?"

She shook her head, her chest heaving with fear. "P-please, sire..."

He considered ignoring her pleading. The blood was like an aphrodisiac, and he wanted her right then and there, but he had also grown bored of his toy. The cowering women before him no longer aroused any desire.

"Go," he said, brushing her aside, and she bowed hurriedly before scrambling out of the room.

"Lady Diascia?" Malcolm inquired as she staggered down the hall.

She stumbled, and Arcus caught her, holding her trembling shoulders.

"It was so horrible..." she sobbed, shivering uncontrollably. Blood dotted her dress and smeared her skin.

"It's all right," Arcus soothed in his gentle way. "Let's clean you off, and this day will be no more than a bad memory."

Takaria's quarters were closest, so they steered her in that direction. Senna shuffled her off to the lavatory to be washed, and she emerged a short while later wearing a clean dressing gown, her long copper-blond hair brushed and draping over her shoulders. She had a fragile, wounded beauty about her.

"Lady Diascia, are you all right?" Malcolm inquired while Arcus rose and helped her to a chair.

"I'll be fine," she replied, her voice shaky. Though she tried to smile, it was a shadow of her previous effervescence.

"If you don't feel well enough to return to your quarters, we can inform Lady Lobelia and—"

"Please don't tell my sister," she begged, and Malcolm furrowed his brow.

"Don't you think she deserves to know?"

"Lebby won't understand. I'll just tell her I won't be seeing the king for a while. She doesn't need to know anything more."

Takaria nodded somberly and turned a stern glance upon the gentlemen. "Your secret is safe with us, Lady Diascia."

Malcolm and Arcus gave reluctant nods of agreement.

"If you would be amenable, I could use an assistant to help me with my husband's accounts," the formidable duchess added.

Diascia blinked. "I'm not really good with complicated stuff like that..."

Takaria made a tutting sound at her timorous words. "You wouldn't have to do anything other than take the notes I dictate and collate paperwork. It would give you an excuse to remain busy at the very least."

Diascia appeared to consider this. "I would be grateful, Duchess. I'll do my best."

"If you need anything, please don't hesitate to ask," Arcus offered, his kindness genuine.

"Thank you, Viscount. I just want to go back to my life before any of this happened."

Easier said than done, Malcolm thought grimly.

Gaius had been the lead physician in the palace, but luckily there were others who had remained behind. They had bandaged Nefion's eyes in gauze as he lay upon the bed in the infirmary, moaning in his sleep.

Lord Rudo Lydo sat by his bedside. "Earl," he said by way of greeting, neither rising nor releasing his friend's hand.

"How is he?" Malcolm asked.

A nurse turned his way. "He'll survive, though it was touch and go for a little while," she whispered. "It'll be a long recovery, and he'll never see again. His eyesight has been irreparably damaged. We have him under sedation for the moment, but the pain must be excruciating."

Malcolm nodded, swallowing his guilt. "Forgive me," he said, though Nefion couldn't hear him.

"You tried. We all know that. But he... he just wouldn't let it go." Rudo's voice was thick with grief, and he lapsed into silence.

Malcolm decided it was best to leave them be. "Let me know if I can help in any way," he said, knowing his words were hollow. The nurse gave him a slight nod before returning to her patient.

Oil and Water

After keeping to the fringes of towns and settlements, Caro was thrilled to book a room at an inn for the night. Morfran had traded in his silver mask for one of black leather which was somewhat less noticeable, though his grim countenance was still unnerving to any who crossed his path.

"If you wish me to remain out of sight while you are in town, I will do so," Morfran offered. "I have no complaints about spending the night under cover of darkness."

Caro shook her head. She refused to isolate her newest comrade. "If you keep your hood up, it will be all right."

Stelian looked disgruntled, and Caro ignored him. He hadn't had a chance yet to get his feelings off his chest, and the animosity was irritating.

Morfran stared at Caro a moment, his unruffled manner leaving no clue as to what he was thinking, then bowed his head. "If that's what you feel is best, I will oblige."

The innkeeper blinked at his trio of prospective guests: a short young female vagabond, a greenhorn, and a man who looked like a hulking beast in black, his cowl drawn so far down only his lips were visible. Caro could imagine they must look like a comedy troupe.

The man shook his head and shrugged, handing over the keys. "One room, best I can offer. There's two beds, plus a cot."

Stelian opened his mouth to object, but Caro smiled sweetly.

"Thank you, that will do fine."

"That's twelve kamsyas, which includes dinner, and another three for breakfast tomorrow morning if ye want it."

"Yes, please. When do you stop serving meals? I would rather have privacy if possible," Caro added, lifting her eyebrow.

The innkeeper swallowed, grasping her meaning. The tall one would no doubt intimidate the rest of his clientele. "Kitchen's open 'til nine and opens again at five if yer gonna make an early start."

She handed over the bronze coins, then the three made their way upstairs. The beds were small, just enough for one person, with a cot squeezed between the wall and the dresser. Caro had to admit it was a little pricey, but decent.

"Cozy," she quipped.

Stelian looked like the last thing he wanted to do was get closer to Morfran. She sighed, deciding she might as well ignore them and let them figure it out.

Dinner was seared pork medallions served with creamy mushroom and garlic sauce—rather more elaborate than Caro had been expecting, but admittedly a pleasant surprise.

"Excuse me," Caro said, holding up her hand, and the innkeeper came over. He had served them himself since the staff had been sent home for the night.

"Is there a problem?" he asked gruffly.

"Not at all. I would like to give my compliments to the chef."

He blinked, then nodded. "Thank you, miss, I will do so. We have no dessert to offer, but he could make you some milk pudding, if you like?"

"That would be delightful."

The pudding was plain but flavorful, baked and drizzled with sweet caramel.

"You like pudding?" Morfran inquired.

"Yes, but my favorite is custard tarts with a dusting of cinnamon," she replied, surprised by the question.

"I prefer chocolate meringue cake," he murmured, and Caro nearly toppled off her chair. The assassin feared by all, the commander whose very glare could freeze a person in their tracks—liked chocolate cake.

"I'm going to take a walk," Stelian declared stiffly, and his chair squeaked across the floor as he rose and stormed off.

"I don't think he likes me much," Morfran said, and Caro frowned.

"You haven't exactly made an effort."

"If you will excuse me, I think I would like to get some air as well. I promise I won't cause any trouble," Morfran added at Caro's suspicious look.

Her footsteps echoed down the hollow stairs as Morfran stepped outside. The night was cool and brisk, shrouded in darkness. Just how he liked it.

He heard a swishing of metal and turned to where Stelian was practicing with his sword in the alley. Morfran held out his scabbard, meeting Stelian's blade.

"You—!"

"I don't know what I've done to offend you..." Morfran tried.

"Offend me?" Stelian seethed. "Your very presence offends me."

Morfran took a slight step back as Stelian advanced.

"Back after she escaped from the garrison, I saw the cuts and bruises. How can you profess to serve her now?"

All the while, Morfran had been holding up his scabbard, diverting blow after blow as he backed up. If this kept up, he'd have to replace it. He planted his feet, standing his ground, and Stelian's arms shuddered from the sudden resistance.

"Her Majesty didn't tell you what happened?"

"She said it wasn't what it looked like."

"But you didn't ask further?"

Stelian scowled but remained silent.

"Contrary to what you might believe, I am indeed loyal to Her Majesty. I was playing along with Zhelyas to get what I wanted from him."

"So?"

Morfran sighed. "At the garrison, I saw the chance to keep her out of danger. But my situation was precarious, so I made a deal with her: she would pretend to be my servant, and I would help her escape when the opportunity arose. I made due on my word, I might add."

Stelian frowned, unconvinced.

"As for that incident... She spoke up rashly during a strategy session with the other officers, so I had to act quickly to maintain both our covers. I hauled her away to give her a merciless thrashing, or so it was believed—but that left me with a quandary. I couldn't very well beat my queen, so I cast aside my armor and gave her a dagger with which to defend herself, and we sparred."

"Sparred?" Stelian repeated.

"Yes." Morfran nodded, the memories trickling back. "I had the upper hand, but I took care not to strike her anywhere which would cause her grievous injury. It wasn't one-sided either," he added at Stelian's dark look. "I concealed my wounds beneath my armor so no one was the wiser, but this one in particular still smarts."

Morfran loosened the straps on his bracer and pushed up his sleeve to show Stelian. The last cut that Caro had inflicted was not yet healed, the skin raw and inflamed.

"So you see," Morfran continued, rolling down his sleeve and refastening the bracer, "everything I did, no matter how callous it seemed, was for her own sake."

Stelian pursed his lips, then gave a short nod. "As long as you continue to protect her, I will fight alongside you. However, there is something you must realize."

Morfran was surprised by his seriousness.

"As a princess, Caro was always surrounded by nursemaids and servants. Then, when she was fourteen, the king decided she needed a bodyguard, and General Luther chose me," Stelian said. "Every day for three years, I rose at the crack of dawn to make sure I was there when she woke up. I escorted her to balls and listened when she needed someone to talk to."

There was a long pause, and Stelian took a deep breath. "I was there when she received the news of her parents' murder, and overheard through the door as her heart shattered into a million pieces. Then the night Zhelyas made his move, I woke her to tell her that for the second time in as many months, her life was altered forever. I will do whatever it takes to protect her."

Stelian met his gaze, and Morfran gave a slow nod.

"I understand perfectly, but don't make the mistake of thinking I have shed myself of guilt. For the crime of injuring her, no matter the reason, I will atone. Even if it costs me my life."

A fist rapped on the door of the room, gloved knuckles dull against the wood.

"Come in," Caro said from the bed nearest the door. She had removed one of her boots and was struggling with the other.

Morfran closed the door, then knelt at her feet. "Allow me." He began to methodically untangle the laces, which had become knotted during the day's trek.

"I heard you and Stelian in the alley. Were you fighting?"

"I did not unsheathe my sword," Morfran said. "I didn't think you would approve."

"Certainly not. And?"

He smiled as she pressed him for an answer. "I still don't think he likes me, but at least the air is clear between us."

"Thank Aryama for that," Caro sighed. She wasn't pleased they had come to blows, but at least the matter had been resolved for now.

She stared down at him as he worked in silence. "Tell me, why do you wear that mask?" she inquired, unable to keep quiet any longer.

"It is not a face I wish others to see," Morfran replied, and slipped off her boot.

"Is it an injury, or...?"

He nodded.

"Will you not show me?"

He looked up at her. "Please do not ask that of me."

Caro had expected him to refuse, but she was taken aback by the sorrow in his voice. "Why?" she could not help but ask.

"Because I am not ready for you to see me as I am."

Morfran rose, placing his palms on either side of the blanket beside her, and leaned forward. Caro craned her neck upward, meeting his dark gaze through the mask. She'd never realized that his eyes, ever in shadow, were blue.

"I promise, once this is over, I will tell you everything." He sank back to the floor, then took her hand and kissed it, the briefest of a feather's touch.

They departed after eating breakfast when the kitchen opened. There were more early risers than night owls, and they gave a wide berth to Morfran in his ominous cowl.

"The eggs were runny," Stelian grumbled, "and the potatoes were too crispy."

Morfran shrugged. "I like runny eggs. The potatoes should have been cooked longer."

Caro rolled her eyes at the banter. Stelian and Morfran, while not quite friends, had reached an accord and were no longer exchanging venomous glares or sarcastic barbs—at least not as often. Caro supposed it was as much as she could ask. She hoped their relationship would improve as time passed, but so long as they weren't at each other's throats, she would be satisfied.

"How far are we from Agassey?" Stelian inquired, strolling down the road with his hands clasped behind his head, elbows flailing.

"If the weather holds, we should be there by nightfall," Caro replied.

Morfran lifted his head and glanced at the horizon. "Better hope it holds. It looks like we're in for a storm."

An ill Wind

"I'm growing tired of your incompetence!" Zhelyas raged as Luther cowered before him.

Veena stood unobtrusively off in the corner.

"Apologies, sire," Luther groveled. "My men have searched every inch of the road for Queen Caro and her retinue, but the task is made all the more difficult without the aid of Morfran—"

Zhelyas's fury boiled over. He crossed the space between them in the blink of an eye and backhanded the general. "Morfran is a traitor and a defector! You will not speak his name again!"

Luther staggered from the blow, a welt rising upon his cheek, then hunched his shoulders in abject shame.

Veena couldn't help but feel pity for the poor man. He'd done all Zhelyas had asked, and this was his reward?

Luther glanced at her, and she evaded his gaze, examining her fingernails.

"Are you so incompetent you can't do anything without help?" Zhelyas spat.

"N-no, Your Majesty. Forgive me."

"Veena!"

She jerked her head. "Yes, sire?"

"You'd better have a more effective way of locating them."

"Of course, my liege," she purred, forcing a smile.

Veena led the way to the tower where she performed many of her spells. Zhelyas paced the room like an angry lion, the hem of his embroidered coat fluttering in his wake. He wore the Artemisian crown upon his head with its curved spires of gold and rubies, unruly black hair drifting across his cold eyes.

"Do you know where they are?" His voice was sharp with impatience.

Luther huddled against the wall, arms crossed close to his body as he watched the ritual take place.

Veena stood in the center, facing the wide arched window. Before her, a metal brazier blazed. Violet smoke curled into the air and spilled down the sides, pooling upon the ground like a noxious mist. She had replenished enough magic to complete this spell, though she would feel the effects afterward.

She closed her eyes in concentration, and the walls of the room rippled with the force of her sorcery.

Like the roiling sky, a deep purple hue
The amethyst sparkles like lightning
Garjan, god of storms, I call upon you
A power so vast and so frightening

Heed my plea, stretch out your hand
Across the heavens, through the land

My body shall serve as your anchor

Those who near the fore shall hide
Will not be veiled from my sight

And those who near the aft abide
Will be cowed by thunderous might

There is no time for refuge
For upon them is the deluge

Veena chanted the spell, tracing an angular rune in the ashes. As she spoke, great black clouds formed, rolling in from the mountains, ominous and foreboding. Accompanying them was a bitter wind, one that chilled to the bone, as if the hand of Death itself were stroking her skin.

The clouds moved unnaturally, seeping across the sky like ink poured from a bottle. Within their depths, violet lightning flashed, mirroring the gems consumed by the flames.

"Why does the sky hate us?" Khalil whined.

Ezalia and Alenard exchanged a puzzled glance.

"Ah, you're from the desert, aren't you, lad?" Alenard said. "Have you never seen rain?"

"Rain?" Khalil repeated incredulously. "I am not an infant. I have seen rain, but this is like the gods venting their anger upon the world!"

His exclamation was overly dramatic, but Ezalia couldn't help agreeing with him.

A minute later, she and the others were running for cover as the storm swept over them, drenching them in seconds. A blind person was not equipped to flee, so Alenard took Ines into his arms rather than risk her tripping in the mud. Ezalia beamed at his gentility.

Luckily, there was still a room available at the inn. It would be a tight squeeze for four people, but they would have to make do. Alenard set Ines down, and she did not appear any the worse for wear. Khalil, on the other hand, was coming apart at the seams.

"Khalil?" Ezalia said.

"I—I'm okay," he breathed, backing up against the wall farthest from the window.

A bolt of lightning streaked across the sky, and thunder shook the inn.

"Aryama preserve us!" Khalil jumped like a startled rabbit and sank into the corner, his hands covering his ears.

Ines navigated the cramped space and crouched beside him. "It's all right," she soothed. "Everybody's afraid of something." She cocked her head in the general direction of the other two.

"Confined spaces," Ezalia admitted sheepishly.

"Snakes." This from Alenard.

Another peal of thunder, and Khalil cringed, shrinking into a little ball.

"You see?" Ines continued gently. "You're not alone."

He looked up, his wide eyes full of tears.

"What's most important is you identify that fear. Once you put a name to it, then you can master it." Ines stroked his back in rhythmic circles. "Take me, for instance. The world is frightening for one who cannot see. Even crossing a street can be a horrific ordeal, yet I do not hide from it, I embrace it."

"So I'm being silly?" Khalil murmured.

Ezalia shook her head. "Not at all. It's nothing to be ashamed of. I bet if there was a snake in the room, Allen would leap on a chair, shrieking like a skittish housewife."

"I would not!" Alenard retorted, and Ezalia snickered.

"Point is, while it would be amusing, I wouldn't think any less of him. And we don't think any less of you for being frightened in a thunderstorm."

"Really?"

"I bet if a massive sandstorm blew through here, you would yawn. That would scare the willies out of me!"

He smiled, apparently buoyed by this logic. "I think sandstorms are kind of pretty."

"Then you've proven my point," Ezalia said with a chuckle. "Now let's try to get some shut-eye. You and Allen can share one bed, Ines and I will take the other. It'll be a little cozy, but we'll manage."

The storm came on faster than anyone expected.

Caro sneezed as she and her two companions sheltered under the eaves of a nearby building. Stelian was asking directions to an inn from a shopkeeper who was closing up early due to her dwindling clientele.

"Are you all right?" Morfran inquired as Caro huddled inside his cloak for warmth.

She nodded, shivering.

"There's no room at the inn," Stelian informed them, rubbing his hands together, "but this gracious lady has agreed to put us up for the night as long as we buy twenty cases of preserves. I told her we can't possibly carry that much, but she insisted."

"We'll take it," Caro said, and sneezed again.

"My name's Pertha," the preserve seller said cheerfully. "This young fellow tells me you need a place to stay. Oh my, don't you look chilled to the bone!"

Morfran glanced down at Caro, his lips thin with worry. "It's cold and raining. Is there any way my lady can have a hot bath?" he asked as they entered the modest residence.

"That'll be another case of preserves." Pertha lifted an eyebrow and smiled at Morfran's nod.

"Thank you," Caro replied, feeling a little lightheaded.

"You can hang your wet garments above the wood stove to dry," Pertha instructed. "Right this way, miss. I'll get that water all warmed up for you."

She stripped off her sopping clothes, which Pertha took away. Caro sank into the hot water, her knees tucked up to her chest, and hoped the others were faring better.

The storm fulfilled its purpose, hunting down Caro and the wayward travelers where Luther had failed. He still bore the mark of Zhelyas's wrath, and Veena knew she would suffer a similar fate if she were unsuccessful.

Magic was more predictable than mere mortal eyesight, and could travel where a human could not in a form that was unassuming yet would strike fear into the most stalwart of hearts. She smiled to herself, reveling in the sorcery as it crackled around her. Nothing was beyond her grasp.

Veena wiped the grin from her face at Zhelyas's dark look.

The one regret she had was Morfran. She never could manipulate him the way she did other men, Zhelyas and Luther included. Morfran's heart was concealed beneath a veil of shadow, deeper than even she could reach. He had been unbound by the fetters other men shackled themselves with, and she missed his presence. Luther was always gloomy and Zhelyas would explode at the drop of a pin; it was exhausting.

Veena kept her expression neutral as these thoughts flitted across her brain.

Still the thunderstorm advanced to every corner of the country. Northward, it went. The storm was her eyes and ears, and she scoured the realm for four particular presences. They had split into three groups: Gaius one, Ezalia another, and Caro and her bodyguard in a third—with Morfran by her side. That was an intriguing development.

Having obtained her objective, Veena spoke the final words, canceling the spell.

The contract is fulfilled
The storm may now disperse
Like the awe it has instilled
May the tether now reverse

The fire died down, the smoky mist abating. Veena, weakened by the effort, sank into a chair.

Zhelyas ceased his pacing and faced her. "Well? Did you find them?" he demanded, with no apparent thought to her welfare.

She shot him a rueful look. "Yes, but there are others with her. She seems to have recruited several allies."

"They are of no consequence. Only the queen matters."

Veena sighed wearily. "They are headed toward Agassey, to the house of Grand Duke Ezekiel, if I were to speculate."

Zhelyas gave a curt nod. "Then that is where we are going."

"All of us?" Luther blurted. The king had not left the palace since he had seized it, nor had he asked Veena to do so.

Zhelyas narrowed his gaze at Luther, who looked like he wished he hadn't spoken. "Since you two can't seem to deliver what I want, I will have to take it for myself."

Luther bowed his head, the welt on his cheek livid in the dying firelight. "Yes, sire. I shall prepare for our departure."

"We leave at once," Zhelyas corrected, then spun on his heel and flounced out.

Luther rubbed his cheek.

"Does it hurt?" Veena asked. "I have some salves."

"No, but thank you. His indifference stings the most—toward us both," he added, and Veena gave a slight nod.

Still, their liege commanded and—for now—she would obey.

Zhelyas waited with marked impatience while Luther secured spare horses and supplies.

"You have the weapons I commissioned?"

"Yes, Your Majesty. A squadron is outfitted, each carrying a dragon-breath, as you ordered."

"Good."

Finally, all was organized and they set off for Agassey.

"Where are they now, that they eluded my forces?" Zhelyas asked Veena as she rode beside him.

"They crossed the bridge and have taken two paths, one to the north, the other to the east, traversing the desert."

"Whatever for? Did Caro think she could recruit allies among your people?"

She gave a shrug. "One of them is with her, but it is unlikely that was her original intention."

Zhelyas turned to Luther.

"Nothing lies that way except Biding, although, if she gained Lord Alenard's support, she might have his private army at her disposal. But it is insignificant compared to the breadth of the royal forces under your command," he added, and Zhelyas pursed his lips at the man's pandering.

Malcolm stared out the window as Zhelyas departed on horseback, accompanied by Luther, Veena, and a fair number of troops.

"Don't get any ideas, Earl," Arvind said lazily from the doorway, and Malcolm spun to face him.

"Your Highness," he said warily.

"While the king is gone, fulfill your duties and don't test my patience," the prince chided. "Remember, you are treading a thin line. Be careful not to cross it."

Tickled Pink

Caro woke in the morning and shuffled downstairs in Pertha's fluffy wool bathrobe and slippers.

Stelian and Morfran were sitting around a table playing cards while their host busied herself about the kitchen, baking and humming a little ditty.

Do I bake cherries? No, no. Do I bake figs?
Do I bake blueberries? No, no. Too many twigs.
Do I bake blackberries? No, no. Better a dye.
Do I bake raspberries? No, no. Not in a pie.
Do I bake cranberries? No, no. Much too tart.
Do I bake peaches? Yes, for my sweetheart!

It was cute, and Caro couldn't help but smile.

"Oh, you're up!" Pertha exclaimed, holding a wooden spoon dripping with fruit puree.

Stelian rose, and Caro eased herself into the vacated chair.

"Are you feeling well?" Morfran inquired, laying down his hand of cards. From what she could tell, he was winning handily.

"Much better, thank you."

"Here you go, fresh out of the oven!" Pertha declared, and whisked three plates onto the table. Upon each was a tart, steam still escaping through the vents poked in the pastry. "Careful, they're hot."

"Since we bought so many fruit preserves, she's baking some into pies so we can eat them along the way," Stelian supplied, testing his tart. He let out a yelp as he burned his tongue.

"That's the rest," Morfran added, gesturing to a big pile of cases. "She says her neighbor has a cart he's trying to sell, so we can load them upon that."

"That sounds like a good idea."

Caro took a careful bite out of her tart. It had cooled enough to eat, and tasted delicious. "Thank you so much for putting us up last night. I hope we weren't too much inconvenience."

"Not at all, sweetie. I was glad of the company," Pertha said with a smile as she stirred a new batch of pie filling. "I was married, but my husband passed away some time ago, and the young'uns all left home and have little ones of their own. So it's just me now." She paused in her stirring, adrift in her memories. "We had forty-two years together and raised six wonderful children. I wouldn't trade those days for anything. I am content."

Caro nodded, recollections of the past trickling back, in particular a day which she hadn't thought of in some time. The sweet aroma of peach tarts. A picnic with her mother and father. Cherry blossoms drifting through the air like pink snow. She had been innocent then, a child, with a child's hopes and dreams. Cocooned in her parents' love, she could never have imagined such a future awaited her.

Caro became aware of Morfran watching her, and she shook her head to allay his concern.

"Your clothes should be dry and warm for you to wear," Pertha said. "It looks like the storm has passed, so you can continue on your way to wherever you fine folks are going."

"Your Majesty," Morfran ventured softly when they were alone.

"What is it?" Caro asked.

"That thunderstorm we encountered was not a natural phenomenon. It was sorcery."

Caro blinked. "Sorcery?"

"Because we have traveled beyond Luther's reach, it seems likely Zhelyas has turned to his sorceress, Veena. I believe she sent out a tracking spell in the form of that tempest."

"Then that means Zhelyas knows where we're headed."

"It seems likely," Morfran said with a grim nod. "What should we do? Return to Alenard's to come up with another plan, or forge ahead to Agassey?"

Caro chewed a nail. "We've come too far to backtrack now."

As suggested, Stelian bought the cart from the preserve seller's neighbor, a kindly old man who gave them a crooked smile as they took it off his hands. They then loaded the cart with the pies and remaining cases. Caro and Stelian climbed aboard while Morfran took the reins.

Stelian dozed off in the back, but Caro scooted up front to sit beside Morfran.

"I've been wondering for a while, but you seem different somehow."

He glanced over at her, his lips parting in surprise at the comment. "How do you mean?"

"When we first met, you were snarky and sarcastic, even intimidating, but... you're not like that anymore."

He let out a little hum, keeping his eyes on the road but his attention fixed upon her. "As my queen, I can hardly be rude to you, as I was back then. But if you want me to, I can practice my sarcasm."

Caro frowned at his flippancy.

"I was playing a part, Your Majesty," Morfran continued somberly. "Perhaps I always have. Assassin. Mercenary. Commander. I was feared, and rightly so, for being remorseless, conniving, and cruel. This mask hid the face of a beast from the world."

He hesitated, perhaps gauging Caro's reaction to his harsh, self-deprecating words. "However, I have dedicated my life to you, my queen, which means I no longer live for my selfish desires."

"I feel like you have been repressing your emotions since you swore yourself to my service. I don't want you to regret what you have done just because you think you should act a certain way."

Morfran slowed the cart and faced her. "I promise, my queen, what I do for you, I do with all my heart. But you are correct: I may have been overly sensitive about how to behave. I believe Khalil told you about my past?"

Caro nodded. "A little."

"What he doesn't know is that when I was a boy, I was taken as a slave by a band of brigands. My kidnapping was engineered by a certain person it took me many years to find. They were the ones who inflicted this wound," he added, his fingers brushing the mask. "I escaped my captors and was rescued by the Sharir. I am not the cowed boy of my youth, but neither can I be the rash commander who pestered you when

318

you were in my company. Just as you have returned to being the commanding queen rather than the submissive maid, so too have I changed roles from callous captor to obedient servant."

Caro nodded, touched by his tragic tale. "Act as you choose, Morfran, if that is your wish. I am grateful to have you by my side."

He bowed his head, and she thought she saw the hint of a smirk in his smile.

"Are we there yet?" Stelian said sleepily, roused to consciousness.

"Just a little farther," Morfran informed him.

Stelian yawned. "Wake me up when we get there."

"A cart! Bless your soul," Ezalia exclaimed as she and her companions trudged up the hill, meeting them at the fork which divided the two routes. Ezalia's road had been shorter, but Caro's group had traveled at a swifter pace with the cart to speed their way for the last leg of their journey.

Caro waved and leaped down, rushing to hug her aunt. Alenard watched with fondness in his eyes while Khalil helped Ines up the steep incline. Morfran nodded to them in greeting.

Stelian rummaged in the back. "If you're hungry, we have pies. And tarts, too."

"How did you manage that?" Ezalia inquired as Stelian emerged with a cherry tart for each of them. Khalil stared at his for a moment and waited for Alenard to take the first bite.

"It's a long story," Caro replied. "Did you get caught in that thunderstorm?"

"Oh yes, it was dreadful. We were lucky to find a room!"

Khalil twitched at the mention of the storm, and Ezalia shot him an encouraging look.

"We couldn't find anywhere, so this lovely preserve seller invited us into her home for the night," Caro explained.

Stelian covered the pies again. "I would have paid cash, but she insisted."

"She's probably trying to sell off her stock," Ezalia said rationally. "My father will see that they don't go to waste."

Caro's grandfather was an unusual man. Odd, perhaps, but brilliant. His eccentricity came from his cultured intelligence, which he had honed like the senses of a hunting dog; he could sniff out idiocy and had zero tolerance for it. She glanced at Morfran, wondering how the two elusive men might get along.

"Once you've rested, we can set off," Caro said, and Khalil nodded, stretching.

"The desert is not so hard upon my feet as this rough gravel. Oh, how I ache."

"Do you want to ride in the cart?" Caro added sweetly, chuckling at his grousing.

"If you intend to walk, I could walk with you," Khalil replied, a little sheepish.

"No thank you, I've walked quite enough. Ezalia, Ines, join me."

"You needn't ask me twice," Ezalia said, and Alenard lifted first her, then Ines, into the cart.

"Now there's no more room," Khalil pouted.

"You could always sit beside Morfran."

Khalil sighed, then pulled himself onto the driver's bench.

"Am I such terrible company?" Morfran inquired with an amused lilt, and Khalil shrugged, slouching in his seat.

Morfran snapped the whip, and the old mule began to plod ahead.

By the time the group arrived at the border of Agassey, Khalil was regaling Morfran with the tale of the frightening thunderstorm which the "gods had set upon them," gesticulating wildly.

Caro was chatting with Ines about their own adventure, glad to be reunited, and she glanced at Morfran, who was curiously silent about the subject. She would have expected him to at least chide Khalil for his wild imaginings, but he didn't say a word.

Stelian and Alenard, walking beside the slow-moving cart, had also struck up a conversation. Somehow the subject had come around to sword fighting and which weapon they favored in battle.

"Of the ranged weapons, I prefer the halberd. It has the best of both worlds, an ax head and a spike," Alenard said.

"But it's so unwieldy and imprecise. I would go with the spear any day," countered Stelian.

"You don't need precision with a weapon that can slice both sinew and steel," Alenard pointed out, and Stelian nodded in reluctant agreement.

Ezalia watched Alenard as he expounded upon his point and sighed.

Caro cocked her head at her aunt, whom she now realized was smitten. "Did something happen between you two?"

"When I mentioned we used to court, I did not elaborate upon the circumstances of our parting." She sighed again, the luster in her eyes dulled by sad memories. "He proposed to me, you see, but I thought I had better prospects, so I turned him down. We haven't spoken since, beyond the requirements of civility at court. I couldn't hold it in any longer and confessed that I wished things had been different—and he forgave me.

We decided to try again, and who knows, maybe things will work out better for us this time."

"I'm sure they will, Auntie." Caro squeezed her hand, overjoyed for Ezalia's good fortune.

"What about you?" Ezalia inquired slyly. "You have Khalil vying for your hand. And Morfran?"

She blinked at Ezalia. "Morfran? Whatever gives you that idea?"

"Oh, I don't know. The way he looks at you sometimes. One can't see his eyes, but his stare is so *intense*."

Caro glanced at his broad back where he sat upon the rider's bench, the traveling cloak concealing his jet-black armor beneath. She had to admit she'd felt a connection in that brief moment when she'd peered behind the mask to his gaze beneath, for the first time clear and unshadowed. But for him to have feelings for her? It wasn't possible.

She shook her head. "Khalil is one thing, and I will consider his suit when the time comes, as I promised his mother. But I don't even know who Morfran *is*."

Ezalia considered this. "Ines, do you have any idea?" she asked.

Ines shrugged. "I am afraid not. That is the only name by which I have known him. If he has another, then I am unaware of it."

Ezalia appeared deflated.

"Anyway," Caro said, clearing her throat, "as I told Hadiya, I don't have time for that right now."

Ezalia smiled, her gaze lingering once more upon her paramour. "You never know. Love may show up when you least expect it."

"Hey, Ezalia!"

Caro was spared any further witticisms by Stelian's excited cry, and she peered over the side to see him waving.

"What do we do now?" he asked.

Morfran slowed the cart to a stop as Ezalia leaped down. "Well, that's not something you see every day."

Caro hadn't heard such an underwhelming statement in her life.

A flock of sheep were minding their business in the center of the road, while the beleaguered shepherd was trying his best to clear the path. It wasn't the sheep lingering on the roadway which was odd, it was the sheep themselves. Their wool was not creamy white—but pink. Bright, garish pink.

Caro hopped out of the cart. "Ezalia?"

Her aunt was laughing so hard she had tears rolling down her cheeks.

Caro approached a sheep and held out her hand, stroking its back. It gave a plaintive bleat, and Caro looked at her fingers. They were now pink, too.

"What in the world...?"

"Well, I'll be. Milady Ezalia!" the shepherd exclaimed, doffing his flat leather cap.

"What's with the pink sheep, Robb?"

"It's that darn muhly grass! Been growing like crazy 'round these parts! Sheep go out to graze on the ley, and next thing you know, they're ruddy pink!"

Ezalia grinned.

"I think they're adorable," Caro cooed, scratching one behind the ears, careful not to transfer any more of the potent dye onto her hands or clothes.

"Ah, didn't see you, miss," Robb said, and bowed his head to Caro. "Doncha worry, I'll get these uncooperative old yows moving soon enough and you can be on your way. Off you go," he said, brandishing his crook and nudging them gently. It took a while, but the flock yielded and began to shift as a group until the road was clear.

"There y'are, milady. Safe travels," Robb said, doffing his cap once more.

They climbed back into the cart, and Morfran flicked the reins.

"Oh, one more thing. If you visit the guv'nor's house, tell that croaker my Milly is doing much better after the baby since drinking his willow leaf tea."

"Croaker?" Caro repeated, flummoxed.

"I think he's talking about Gaius," Ezalia murmured, then waved back. "I'll be sure to do so, and congratulations!"

Robb gave an embarrassed smile, then noticed a sheep was straying from the rest. "'Ey you, get back here!"

Caro watched over her shoulder, then turned to the front of the cart. She was relieved that Gaius, and hopefully Lottie too, had made it to Agassey, and was looking forward to seeing them again.

The cart plodded along at its leisurely pace. They passed many more fields with flocks of white sheep moping about.

Khalil was filled with marvel. "I have never seen such creatures before!" he said excitedly. "We raise goats and sometimes big-horned cattle, but these balls of fluff are so cuddly."

"I'm not surprised. Sheep are far too indolent and stupid"— Ezalia added as one flopped over, then couldn't get up again— "to survive in the desert. However, they thrive in mountains, and provide quite a challenge for their shepherds because they can navigate the rocky outcroppings."

The group reached Ezekiel's estate, and Caro was surprised to see several fluffy beasts grazing upon the wide stretch of lawn.

"More sheep? Here?"

Ezalia chuckled. "They're excellent at keeping grass trimmed. Let them graze for a few hours and it will never need to be mowed."

A road of smooth paving led to the estate of the grand duke at the top of the hill. It was a massive, stately building of dusky red brick with elaborate lintels over the windows. Tall bushes and trees framed the entrance beneath a circular porte cochère, flanked by tall white columns with ornate cornices and lit by soft golden lamps.

Caro's grandfather kept to himself. Even at her Accession, he had done his duty and sworn his allegiance but had not lingered after the ceremony. He had attended her parents' funeral, however; she recalled seeing him with a stoic look throughout the service, lined face impassive and stern in his grief at his youngest daughter's untimely death. Then he had departed the next day.

The man who stood at the door was tall and slight, of advanced age, but his vitality was not dimmed. He was dressed in a gold waistcoat and burgundy jacket, leaning upon a ram-headed cane, the symbol of the grand duke's house. His face was thin, with a hooked nose, a stern chin, and eyebrows that looked like they were sculpted in a permanent scowl. His hair was pure white, combed back from his widow's peak, and fell elegantly upon the collar of his coat.

"Your Royal Majesty, Divine Queen of Artemisia."

Caro inclined her head, slightly flustered. She hadn't been addressed by her full title in some time. "Your Grace, Lord of

Agassey and the Highlands of Rothelin," she replied with equal formality.

Ezekiel bent his back knee and bowed almost to the waist. "I am grateful you have sought me out, Your Majesty, and returned my precious daughter home." The seemingly permanent scowl melted as he laid eyes upon Ezalia. "Please come in and warm yourselves. You must be chilled and famished, and my house can remedy both."

Caro nodded at his exceeding politeness, yet it did not seem facetious as Oswin's had.

"Alenard, my boy. It is a pleasure to see you," Ezekiel greeted with a smile, shaking hands and hugging Ezalia's former/current beau.

He nodded politely to the others, lifting a mild eyebrow at Khalil, who escorted Ines. Then his brows returned to their usual place, even more furrowed.

"Naturally, all your companions are welcome, Your Majesty," he said, sizing up Morfran, who had taken up the rear of the queue. "But I must question the wisdom of including among them one who was, until recently, a servant of the *vile usurper* himself." Ezekiel spat the words as if they were repugnant upon his tongue.

"Morfran serves me now. I do not wish to dictate to you, Your Grace, since I hold you in the highest esteem—but the commander has sworn loyalty to me, and I have accepted his fealty. As such, he is to be afforded the same respect as any of my retainers."

Ezekiel appeared taken aback by her unyielding tone. "My apologies, I spoke out of turn. Commander."

"I am honored, Your Grace," Morfran replied humbly, bowing low.

Ezekiel seemed somewhat mollified by his humility, though his brow was still creased in suspicion. Caro had the distinct feeling this was not the end of the matter.

It appeared that like Oswin, Ezekiel favored dark wood and red in his decor, but instead of the baron's gaudy tastes, the grand duke's carpets and furnishings were of a refined crimson. Rather than oppressive, it was warm and cozy, and Caro instantly felt at ease.

"Milady!" The familiar voice reached Caro's ears.

"Lottie?"

The maid raced through the hall, holding her skirts. Her ringlets were no longer so neatly curled, nor her uniform starched and pressed, but she was positively beaming. Caro's heart swelled with joy, and she searched for Gaius.

"Heya," he said, her gaze landing upon his handsome face and easy smile as he leaned against the banister.

"You made it!" Ezalia exclaimed.

"You wouldn't believe what we went through to get here," he said, sighing dramatically.

Ezekiel cleared his throat, silencing their rapid-fire conversation. "I believe introductions are in order. I would appreciate knowing the names of all the guests residing under my roof."

"Of course, Your Grace," Caro replied, indicating each of her companions. "After splitting up from Gaius and Lottie, I departed with Ezalia and Stelian, and we ventured into the Esaphis Desert. There, we encountered the Omaira tribe and met their prince, Khalil. In exchange for lending their support, I agreed to let Khalil accompany us."

Gaius appeared to be mentally ticking off his fingers, while Lottie was staring at the handsome desert prince, a light blush coloring her cheeks.

"We then traveled to Biding to seek Alenard's goodwill." Caro glanced at Morfran. "While there, the commander revealed he had turned on Zhelyas and devoted himself to my service. Ines accompanied him as his confidante, and naturally joined us as well."

Ezekiel gave a crisp nod, scanning each of their faces. "There is no need to stand on ceremony. Make yourselves comfortable. Guest rooms will be prepared to your preferences; you need only convey them to my steward."

"Thank you, Your Grace," Caro said on behalf of the others.

"If I may speak with you for a moment, Your Majesty, it will not take long." Ezekiel shut the heavy door of his office, then turned to Caro.

"I never had the chance to express my condolences for your parents' death," he began. "Your father was a wise and good king. And your mother, my dear Cecilia..." His voice cracked, and he collected himself with evident difficulty. "My rank does not allow for great shows of emotion, but here in private, I can be just your grandfather, grieving the loss of his beloved child. I assure you, without a shadow of a doubt, that I shall do whatever is in my power to avenge their deaths and restore you to the throne."

He sank to one knee, leaning upon the cane for support. Caro's heart broke to see her noble grandfather abasing himself so.

"Rise, Lord Ezekiel," she said gently. "I ask only that you be my pillar of strength and advise me when I am lost and unsure of how to proceed."

Ezekiel rose and gave a crooked smile, his eyes twinkling beneath his heavy brows. "You are so much like your mother," he said fondly. "Impulsive, a little reckless, but with a heart as big as the sky."

Caro embraced Ezekiel, flustering the indomitable old duke, and he wrapped his arms around her.

"I am truly grateful you sought me out. It means more than you know."

There was a long moment of silence after this heartfelt declaration, and Caro could tell a fond reunion was not all he had called her into his office for.

Ezekiel cleared his throat. "Your Majesty, I respect your wishes. You know that," he began, and Caro sighed inwardly.

"I suppose this is about Morfran?"

The name caused a dark scowl to bloom on his face. "Will you hear me out?" Ezekiel asked, his lips set in a thin line.

"Very well, Your Grace. Because we have come here for your aid, it's only fair you be allowed to air your grievances."

Ezekiel gave a slight nod. "As I have been here since the funeral, I only heard what transpired in the capital through secondhand means," he continued. "After your escape, Zhelyas established his dominance with a swift demonstration, and one of the nobles was executed for defying him."

This was news to Caro, and she was saddened at the loss of one of her court, but she had steeled herself against the possibility.

"Did Morfran kill him?" Caro asked, though she dreaded the answer.

"No," Ezekiel admitted. "However, while General Luther was tasked with finding you, Commander Morfran was dispatched as Zhelyas's thug, subduing the populace. There were even rumors he was conducting a secret investigation within the palace."

Morfran had said as much back at the garrison. He was greatly feared as a former assassin, so it stood to reason Zhelyas would have hired him for unsavory purposes.

Ezekiel had fallen silent, and Caro realized her conflicted expression must be intimidating. "Go on," she said.

"When Gaius arrived, he related to me what had occurred at Ockbridge, and how you were taken prisoner by Commander Morfran. He expressed some disbelief, I might add, that the man had released you without incident, and I must confess I share his feelings."

Ezekiel was growing close to a breach in etiquette by interrogating a royal personage, but Caro couldn't blame him.

"Upon discovering my identity, Morfran struck a deal with me," she explained. "I would pretend to be his servant, and when the chance presented itself, he would help me escape."

Ezekiel looked mildly aghast at the notion of a queen doing manual labor, but he apparently decided to gloss over that point. "And?"

"Things didn't exactly go smoothly, but he was tolerant of my mistakes and protected me from the other officers. He had multiple chances to punish or mistreat me, and I wouldn't have been able to do anything about it, given the precarious position I was in. My fate would have been far worse had he turned me into Zhelyas, but he didn't do that either. When he received word Luther was approaching, he fulfilled his promise and let me go." Caro paused. "That's why, when he showed up at Alenard's estate and swore his allegiance—I believed him."

"But weren't you the slightest bit concerned?" Ezekiel pressed. "How could you be convinced so easily of his sincerity?"

Caro pondered the question. "There were two additional factors, and you've met both of them."

Ezekiel frowned. "I have?"

"First, Khalil, the prince of the Omaira tribe from the Esaphis Desert. He told me Morfran was once a member of an

330

assassin clan called the Sharir, but he also related a story about a young boy whose tears Morfran soothed."

"And the other?"

"The blind woman, Ines."

"I admit, she has puzzled me as a choice of traveling companion," Ezekiel mused. "I believe you mentioned she was Morfran's confidante?"

Caro nodded. "She looked after me at the garrison. When I asked why she served Morfran, she confided that he had saved her life, rescuing her when she was lost and alone. When he came to pledge his service, he brought Ines with him rather than leave her behind. Whatever anyone might say about him, I have faith in her intuition most of all."

Ezekiel worked his jaw, digesting her words. "You're certain you trust him?"

"I am," Caro replied.

"Then I will not question your decision again, Your Majesty," he said, bowing. "Though you will forgive me if I reserve judgment for myself."

"I understand from Lord Gaius you require funding for this venture Vittorius has proposed," Ezekiel said. "I have numerous connections, and there are many who owe me favors."

Caro had no doubt of that. The old man was as shrewd as his daughter. "Thank you, Your Grace, but it would be best to pursue such avenues discreetly. I don't want to alert Zhelyas to my intentions."

"What about a ball?"

Ezalia blinked at Alenard, who had made the unexpected suggestion, then nodded. "A ball is a good idea. Father would be able to converse with his contacts in relative privacy. Isn't the Springtide Ball coming up soon?"

"Yes, in a little over a week's time," Ezekiel replied.

"That's perfect. It's a masquerade, so none of us would be recognized. You should be right at home, Morfran." Ezalia added with a slight smirk.

He pursed his lips at her subtle barb but didn't reply.

"What about Zhelyas?" Caro inquired. "If he were in attendance, we wouldn't recognize him either."

Alenard shrugged. "Don't worry about him. He's been holed up in that castle for weeks."

"I wouldn't be so sure," Ezekiel said grimly. "I have received word from my agents that Zhelyas, Luther, and the witch are on the move."

"I see," Caro mused. It seemed to confirm Morfran's private suspicions about the storm's nature. "I still believe it's worth the risk. Your Grace, can you arrange for personal invitations to be sent out to those you feel will be amenable to my cause? It might be an imposition, but I would like them to know what they are getting themselves into."

"That is an excellent idea. If Your Majesty permits, I shall draw them up immediately. Ezalia, if you would assist."

Ezekiel bowed, and they set off to his office.

"A bal masqué..." Morfran murmured.

"You don't like parties?" Caro inquired.

"It's not that I'm averse to them, though I am admittedly not fond of crowds. I simply have not attended one in quite some time."

"Caro, what's a masquerade ball?" Khalil inquired, perplexed.

"A ball is a gathering where people get together to chat, exchange gossip, and often dance," Alenard explained with the air of a professor reading from a textbook. "The children of nobility are often debuted to society during these events, and alliances are formed between eager parents hoping to match them up with others of their social station."

Khalil scratched his head and nodded for Alenard to continue.

"A masquerade ball has the added intrigue of the guests being required to wear masks to obscure their faces. Sometimes it is for the sake of entertainment, and they do not try to conceal their identity; for others, it is a way to interact with no preconceptions. Some masks make it virtually impossible to tell who the other person is, while others are decorative and can be removed at will—such as by a coquettish lady luring a lover."

Caro thought she spied a longing glint in his eyes, as if Ezalia had done the same thing years ago.

"Few can afford such pageantry, and I believe masquerade balls have fallen out of favor at the royal palace, but they have always been a luxury of the Ducal Court of Agassey."

Khalil glanced up at Morfran, who remained stone-faced. "I see," he said, smiling. "So we get to pretend to be someone other than who we really are for a night."

One Man's Poison

Ezekiel mulled over his discussion with Caro. He couldn't make sense of it. In many ways, she was still a child who hadn't seen the true cruelties of the world, despite suffering so much already. He wanted to protect her from further pain, but how could he, when every word sounded like an old man's foolish worries?

He was sitting in his favorite spot on the porch, drinking his morning coffee and looking over his domain, the land he loved so dearly. There was a presence in the doorway, and he faltered, wondering how he should announce himself to a blind woman without startling her.

"Your Grace, I didn't mean to disturb you," Ines said smoothly, sparing him the attempt.

"Lady Ines, was it?"

She chuckled, a musical and gentle laugh. "Just Ines, Your Grace. I am no lady."

He hesitated. "You look familiar, Ines. Have we met somewhere before?"

"I'm afraid that would be quite unlikely."

Ezekiel nodded, but he couldn't quite shake the strange sense of recognition.

"Agassey truly is beautiful," Ines said, bringing his thoughts back to the present, and Ezekiel's eyes scanned the horizon. Endless rolling green hills, dots of white sheep tended by their shepherds, a glassy winding river, the opera house in all its magnificent glory.

"I do agree, but...?" He trailed off, realizing his question would be intolerably impolite.

"How do I know, when I can't see?" Ines finished with an amused smile.

"Forgive me, that was rude."

"Not at all. However, just because I have been deprived of one sense, does not mean I cannot discern beauty with the others." Ines turned her face to the sky. "The sun is warm and pleasant, not oppressively hot. The air smells clean and fresh, and a crisp breeze tickles my skin. I hear the bleating of the sheep, the soft rippling of water, and the dulcet tones of music in the distance. All of this is beauty, Your Grace. I simply perceive it differently."

Ezekiel stared at her, dumbfounded, then realized he should say something. "I understand now. I beg your pardon."

Ines smiled. "I can tell you are a good man, Your Grace. You care for these people, and the queen, deeply. You have a strong sense of responsibility and morality, which is doubtless why you shared strained words with Morfran when we arrived."

"You heard that?"

"I did."

Ezekiel deliberated over his next question. "Her Majesty tells me you served together in the garrison. Tell me, what did you think of her then?"

Ines sat down in the chair beside him. "She was lonely. I didn't know she was the queen at the time, but she had already endured something so traumatic it set roots in her soul. She blamed herself and she wept, even when she thought I couldn't tell. But even so, she displayed remarkable strength. I admired that, and I missed her when she left," Ines confessed. "When we were reunited and I found out she was the queen, it made me respect her even more."

"Commander Morfran didn't tell you beforehand?" Ezekiel inquired, puzzled.

"No. Why do you ask?"

"It wasn't strange? For him to announce you were leaving, without telling you where you were going or why?"

Ines let out a soft sigh. "I trust him implicitly, Your Grace. I always have."

Ezekiel had an inkling why Caro placed so much faith in this woman's wisdom. He found himself doubting every thought that had crossed his mind since Ines's arrival, and it humbled him.

He rose. "I am grateful, Ines, that you saw fit to confide in me. If I have caused offense, I ask your forgiveness."

"None taken, I assure you."

Ezekiel passed Morfran in the hall, and the black-clad man bowed low. He had been wearing a leather mask when he arrived, but had returned to the silver one for which he was so famous since he no longer feared being recognized in the townships along the way.

"Commander," Ezekiel said stiffly, and his conversation with Ines drifted back to him. "I admit it is somewhat difficult for me to reconcile the image of the queen's loyal servant with your fearsome reputation, but both Her Majesty and your companion have convinced me of your sincerity. I will therefore place my trust in you as well. Don't disappoint me— or the queen."

His voice had a hard edge, and Morfran bowed again, slightly deeper as if to profess his solemn oath.

"You have my word, Your Grace."

"Ines?" Ezalia inquired from the door. "I saw you talking with my father. Is everything all right?"

Ines smiled, her tense shoulders relaxing. "Everything's fine, Ezalia, thank you."

Ezalia wrapped a shawl around her bare arms and rubbed them vigorously. It was the onset of spring, but there was still a lingering chill of winter in the northern highlands.

"I'm glad to hear it. He looked rather chastened, actually. Not many people can do that." She chuckled. "I'm impressed."

Ines placed her hand on Ezalia's. "Your father's a good man. I can tell where you get your kindness from."

Ezalia cherished her warm touch and flattering words. "What were you talking about anyway?"

"Morfran," Ines replied, and Ezalia let out a knowing sigh.

"I wondered when he would broach that subject. What did you tell him?"

"Everything I know," Ines said with a small shrug, "which I confess isn't much. I trust him because he saved my life without asking for any reward. A blind woman is hardly a useful companion for an assassin, but he's kept me by his side all this time."

"Does he trust you in return?" Ezalia inquired, intrigued.

"Yes." Ines nodded. "I wasn't lying when I said I don't know who he is. I've only ever known him by the names Morfran or Mukhif, which was his Sharir name long before we met. He is haunted by the trauma in his past, and his devotion to Queen Caro is genuine. But other than that... he's only revealed fragments."

Ezalia's curiosity was piqued. "Such as?"

Morfran emerged to find Ezalia waiting for him in the hall. He had been aware she was watching him, her gaze following as he passed by, but he hadn't anticipated such a bold move as this.

"Is there something I can do for you, Duchess?" he asked with just the right trace of deference.

She leaned against the wall, arms crossed, and jerked her head toward the stairwell which led to the roof.

Morfran nodded and followed. "Why are you dogging my steps?" he inquired somewhat more forcefully.

"I know who you are," she stated.

He kept his expression neutral. "Do you?"

"It took me a while to piece together, but the puzzle is fitting into place."

Morfran stared at her, reading the truth in her eyes. "I would advise you not to confide your suspicions to anyone else. My identity is a secret for a reason, not merely my pride. I'm sure you realize that—*if* you have correctly deduced it."

Ezalia smirked, seeing past his façade of indifference. "So what now? Will you kill me?"

"No," he said gravely. "I swear all will be revealed when the queen sits once more upon the throne which is rightfully hers. I respectfully ask for you to wait until then."

Ezalia nodded. "Very well, my lips are sealed. I just wanted you to be aware someone will hold you accountable for keeping Caro in the dark."

"I shall bear that in mind, Duchess. Now, may we go back inside? The weather is foul out here."

As they parted, Morfran couldn't help feeling a trace of worry. If Ezalia had put the pieces together, others might as well... perhaps even Caro?

He shook his head, dismissing the notion. He had never met a person as cunning as Ezalia, and didn't think anyone else could leap to the same conclusions. Morfran was content his secret was safe.

Dirty Linen

Arvind was sore and exhausted. He slouched in his chair and leaned his head back, rubbing his neck.

"A moment, Your Highness?"

His eye twitched, and he glanced at the door to see a noblewoman standing there. She was not of high rank, the niece or some such of a foreign dignitary. She had sharp features, dark hair swept up with emerald hair pins, and piercing deep green eyes.

"Lady Lobelia Anthusa, isn't that right?" he inquired, searching the crevices of his brain for her name. He seemed to recall she had a younger sister, Desca or something.

"That's correct."

Arvind sighed inwardly. He was too tired to put up with this. "What can I do for you?"

"It's not what you can do for me, but what I can do for you," she replied with a seductive lilt, and sidled up to his desk. "I have a secret, you see."

She was wearing a dress of forest green, so dark it was almost black, and the fabric shifted in the light as she moved. She sat upon the edge, tracing the wood grain with the tip of her painted fingernail.

"Oh?" Arvind gave his most charming smile, even though he wanted to strangle her. "Do tell."

Lobelia licked her lips. "It's about Earl Malcolm Dahl. He's been very *naughty*."

Arvind narrowed his eyes as she related the details of the coalition and the activities which had been undertaken in his absence.

"Now see, I don't want to be the one to spread bad rumors, but the earl's going about telling people you can't be trusted. I can't imagine why he would say such indelicate things."

He had been aware of many of the facts she told him, but this came as a particularly unpleasant surprise. "Thank you, Lady Anthusa. I am most grateful for your confidence."

She smiled and slid off the desk. "It is my pleasure, Your Highness." She gave a bow, then sauntered out of the room.

Arvind's entire body trembled with fury. "Bring me Earl Dahl," he snapped to his guards, and paced until they returned with their detainee in tow.

Malcolm flinched as Arvind's fist slammed the desk. "What did I tell you?" he growled. "You were to mind your own business and not breathe a word of what you knew."

"I didn't mean—"

Arvind cut off Malcolm's protest with a sharp gesture and waved the poetry book in his face. "I was aware of what you've been doing, your secret little humanitarian act, and I permitted it. But when you undermine my authority, you breed disrespect!"

He paused to collect himself. "I think it's time you learn the consequences of defiance."

Lobelia smirked to herself as she overheard the terse exchange, then ducked out of sight as Malcolm was dragged down the back hall toward the dungeon.

"Perfect."

"What's that?"

She turned at the voice and smiled at the man standing before her. "Ah, Major, were you eavesdropping on me?" she teased.

He leaned languidly against the wall, subtly invading her personal space. "Never, my dear," Sejic jibed back. "Everything is going as planned, then?"

"Malcolm just needs a little push, and he'll be putty in my hands."

"As long as that's all it is," Sejic said, a trace of jealousy coloring his tone.

Lobelia curled her arm around his neck. "I couldn't have done this without you. You were the one who figured out their little plot."

"So what do you intend to do now?"

"After Malcolm returns from the punishment inflicted by Arvind, he'll be much more pliable. I'll assure him of my continued fidelity, and then tip the scales ever so slightly in my favor. It won't take much. The entire castle is abuzz with tension, the nobles most of all, and those involved are already paranoid of being discovered. A little shift in their priorities—from philanthropists to renegades—will be easy."

Lobelia licked her lips, flush with triumph. "For supplanting the usurper, we will both be rewarded beyond our wildest dreams."

Delusions of Grandeur

Caro nervously adjusted her mask as she made her way into the opera house. Every inch was dripping with gold leaf and gleaming champagne-colored marble, the vaulted ceilings embellished with intricate mouldings and murals to rival those in the palace itself, all depicting music and the arts. Gilded statues of graceful nymphs danced upon the stairways whilst lifting great candelabras into the air, guiding visitors up the lush green carpeting and casting everything in a warm, crystalline glow.

As the Springtide Ball was a celebration to welcome the new season, the building was bedecked in an endless array of flowers which had been grown in a greenhouse to maintain their pristine beauty against the lingering traces of frost. At every corner was a lush arrangement of vibrant pink and yellow blossoms in sculpted marble vases, while garlands cascaded down the railings and twined around the pillars.

The lively music of the viola, cello, and harp trickled into the hall, accompanied by the haunting notes of a glass armonica. Even though the ball had started in the evening, it was so bright it could be the middle of the day, and Caro was awed by the dazzling beauty.

A portrait stood by the entrance to the ballroom, and she slowed to gaze up at it. The woman was wearing a long, theatrical cobalt dress and a silver circlet in her coiffed hair, dark brown curls trailing over one shoulder. Her deep blue eyes seemed to stare out of the painting, a serene smile on her lips.

"My mother, Mavella," Ezalia said, placing a hand on Caro's shoulder.

"My grandmother?"

Ezalia nodded. "This building was in disrepair, so Father purchased its debt and had it restored for her as a wedding gift. He went to every single one of her performances," Ezalia said wistfully. "Ceci and I played here as children. It was a like a second home to us, and I'm happy you get the chance to see it. Mavella died when you were little, but she loved you."

Caro lifted a finger, tracing the portrait's features from afar. They were softer and more refined than her own, but still she felt like she was looking in a mirror.

"Will I be that beautiful when I'm older?" she wondered aloud.

Ezalia lovingly tucked a stray curl back into place. "You're beautiful now, dear."

Caro had preferred to wear trousers since her flight from the capital, but she had to admit she felt rather elegant in the ball gown. The pale gold satin set off her green eyes, and her hair was braided with jeweled combs in such a way it wasn't immediately apparent it was cut short. The ensemble was far too plain to be compared to her royal attire, but its multiple petticoats, underpinnings, and flounces made Caro feel once more like a queen, not a fugitive on the run.

Ezalia's stunning gown was white, the bodice overlaid with red lace matching the crimson roses and feathers in her raven hair. Ines wore a simple lavender dress with tumbles of tulle cascading down the skirt. Lottie, thrilled to be attending a party, was wearing a dress of cheery apricot with tiered bows, her ringlets once more perky for the occasion.

Not to be outdone, the men wore elegant outfits that equaled, or even rivaled, those of the female patrons. Alenard's suit was red with a draping white lace cravat and a large red hat—the opposite of, but perfectly matching, Ezalia's dress. Khalil had been delighted to discover that fashions reminiscent of his people's in the desert were popular at such festive occasions, and so had no trouble finding a high-necked tunic and pantaloons in sky blue with silver trim. Stelian had opted for a more muted blue, the cut of his jacket resembling that of a soldier, but with far more lace than would be practical for combat. Gaius's coat was pale yellow with gold braid upon the sleeves, his long blond hair tied back with a trailing ivory ribbon.

As the host, Ezekiel's outfit was the most flamboyant: a long coat of deep green velvet accented with violet and a purple satin cap with a fountain of vibrant peacock plumes. He carried his usual cane, though tonight it was topped with the long nose and bells of a jester. Everyone would recognize him, but that was precisely the point.

Gaius waved off another hopeful partner. "My card's full."

"You should dance with one of them," Ines said. She looked radiant in her lavender gown; the color suited her pale features.

"You wouldn't guess it from my innate grace, but I have two left feet when it comes to dancing," he replied cheerfully. "Unless you wish to dance? Then I'm all yours."

Ines shook her head. "I cannot dance, my lord. Surely that must be obvious."

He had observed the blind woman was uncomfortable in such a crowded space and had been hesitant to join in the revelry, only doing so at Ezalia's prodding.

"Sure you can," Gaius said, and stepped closer. "You needn't see your partner to dance. Just *feel* them."

He lifted her hand in his own, then pulled her close with the other. Her heart was beating madly, pulsing against his skin.

"There. Now feel when I move." He slowly stepped backward, and she took a hurried step forward. "Now back." He moved toward her, and she shuffled backward. "See, that was easy. You're a natural."

Ines smiled, a dazzling expression that lit up her face and outshone all the lights in the room.

They danced that way for a time. It wasn't elegant in the eyes of a critic, but Gaius was delighted at Ines's sheer joy, as if she had discovered a new sense of freedom.

She stopped finally and took a deep breath. "You have worn me out, Lord Gaius. I think I must rest awhile."

"I'll join you, if you can suffer this old fool's company. Besides, I wouldn't want to leave a lovely lady alone. That would be ungentlemanly."

"As long as you don't mind," Ines murmured.

Gaius snatched two champagne flutes from a passing waiter, placing one in her hand. "Not at all. It's more fun to watch everyone else, anyway."

Nearby, he spotted Lottie standing at the edge of the dance floor, looking nervous.

Stelian cleared his throat and held out his hand with a short bow. "Would you like to dance, Lottie?" He shifted his gaze, blushing. When he looked back, she was smiling.

"Sure," she said sweetly.

Neither of them knew how to dance well. As a bodyguard, Stelian only took part in balls when obliged to, and as a maid, Lottie had served rather than participated in such events at Oswin's estate. Still, they looked adorable together, trying to keep step with the music, Stelian wincing occasionally when Lottie trod on his toe.

Gaius's attention turned to Ezalia, who was spinning with Alenard on the dance floor in rapturous bliss. He'd never seen her so happy before, and was pleased she had been reunited with the love of her life. Once upon a time, he might have longed for that role himself, for she was a shining star at court, unpretentious and witty, but now he valued her friendship more than anything.

So deliriously in love were the two, that they occasionally bumped into another dancing couple. Ezalia would give a hurried apology, then giggle with Alenard at the social faux pas.

Gaius glanced around for Khalil and finally spotted him in a corner nearby, surrounded by a gaggle of adoring women. They kept saying how handsome and exotic he was, "a true desert prince." Gaius was flummoxed by their fascination, then remembered the recent tawdry novel by that name and chuckled inwardly, wondering if the poor boy had any clue.

Across the room, Gaius noticed Ezekiel was working his contacts as he'd promised. Caro stood off to the side, and they were deep in conversation with a woman in an iridescent orange gown. He recognized her as Baroness Uyria Ilyana of Dalry, a keen businesswoman and one of the wealthier landowners after Oswin.

Gaius let out a relieved sigh, and Ines cocked her head. "Ezekiel's doing his part. Let's leave the others to their fun."

Caro stood discreetly by Ezekiel's side as he plied the favors of his acquaintances. Some were surprised at the request, others outwardly hostile, but most were simply scared.

The Baroness Uyria Ilyana of Dalry, the most recent of their potential allies, shook her elegant head. She wore a gown of vibrant orange, the jewels studding her mask bright against her deep red hair.

"I'm deeply sorry, Your Majesty, but I cannot risk it. We've all heard what the king did to Oswin, but he was only punished because of his association with you. I have no wish to share his fate. If we keep our heads down, he'll take no notice of the rest of us."

"But surely—" Caro tried, and Uyria agitatedly fluttered her fan.

"My sincerest regrets, Your Majesty. Your Grace." With that, she gave a bow and swept off.

Caro sighed. That seemed to be the prevailing opinion, and even her grandfather, previously confident in his own clout, looked a little downtrodden.

"I'm sorry. I thought we would be able to convince at least one," he apologized.

"It's not your fault. I can hardly blame them. They have no stake in this," Caro said wearily. "If you'll excuse me, I'm going to sit down for a moment."

She made her way to an empty chair and sank into it morosely. Ezalia and Alenard were twirling upon the dance floor, as were Lottie and Stelian. Khalil was chatting animatedly with a number of ladies, while Gaius had struck up a conversation with Ines.

Caro hung her head, her chin in her hands. Why had she thought this would work? Because Alenard and Ezekiel had joined her, she had hoped others would do the same. She was naive. Of course her resistance against Zhelyas seemed hopeless, so nobody wanted to earn the ire of the usurper king. They were concerned with their own affairs, and she had nothing to offer as a reward for their fealty.

"May I have this dance?"

Caro looked up at the voice. In contrast to his usual armor, Morfran was wearing a sleek black jacket trimmed with purple ruffles and a maroon gem set at the center of his lace cravat, as well as a cloak of the most luxurious amethyst silk that rippled like wine in the candlelight.

However, it was his mask that inevitably drew her eye. Formed of glossy black feathers gleaming violet and indigo, it descended his cheeks, while the top jutted upward in the shape of raven's wings. While all the patrons, herself included, wore masks that complemented their attire—his was mesmerizing.

"Me?"

"If you so wish, milady," he said with a hint of a smirk about his lips.

Caro smiled, blinking away her tears. "That would be lovely."

They took their positions on the floor, and she placed her hand in his, lifting the hem of her skirt while he wrapped his arm securely behind her back.

Caro had learned to waltz at an early age. It was required for any lady of noble birth, but she had only danced with her instructors or young men of court—and never so closely as this. She felt a flush creep up her cheeks, and she was grateful for the cool evening breeze which wafted through the open windows.

"Are you unwell?" Morfran inquired.

"The scent of gardenias makes my head spin a little, that's all."

"That's a relief. I wouldn't want the dancing to make you dizzy."

His voice was light with amusement. Caro had seen so many sides of the man, but even when he was confiding in her, he always seemed guarded. Tonight, it was as if he'd shed all his illusions along with his black armor and was truly free.

Was this the real Morfran? The one Ines had described in her account of the past? Or the one who would give a sweet to a little desert boy to soothe his tears?

Caro fell easily into step with his stride as they glided across the floor. The way he held her in his strong arms was just like when she had ridden with him out of the garrison. Somehow, she knew he would keep her safe.

"I beg your pardon," a woman said tersely as Ezalia spun into her path.

"My apologies," Ezalia replied, then turned back to Alenard, giggling like a schoolgirl. "This is going on my permanent record: Lady Duchess can't keep up basic etiquette."

Alenard smiled. "Lady Ezalia has never done what everyone would consider 'proper.' She's fearless and beautiful, and that's what I love about her."

He leaned over to peck her on the nose, but at the last moment she tilted up her chin, catching his lips in a kiss.

The music slowed, and so did the pace of their dancing. Ezalia was relieved for the brief respite; she was quite breathless. The melody was a romantic one, and she and Alenard fell in step.

"This used to be our favorite song, remember?"

Ezalia nodded, the painful memories a mere twinge in her heart now. It was from the opera her mother used to perform,

Gisela and Darim, the instrumental version of the aria sung by the leading lady to her lover.

"Oh, that reminds me," Alenard said. "Do you remember back at the house, when we were talking about that legend and I was doing some research into it?"

That had been the night they had reaffirmed their love for each other. How could she forget?

"I finally remembered the final piece of the historical account."

Ezalia perked up. "Oh?"

"While the princess agreed to marry her betrothed, he could not forgive the king for sparing the desert rogue. Sometime later, during a hunting party, the king was killed, shot through the heart with an arrow. Her fiancé vanished that day, never to return. The haste with which he fled led many to speculate he was the culprit, and had murdered the king out of spite; after all, he was known as the best archer of the group," Alenard elaborated. "The princess took the throne and married another noble to further the royal line. She reportedly wrote in her diary that she had never forgotten her beloved desert rogue, but would obey her late brother's edict and not seek him out, even when she was free to marry. Her kingdom was looking to her for guidance, and that was her love now. When we were children, we went looking through the library here in the opera house, and that sparked my interest in the legend."

Ezalia's thoughts were no longer rooted upon their conversation. Something about the tale had struck a chord, and her thoughts were spinning.

She kissed him on the cheek. "Pardon me, love, but there's something I need to look into. I'll be back soon."

"Alenard? Where's Ezalia?" Gaius inquired as the lone member of the pair slunk off the dance floor, looking somewhat bewildered.

"She said she had to go do something. Then 'poof.'"

Gaius handed him a glass of spirits and patted him on the shoulder. "Women, eh? What can you do?"

"Ahem."

"Sorry, Ines, no offense."

Ezalia hated to leave Alenard standing alone on the dance floor, but that story had roused long-forgotten memories of times spent before they had fallen in love and been split apart by circumstance.

They had both been young when they first met, and constant companions throughout their youth. Alenard was passionate about history and so, when Ezalia had swiped the keys to the library annex where her father stored all his rare books, he had been most eager to see them.

Ezalia scoured the shelves, trying to conjure up those days long past.

"Your father has read all these?" Alenard had said, amazed.

"I doubt it," Ezalia replied, pleased at the effect her gift had upon her friend. "Some of them he acquired only recently, while others have been here for ages, so the ink is fading and even the titles on the spines are nearly unreadable."

She watched as Alenard perused the shelves. Ezekiel did not do something so crass as sort things alphabetically; his system was far more esoteric and complex than Ezalia could ever hope to decipher. He did, however, tend to group things thematically. Alenard paused in front of the historical fiction section, the adventure novels of which he was so fond.

"*Ladder of Swords*..." he murmured, indicating interesting titles. "*The Sunstone... The Mottled Wing... The Archer.*" He picked up the last book and flipped through it.

Ezalia ambled between the shelves, selecting *The Woman in Violet*, which sounded intriguing. She returned to his side a short while later, as he was replacing *The Archer* upon the shelf.

"Interesting?"

"Quite."

He hadn't said anything further, his attention diverted by another promising read. "Where is that book...? Ah, there."

Now, Ezalia spotted the tome she was looking for at the end of the shelf where it had been waiting for decades, after *Ladder of Swords* and *The Sunstone*. She flipped through the brittle pages, searching for a clue.

As Alenard had implied, *The Archer* was an account of the events which had inspired the legends. Written from the perspective of a firsthand observer, the author told of the princess's affair with the rogue, their parting, and the hunting incident with the king followed by her fiancé's flight—but it didn't stop there. The book posited the fiancé had then fled to a neighboring kingdom and married the daughter of a merchant, gaining fortune and prestige. And his name was...

Her finger lingered upon a particular paragraph. "So long ago... Could it be so simple?"

Ezalia recalled that a few months before the murder of Caro's parents, Gaius was attempting to instill into the young princess a sense of reverence for her family line. History had always been her weakest subject, so he had hauled out an old tapestry which hung in an abandoned, drafty part of the castle.

Caro coughed, wafting away the clouds of dust that billowed off the fabric as Gaius unrolled it. "Is this going to take long? I'm supposed to be sparring with Stelian."

"It will take as long as it takes," he chided, and Caro turned to Ezalia.

"History is important too, Caro," she said. "It may be in the past, but the events still affect us to this day. We can learn a lot from previous kings and their mistakes, so we don't repeat them."

Caro sighed, defeated.

"Here is where you are, and your parents, Their Royal Majesties. Hmm... There isn't much room left at the bottom. You may need to commission a new tapestry when you are queen," Gaius mused, staring at the small patch of blank fabric.

"Why don't we just sew more at the end?" Caro suggested, and giggled at Gaius's affronted look.

"This tapestry is a work of art!" he proclaimed, puffing up his chest. "Look here, this is your mother's family, Duchess Ezalia Mavella, her sister, and Grand Duke Ezekiel Garsiv. Perhaps you should tell him his descendants won't fit any more, so sorry."

Caro chuckled. "Point taken." She bent over the tapestry, careful not to lean on the surface as Gaius sucked in a sharp breath. "So how far back does it go?"

"All the way to your great-great-great grandmother's time," he said. "Queen Malianme." He indicated the top of the tapestry which formed the highest "branch" of the tree.

"What's this?" Caro pointed to the second set of "leaves," where the fabric looked to have been damaged, the weft threads hastily rewoven.

"I never noticed that before," Gaius said, scratching his head. "A royal scandal, I suppose? Records from that time are spotty, but Queen Malianme's son Guillam died without an heir, so his sister Guinevre became queen in his stead, issuing the current royal line."

Caro peered closer, her nose brushing the fabric to read the name which had been scratched out. "Tarthan... Ralston?"

Ezalia remembered hearing a sound at the door, but when she had looked, nobody was there. Zhelyas must have been passing by and overheard the lesson. It wouldn't have been out of the realm of possibility that Caro would make the connection between the disgraced Tarthan Ralston and his descendant Zhelyas Ralston. Still, it was unlikely. Ezalia and Gaius were forever reminding her of the names and titles of those nobles she was to receive at soirées.

But for Zhelyas, likely unaware of his own scandalous history until then, it must have planted a seed of doubt in his mind. He had pursued the matter, discovering the truth for himself. If Tarthan hadn't fled, he would have been Guinevre's husband, and by some stretch of logic—Zhelyas would be king.

Ezalia wondered how he had felt every time one of the court ladies gushed about *The Desert Prince* or the critics celebrated another masterful performance of the opera. It must have eaten him up inside until he grew bitter and vindictive. The king and queen stood in his way, so they had to go. Then when Caro, a mere seventeen-year-old girl, became queen, that was the opportunity he needed.

Her gaze scanned the page, registering the contents. She hesitated, then ripped it out.

The conductor declared a short recess for the musicians to take a well-earned break.

"Shall we rest as well?" Morfran suggested.

Caro nodded. Her feet were sore, but she was having a wonderful time. She had almost forgotten why they were at Agassey in the first place. She sat in a chair on the sidelines and wiggled her toes in her shoes.

"I didn't think you would be such an excellent dancer."

"As are you, milady," Morfran quipped back at the jibe, sinking into the seat beside her.

Caro smirked. "Well, I *am* a queen. What's your excuse?" She whispered so only he could hear, and he smiled at her pompous words.

"Parties can be like battlegrounds," he replied. "Alliances are formed, deals made, and fates sealed, all within the space of a single evening."

Caro stared at him. She had never envisioned a ball as such a momentous occasion. Even with his light tone, she wasn't sure if he was joking. "I'm sure you have danced with many rich and beautiful ladies," she said coyly.

The corner of his mouth twitched. "Ah, but who else could compare to my own?"

She was about to inquire as to his precise meaning when the conductor climbed onstage to announce the music was resuming.

"Shall we?" Morfran said, rising and offering his hand. "Or perhaps you would like to dance with another young man? I have seen many watching you admiringly."

Caro placed her hand in his. "They'll just have to be disappointed."

As Zhelyas sauntered into the ballroom, his attention was drawn by a woman who had entered mere moments before. She appeared out of breath and held a yellowed page of parchment in her hand. He barely glimpsed it as she folded it up and tucked it into her dress.

Putting these events to the back of his mind, he turned to Luther. "Find out what you can. I want to know if Caro has been seen around these parts and whether Ezekiel is helping her, as I suspect."

Luther nodded in his skull mask and disappeared into the crowd.

"Do you have any doubt?" Veena inquired, looking every part the witch in her striking wine-red gown.

"He's Ezalia's father, so I have to assume he'll take Caro's side. However, if there is even the smallest chance he could be convinced to become my supporter instead, it would be worth it. The Grand Duke Ezekiel Garsiv is an influential name to have on one's side."

Zhelyas's forehead began to sweat beneath the mask. Leather and gold with the face of a horned beast, he hadn't been able to resist it for the occasion—although he wondered in retrospect if it was perhaps too obvious. He didn't care. Even if Caro and her cohorts guessed who he was, they couldn't escape him in such a public venue.

His thoughts returned to the strange actions of the woman from before, and his gaze searched the hall for her. She had made her way across the room and was now interrupting a couple who were dancing. Rather than cut in, however, she took the girl by the hand and led her to the sidelines.

Curious, Zhelyas skirted the edge of the dance floor, ducking behind a pillar a few feet away as she withdrew the paper from her dress and unfolded it, her hands shaking as she spoke. What Zhelyas saw made his blood run cold: the couped head of a growling wolf, displayed upon a pair of crossed swords.

The Ralston crest.

"Hey, Ezzy," Gaius greeted, lifting his champagne flute. He appeared to be tipsy, and she wondered how many glasses he'd had.

She was still clutching the incriminating page in her hand, and she folded it up, tucking it in her bosom. "Where's Allen?"

"Seeing he was free, your father recruited him to back up his donation pitch."

Ezalia glanced across the room to where Ezekiel was chatting up another of his acquaintances. Alenard was by his side looking utterly bored, yet trying hard not to show it. She wanted to rescue him, but she had other worries on her mind.

"Where's Caro?"

Gaius jerked his head toward the dance floor. It appeared Morfran and Caro had been taking a break on the sidelines as the musicians rested their instruments. Now that the music was starting back up, they were resuming a waltz.

"Getting rather chummy, aren't they?" Gaius mumbled.

Ezalia frowned, conflicted. It was then she noticed three new guests enter the ballroom. Two men and a woman, all in impeccable formal dress and masks fit for the occasion—but for some reason they made Ezalia uneasy.

The first wore a long, black velvet robe trimmed in gilded lace, a triangular hat, and a mask of burnished gold with large protruding horns. On his arm was a woman in a silk gown of deep burgundy, with a black veil and a delicate lace mask resembling bat wings. The third was a man with orange pantaloons, waistcoat, and a box hat with a long tassel, his white mask disconcertingly shaped like a skull with diamonds for teeth.

Ezalia glanced at Khalil, who looked like he was about to faint. "What is it?" she whispered as he disentangled himself from his gaggle of admirers.

"That's Veena," Khalil replied, his eyes wide.

"Veena?" Ezalia vaguely recalled the name of the woman in Hadiya's warning. "So then... that must be Zhelyas, and Luther with him."

"Do you think they've noticed us?" Khalil asked.

Ezalia shook her head. "Just don't make a scene. Quietly inform the others, and I will tell Morfran and Caro."

"Ezalia, what is it?" Caro asked, unnerved by her aunt's intensity.

"I need to tell you something," Ezalia replied in a hushed voice. "First, though—Morfran. You can trust him. From now on, don't leave his side."

Caro furrowed her brows. "What do you mean?"

Ezalia ignored her, glancing around like a nervous rabbit. "It's not safe to talk here."

As Ezalia pulled her farther from the ball, Caro found herself in an unfamiliar place. "Where are we?"

"This door leads to the crossover where the diva can dash to her dressing room after her performance, then join the guests at the post-opera soirée without having to evade all her adoring fans. We're behind the stage with all the rigging for lighting and backdrops."

Caro stopped in her tracks. "What's this about, Aunt Ez?"

"I've discovered something that could explain everything."

Just then, there came the sound of heavy footsteps.

"Damn, he's here," Ezalia cursed, grabbing Caro's hand and racing up the steps.

Morfran was wondering why Ezalia and Caro were taking so long, when he was approached by Gaius.

"Lovely party, isn't it?" the physician said with false cheer.

He frowned, and Gaius leaned close.

"Turn around. Khalil says that's Veena. Do you recognize her?"

Morfran resisted snapping his neck and forced himself to glance casually over his shoulder. She was wearing a modest dress and a black veil draped over her ivory hair, but it was her. "Yes, that's the sorceress Veena."

"Ezalia went to tell Caro," Gaius supplied.

"Then why haven't they come back?" A more disconcerting fact occurred to Morfran. "If Veena's here, then Zhelyas must be, too." He bit his lip hard. "Go find the grand duke and see what's to be done. I'll get Lady Ezalia and the queen."

Ezalia and Caro were rapidly running out of scaffolding.

Zhelyas pounded up the stairs behind them as they reached the edge of the platform and peered down. Approximately ten feet below was an alcove where ropes and winches were stored, along with a large stack of canvas material.

Caro sized up the distance, wondering if they could jump it. She turned to see Ezalia staring at her.

"You wouldn't run away, even if I asked you to."

"What—?" Caro's question was cut off as Ezalia squeezed her shoulders, then pushed.

"Forgive me," Ezalia whispered.

Eyes wide with shock, Caro toppled backward off the platform.

Zhelyas mounted the final few steps and stared at Ezalia, perceiving what she had done. He glanced over the edge at Caro, who lay unconscious upon the pile of canvas below, then advanced upon Ezalia, his sword drawn. She backed into the wall behind her, the blade's tip pressed into her sternum.

"Give me the document."

Ezalia hesitated a moment, then reached into her bosom and pulled out the paper.

Upon the page, amid the incriminating evidence, was the Ralston crest. In the days of Guinevre, Ralston had been a distinguished noble family. Over the intervening years, the fashion of noble names had been replaced by parental lineage and the surnames dropped and made defunct. After that fateful day, Zhelyas had discovered Ralston was a hereditary name passed down to his father. He had inherited it too, along with the burden of his ancestor's crime.

Zhelyas snatched it from her hand and read it, his eyes darting across the page. "Is this the only copy?" he demanded, waving it in her face.

"Yes, I tore it from the book." The ragged edges were clear proof of her claim.

He crumpled it up in his fist, then it burst into scarlet flame. "Show me," he hissed, nudging the sword to emphasize his point.

"Fine," Ezalia said with a sharp sigh. "Follow me."

Ezalia led Zhelyas through the scaffolding to the rear of the auditorium. Ever present was the warning of the sword in his grasp, and the unknown quantity of the magic he now wielded.

When they reached the library, she unlocked it, then led him to the annex.

"You know this place well."

"My mother was a renowned opera singer, and she often performed here."

"How sweet," Zhelyas said snidely.

Ezalia ran her fingers along each of the faded spines until she found the one she was looking for. She felt a brief pang of remorse as she handed over one of her father's precious books, but she'd learned all she needed to. Now she had to stay alive to pass on that knowledge.

Zhelyas flipped through it recklessly, his expression growing darker, until he found the place where she had torn out the page.

"I know who you are, Zhelyas Ralston."

Zhelyas looked up and set the book aflame, the pages curling as they were consumed by magic fire. "And now you must die, Duchess."

Ezalia smirked at the hollow threat. "Did you think I came here without an escape?" she said, shaking her head with mock disappointment. "I have played in this building since I was a child. I know all its secrets."

While he had been distracted by his conquest, she had felt along the base of the middle shelf, fumbling for a concealed lever. Now, she thumbed the device, triggering a sliding panel to open in the wall, and darted inside.

Zhelyas howled with rage as it sealed itself behind her.

There was a sharp banging, presumably as Zhelyas struck the door with his sword, then a sizzling sound as he tried to use his magic fire to sear the pressed metal—with little success.

It was a tighter fit than when she was a little girl playing with Cecilia in the library, both of them hiding from the adults. Ezalia missed her little sister and those carefree days spent together, but her niece needed her now. She shifted to her knees in the cramped space, swallowing the unease it engendered, then scooted down the passageway that connected it to the adjoining room.

Ezalia emerged in a musty storage closet stuffed with long-forgotten props and costumes. The blue dress from her mother's portrait hung in the corner with the silver coronet, as well as the backdrop of a romantic starry night.

She settled herself amongst the trappings and planned her next move. She would lie low for a while until Zhelyas's energy was spent and he wearied of searching for her, or was pulled away by other matters. Then she would rejoin Caro and the others and reveal the earth-shattering secret she had discovered.

Morfran followed the trail to the rear of the opera house.

"Your Majesty!" He listened, then called out again, "Queen Caro!"

Morfran heard a groan and mounted the steps of the scaffolding two at a time. He saw her then, in the alcove below. He leaped down and crouched by her side.

"Are you all right?" he asked, supporting her as she sat up gingerly.

"Zhelyas..." she managed, winded. "He's here, and he chased us..."

Morfran frowned, his worst fears confirmed.

"We have to rescue Ezalia." Caro attempted to stand, but she swayed on her feet.

"You're too unsteady to go anywhere," Morfran remonstrated, catching her before she fell.

"But—"

Ignoring her spluttering protests, he swept her into his arms. "If Zhelyas is at the ball, then we need to get you to safety at once."

Zhelyas, livid at Ezalia's trickery, returned to the place where Caro had tumbled off the edge—but she too was gone.

He stormed back into the hall. Luther had rejoined Veena, and they shared a nervous glance as he strode toward them.

"We're leaving," he snapped without slowing his pace, and they hurried to follow.

Once outside, Zhelyas spun toward the opera house, seething with rage. "Burn it to the ground!"

Veena gave him a scathing look. "I will not be responsible for the loss of so many lives. This is your doing, not mine."

Under Veena's tutelage, his magic had grown powerful, but not for a task so massive as this. He turned to Luther.

"B-but it's a historical landmark—" Luther stammered, trembling as Zhelyas fixed him with his murderous gaze.

"I don't want a single splinter remaining. Is that clear?"

"Y-yes, sire."

Luther gave a shaky nod and called forth the soldiers under his command. Each had been outfitted with a portable weapon designed to replicate the fiery breath of a dragon. They were particularly destructive, and Zhelyas watched with sinister pleasure as the tongues of flame were expelled from the maw of the metal beast, spreading rapidly across the ground and up the walls, devouring it whole.

Alenard and Gaius were discussing what to do next when Ines looked up, closing her eyes and furrowing her brow.

"Something's not right."

"What do you mean?" Gaius asked. She had been silent since the revelation that Zhelyas had appeared in their midst.

"There's an unpleasant smell."

"Unpleasant how?"

"Maybe... like a lamp which has tipped over and spilled its oil."

Gaius stared at her a moment, then lifted his chin and sniffed the air. "It's very faint. I'm amazed you could pick up on it."

"It's what I do," Ines quipped, then sobered. "But what is it?"

He pondered, then met Alenard's alarmed gaze. "You don't think—?"

"He wouldn't!"

Gaius felt a pit form in his stomach. "Tell Ezekiel we need to get everyone out of here. I'll wait for Morfran."

Alenard, with Ines on his arm, crossed the room to where Ezekiel was sitting by the fireplace and whispered in his ear.

The grand duke paled until he was white as a sheet, then rose and clapped his hands loudly. The musicians ceased their music, stray notes whining into silence.

"May I have your attention. I'm sorry, but there seems to be a bit of a disturbance outside. Please leave the hall quickly and in an orderly fashion."

"What's going on?" Khalil inquired of Gaius, looking around as people began to shuffle to the door.

"No time to explain. Get out of the building now."

"For the love of Aryama, *fire*!" someone in the outer hall cried, and screams followed back to the ballroom. A stampede threatened as the panicked patrons began to race for the exit.

"I said in an *orderly fashion*!" Ezekiel bellowed above the crowd, banging his cane sharply upon the marble. "There is plenty of time for everyone to make it out safely! Help your neighbors and those who may be less mobile, and remain *calm*."

Quelled by his commanding rebuke, the shaken attendees proceeded to the door more composedly than before.

"Pardon me," Alenard said, scooping Ines into his arms.

"What about the others?"

"They'll be along soon," he assured her as he wove through the crowd.

Ines held onto his neck, trembling. "I can feel the heat of the fire, hear the frantic cries—but I can't do anything."

"You smelled the fire long before anyone else would have and saved all these people. None of us would be alive if not for you."

Lottie and Stelian made it out next, along with Khalil, who stared at the soldiers setting fire to the building.

"Are they using... magic?" he whispered.

Lottie couldn't bear to watch and buried her face in Stelian's shoulder.

"They're dragon-breaths," Alenard replied grimly, setting Ines on her feet. "To the uninitiated, it would indeed look like magic. It's a device which shoots bursts of liquefied flame, and is among the most devastating weapons ever invented. King Roland banned their use, but it seems Zhelyas has unearthed them from the foundry."

Khalil looked equal parts awed and horrified.

"The accelerant is what you smelled, Ines," Alenard added. "It's a flammable oil similar to the type used in lamps, but thicker and more viscous."

She nodded, holding tight to his arm.

"You must be a *kahina*, a priestess like my mother, to have such keen insight," Khalil said, gazing with wonder at Ines.

The rest of them could only watch as the soldiers utilized the horrific contraptions with merciless efficiency, setting the magnificent opera house ablaze.

Morfran had almost reached the ballroom when the sounds of panic assaulted his ears. The air felt heavy and sticky, and he spotted the head of the blond physician above the rest of the thronging crowd.

"Lord Gaius?"

"Oh, thank all the stars, you found her!" Gaius exclaimed. "Zhelyas has set fire to the opera house. We have to evacuate!"

Carrying the half-conscious Caro, Morfran followed Gaius and fled the burning building. The others were waiting outside and expressed similar relief upon seeing Caro safe and sound.

"What about Ezalia?" Alenard inquired. By now, all of them save Morfran had removed their masks, and his worry was clear.

Morfran shook his head. "I'm sorry, my lord, I don't know. When I reached Her Majesty, Lady Ezalia was nowhere to be seen."

"What's happening?" Caro murmured, rousing.

"Your Majesty..." Morfran said, looking down at her, then grimaced as she dug her fingernails into his arm.

"Ezalia! We can't abandon her!" She managed to wriggle free and run toward the building, stumbling over her long skirts, heedless of the danger.

Morfran raced forward, grabbing her shoulder and holding her back. She had more strength than one would expect from a teenage girl, and he planted his feet, wrapping both arms around her as she strained against him.

"Release me!" she cried, tears streaming down her face. "We have to go back for her! I *order* you to go back for her!"

Morfran remained steadfast despite her distraught commands. She fought and clawed at him to break free, but he wouldn't let go.

"Your Majesty, please," Alenard said, his voice cracking. "There's nothing more we can do."

Caro slumped in Morfran's arms, her resistance spent.

"We need to leave," Khalil urged. "Veena and the others will find us if we stay here."

His words seemed to pull the rest out of their grief-stricken shock.

"Yes, you're right," Gaius said.

"Where can we go?" Stelian asked, Lottie still sobbing on his shoulder.

"My family has a place nearby. It will be empty, and we can lie low there for a while," Alenard suggested hoarsely.

Morfran nodded, glancing down at the burden in his arms. Exhausted from the ordeal and her struggle, Caro had fallen asleep.

Sleeping Dogs

Less than twenty minutes had passed since Ines's timely deduction, but the fire had already consumed half the structure, lit by a horrible glow like the orange aurora of a premature dawn.

The heat pouring off the building was so intense that everybody had taken shelter. Even the soldiers had retreated, their terrible deed done. The partygoers, formerly celebratory, were now standing upon the lawn, huddled together in shock and grief. Those, like Ezekiel, who dared to remain, stood well away from it, the wall of oppressive heat beating down upon them. He stood in the courtyard in his finest evening attire, his face lined with the pain that suffused his heart.

The firefighters with their meager water pumps could do little as the conflagration engulfed the opera house. By morning, the beloved building would be a blackened skeleton, the resplendence it once held unrecognizable. Ezekiel could see it in his mind, gold leaf chandeliers and sculptures melting, years of backdrops and costumes set ablaze, the massive red velvet curtain swaying as flames licked from the stage. All his memories destroyed in mere moments. Tears stung Ezekiel's eyes from regret mixed with the ash choking the air.

The one small beacon of light was that somehow, astonishingly, every one of the bal masqué's guests had emerged from the building before the spreading flames cut off the exits. A few of them bore minor burns, but it could have been a tragedy of epic proportions.

Ezekiel, though devastated by the loss, knew who to thank for this miracle. He only hoped she and the rest of her companions would take comfort in that, where there was little else to be found.

"Grand Duke Ezekiel Garsiv," Zhelyas greeted, approaching him upon the lawn.

"Was this your doing?" Ezekiel asked brusquely, deliberately omitting any form of aristocratic title.

Zhelyas shrugged. "It seemed to me some suspicious things were going on at this ball. Tell me, have you seen your daughter, the Duchess Ezalia Mavella, about? She might have been traveling with the exiled queen."

He lifted an eyebrow with an air of ease, and Ezekiel swallowed his emotions, refusing to rise to his bait.

"Who can say?"

"The queen was in attendance," Zhelyas said pointedly.

"So were two hundred other guests, all masked and anonymous."

Zhelyas pursed his lips, then nodded, apparently unwilling to go toe to toe with the grand duke on his own turf. "Very well, I shall accept your word. This is a terrible tragedy. It's a wonder lives weren't lost."

Ezekiel let out a noncommittal grunt. "If you will excuse me, I need to see to my guests and ensure they are sent home."

"Of course," Zhelyas purred. "I must invite you to the capital one day, Your Grace. We should speak more."

"I'm sure I will be passing that way soon," Ezekiel replied, then bowed barely within the limits of decorum.

Zhelyas recalled his troops and strolled out of the courtyard.

"Pompous ass," Ezekiel muttered, grinding his teeth.

Glass Houses

Caro glared at Morfran, who knelt before her. "You disobeyed my direct order."

"My first concern is always for you, Your Majesty," he replied quietly.

"Even against my command?"

He hesitated. "Yes. I'm sorry—"

"I don't want to hear that from you!" she snapped. Tears stung her eyes and her chest was tight, like it was trapped in a vise. "You don't have the right to say those words. You left her. You left Ezalia to *die*! How can I ever forgive you?"

She swallowed, her voice thick with the anguish and anger that filled her heart. "Ezalia was everything to me. She was always there, even when her own heart was breaking, and she never asked for *anything* in return. You pretend to know what's best for me, but if you did—you'd know it was her."

Caro pressed her lips together, trying to hold it in. "Get out."

"Your Majesty—"

She gestured sharply. "Just... go."

She turned away, and he rose, bowing out of the room.

Gaius and Stelian were waiting outside.

"Is she all right?" Gaius asked. He had removed his jacket and rolled up the sleeves of his shirt, while Stelian still wore his military-inspired outfit, flounces of lace draping from the cuffs.

Morfran hung his head miserably. "She threw me out."

Gaius patted Morfran on the shoulder. "Come on, you need a drink. Stelian will stand guard."

Morfran gave a slight nod and allowed himself to be steered down the stairs to the kitchen, which Gaius had turned into a makeshift clinic.

"Sit. I have some spirits here, I think."

Morfran stared as he rummaged through his medical bag.

"For use as an anesthetic, naturally," Gaius said with a smirk, and poured them each a cup.

Morfran stared glumly at his drink.

"She's not angry at you in particular. She's mad at the world, and she's lashing out at anyone within reach. Don't take it personally. She needs time."

"And you?"

Gaius leaned back in his chair. "Ezalia and I were friends for many years. I need time, too. Alenard... Well, he's just trying to keep from falling apart. They reconciled so recently."

"So I gather."

"Everybody needs to mourn in their own way."

Morfran tipped the cup of amber spirits, watching the liquid shift within.

"Regardless, the room beneath Caro's is empty. It'll be chilly overnight, but you'd be able to observe her window from the yard."

Morfran blinked up at him, uncomprehending, then nodded. "Thank you, Lord Gaius, I will take you up on that offer."

He drained the cup, then made his way down the hall. He didn't even bother to turn on the lamp, but stepped outside and peered up, pulling the amethyst cloak tight around his shoulders. Just as Gaius had said, he could see the light from Caro's window.

"Your Majesty? Caro?"

She barely recognized the gentle voice through the sound of her own sobs.

"It's Ines. I'm coming in."

Caro was curled up on the bed, her arms wrapped around her knees beneath layers of petticoats. She looked up to see the beautiful blind woman enter the room, resplendent in her lavender dress.

Tracing her fingers along the wall, Ines found the bed and sat upon the edge. "I only knew Ezalia for such a short time," she began softly. "I don't share the same memories as you, but still, I think I understood what kind of person she was."

Half of Caro wanted to be left alone, and the other half wanted so deeply to talk about her aunt with someone. It hurt, but it was the kind of pain that made sense, and her heart felt a little lighter.

Ines's hand reached across the covers and touched her own. "Ezalia wasn't perfect, but she loved you as if you were her own daughter. She would have done anything for you if it was in her power, even protected you from the world and all this sorrow you've had to bear. She wouldn't want you to grieve for her."

Caro's eyes welled with tears, and they streamed freely down her cheeks. "It's all my fault, Ines," she said, her voice hoarse. "I yelled at Morfran because I couldn't bear the guilt. It's crushing me. She wouldn't have been there if not for my

foolish plan. I knew Zhelyas was coming, but I never thought..."
She trailed off, dissolving into tears.

Ines wrapped her arms around Caro's trembling shoulders and shushed her softly.

"I miss her," Caro whispered.

"I know. I do, too. But when someone you love leaves you, they stay with you. Ezalia will never be far away."

Caro snuggled into Ines's warm embrace, desperate for a comforting touch.

Caro stayed in her room all the next day. Stelian delivered her meals and, despite not having much of an appetite, she managed to eat a little. Ezalia would have wanted her to.

Each thought of her beloved aunt brought a fresh wave of tears. She had wiped them away so many times that her eyes were red and puffy and her satin dress stained with drops of saltwater, ruining the fine fabric. Ezalia would have gently dabbed her tears with a soft handkerchief, then held her close, whispering words of love and understanding.

She had never judged Caro for a single thing. She had been stern at times, but always patient. In many ways, she had been more of a mother than Cecilia, sharing with Caro the secrets of growing up, of dancing and romance, and all the things a young woman needed to know.

How could Caro go on without her? But Ezalia had her own reasons for wanting to support the rebellion, not only her love for Caro, but her country's queen. Like her father, Ezalia was principled and would do whatever it took to see the usurper defeated and Artemisia once more at peace. Caro would be disgracing her aunt's memory if she let her sacrifice be in vain.

As much as Caro wanted to curl up in a little ball and hide under the covers, she knew she couldn't stay cooped up forever. Mustering her courage, she decided to go for a walk to clear her head. Maybe some fresh air would help put things in perspective.

Alenard's house was modest as noble villas went, white with pale green siding, but it was cozy. In the back, just off the kitchen, was a small garden, and Caro found herself drawn to its tranquil atmosphere. She glimpsed a flash of purple. In the midst of the weeds were blooms of jewel-like flowers.

"They're irises," Alenard said, and Caro jumped. She hadn't even realized he was there. Since the villa was his family home, he had traded his vibrant red brocade for a more somber black suit. "I'm sorry, I didn't mean to startle you."

Caro shook her head. "Irises? At this time of year?"

It was only the onset of spring, but the flower usually found in the summer months was in full bloom.

"The climate in the highlands is harsh, but there are a few plants that thrive—such as these winter irises. Even in the most difficult of conditions, they persevere, seemingly defying the frosty chill." Alenard smiled sadly. "They were Ezalia's favorite flowers. I think they fit her well, don't you?"

"I do," Caro replied, her throat stuck.

"I will be departing shortly to speak to Lord Ezekiel, and I think I'll take one with me. How about you, Your Majesty?"

Caro nodded, and Alenard knelt before the bed of irises. He cut one at the ground, then snipped off another blossom near the top.

"Let me help you with that," Caro said as he fumbled with his jacket buttonhole. She took the delicate flower and affixed it to his lapel.

Alenard gave a nod of thanks, his eyes brimming with unshed tears. "This one's for you," he added, bowing and handing over the long-stemmed flower.

Caro held it to her heart.

Gaius looked up as she entered the kitchen. He stared for a moment at the iris, then nodded to himself. "Let's find you a vase. I'm sure I saw one here somewhere."

Caro sat as he rummaged through the cupboards, grateful she didn't have to ask.

"That's better," he said as he placed the iris stem into a long, fluted glass with some water and set it on the table. "I was about to have some tea to relax me before bed. Would you care for some?"

"Yes, please."

Gaius picked up the copper kettle with a cloth and poured water into two cups. Small bags floated to the surface as he carried them to the table.

Caro cradled the cup in her hands, the delicate notes of the lavender tea drifting up to her nose and soothing her.

They sat that way for a long time, Caro sipping her cooling tea and staring at the iris. After a while, she started to feel drowsy.

"I think I'm going to turn in. Thank you, Gaius."

"You should take the flower with you," he suggested as she rose. "That way, you'll have pleasant dreams."

Alenard passed Morfran as he exited the garden. "Commander."

"Margrave," Morfran replied warily, stepping away from the tree he was leaning against and bowing to him. He and Ezalia had been lovers, and Morfran wondered if the usually mild-mannered man would lash out at him, as Caro had.

"You told me once you would make amends for invading my house."

Morfran nodded, and Alenard's lip trembled.

"Kill him. The man who murdered my beloved. Then I will consider your debt repaid."

His voice was remorseless and colder than Morfran had heard it before.

"You have my word, my lord," he replied. "When next we meet, Zhelyas will not live to see another day."

"I will hold you to that. Good evening, Commander."

Morfran bowed again as Alenard swept off, then he returned to his vigil.

Caro was still melancholy the next morning, but sleep had rejuvenated her. The winter iris seemed to have done its job, and she had been mercifully untroubled by nightmares.

There was a small knock on the door, and it creaked open slightly.

"Oh, Caro, you're awake," Lottie said, peering through the crack. "I brought some new clothes."

"Come in. I was just getting up."

Lottie smiled and scooted inside. "Gaius rummaged through the closets to find something more suitable than party attire," she explained sheepishly. "Lord Alenard's mother was a bit taller than either of us, but these should suffice."

Caro hadn't even thought about changing. Except for Alenard, everybody had still been wearing their garments from the ball, though Ines had helped her strip off the bulky petticoats so she could sleep more comfortably.

"Gaius asked Lord Alenard to bring our things from the grand duke's, but he thought you might want to greet them in clean clothes."

Lottie was wearing a pair of brown trousers and a ruffled cream blouse, blond ringlets flowing free. It was a good look for her. She seemed so much more self-assured than the skittish maid Caro had met mere weeks before.

"Here, we should get you out of that dress."

Caro nodded and let Lottie unlace the back of the bodice, slipping her arms out of the sleeves and letting it fall to the floor. It felt like she was shedding a cocoon. The outfit Lottie had chosen for her consisted of tan pants, a jade brocade vest, and a white button up shirt.

"I suppose you regret coming with me now," Caro said softly as Lottie fussed over her.

Lottie creased her forehead. "Of course not," she said. "You gave me, an insignificant nobody, a chance to make a difference, and now I'm not just a maid anymore. As a nurse, I can really help people. I'm grateful. You can't blame yourself for what happened."

"But it was my fault. How can I make amends for that?"

"By saving us," Lottie replied simply, taking Caro's hands in her own. "I have faith in you. That's why I rescued you from Oswin and disguised myself to distract Luther. So please don't doubt yourself, because I never will."

Caro couldn't help but be cheered by the girl's sincerity. She'd never had a friend her own age before.

"Now, your hair is quite the mess, if you don't mind me saying," Lottie added brightly. "Let's get you cleaned up before the grand duke arrives."

Lottie hummed a little tune as she brushed out Caro's curls. It might have been one of the songs playing at the ball; she couldn't quite recall.

Her thoughts strayed to Morfran, and she glanced out the window to see him standing outside in the cold. Even after her cruel words, he still refused to leave her side.

Caro nodded to Stelian as they left her quarters. "Thanks for waiting for me. Do you think there's anything for breakfast?"

"Gaius has been cooking," he replied as the girls followed him downstairs. "I offered to help, but he said I was better off here."

Caro paused before the door of the room beneath her own. "Go on without me. I'll be just a moment."

She waited until Stelian and Lottie were gone, then stepped inside. "I know you're there, Morfran."

"Your Majesty," he ventured, bowing uncertainly as he emerged from the shadows.

"I don't blame you." Her heart ached as she spoke the words she needed to say. "It wasn't your fault, it was mine, and I will carry that guilt for the rest of my life."

He knelt at her feet. "Lady Ezalia and I were comrades, friends even. Please believe me, if I could have saved her, I would have done anything."

"I know." Her voice sounded forlorn even to her own ears. "I'm sorry for accusing you. That was unworthy of me."

Morfran rose and gazed down at her, blue eyes sorrowful behind the feather mask. "You never need to apologize to me, Your Majesty."

Even though Morfran had said he didn't hold a grudge, she still felt bad for reprimanding him. But she couldn't keep bottling up her feelings or she would explode.

She peeled off his gloves and rubbed his hands together between her own. "You'll catch a chill if you stand outside like that, and then I'll be the one taking care of you," she said gently as he stood transfixed by the gesture. "I won't throw you out again, so stay by my side from now on."

Cold Comfort

Alenard traveled through the back roads of Agassey toward Ezekiel's manor. He had spent many a summer with the grand duke's family as a youth, so he knew the place well, and had whiled away the hours exploring as a curious lad, playing soldiers and pirates, sailing folded paper ships upon the river.

The days were so innocent then. He remembered the first time he had met Ezalia and allowed his thoughts to drift, the faithful stable horse picking his way down the familiar paths.

Agassey was the hereditary demesne of the grand duke, just as Biding was the margrave's, but it was much more vast, encompassing not only the surrounding countryside, but also the desolate highlands of Rothelin. Alenard's family had always been close allies of Ezekiel's, and so they kept a villa for their own private use, under the condition they would visit the manor on occasion.

It was on such a day that the then-Margrave Giness Aberforth took his wife and young son to meet the grand duke and his family. Alenard had seen the older nobleman once or twice at social events, and the grand duchess had performed in an opera which he found rather dull at the time.

"Your Grace." Alenard bowed politely in the hall, and his father gave him a nod of approval.

"Welcome to my house, young Lord Alenard," Ezekiel said warmly.

Mavella stood on the landing, looking as radiant as if she'd stepped off the stage. Beside her were two girls approximately his own age.

"May I introduce my daughters, Ezalia and Cecilia."

The girls curtsied as their father spoke their names. Cecilia, the younger one, had a pointed chin and green eyes, her black hair coiffed so not a strand was out of place, and she appeared to be reveling in the attention. Her elder sister, Ezalia, had softer features, with black curls tumbling about her shoulders. She met Alenard's gaze, and he felt he would be swallowed up in those sapphire pools.

A small green frog leaped from within the folds of Ezalia's gown, and she giggled as it hopped down the stairs. Impulsively, Alenard caught it, cupping the frog gently in his hands as Ezekiel looked mortified and Mavella gave her daughter a stern word of reproach.

Ezalia nodded obediently to her mother, then glanced over her shoulder at Alenard, who had released the frog outside. She smiled, her eyes twinkling, and he blushed. At his age, the rigors of propriety and the talk of family alliances through marriage were tedious adult conversations, best to be ignored. But he couldn't help thinking: if he were to marry a girl someday, it could be Ezalia.

If she hadn't denied his suit years later, would anything be different? The young queen had relied on her aunt, and he believed Caro wouldn't be the same young woman, the same queen, without Ezalia's influence to guide her. It was of small comfort, but it was all he had.

Secrecy was paramount, so Alenard slowed his horse as he drew closer to the manor. Dismounting, he kept out of the lanterns' glow as he headed to a side door in case Zhelyas's agents were prowling around.

Alenard rapped on the door softly and was greeted by the butler.

"Lord Margrave."

"I need to see the grand duke."

The butler nodded, holding the door. Alenard slipped though without removing his coat and made his way to the sitting room, where he knew Ezekiel would be at this time of the evening with a glass of sherry and a book.

Tonight the sherry was whiskey, the book abandoned as the grand duke stood facing the center of the room, lost in thought. A letter sat beside him on the table.

"Your Grace," Alenard said, drawing his attention.

Ezekiel turned to him. "Any news?"

"Her Majesty, the queen, is safe. She and the rest of our companions are currently hiding out in my old family villa. It was the only thing I could think of..." he added, trailing off, and Ezekiel nodded.

"You did the right thing. There's no telling whether or not Zhelyas's spies would dare defy my authority and encroach upon the manor," he said brusquely, then he grew quiet. "And Ezalia?"

Alenard shook his head and bowed, unable to bear the desperate hope he saw mirrored in her father's eyes.

"I regret to inform you, Your Grace," he began, wearing the formality like a shell around his wounded heart, "there is little chance the Lady Ezalia survived the flames. If she had, surely she would have sent us word, but there has been none."

His throat felt raw and he pressed his lips tightly together, focusing on his mission. "I am here on Her Majesty's behalf to ask if you would come to the villa to discuss the future of her rebellion. If you are still willing, that is?"

His solemn words were met with silence, and he glanced up hesitantly—but it appeared the grand duke was no longer listening.

Ezekiel barely comprehended what Alenard was saying. His world had shattered, and he collapsed into the chair, unable to stand.

Alenard looked like he had been crying for hours, and tears pooled in his eyes as he delivered the news of Ezalia's death.

His beloved daughter... was gone. Ezekiel buried his head in his hands.

First Cecilia had been murdered with her husband, then Ezalia burned alive in the opera house which had been his refuge. How much more could he bear?

"Your Grace?" Alenard whispered, and Ezekiel realized he had asked a question.

"My apologies," he said, recovering himself, though he struggled to speak. "Yes, I will call upon the queen."

He rose unsteadily, leaning upon the cane as if it were the one thing keeping him from plunging into despair. "I will retire now. Please stay the night, Alenard. You must be weary."

Alenard nodded, his own sorrow etched upon his face. The man whom Ezekiel had hoped would become his son-in-law someday. Now that day would never come.

Ezekiel squeezed his shoulder, then mounted the stairs, each step more painful than the last, until he reached his room. He shut the door with the last ounce of his strength, then staggered to the window.

The curtains were damask, pale gold patterned with deep plum. Ezalia had picked them out, and he had expressed doubt that they would complement the taupe walls and furnishings. Of course she'd been right, and they matched perfectly. She had always been right.

He gripped the heavy fabric in his hands, feeling the smooth, metallic threads beneath his fingers, remembering the softness of Ezalia's hair.

"Oh, Mavella," he sobbed. "What I wouldn't give to hear your voice again. Now, I've lost you and both our daughters."

Ezekiel sagged against the curtains, his cane clattering to the ground. "If Cecilia hadn't married the king, she wouldn't have been there that night, and Ezalia wouldn't have died at the hands of her murderer. But then..."

An image flickered across his mind. Cecilia's green eyes in a small, delicate face, eyes which had seen so much suffering in her young years, but never seemed to lose their light.

"Caro," he whispered. If fate could be changed, then he wouldn't have his granddaughter, the one spark of hope for his wounded heart. He had nothing left to live for—nothing but her.

"Mavella, give me strength to make you and our daughters proud. And perhaps, I can fulfill Ezalia's final wish."

Alenard arrived a day later with Ezekiel in tow.

"Did you have any trouble?" Gaius inquired.

"Zhelyas has left the area for now," Alenard said. "He stationed a squadron to keep the city under observation, but though he spoke with His Grace after the ball, there is little more he can do. So far from the capital, he has fewer resources, and if the folk of Agassey find out he burned down their opera house, he might have a full scale riot on his hands."

Ezekiel nodded at Alenard's assessment, holding his cane in the crook of his elbow as he pulled off his gloves.

"Your Grace," Caro said, remorse suffusing her voice, "forgive me for bringing such sorrow upon your land and family."

"I knew what I was getting into when I agreed to help you, and this has not changed my mind," Ezekiel said firmly, though his voice was strained.

"But Ezalia..." Caro murmured, the words sneaking out.

"Your Majesty, my daughter believed so strongly in you and this mission that she was willing to make any sacrifice. In her place, I shall strive to uphold her ideals." He shook his head gravely, his own sorrow evident in the weary lines of his face. "I should be apologizing for these lamentable events, my queen. It is the duty of a servant to bear the burden of his master."

Ezekiel bowed low, and Caro nodded, both chastened and touched by his conviction.

They settled in the foyer of Alenard's family villa, Caro across from Ezekiel, who perched in a chair, arms crossed.

"Due to the circumstances, several like-minded associates have sought me out. Lady Uyria is among them, and she is eager to welcome you upon your return through her land. It would be the most expedient route to take back to the capital."

That was surprising. Uyria had been adamantly opposed to helping Caro before. It seemed the tragedy of that night had changed all of them.

"I am relieved to hear that."

"I have also secured funds, which I have transferred into Duke Vittorius's account. In addition to the writ Gaius already deposited, he should now have ample currency for his purposes."

Ezekiel waited for Caro's nod. "This brings me to my next question. Alenard, I understand your army is on standby awaiting orders?"

"Yes, Your Grace," Alenard confirmed. "I only need to send word to Lance, and they will be ready to depart."

"And—Prince Khalil, is it? From what I gather, you accompanied Her Majesty as a gesture of good faith?"

"That's right. My mother Hadiya, chieftess of the Omaira clan, has pledged the support of our warriors."

Ezekiel nodded to himself. "A map, Gaius, if you would please. And find some nuts or seeds."

Gaius disappeared into the library and brought back a book of maps, while Khalil went in search of place markers.

"Will these do?" he inquired, returning moments later with a basket of sewing supplies, a box of colored beads and buttons among them.

"I had forgotten those were here," Alenard said, amused. "Mother liked to swap out Father's plain shirt buttons for fancier ones when he wasn't looking."

Gaius flipped through the various maps. "The former margrave was quite the cartographer. These are very detailed."

He found one he seemed to like and spread it upon the table. Caro rested her elbows on her knees as Ezekiel leaned over the map intently.

He placed a handful of blue beads at Biding. Another handful of red went in the desert, a couple of green in Agassey, and a few violet outside the capital. He then took a scoop of black beads and spread them out between the capital and Ockbridge, the majority centered on the castle.

"The blue beads are Alenard's army," he explained. "The red are the clan warriors; the green for us; and the violet are the mercenaries Duke Vittorius has employed."

Ezekiel then indicated the black beads. "That leaves us with Zhelyas. He has the full complement of the royal Artemisian army, led by General Luther. I have heard that after Oswin's arrest, a division of troops was stationed at his manor, while the remainder of the army is ready to mobilize whenever Zhelyas commands."

Caro lifted her hand to her lips, thinking. "We need to make sure we join our forces before we march on the capital. Ideally, before we reach Oswin's. If we could take Ockbridge, then we would control that critical passage."

Ezekiel contemplated her tactics.

"Khalil's men will come south from the desert, which would lead to Frok," Caro continued. "Veena, Zhelyas's sorceress, might have guessed the purpose in Khalil's accompanying me, but she may underestimate the extent of Hadiya's commitment."

She looked to Khalil for confirmation, who nodded. "I don't think it has factored into her calculations. She likely believes I tagged along on a whim."

"Then Khalil will travel to Hadiya and return with the clansmen she promised," Caro concluded, shifting the red beads downward. "Next, the most efficient course for Alenard's men would be to skirt around the outer edge of the desert, parallel to our own path."

Alenard nodded his assent. "I will send word to them right away."

"Remember, they have to reach Ock at precisely the right time," Caro cautioned. "Khalil, how long will it take your people to prepare and make the journey?"

Khalil pondered, staring at the map. "Twelve days, fifteen at the outside."

"Then, taking into account your own travel time, let's say three weeks to be safe. Alenard, can your army make the distance in that period?"

"If Lance hasn't been bone idle, I think it's possible."

"I insist Alenard remain behind to advise Your Majesty," Ezekiel said firmly.

"Then I will dispatch Stelian to deliver the deployment orders," Caro declared. "Khalil's men and Alenard's will converge, closing in from behind and cutting the soldiers stationed at Oswin's off from reinforcements. Then Ockbridge will be ours."

"Before you go," Morfran said, handing Khalil a small scroll, "see if your mother can contact the Sharir. Given the stakes involved, they may lend us their aid."

"I will do what I can, Mukhif," Khalil assured him, peering at the indecipherable script on the slip of parchment.

Once Bitten

"Well? I trust you have been appropriately chastised."

Malcolm knelt upon the cold stone floor, knees stiff, his wrists affixed to the wall with chains. His body ached from the beating by the guards, but he was almost certain nothing was broken. They had been careful not to touch his face so he would be able to hide the evidence from his peers, but the rest of him was covered in ugly purple bruises.

He glanced up at Arvind, who stood in the cell, arms crossed.

"I..." Malcolm trailed off, meeting the prince's livid silver gaze, then lowered his eyes. "Yes, Your Highness."

Arvind frowned, then coughed, wincing in pain. As he clutched at the fabric of his unbuttoned shirt, Malcolm glimpsed the scar which knitted the skin above his heart.

Magic. Even the word sent shivers down Malcolm's spine. Since that night, Arvind had sequestered himself in his office, rarely emerging. Unfortunately, he'd heard about Malcolm's little misstep and decided he needed a scolding.

Malcolm wondered what sort of man would go through such excruciating pain, holding tenuously to life to get what he craved most. A monster.

Arvind recovered, tugging his shirt straight with a steadying breath. "As long as you remain discreet, I will not inform the king of your other activities. However, you will report them to me from now on. You needn't tell the others of my involvement, but you will not sully my name again."

Malcolm was keenly aware he was now in the prince's debt. Arvind ordered Malcolm's release, then retrieved his possessions, including the book of poems.

Oh, how I long for the day
When I might see you again
The promised walk along the shore
In childhood's meadow we play
Dancing in the rain
Forgotten memories of yore

"Who writes this rubbish?" he scoffed, reading one of the pages aloud. "I suppose it contains some hidden message?"

Malcolm nodded, massaging his wrists, which had been rubbed raw by the shackles. "The poet is said to have been your ancestor Queen Malianme herself, writing under the pseudonym Mallory Blanc," he explained, wishing he didn't have to betray Radella's brilliant scheme. "One of us arranges the details of the mission according to the stanzas in a poem, then hands off the book to someone else to oversee its execution. The particulars are passed along so one person alone is not responsible, and there is no other record."

"Hmm, clever," Arvind said, stroking his chin. "I must admit I'm impressed with your ingenuity."

He snapped the book shut and handed it back to Malcolm. "I meant what I said. I will endorse this, but each action will be confirmed with me *before* it proceeds. If I have cause to suspect you are deceiving me, I will put a swift end to it, and all involved will face the consequences."

Malcolm left Arvind's office and wandered back toward his quarters.

"How are you?" Lobelia inquired, coming alongside him in the hall. She handed him a cup of tea, and he inhaled the invigorating aroma of lemon verbena.

Malcolm shook his head, hiding the pain. "Just a head cold. I don't do well this time of year in such a drafty castle. I'm sorry I concerned you."

"You don't need to lie. Sejic told me of the punishment you received at the hand of Prince Arvind," she said softly with a pitying sigh. "It's deplorable."

Malcolm gave a weary nod, the experience still quite fresh in his mind.

"If there's anything you need, please don't hesitate to ask," she added, giving his hand a gentle squeeze. "We're all in this together. I've already spoken with the countess and offered to take your shift tonight, so get some rest."

Malcolm didn't need much convincing. His body hurt all over, and he was practically dead on his feet. Resuming his duties immediately after a beating would take a toll on anyone, plus the added stress of having to conceal his pain lest the prince be disparaged again. He knew Arvind would not be so forgiving next time—not to him, and not to the other conspirators. He was almost relieved he didn't have to hide it from Lobelia.

"I appreciate your consideration, Lady Anthusa. And thank you for the tea as well."

One thing Malcolm couldn't figure out was why the prince was allowing it at all. He had said he would permit their actions to continue, stressing discretion, but it seemed out of character somehow. He'd been the first to bow before the usurper, after all.

What could Arvind possibly hope to gain? Control? Perhaps he planned to seize the throne for himself after the obstructions had been removed from his path, and having them in his debt would further those aims. But he didn't really seem the type to be so shrewd.

No, there was a simpler answer: fear. If it came to light, Zhelyas would likely blame Arvind for not doing his job and letting the nobles run free. By keeping it to himself, he not only protected his own interests, but held power over those who were involved, including Malcolm. Surely it would mean death if they were discovered, so he had to remain in the prince's good graces—and Arvind had a suitable scapegoat if the need arose.

Malcolm spied Arcus across the hall, looking somewhat nervous.

"Did you get a message, too?" Arcus whispered, beckoning him over.

Malcolm furrowed his brow in confusion, then withdrew a small card. "You mean this? It was slipped under my door this morning."

"What does it mean?"

It was certainly a puzzle. A plain white notecard with elegant script and a cryptic poem. The poem was similar to those in the *Reminiscence* book, though not as refined, so he assumed it must be from one of their fellow compatriots.

When the moon is high
And the lamps are low
There shall be a meeting of the mind
Where the wine's run dry
'Neath the moon's white glow
The final hour of the day's rewind

"The final hour" implied just before midnight. "Where the wine's run dry," though, that was an odd clue, and Malcolm pondered its significance.

It must be something painfully obvious if he and Arcus were expected to decipher it. Malcolm had been surprised to find someone else had received the same note, and he wondered how many others had been sent one, too.

"The wine, though..."

He had it: it was a pun. A "dry wine." The castle had two wine cellars, but the second hadn't been used since the newer was constructed, and was left empty except for storage. It had been built underground in order to maintain the delicate temperatures required, and there was only one place where the moonlight would reach, from a gap high above carved into the stone.

Malcolm glanced at Arcus, and his friend nodded, suggesting he had reached a similar conclusion.

Under cover of darkness, Malcolm made his way to the wine cellar, curious as to who had summoned him. He was not the only one. A dozen of his fellow conspirators were all gathered, standing beside vacant casks and pallets of empty bottles.

Rudo was in attendance, as was Nefion, who had recovered enough strength from his ordeal to leave the infirmary, though he hobbled along with his friend's assistance, a bandage wrapped around his mutilated eyes.

"It's dangerous for all of us to meet like this," Radella said, shifting her feet nervously. She was in her nightclothes, as were many of the others, so they could scatter to their rooms if they were spooked.

Takaria was noticeably absent, though it was unclear whether she had refused the summons out of disinterest or, more disturbingly, had deliberately not been invited. The latter possibility made Malcolm uneasy.

They all whispered among themselves, eager to know the identity of the one who had invited them.

Arcus stroked his chin. "Doesn't this seem a little too convenient?"

"What if we were lured here by the king?" Radella added with slight panic in her voice.

Arvind hadn't indicated any intention of reporting their activities, so the use of the poem would have been contradictory, and Zhelyas didn't strike Malcolm as the type who would use such a subtle method to gain retribution.

"Unlikely," Malcolm concluded. "He would need to have intimate knowledge of our methods. This is from one of us."

He glanced at the faces of those gathered, trying to place who else might be missing.

"Greetings, gentle noblemen and ladies," a sultry voice said, and a figure stepped out from behind a dusty cupboard.

"Lady Anthusa?" Arcus inquired, voicing Malcolm's bewildered thoughts.

"The very same," Lobelia replied with an amused smirk. "You must pardon me for this abrupt summons, but I assure you I will make it worth your while."

Malcolm was at sea. "What exactly is the point of all this? Why did you bring us here?"

"I have a proposition." She smiled, meandering through the small crowd with dainty steps. "It isn't right, the way the prince is pandering to the king, and the usurper hasn't exactly endeared himself to his subjects either. It's time we did something about it. All of you have resources, and I admire your philanthropic goals, but there are better uses they could be put to."

Malcolm was starting to get a queasy feeling in his stomach.

"The poor queen is out there, on the run, a fugitive from her own forces, with no friends and no hope. Imagine if she were to return home, her beloved court having saved her from such a wretched fate. Everything would be as it was, and she would be deeply grateful."

"What are you trying to say?" Arcus asked, furrowing his brow.

"Why, only that we play to our strengths and use our connections to do more than help a few citizens escape. We are the nobles of Artemisia. If we banded together, how could Zhelyas possibly stand against us?"

"Are you out of your mind?" Radella stared at her with disbelief. "You must be mad."

"You've seen what Zhelyas will do if his rule is challenged," Malcolm agreed, urging caution.

"He's right," Arcus added. "What could we hope to accomplish alone?"

Lobelia gave a sly smile. "Not alone. Major Sejic is with me. Isn't that right?" She crooked her finger, and Sejic stepped forward.

"Of course, Lady Lobelia," he replied, and there were whispered murmurs. "All the men under my command are loyal to me, and I can modify the duty roster. Zhelyas will be denied the support of the general's men at key strategic locations, and the rest will be easily overcome."

Malcolm stood his ground. "I won't condone such a rash move. What you're planning could get us all killed."

Lobelia turned her gaze to him, and he was startled to see it was full of pity. "Oh, Earl, you know I'm right."

"What does she mean?" Radella asked, also turning to stare at him.

"You didn't tell them?"

"Lady Lobelia, I don't think—" Malcolm tried, but his discretion was in vain.

"The prince, whom you all believe has your best interests at heart, had the earl beaten for a petty disagreement."

A chorus of gasps followed this revelation.

"Is this true?"

Malcolm looked down, unable to meet Radella's accusing gaze. He had told the others he'd confided in Arvind, and Radella had been especially relieved.

"But he's been helping us," Arcus interjected rationally, though he too sounded doubtful.

"Has he really?" Lobelia countered. "Or is he pretending in order to keep you all under his thumb? Are we going to continue believing his lies like frightened sheep? Either you sit back and do nothing, or make a stand. Those are your two choices."

Lady Lobelia Anthusa was a minor noble, but Malcolm had to admit she was a powerful speaker. As much as he wanted to object, the lingering memories of the pain made him want to agree.

Arcus already seemed swayed by her logic, especially given Zhelyas's abuse of her sister Diascia, for whom he had developed feelings.

"Nefion, this is our chance," Rudo urged, but his friend shook his head.

"I've suffered Zhelyas's wrath firsthand. That's enough for me."

Malcolm took a deep breath. "For the sake of our alliance, I'm going to give you some time to reconsider. I suggest you all think carefully on this, and on the consequences should you fail."

Lobelia faced Malcolm challengingly, her fierce green eyes glittering. "You need to decide which side you're on, Earl. Are you a sheep? Or a wolf?"

Ignorance is Bliss

The most common locations for entering or exiting the Esaphis were through the border towns where one could procure supplies and provisions for the journey ahead, but Khalil had lived in the desert all his life and knew there were many lesser-known paths. However, they were not without their risks. The weather was unpredictable, and sleeping without a tent would leave one exposed to the elements. If a sandstorm arose, it could flay the flesh from a man's bones unless he had shelter of some sort.

Despite that, brigands presented a far greater hazard. His tribe, the Omaira, was one of many, all vying for livestock, riches, resources, and territory. Some were comparable to his own and had good relations with his mother Hadiya. Others were little more than thieves, vultures feeding off the weak.

The desert was full of danger, and Khalil was ever wary. Journeying with Caro had made him somewhat complacent, though, and he missed the telltale ripples that would indicate a sand crawler was nearby.

The speckled brown snake sprang out of the sand mere inches from his foot. Khalil took a hasty step backward and toppled over, facing the serpent as it emerged, its head undulating back and forth, green eyes fixed upon him hypnotically. As a child, he'd thought sand crawlers were the most beautiful creatures in the desert, but his awe was less for their beauty at this moment.

It reared its head back to deliver its fatal venomous blow. Suddenly, the metal spike of a spear impaled it through the neck.

Khalil looked up to see one of the Zarqa clan staring down at him from atop a horse, blue sash clearly visible.

"Well, hey, lookie here. Good thing we were around, or you'd be a goner," the man chuckled, his two fellows leering. "You're Hadiya's kid, aintcha? Our chief's gonna be mighty pleased."

The man yanked the spear out of the ground and pointed it at Khalil. "Get up. And would you mind handing me the snake? That's a good boy."

Khalil arrived at the Zarqa camp, tired and weary. His hands had been bound in front of him by his captors and the rope tied to the horse's saddle. They dragged him to the largest tent and presented him to their chief. Khalil recognized the man as Anwar, a fierce, merciless brute.

"Well, well, Khalil. What are you doing out here all by yourself?" he jeered. "This is my territory."

"Since when?" Khalil retorted, and the chief struck him.

"Since I say."

Khalil bit his tongue against the pain and humiliation.

"Did you find anything on him?"

He had changed his clothes before entering the desert, so there was nothing to suggest where he'd been. Except...

"Only this, *Sayyid*," the man with the spear said, handing over Morfran's scroll.

Anwar unrolled it and stared at it with irritation. "Rubbish," he declared, tossing it away. It rolled perilously close to the fire.

"Wait, that's—!" Khalil cried, and the chief spun and walloped him again.

"Nibal! More wine!" Anwar bellowed, apparently bored with tormenting Khalil.

His thin-faced servant obeyed, casting Khalil a suspicious frown.

Deciding to exact as much misery as he could upon the son of his hated rival, Anwar booted Khalil out of the nice warm tent, and he sat shivering upon the cold sand, his wrists tied around a tall stake.

"Want some?" the spearman offered from where he sat by the fire eating dinner.

He placed a plate in front of Khalil, cheese curds in a colorless sauce. The head of the snake was perched on the very top, dead eyes staring back at him.

Khalil picked up the snake with his bound hands, then ripped its throat open with his teeth. The man sniggered at the display. Let him laugh. The snake would have bitten him; now he was eating the snake. That was what it meant to survive in the desert.

"Captain, someone is here to see you."

Lance looked up from reviewing the day's papers and nodded.

The page stepped aside, admitting a young man. He recognized the youth as being a member of Queen Caro's entourage but didn't recall them ever being introduced.

"Captain Lance?"

"Yes?"

"My name is Lieutenant Stelian. I am here on behalf of the queen and Lord Alenard to see to the deployment of your forces."

"Why didn't the margrave come himself?" Lance inquired, a little irked at taking the orders of a boy.

"He is required by the queen to advise her," Stelian replied brusquely.

"I see. My apologies, Lieutenant. I did not mean to cause offense."

Stelian let out a relieved sigh. "None taken, Captain."

"Where are the margrave and the others now?"

"At Dalry, hosted by the Baroness Uyria Ilyana," Stelian said, and Lance blinked, surprised.

"And you traveled all this way?"

"As swiftly as I was able."

Lance had a grudging new respect for the boy. That was a long journey, and from the state of him, he appeared to have done it without stopping for rest.

"You have my gratitude for arriving so expediently, Lieutenant. It will take at least a day to prepare the men to leave. Please eat and take some rest before you keel over."

His words had the effect he intended. All the tension melted from Stelian's expression and posture, and he slouched, visibly exhausted.

"I'll just get a few hours," he agreed. "Then I'll come help."

Although Lance was frosty to Stelian at first, he soon warmed to the boy. In many ways, he was much like Alenard had been as a youth, impetuous and headstrong but with a strong sense of duty.

Stelian looked over the supplies manifest while Lance doublechecked the wagons. "How are we progressing?"

"Everything is more or less ready to go," Lance replied. "Provisions are cataloged and packed, weapons and armor prepped, the soldiers already resting and rising in shifts."

Stelian gave an approving nod.

"Eager to return to your queen?" Lance inquired.

"So much has happened. I hate leaving her," he admitted.

"Did you get help from the grand duke?"

Stelian nodded, but he seemed troubled. "Yes, but in the process, Lady Ezalia was lost."

Lance's hand froze. "What?"

"The queen and the rest of us were attending a masquerade ball, and Zhelyas followed us there. He burned down the opera house... with Lady Ezalia still inside."

Stelian finished his sorrowful story, and Lance shook his head.

"Poor Lord Alenard," he murmured. "Even as a lad, he loved that lady, and time did not dull his affections. He must be suffering, and the queen, too."

"Lady Ezalia was important to all of us, but none more so than Her Majesty. She's trying hard to focus on the battles ahead, but I still see tears in her eyes when her thoughts turn to her aunt."

Lance gave a determined nod, tightening the straps over the tarp. "Then we'll make haste to return to their sides."

Stelian fell silent, then jumped as a gigantic black stallion nudged his shoulder from a nearby stall, staring at him.

"Been taking care of that fellow Morfran's horse, too. Don't worry, he's a mild fella. Gentle giant, eh, Eclipse?"

"Eclipse?" Stelian repeated, lifting a doubtful eyebrow.

"That's his name. Still won't let any of us ride him, though. He's got high standards." Lance chuckled. "Bet you're champing at the bit to see your master too, eh, boy?"

Eclipse stamped his hooves and whinnied as if in reply.

Troubled Waters

Countess Uyria Ilyana was a gracious hostess, as Ezekiel had said she would be. She was also the most fashionable woman Caro had ever met. Whenever she graced the court with her presence, it always caused a stir. Wearing only the finest clothes and jewels, she didn't follow the latest style—she dictated it.

Uyria had the same merry brown eyes as her cousin Radella, though her hair was a deep red, sleek and entwined in a twisted updo. Her luxurious maroon dress with ribbons and dyed lace trim was a complementary shade, while a garnet and ruby parure glittered in the candlelight.

"Your Royal Majesty, welcome to my humble home."

Caro nodded her thanks, though the stately house didn't quite seem to fit. Unlike Oswin's, which had been square and squat, Uyria's manor was wider than it was tall, white with mauve roof tiles and burgundy shutters. A veranda with delicate curled railings stretched around the façade. Shrubs of hydrangeas with clusters of pastel blossoms filled the veranda. It was almost like a scenic painting.

Uyria stepped aside for them to pass, gesturing invitingly. The decor inside was all in a pleasant tones of golden-brown, pink, and ivory.

"Thank you, Lady Uyria, for your hospitality. The grand duke has lauded your generosity, and I am grateful."

"It is my pleasure," Uyria purred, bowing.

Then she frowned, looking Caro up and down with a mix of displeasure and pity. "Goodness, this will not do."

"Pardon?"

"You must get changed at once! Such attire does not befit a noblewoman of your stature. You must be desperate to get out of those filthy rags!"

Minutes later, Caro had been swept up the stairs by Uyria's insistently fluttering black lace fan, past a portrait in stained glass, and into a room where maids set upon removing her traveling clothes.

"Lady Uyria, I appreciate the thought—" Caro tried as she was trussed up in the most regal of gowns outside the capital, fancier even than the one she'd worn to the ball.

Uyria waggled her finger and tutted, "A queen must always look her best."

Caro could hardly argue with that unassailable logic.

Uyria tsked as the maids struggled to find something to do with her short curls. "It is a shame. A woman's hair is her pride."

Caro didn't want to tell her that was precisely why she'd cut it; she was afraid the poor woman would be aghast at the "indignity" of it all.

Once the servants finished their work, Caro turned in front of the mirror to the delight of her hostess. She was wearing so many petticoats and layers of frills she looked like a frosted mint cupcake.

"As a nurse, I suppose I will have to accept the suitability of that uniform of yours," Uyria commented to Lottie, then glanced away, oblivious to her disappointment. She then turned to Ines. "However, you are a beautiful woman. I'm sure I have something that would look divine on you."

"Pardon me, milady," Ines said politely. "But as I cannot see, an elaborate dress would be difficult for me to maneuver in, and a long hem would only trip my feet."

Uyria seemed to be stymied for the first time at her calm reasoning, then acquiesced and provided Ines a much simpler gown—to Caro's mild chagrin—in a flattering shade of rose.

Of the men, only Alenard was of significant birth to warrant her scrutiny, and while he did not have to change, she declared resolutely that his jacket must be pressed. Caro grinned at him, happy to not be the only person whom the formidable noblewoman had fixated upon, and he gave a half-hearted frown at her levity. Uyria was apparently too intimidated by Morfran to comment on his imposing black attire, while Ezekiel, in her opinion, was "the epitome of the fashionable man."

Ines stroked the gown. "I like the feel of the fabric. It's very soft," she murmured to Caro. "What color is it?"

"Pink," Caro replied, not quite sure how to answer the question, but Ines merely smiled.

"Like the dianthus which smells a little like cloves. I was born blind, and have never been able to see, but I can rely on my other senses. I associate colors with flowers, for instance, because I can understand their beauty by how fragrant they smell."

Caro was stunned by this heartfelt revelation.

"Let's take a walk, and I'll show you what I mean."

At the back of Uyria's manor was a lush greenhouse, glass segments fitted neatly inside a wrought iron frame. Arm in arm, the two women meandered through the greenery.

"Over there are roses. They come in every hue of the rainbow, and each one has a slightly different yet equally lovely scent."

Caro was amazed Ines could pick out their fragrance among the myriad of other blossoms.

"I recall Ezalia told me my dress at the ball was a lavender color. I do love the soothing smell of those wildflowers." Emotion flickered across Ines's face at the mention of the ill-fated party. "Over there are daffodils, which are yellow, I believe, and blue hyacinth. And the lilacs are in full bloom. Their heavenly fragrance reminds me of the sweet taste of honey."

Caro nodded, finally understanding.

"I have learned to find joy in the world, even if I cannot see it. I have adapted to survive, and Caro, you must adapt as well."

She frowned slightly, knowing where this was heading. "I'm not sure I can."

Ines stroked Caro's arm reassuringly. "In my case, I am the only one affected by my choices, but you don't have that luxury. I don't envy you, but you know you're not alone."

"So this is where you are."

Caro turned to see Uyria carrying a tray with a rose-patterned tea set and a tiered plate with strawberry shortcake and scones with clotted cream.

"Would you join me for some tea?"

Caro guided Ines to a bench with chartreuse cushions while Uyria set the tray on a small white wicker table, pouring the fruity tea into the delicate porcelain cups. The tea smelled faintly of peach and was pleasantly subtle.

"I wanted to apologize, Your Majesty," Uyria said, wringing her hands in her lap. "What I said at the ball... It was unpardonably rude."

"Please think nothing of it, Lady Uyria," Caro replied, wincing inwardly as she recalled how much the words had stung.

"I dismissed you so easily. I didn't realize the extent of Zhelyas's cruelty, nor his utter disregard for his subjects. I understand from Ezekiel that if not for Ines's timely intervention, we would all have been killed. In the end, Lady Ezalia was the sole victim." Uyria bowed her head. "I am ashamed, my queen. Forgive me."

Caro was touched by her remorse. "None of us could have anticipated Zhelyas's actions that night," she said kindly. Her voice cracked at the mention of her aunt, and Ines secretly squeezed her hand. "I am grateful for your support in this trying time."

Uyria nodded, her painted lips turning up in a melancholy smile. "Anything you need, do not hesitate to ask."

As she was venturing upstairs to her room after dinner, Caro was drawn to the stained glass window and paused upon the landing. A woman with red slices of glass for hair and an emerald-green dress sat upon the bank of a winding river holding a lyre and gazing pensively into the distance.

Uyria came up the steps beside her. "You like it?"

"It's beautiful. Who is it?" Caro asked.

"People sometimes think it's me, but despite my reputation, I'm not quite that vain." She gave a wry chuckle. "I've always loved the story of Aryama and Mahira. She was the goddess of fire, and he was blessed by the moon goddess with the powers of water. Legends say when she was missing him the most, she would sit by the river and play, hoping he would hear her song wherever he was. She just happened to have red hair like mine."

Uyria had always seemed a little flighty and absentminded, and Caro was moved to see a new facet of the baroness.

"I was married once, you see, a long time ago," she admitted, tracing the fragments of colored glass with her fingertips. "His name was Pharos, and not a day goes by that I don't miss his presence. Like Mahira, I sit by the river and hope my thoughts reach him."

"I'm sorry. It must be a painful reminder," Caro said.

"That's precisely the point, Majesty," Uyria replied, shaking her head. "As long as we don't forget those we've lost, they will always be with us. And so the memories, while sorrowful, are also a comfort."

Ines had said something similar back at the villa, but Caro hasn't quite understood what she meant until now. To purposefully remind oneself of a loss seemed needlessly cruel, but it was a balm for Uyria's soul.

Caro touched the pieces of glass that represented the reflective water, the same blue as Ezalia's eyes. "Though I loved her dearly, I knew so little about my aunt. Would you tell me what you remember of her?"

Uyria seemed slightly surprised by the request, then smiled and gave a patient nod. "I would be glad to. Ezzy was a good friend."

Together they shared in reminiscences of Ezalia, and somehow Caro's heart felt lighter. The memories no longer hurt so much, though they still brought tears to her eyes. They would for a while yet—even Uyria's eyes glistened when she spoke of her lost love from long ago—but in time, she wouldn't look for Ezalia around every corner. And perhaps one day, she would forgive herself for what she could not do.

Spilled Milk

Vittorius's journey to Salissard was more difficult than when he'd served as Minister of Trade as opposed to being branded a traitor, but he still had enough contacts to make it there in decent time. He'd traveled to the country before to trade for furs, spices, and jade; now he was here to barter with mercenaries.

He drew his cloak tight as he stepped off the long, narrow boat, shivering in the shadows of the snow-capped mountains looming above like great impassive statues.

The settlement of Kvalheim was small but well protected, with a defensive stone wall surrounding it on all sides. Through the gate were various small buildings, as well as an elevated guard tower to warn of threats coming from land or sea.

"She will see you now," a young woman said.

Vittorius nodded and entered the hut. It was a strange, triangular structure constructed entirely of wood and peat, with a moss-thatched roof to insulate the house from the bitter cold.

A bench rested against the opposite wall, carved into the stylized form of twin dragon heads, and a woman sat upon it, expecting him. She had long red hair braided at the front and sides, the rest cascading in a fountain down her back, and wore a muted violet dress over a gray, long-sleeved tunic. A brown wool cape trimmed with fox fur draped around her shoulders, affixed by gold brooches and strings of amber and flameworked beads.

Vittorius took a deep breath to steady his nerves. He had promised his niece he would come to Salissard to seek aid on her behalf, but he couldn't have prepared himself for the feelings it would engender.

He sat on a small stool while the woman stared at him, her fierce emerald gaze boring into his. "Duke Vittorius," she said, her voice as cold as the chill in the air outside, "we have not seen you around these parts in quite some time."

"I was sorry to hear of your father's death," he began. "He was a strong *sjef*, and I respected him greatly."

"Enough platitudes. Get to the point," she snapped. "What do you want?"

"I have come to ask a favor—"

"Of course you have," she said tersely. "Why else would you return to your wife's house after you stole her from her people?"

Vittorius bristled, both angered and saddened by the accusation. "Iduna came with me willingly, Rusila. You know that," he said, forcing his voice to remain level with some difficulty.

"Yes, and then she *died*. Father never forgave you for that, and neither have I."

"Not a day goes by that I don't miss my wife. Her death weighs heavy upon me, as it does our child, who now has children of her own. Your sister may be gone, but her legacy endures."

Rusila's expression softened at his fervent words.

"I cannot say what your father would have done, but I hope you have the grace to forgive the past and let me speak," he continued, placing his hands on his parted knees and bowing his head deeply.

"Very well," she said curtly, though some of the vehemence had melted from her tone. "I will hear you out, Duke. First, I'm sure you must be hungry. Come."

Vittorius could hardly refuse an invitation from the shield-maiden who had been elevated to the position of *kvinne* of the Solveig clan upon her father's death. In Salissardian culture, it was not a hereditary position, but one that spoke to the great faith and trust her people held in her.

Vittorius waited for Rusila to seat herself before sitting beside her on the floor near the hearth. It was rectangular, with raised sides to prevent the spillage of coals, and a pot of stew was suspended from a trio of crossed poles; his mouth watered at the smells steaming from it. Iduna had cooked some of her people's traditional foods occasionally, though ingredients were difficult to come by, and he had forgotten how much he missed them. He pretended to rub a bit of ash from his eye to conceal the tears he wiped away.

Two young women served them, one with pale blond hair, the other tawny gold.

"My daughters, Hetha and Wisna," Rusila introduced.

Hetha ladled out the stew into pewter bowls, while Wisna tore off pieces of freshly baked rye bread. The stew was a hearty mixture of venison and rabbit with root vegetables, mushrooms, and a rich creamy broth, and for dessert they were served a buttermilk raspberry pudding.

"I'm sure you are aware of what is transpiring in Artemisia," Vittorius said once they had finished their meal.

The two of them were relaxing by the softly smoldering fire, with a mug of hot mulled cider which warmed them from the inside.

"Yes," Rusila replied, nodding. "Disturbing circumstances. But even if I sympathize, you know we cannot lend military aid..."

"That's not why I've come. I have another request."

She lifted an eyebrow. "Go on."

"I recall the Solveig clan had good relations with the Braxley, who are willing to hire themselves out as mercenaries, if I'm not mistaken."

Rusila looked at him askance, and he wondered what she was thinking. "You'd better be thankful we're family, Vittorius. Not many outsiders would make such a suggestion and receive a favorable answer. However, that will be Holger's decision, not mine." She paused. "He is also my husband, so I trust you will see him unharmed in this little venture of yours."

Vittorius felt a pang at the mild note of censure in her voice. "I will do my utmost."

She sighed wearily, glancing at her daughters, who were clearing up the remains of their dinner. "What is your proposal, then?"

"I have with me a contract promising eight thousand Artemisian rukmas, the equivalent of thirty-six thousand silver eyrir in your currency, half payable in advance. That would fund the services of the warriors and the supplies they would require. An additional two thousand rukmas is set aside for any amendments, as well as reparations for their families should they not return."

Rusila leaned back, steepling her fingers. Vittorius was aware a sum of that amount was not only fair, it could go a long way toward outfitting a settlement such as Kvalheim with much-needed necessities.

Rusila nodded to herself and rose, fluffing out the fur collar of her cape. "I will return in a week."

Vittorius opened his mouth to protest, scrambling to his feet, but she held up a hand.

"I cannot make a decision without consulting Holger first. Remain here and await my answer. Don't worry, Hetha and Wisna will keep you safe," she added with a slight smirk.

Vittorius had no doubt the daughters of such a formidable shield-maiden would be sufficient protection, but he was still concerned. "You know I don't have much time."

Rusila's grin widened, as if she were enjoying her own private joke. "If your proposal meets with Holger's favor, then travel back to Artemisia will be much swifter than your journey here, wouldn't you say?"

Silver Lining

Khalil jerked awake. How long had it been since his capture? Days? A week? Longer? Tears of shame stung his eyes, and he mercilessly wiped them away with the heel of his bound hand.

"I'm sorry I failed you, Caro," he murmured.

Pausing in his self-remonstration, he heard voices from inside the tent.

"How much do you think we can get for the whelp?" Anwar was asking.

"Six goats at least. Maybe ten," Nibal suggested.

"Ten goats?" Anwar roared. "For the life of her son, Hadiya had better give me fifty—and that lovely young ward of hers!"

Khalil gritted his teeth at the man's gall.

"*Sayyid*, there's a messenger to see you."

"I'm here to discuss a price for the prince," said a sultry voice.

Khalil peered through a tiny crack in the tarpaulin. He thought the person sounded familiar, but their features were obscured by a hood.

"Excellent," Anwar said. Khalil could imagine him rubbing his sweaty hands together greedily. "Do go on."

Before Khalil could make out more, a guard cuffed him on the back of his head. He huddled against the pole as Anwar and his guest retreated into the privacy of the back and continued their conversation in hushed tones, out of his hearing.

"Up ya get!"

Khalil blinked blearily as he was kicked awake. Sand had settled in his eyes, and he tried to rub it away as he was dragged into the tent. It was still dark, hours yet until sunrise.

"So, looks like I'll be getting a good price for you," Anwar chuckled, "but not from your mother. Some witch offered me a much more tempting reward when she found out you were for sale."

He couldn't mean... Veena?

"Get the whelp ready to travel. I'll practice my heartfelt apology to his mother for failing to save her precious boy. Maybe she'll still give me the girl for my trouble?"

He stroked his beard with a lascivious grin, and Khalil's blood turned to fire.

"You swine!" Khalil lunged for Anwar, wrestling him to the ground, bound hands grasping at his thick, fleshy neck. "I'll have your guts for my sandal strings if you dare lay a finger on Fatima!"

It took three men to pull Khalil off Anwar. They pounded him in the ribs, forcing him to his knees.

"That wasn't very smart, boy," Anwar snarled, readying his whip. Three leather thongs with metal tips glinted in the lamplight. "She must be good, though." He licked his lips. "I'll be laying more than just a finger on your pretty harlot."

Khalil trembled with fury as Anwar raised the whip above his head. He flinched, expecting the strike.

Suddenly, Anwar let out a howling cry as a short, thin knife pierced his palm. He dropped the whip and clutched his profusely bleeding hand. "Who threw that?"

A man stood in the entryway, wearing black from head to toe. The lower half of his face was covered by a scarf, leaving only his dark eyes visible—but somehow he reminded Khalil of Morfran.

"*L-La Firar...*" Anwar whispered, his eyes wide with terror.

"Release the boy, Nibal," the man ordered in a soft voice, and Anwar's thin-faced servant cut Khalil's bonds, helping him to his feet.

"You're Sharir," Khalil said, awed.

"That's right," *La Firar* replied, pulling down his scarf. It was the traditional title of the assassin's leader, a word that fittingly meant "inevitability."

He was handsome in an intimidating way, with heavy brows over penetrating deep blue eyes. Long black hair was brushed back from his face and hung about his shoulders, and his facial hair was neatly trimmed. His expression was neutral but intense, and Khalil could see how he commanded a clan of feared assassins. Any man would be cowed by a single glance.

"My name is Jabez. I received Mukhif's letter, which my man here liberated." He gestured to Nibal.

"You did?"

"Mukhif says you are his traveling companion and trusted friend. I could hardly leave you to be devoured by these mangy jackals."

Khalil sighed with relief, earning a sharp rebuke from his injured ribs.

Jabez glanced into the corner to see a hooded figure, the same one Khalil had glimpsed speaking to Anwar earlier. It was Veena, as he'd thought. Wisps of ivory hair drifted from beneath her hood as she lifted her arm, a ball of azure magic hovering in her hand.

"Leave him be, Sharir. He's mine."

She threw the sphere, which shattered in an explosion of sparks as Jabez countered her magic with his own, deep indigo.

"You were banished from the Esaphis by my predecessor and commanded never to return under pain of death."

"Oh?" Veena said innocently. "What crime have I committed, oh great *La Firar*?"

Jabez scowled. "Your sorcery is heresy. Magic belongs to the earth. It must be respected and the price paid. You have no concept of that balance, and use it only for your own selfish ends."

"You know nothing about me!" Veena hissed.

She drew a circle in the air, and shards of blue light shot from her fingertips, flying erratically like stinging insects. Jabez waved his hand, calling forth a wall of shadow, and each of the illusory wasps burst into indigo flame.

The shadows solidified into black feathers, hurtling through the air toward her. Veena dodged as the feather daggers struck the tarpaulin behind her head, then dissolved into dust.

She pulled a piece of charcoal out of her pocket and held it in her palm, chanting a rapid incantation.

Oh Mahira, I summon thee, goddess of fire
I offer this token, may my foe feel your ire

With her free hand, Veena drew a V-shaped emblem in the air, intersected by a vertical line. It turned red, the rock glowing as if it were at the heart of a raging inferno.

Blinding orange flames surged across the sands, and Jabez leaped out of the way, drawing his sword and slicing them with an arc of shadow.

From a crouch, he launched himself toward her, but Veena discarded the cloak and flipped gracefully out of his reach. She landed as nimbly as a desert cat, her lips curled into a grin.

"I could dance all day, Sharir." She stood there confidently with her hand on her hip, taunting him, the red silk of her dress and her ivory hair blowing in the hot breeze.

"I tire of this," Jabez said coldly.

He narrowed his fierce gaze, and shadows gathered in the tent, creeping down the walls and slithering toward her like a writhing mass of obsidian snakes.

"I would suggest you are no match for me, sorceress," he warned. "Leave now, and I will not pursue this transgression upon my domain."

Veena tensed, sidestepping as she unleashed her spectral fire upon the serpents, but it had no effect. For a moment Khalil thought she would retaliate, but she merely scowled and vanished in a puff of blue smoke.

The shadows dispelled, Jabez sheathed his sword with a sigh and turned back to Khalil. "As for you, you were looking for trouble."

"That's right!" Khalil exclaimed, pushing Veena to the back of his mind for the moment. "Queen Caro sent me to make good on my mother's promise! I hope I'm not too late."

"That too was in Mukhif's letter," Jabez said calmly, though his voice took on a strangely sinister tone. "However, I have no obligation to help you further."

"What?" Khalil asked, leaning on Nibal as he hobbled out of the tent.

"I rescued you because you are Mukhif's friend and Chieftess Hadiya's son, but that's all. Your mission and the fate of the queen are outside my purview."

Nibal, apparently a doctor, made Khalil sit upon an overturned bucket while he poked and prodded in a more or less gentle way. "The ribs aren't broken, just bruised. They should be bandaged when you return to your tribe, but you're not in any immediate danger," he said gruffly.

"I won't abandon you in the desert. I'll give you supplies to continue on as planned," Jabez elaborated, crossing his arms. "But this is where our journey ends."

"Too much time has passed already. If I don't get to my mother soon, Caro's plan will fail. She's counting on me. I need your help," Khalil pleaded.

"I must admit surprise at Mukhif aligning himself with the young Queen of Artemisia. I very much wish to meet her," Jabez mused. "However, I know nothing of whether she is worthy."

Khalil's mind flailed. "How I can prove that?"

"You would do so, as her proxy?"

"Yes!" Khalil exclaimed. "Anything."

Jabez stroked his chin thoughtfully. "Very well, I'll give you the chance. If you succeed, I will assist you in your mission. Agreed?"

Khalil frowned, conflicted. It had been weeks already, and Caro was relying on him to bring his warriors to her aid. But if he could somehow prove himself to the Sharir...

"All right. I'll do it."

Jabez gave a slightly menacing smile. "Good."

"Are you sure about this, *La Firar*?" Nibal whispered, and Khalil glanced at the two assassins.

Jabez nodded. "This is a test of worth given to Sharir initiates, however I think it will serve its purpose. This is your last chance to turn back, Prince Khalil. If you fail this test, not only will you not reach your mother in time, you may even lose your life."

Khalil swallowed and nodded numbly. "I'm ready. I have to keep my promise to Caro, whatever it takes."

Jabez's lips turned up at the corners. "Very well. There is a cave beneath us and a system of tunnels. I will be waiting where they let out at the other end. Take as long as you need; however, you are aware of the time constraints most of all. I trust I will not be waiting long."

Khalil gave a determined nod, trying to settle the butterflies in his stomach.

Jabez gestured to a hole in the rocky ground into which Nibal had dropped a long rope. Khalil rubbed his hands together to warm them, then grabbed the rope and slowly lowered himself down. He jumped the last foot and landed in the packed sand.

Nibal pulled up the rope, and Khalil suddenly understood why Jabez had said it was his last chance to turn back.

"Take this," the Sharir leader said, and Khalil looked up, catching a small tinderbox. "Remember, Prince: nothing is as it seems."

With this last cryptic warning, Jabez vanished from Khalil's line of sight, and he heard the two men's footsteps as they returned to their horses.

"Do you think he can do it?" Nibal inquired, sounding doubtful. "The boy is no Sharir."

"He has no choice," Jabez replied simply. "And yet I wonder if he is up to the challenge."

Khalil frowned at their discouraging exchange, then turned his thoughts to the task at hand.

Caro. She was all he could think about. He needed to fulfill his promise. Khalil lifted a torch from a bracket on the wall and lit it with the materials in the tinderbox.

The passage ahead was dark. He took a deep breath, then advanced.

It was a long walk, and Khalil was conscious only of the crackling of the torch, the flopping of the soles of his sandals in the sand, and the sound of his own breath in the pervasive silence.

Eventually, the tunnel branched out, but it wasn't a simple choice of one path or the other, he realized in frustration after backtracking over a dozen times. Each tunnel split into another, until he found himself in a labyrinthine maze. It would take hours, days even, to find the right route through trial and error.

He bit his lip, thinking. This was a test of worth; surely stumbling through blindly wasn't the point. He frowned at the dizzying maze before him, then at his torch, and back again.

What had Jabez said? *Nothing is as it seems*.

The torch was meant to light his way in darkness... but the Sharir were creatures of the night. What if the torch was only a hindrance to his progress?

He dithered a moment, hoping this was the right move, then doused the torch in the sand.

The cavern was plunged into darkness so intense he couldn't see a thing—then small patterns of blue light appeared on the walls of the rightmost tunnel. Khalil crouched and peered close, mystified. Was it magic? No, rather some sort of luminescent lifeform which had attached itself to the rock. In some of the more moist areas of the desert after a long rain, Khalil had seen mushrooms that glowed orange at night, and he imagined these must be similar.

Khalil followed the ghostly path of light, feeling a swell of pride that he had guessed correctly about the torch. But the test wasn't over yet. The tunnel opened into another cave where there was an underground spring. Standing in the spring were two massive life-size statues, proud desert warriors.

Khalil scoured the crystal-clear water, also glowing blue, but didn't see any creatures that might try to poison or eat him. Carefully, he slipped into the spring up to his knees as he waded toward the statues. Behind each of them was a dark spot in the water, a passage through the stone leading to another cave, and Khalil had a bad feeling.

Again, this was a test of worth, not of chance. Jabez had warned him this trial might prove fatal—if he picked the wrong one, it was likely he would drown before he realized his mistake. But how would he know which was correct?

He waded out of the spring again and began to search the area for clues. There was a flat area by the entrance, like a plaque. He dusted off the sand, but it appeared to be blank.

He had an idea and, returning to the spring, cupped his hands and filled them with water, then poured it over the spot. Before his eyes, words appeared, the script darkened by the moisture.

It was an old desert proverb: "The eye is the mirror of the soul."

Khalil frowned, rereading it. What did that mean? What eye? The only other eyes in the room were those of... the statues. He lit the torch again.

He peered deeply into the stone warriors' faces, but could not see anything that made them different. If the clue was referring to a literal mirror, then he would need to reflect the fire off its surface. But what could he use to focus the light?

It had to be something in the room with him, or the test wouldn't be fair. After what seemed like another hour of fruitless searching, a glint attracted his attention. The spring was glowing blue because of the organisms attached to the clear, rounded stones beneath his feet, but there were other pinpricks of light he hadn't noticed before.

Careful not to get the torch wet, Khalil crouched in the pool, his hands feeling along the bottom. His fingers wrapped around a stone that was smooth and slightly sharp, and he lifted it out of the water. It was a faceted crystal nearly indistinguishable from the rest, and it was exactly what he needed.

Khalil returned to the statues and, lifting his torch, angled the light so it refracted through the facets of the crystal into the eyes of the right statue.

Nothing happened. He moved over and tried the same with the left. The light was faint, but it reflected back at him from mirrors embedded deep behind the statue's eyes.

The left passage it was. Unfortunately, the torch which had served him so well couldn't come with him, so he doused it again and left it at the side of the spring. Then he took a deep breath and held it, diving into the water.

Though a desert dweller, Khalil was a strong swimmer. He had tested his endurance often in the oasis spring near the Omaira camp; breath control was especially critical when hunting small, skittish creatures that might bolt at the slightest sound.

He kicked furiously, following the underwater passage that stretched farther than the eye could see. His lungs started to burn with the effort of holding his breath, and a bubble escaped his lips. He pressed them together tightly, willing his aching muscles to continue on. He couldn't fail now, not when he'd come so far.

Doubt flickered across his brain—perhaps he'd chosen the wrong passage after all? Then it opened up above his head and he ascended, legs flailing, fingers clawing to reach the top. His head broke the surface and he gasped, refreshing cool air rushing into his lungs.

Khalil treaded water for a moment, savoring the sensation of breathing again, then swam, feeling for the edge with outstretched hands. He waited for his vision to adjust to the darkness, but he remained as if struck blind in the pitch-black room.

Cold and wet, he crawled to the wall. He found a sharp rock and bashed it against the stone, creating a sort of nick by which he would know he had found his way back to his starting point. He then resorted to feeling his way by touch with deliberate slowness so he didn't miss any small detail which could explain the purpose of this place.

Khalil paused in his search as his fingers met empty air. A tunnel? He made a mental note of it and shuffled forward, feeling for the other side. A short while later he found another tunnel, and then a third. He didn't know how much time had passed, but he eventually felt his way along the entire perimeter of the room, back to his marker in the rock. The only defining features of the chamber were the three tunnels, but they stretched in seemingly opposite directions, and with no light to guide him, he had no hope of finding his way.

He felt a shroud of hopelessness settle upon him, and he sank against the wall, shivering. Was he doomed to fail here? Would Jabez come down and find only his body, robbed of both his life and his honor?

No. He couldn't give into despair.

Caro's sad smile and her sweet laugh came to him, echoing in the cold stillness. Even if they would not be wed one day as his mother hoped, she was still his friend. She had lost so much and been deceived by those she trusted; he couldn't afford to fail her now.

With forced determination, Khalil pulled himself to his feet, re-examining his options. This must be a test as well, he decided. If so, what was the point? The first had been a test to look beyond the obvious and trust the clarity brought by the darkness, surely a tenet taught to adherents of the Sharir. The second, to trust his ingenuity in solving a problem with no immediately apparent solution. And the third...

His mind worked wildly, trying to think of something that could solve this puzzle. A source of light perhaps? Or maybe some markings in the tunnels themselves? Then he realized that was exactly what he shouldn't do. This wasn't a riddle to challenge his cleverness or wisdom—it was a test to trust his instincts.

Khalil slowed his breathing, forcing his beating heart to quiet in his chest. He touched the walls of each of the tunnels, tracing them with his fingertips. The middle one felt infinitesimally warmer and dryer than the others. He craned his head forward, listening.

What did he hear? Nothing. No, there was a faint sound, like wind. What did he smell? The subtle scent of the desert. He took a few steps into the tunnel. The air tasted a little different, too. Saltier. He wondered if Ines would be proud of him for using his senses other than sight.

Khalil's instincts told him this was the correct tunnel, and he plodded forward down the seemingly endless path toward his destination. Eventually, the tunnel curved upward, and a small halo of light invaded his vision. He blinked and moved toward it, increasing his pace. He tripped in his haste, but he didn't care.

Khalil barreled out of the cave at a full run, and nearly knocked Nibal over. "I did it!" he exclaimed, and collapsed against the physician, panting.

Jabez leaned against the stone wall, polishing his curved dagger, which he tucked back into its sheath. "I have never been more pleased to be refuted, Prince. You have proven yourself worthy—and by extension, the queen."

Khalil's heart pounded, and he bowed to the Sharir leader. "So you'll help me?"

Jabez nodded. "I gave you my word. Come, we will deliver you to the Omaira. There may yet be time to make your rendezvous."

Hadiya stared out across the desert. She had risen early, awakened by a change on the wind. At first, there seemed to be nothing, then a small company emerged from the dark line of the horizon.

"Khalil," she greeted warmly as the horses slowed to a halt. He looked a little weary, but otherwise unharmed.

He dismounted gingerly from his seat behind the lead rider, then turned and bowed. "Thank you, *La Firar*."

Jabez nodded, then glanced over Khalil's shoulder. "Chieftess Hadiya."

"I'm grateful to you for rescuing my son," she replied. She did not bow her head, but lowered her gaze briefly in respect.

"I understand from the prince you have an arrangement with the deposed Queen of Artemisia."

"I do," Hadiya confirmed.

"Then you had best make preparations. If you can ready your forces to depart in a day's time, I shall return on the morrow and we will set out at first light."

"You're going with them?" Hadiya inquired, wide-eyed, and Khalil looked surprised as well.

Jabez gave a short nod. "I am. The letter I received made me curious. Besides, your son underwent a Sharir trial and passed. I owe him that much."

His oblique reference puzzled Hadiya, but she nodded. "I'm sure the queen would welcome your aid, *La Firar*. I will prepare my people."

"Tomorrow, then."

Jabez and the other man in black turned and rode away, vanishing once more into the dark.

I'm so happy to have you back," Hadiya said, overjoyed, and hugged her son. "Tell me everything."

"There is so much to tell, I scarcely know where to begin!"

She listened with rapt attention as he recounted his adventures and exploits. Hadiya was sad to hear of the fire at the opera house and Ezalia's death. She had become rather fond of the woman during their short time together.

"When *La Firar* received his kinsman's message, he came to rescue me. I begged him to help me fulfill my mission as per the agreement I made with the queen," Khalil explained, filling in the gaps. "He would only do so if I proved my worth, and so I did."

"I'm proud of you, dearest," Hadiya said, stroking his cheek. "I wish you could stay, but I honor my promises as much as you."

Khalil nodded. "So you think we can make it?"

"Another day, and everything will be set." She paused, thinking. "There's one thing I don't understand, though. You were carrying a message for *La Firar*? From whom?"

"He calls himself Morfran, but we and the Sharir know him as Mukhif. He's the one who wears the silver mask."

Hadiya nodded. "I see. So this Morfran is now your ally?"

"I guess." Khalil shrugged. "He was working for Caro's enemy, then turned to our side. He's utterly devoted to her now. Mukhif's not a particularly friendly fellow, but a strong warrior and a reliable companion."

Time is like a sword; if you don't cut it, it will cut you.

The old idiom rang in Hadiya's ears, and she felt it keenly. For her son to be traveling companions—friends, even—with such a man, was quite a twist of fate.

"How the wheel of destiny turns," Hadiya murmured.

The next morning at precisely dawn, Jabez appeared with three of the Sharir. Scarves were pulled up over their faces, their bodies shrouded in black clothing. Each wore a scimitar belted around their waist beneath a long cloak and a short dagger at their side. Khalil could only guess at the number of concealed weapons they also carried.

"*La Firar*," Khalil greeted, bowing his head in deference to the famed lord of assassins.

"Prince Khalil," Jabez replied, "I have come as agreed. This is Husam, Sakin, and Nibal, whom you have already met."

Four might seem to be an insignificant number, but the Sharir were deadlier than desert cobras—even one would increase their odds.

"Are your forces ready to depart?" Jabez inquired, directing the question to Hadiya, who gave a slight nod.

"Yes, everything is prepared." She gave her son a parting embrace. "Please pass along my well wishes to the queen, and my condolences for Ezalia's death. It must weigh heavily upon her. She will need all the support you can give."

"I will, Mother," he replied.

He mounted his camel as Hadiya saw to the final arrangements, ensuring everything was in order for the large detachment of warriors she was sending to Caro's aid. Khalil was anxious to depart and tapped his finger on the saddle, sending conflicting cues to his confused camel.

"There's still time," Jabez chided. "Getting overwrought won't help anyone. You have done everything you can. We must trust to fate now."

He nodded numbly.

"I wish you the speed of the wind," Hadiya said finally. The familiar farewell sounded nostalgic and sad to Khalil's ears.

On the Fence

Arvind was facing the window, his fingers laced behind his back.

"I've just received some unsettling news," he said, turning to Malcolm. "It seems Lady Lobelia Anthusa is planning an insurrection."

"Your—"

Arvind seized his collar, throwing him against the wall. "Did you know about this?"

His head throbbing dully, Malcolm lifted his hands in surrender, trying not to antagonize the irate prince. "I swear, Your Highness, I had no part in it."

"Explain how this happened."

"With intelligence gleaned from Major Sejic, Lady Lobelia discovered what we were doing. She expressed interest, so I welcomed her into our ranks, but she's used her charisma to stir the nobles into a frenzy. With the added influence of the major, she has quite a number of supporters."

"Why didn't you tell me?" Arvind hissed through clenched teeth.

Malcolm sighed, defeated. "I thought they were empty words, that it would amount to nothing—but I was wrong."

Arvind stared at Malcolm, then released him.

"What do we do now?" Malcolm asked timidly.

Arvind let out a short laugh. "You mean, do we tell the king? What alternative do you think we have?"

"But he'll punish Lady Diascia, even though she's done nothing wrong."

"Are you concerned more for her life or your own?"

Malcolm swallowed. "That's a difficult choice to make."

"Not for me," Arvind retorted. He leaned on the desk and tapped his finger rapidly upon the surface.

"Please, Your Highness, give me some time," Malcolm pleaded. "I'm sure I can resolve this peacefully."

Arvind's finger stilled. "Fine. I don't want to see this spiral out of control any more than you do. But I won't be the only one who'll face the king's wrath if he discovers this, you can be sure of that."

The Way the Cookie Crumbles

Morfran mopped off his face with a wet cloth, his mask sitting beside him on the dressing table. He stared at it a moment, lost in thought.

"I brought more towels," Lottie said, slipping through the door.

Her eyes widened as she glimpsed him without his mask, and she spun, hugging the towels close to her frantically beating heart; Morfran could hear it in the stillness.

"I—I'm sorry."

"It's all right." Morfran let out a soft sigh. "I didn't mean to frighten you."

Lottie gave a silent nod and turned around, her gaze flitting up to his face, then to the floor. "Does it hurt?"

"The memory of the pain is with me always," Morfran replied somberly, running his fingertips across the mask's cool metal surface. "But no, it doesn't hurt."

Lottie swallowed, then forced a smile. "You didn't scare me. I was surprised, that's all."

"Thank you, Lottie."

She set the towels by the door, then hurried out of the room.

Morfran sighed, then faced his reflection in the mirror. Like an enemy he couldn't escape, his face followed him always.

He was accustomed to the reactions by now: fear, followed by horror, and then loathing. Still, Lottie had a good heart, and though she was afraid, there had been no disgust in her gaze. An expression he'd seen all too often.

He closed his eyes, recalling the past. So long ago, and yet the memory came with perfect clarity.

"What is this slop? Useless whelp, can't you even cook a decent meal?"

The man growled and swept his hand across the desk, scattering the bowl of gruel—and an open bottle of vivid orange liquid which skidded off the surface, spilling its contents upon the unfortunate boy.

He fell to his knees and cried out in agony. The man gripped his hair and yanked his head back, examining the damage. The boy had closed his eyes in time to save his vision from the corrosive acid, but his face was disfigured on one side and would have extensive scarring.

"That'll learn you, brat!" he snapped, and tossed the boy roughly aside.

Morfran still remembered the humiliation more than the actual pain, which had set deep roots within his soul. He had realized he meant nothing to the slavers. To them, he was only a beast who would be put down if it outlived its usefulness. He'd put *them* down first.

He escaped soon after that incident, sliding beneath the wire that encircled the camp, gritting his teeth and biting back the tears as it ripped through his flesh. Once out, he ran for hours, until he didn't know where he was or how much time had passed.

It was then they found him. The Sharir. They looked at a boy whose body was bruised and beaten, and did not see a worthless slave—they saw a warrior. And that was what he became.

He took the name Mukhif, for the first tenet of their society was to abandon the name with which one had been born, and he was all too happy to cast it aside. His training was hard, his body aching and weary, but he was not a slave or an animal; he was bettering himself, and they nurtured his innate talents. Soon, he was the strongest and fastest of them all. His devotion impressed even *La Firar*, and it wasn't long before he was accompanying the elite on their toughest missions. Nothing could break him, not pain or even torture.

He returned to the brigands who had held him captive, and with newfound ease, he slaughtered them all without remorse or mercy. The leader who had burned him, Morfran left for last. As the cur pleaded for his life, he confessed it was an Artemisian noble who had engineered his kidnapping. Morfran listened dispassionately to his pleas, then slit his throat with his own dagger, the dagger which had been stolen from Morfran that very night.

But even the solitary life of an assassin could not sate his appetite for blood, so he broke away, becoming a rogue mercenary for hire and taking yet another new name. Over time, "Morfran" had become synonymous with "Death."

He hid his face in his hands, the memories returning unbidden.

"Are you all right? I heard Lottie racing down the hall."

Morfran sighed. "I scared her without meaning to."

His voice was laced with sorrow, and Ines held out her hand, cupping his cheek. She smiled up at him. Though her gaze was unfocused, it was kind as always.

It was during the darkest point of his life that Morfran met Ines. A pure soul, broken and abused just as he was, yet having endured. She followed him like a silent, pale shadow, his one companion in the harsh reality which he had created for himself. She never asked what he was planning or what he intended to do, she merely placed her trust in him. She was the one person who had seen the darkness inside his heart and had not flinched from it.

That first night after he rescued her, Ines had come to his quarters.

Morfran looked up as she padded into the room. "Why are you here?" he asked.

"You saved my life."

"You owe me nothing, and I have no wish for a lover."

She smiled enigmatically. "I have not come to offer myself, but to *see* the face of my rescuer."

He was hesitant, but did not resist as she slid off the mask and touched his disfigured skin with her fingertips.

"A strong chin, broad jaw, brows creased with worry, and sad, lonely eyes."

The features she described were his own, yet even he could not see beyond the scarring in the mirror. He felt as if she were tracing the very contours of his soul.

Since then, she had rarely left his side, and when he departed, she was always waiting for his return. Many thought they must be lovers, and Morfran let them. Such assumptions, however false, provided Ines with a modicum of protection, for who would dare touch the woman of the man called Death?

Only Ines had never cared about his reputation. He saw himself in her sightless eyes, and it humbled him. He realized then his path had strayed, marred not by the scars on his body but on his heart.

"Where are your thoughts, Morfran?" Ines inquired with a small smile, as if sensing the dark turn his reverie had taken.

"Just the past, Ines."

"It's okay to remember it once in a while, but don't stay there. You have a more important mission now, isn't that right?"

Morfran chuckled and took her hands. "Yes, you reminded me of that back then, too. I wouldn't be here if not for you."

She beamed up at him, her beautiful face radiant.

Maybe it wasn't too late. Perhaps his black soul might even find redemption.

Roll the Dice

Caro sat in her billowy dress and sipped her tea, anxiously awaiting news.

Sipping tea seemed to be a thing for ladies to do in Uyria's mind. If Caro was at the palace, she would naturally mince about looking gorgeous and attending lavish parties. As it was, Caro spent an inordinate amount of time drinking tea and engaging in idle gossip.

She was also bored out of her skull and desperately wanted to stab something.

There was a commotion at the door, and Gaius admitted a haggard and worn-looking Stelian.

Caro nearly jumped out of her skin with delight and rose, rattling the china on the tray. Uyria let out a small huff of disapproval at Caro's unladylike haste and the boy's scraggly appearance.

"Your Majesty," Stelian began breathlessly, "I have returned with Lord Alenard's army. Captain Lance and the troops are camped out at the edge of Lady Uyria's property, where they should keep out of sight of patrols."

"Thank you, Stelian," Caro said, and nodded to Alenard. "Please see they have everything they need. Once Khalil arrives, we will discuss our next plan of action."

"He's not here yet?" Stelian inquired.

Caro shook her head. A day had passed since their agreed rendezvous, and it was apparent something was wrong. Khalil and his clan had yet to appear or make any contact.

Had something happened to Khalil in the desert? A glance at Morfran indicated he too was concerned.

"I'm afraid we can do nothing more than wait," Ezekiel declared sternly.

Caro nodded and prayed nothing had happened to her friend.

"What of our supplies?" Lance inquired, looking over the documents the quartermaster handed him.

"We brought enough with us from Biding for two weeks, plus dried goods for a longer journey, and Lady Uyria has furnished us with stores from the barony."

"Good."

There was a popping sound, and then an explosion rocked the camp.

Lance burst out of his tent as the cries of his men rose into the air. "What in blazes...?" he cursed, stepping over debris.

"Sir!" His chief warrant officer stood to attention.

Lance surveyed the destruction. A plume of smoke was billowing up from the charred remains of a wagon, and soldiers were running back and forth, throwing buckets of water on the smoldering wreckage.

"What happened here?"

"Some spies infiltrated the camp and tried to sabotage the supply wagons. We managed to put out the fire, but they escaped in the chaos."

Lance gritted his teeth. "Clean this mess up, and get ready to move out!" he ordered gruffly. "It seems the battle we've been waiting for is down to the short strokes."

"Milord!" a breathless Lance cried, bursting through the door.

He flushed crimson as everyone turned to him from the dinner table, the knitted scar over his eye standing out against his red skin.

"Out with it, man!" Gaius snapped.

"Forgive me, Lords, Ladies, Your Majesty," he said hurriedly, "but I have terrible news. As we feared, the forces stationed at Oswin's have gotten wind of our presence."

"How do you know this?" Morfran inquired.

"I regret to report a couple of spies snuck into the camp and set a fire. However, the men on watch could not capture the interlopers."

"Then the enemy knows of our whereabouts. They may even suspect our strategy," Alenard mused, and Lance bowed his head.

"Forgive me, milord, I have failed you."

"No." Caro rose, her meal forgotten. "We only fail if we do nothing. There is no time left to wait for Khalil. Alenard, prepare your forces to ride out. If they plan to make a move, then we will meet them in battle, and we will prevail."

"Yes, Majesty!" Alenard exclaimed. He retrieved his coat and headed for the door, Lance scurrying at his heels.

"Gaius, I want you to take men to evacuate the towns and set up a camp for the displaced citizens."

Gaius bowed, and he too disappeared.

"Are you sure?" Morfran asked quietly, so only she could hear.

Caro shook her head, her expression grim. "We have no other choice."

Alenard took command of his forces, stationing them at the entrance of the now-empty town of Ock, which was to become a battleground.

Caro was not to be on the front lines, though she dressed like a soldier to bolster the troops' morale as they passed by the place where she sat astride a regal-looking horse. She was their beacon of light, their hope for a peaceful future. She smiled encouragingly though her heart was heavy, knowing what she was sending them into.

Once they had filed off to their positions, Caro returned to the manor, where a temporary base of operations had been established in the drawing room.

"I want you to accompany Alenard into the field," she instructed Morfran. "Your expertise and prowess will be an invaluable asset, and may tip the scales in our favor."

He appeared reluctant to leave her side but nodded obediently. "As you wish, my queen."

Ezekiel had brought the map from Alenard's villa in Agassey, fastening it upon a board of porous wood. Various colored pins were poked into the map, replacing the beads. While the movements of the rest of her forces had been adjusted, the red pins were still in the desert, their fate and location uncertain.

"What has become of Khalil, I wonder?"

Ezekiel gave her a stern look. "Did you not say during your impassioned speech that Alenard's troops would win, regardless?"

"Of course," Caro replied, frowning at his candor. "However, it will be at a greater cost than we anticipated."

She winced. Referring to men's lives in terms of "acceptable losses" set her teeth on edge, but she was a queen and that was the reality of war. She could do her best to mitigate the casualties, but she could never eliminate them.

"The plan still hinges on Khalil making his appointment. I just hope that by some miracle he arrives in time."

Time and Tide

Alenard issued orders to stand firm and resisted wiping the sweat from his brow.

He glanced to where Morfran sat astride his massive stallion, looking unruffled and cool as always. Alenard almost envied him.

Zhelyas's forces had arrived at their location en masse, no doubt hoping to overwhelm them with sheer numbers.

"What do you think?" Alenard inquired of Morfran, who was staring at the approaching army.

"They are many, but your men are well trained."

Alenard nodded, buoyed by that frank assessment. Morfran was not known for hollow flattery.

"What now, my lord?" Morfran inquired, yielding to Alenard's authority on the battlefield.

The margrave felt a little uneasy at commanding such a seasoned warrior, but cleared his throat. "We advance and meet them halfway. We cannot allow them to take the bridge, or all will be lost. Our queen is counting on us."

Lance blew into a horn.

"Advance!" Alenard cried, and the soldiers fell into step, weapons drawn.

Despite Morfran's optimism, however, Zhelyas's soldiers proved difficult to overcome. True, Alenard's men had trained for battle all their lives, but there were too many of the enemy in such an enclosed space, and they were soon corralled into the city.

Alenard and Morfran, fighting side by side, backed up onto the bridge. If things continued like this, it looked like their side would win, but with far higher casualties than projected—a fact which Alenard knew Caro was painfully aware of.

Alenard's drifting thoughts were rattled back to reality as an enemy sword came crashing down toward him. There was a clang of steel, and Morfran's blade blocked the strike, cleaving his opponent in two.

"Focus!" he snapped, the first sign of irritation he'd shown since the battle began. Even his icy composure was cracking under the strain.

Alenard gritted his teeth, and they faced their enemy back to back. They were trapped.

Out of nowhere, a loud droning tone sounded, unlike any Alenard had heard before, and he turned his gaze to look for the source. Such distraction might have cost him his life, but Zhelyas's men were equally surprised. They stared into the impenetrable shadows on the other side of the bridge.

A moment passed, then the silence exploded with a war cry—and a warrior on a lean steed, the kind used in the desert.

"Khalil!" Alenard gasped as the lead rider came into view, his scimitar drawn.

Khalil lopped off the head of a soldier standing in his way, racing along the bridge to their aid. To Alenard's amazement, he was followed by no less than five hundred warriors, armed and cutting a swath through their foes. They all wore armbands or scarves of red, marking them as members of Khalil's tribe, the Omaira—except for four lone figures. Clad in black with fabric covering their faces, they seemed to fight with deadly efficacy. Alenard thought he heard a gasp of recognition from Morfran, but could not be certain in the heat of battle.

With the timely arrival of their reinforcements, Alenard and his troops regained their foothold, routing Zhelyas's diminished forces and pushing them back. They either surrendered or fled, scattering to the wind.

"We've won!" Lance blurted, racing into the house, then bowed apologetically for his outburst.

Caro had been discussing contingencies with Ezekiel, and their conversation was cut short.

"What?" Ezekiel said, blinking in surprise despite his earlier admonition.

"Prince Khalil showed up in the nick of time, Your Majesty, and the day was saved."

Caro heaved a sigh of relief, and Ezekiel collapsed into the nearest chair.

"I hear congratulations are in order," Uyria said, bustling in. "We should have wine to celebrate."

"Perhaps later, Lady Uyria," Caro replied. "Please serve some for His Grace. I must see to my troops."

Outside the town, Lottie and Gaius were tending to the wounded in white medical tents which had been erected during the hostilities. Gaius gave Caro an encouraging nod and a smile as she passed.

Other soldiers had retrieved their fallen comrades from the battlefield and were loading them upon wagons with reverence, to be taken back to Biding where they could be buried in their home soil.

A little farther on, several men knelt upon the ground, hands bound behind their backs.

"Your Majesty," Alenard greeted her, and bowed low.

"An excellent outcome, Margrave. You and your men should be proud."

"I am honored, Your Majesty, though I cannot claim all the credit." He jerked his head toward Morfran and Khalil.

"So who might these be?" Caro inquired.

"Enemy soldiers who surrendered rather than be killed," Lance replied with mild distaste.

"However, we are uncertain what to do with them," Alenard admitted. "We had assumed they were all loyal to Zhelyas's cause, but it seems that's not the case. We could execute them as traitors to the throne..." He trailed off as she frowned. "But I did not think you would approve."

Caro knew it was the wisest course of action given their limited resources. She couldn't burden Uyria with prisoners, but neither could she bring herself to kill her subjects when they had done nothing more than follow the one who now held all the power as king. Although their loyalty had been misplaced, it was still loyalty.

She had an idea. "They were all stationed at Oswin's, isn't that so?"

Alenard nodded. "After the baron's arrest, Zhelyas appropriated the manor as a military base. Up until a short while ago, he was there with Luther, but it seems they've since left."

"Then to serve that purpose, Oswin's lands must have been furnished with the necessary supplies. Station some guards, and that will become our prisoner of war camp."

Alenard scratched his chin. "Its location is favorable for our purposes, even as we move closer to the capital. I shall do so right away, Your Majesty."

He bowed, and Lance began rounding up the prisoners to deliver them to their new home.

"Cutting it close there, Khalil," Caro teased as he approached, accompanied by a figure in black.

"Sorry, ran into a spot of trouble. Oh, Mukhif." He waved at Morfran, who turned his way.

Morfran's gaze grazed by him to the stranger.

"Ah, this is—"

"Jabez," Morfran said tonelessly.

"Mukhif."

It was evident the two were acquainted by their tense voices and manner.

Khalil shuffled to the side awkwardly, then he grinned, sweeping Caro into the air.

"Put me down. This isn't becoming," she said, laughing.

He set her on her feet, still smiling with elation.

"What happened to you?" she asked.

"It's such a long tale," he said, shaking his head with exasperation. "Fool that I was, I got myself captured by a rival tribe who wanted to sell me for some goats. But one of them was a spy for the Sharir, and he delivered Mukhif's letter to his boss, who came and rescued me. That's him."

"So the Sharir came," Caro murmured, glancing at the man. "I wonder why?"

Khalil shifted his feet. "He said he was curious about you."

Caro cocked her head, returning her attention to their conversation. "Did he now?"

"So I see you have inherited the title of *La Firar*," Morfran was saying to the stranger.

Jabez nodded. "Yes, *La Firar* Almusakat passed away a few years back."

"I am sorry to hear that," Morfran said, and sounded genuinely mournful at the news. "I wish him peace in the afterlife."

The two men shared a moment of silence in respect for their former comrade.

"I received your intriguing letter," Jabez mused. "It was quite a surprise."

"I wasn't sure if you would answer."

Jabez smiled. "The boy proved himself deserving on behalf of your young queen. It is she who I have come to meet."

Morfran's lip twitched at his genial tone.

Caro stepped forward, deciding this was her cue, and Morfran gestured at her approach.

"Your Majesty, may I present *La Firar*, the chief of the Sharir."

Caro stared up at the man dressed in black from head to toe. He had pulled down his scarf, and his face was lean but strong, with the coloring of the desert people and dark indigo eyes.

He seemed to wait a moment to see what she would do, then bowed low. "Your Majesty. Please call me Jabez."

"Honored to meet you, Jabez," she said. "I am grateful for your timely assistance during this conflict, and for aiding Khalil, who I understand was waylaid in the desert. Without you, this battle would not have gone so well for us."

Caro spoke of her appreciation, yet without an ounce of deference. A tribe of assassins would not respect her for being meek and amiable; she had learned as much from her first encounter with Morfran.

Jabez nodded, apparently impressed. Although Hadiya and Khalil showed the Sharir reverence, they were not in the desert. This was her kingdom, and she was the law here.

"It was our pleasure, Your Majesty." A smile creased Jabez's face, and he looked at Morfran. "It befits you to have found such a worthy queen to serve."

Morfran bent his head in acknowledgment, and Jabez turned his attention back to Caro.

"If it would please Your Majesty, I and my people wish to accompany you on your journey. If this Zhelyas is as much a cur and coward as Khalil has made him out to be, then he should not be sitting upon your throne."

"I appreciate your offer, Jabez, and accept both your cooperation and your counsel," Caro said. "I would ask that when we discuss our next plan of attack, you join us. I would value your insight."

"I would be honored, though you hardly seem in need of advice. This stratagem was well thought out and executed, despite our unavoidable delay. Your forces might have been able to hold the bridge even had we not arrived."

"Perhaps, but at a significant loss of men. There is a much greater battle ahead, and I do not wish to tax my resources so soon."

Jabez stroked his chin. "Wise. Very well, I shall attend upon you at your pleasure, Your Majesty."

Caro let out a long sigh after Jabez had left. It was exhausting keeping up a conversation at that level of formality and caution.

"So those are your people, the Sharir," she said, turning to Morfran.

"Yes. I had hoped they would come, though I would not wish for them to cause any inconvenience for you. The Sharir are used to being the 'top dogs,' so to speak."

Caro shrugged, working a kink out of her neck. "I wouldn't worry about that. Jabez is cunning and I will keep a close eye on him, yet I do not sense any deception in his words. Will that be a problem for you?"

"What do you mean?"

"You know each other. I could tell from the way he spoke to you with such familiarity. And you seemed to be a little on guard."

"Even wearing a mask, you can see right through me." Morfran sighed, resigned. "Jabez and I were recruited by the Sharir at around the same time. We were rivals for accolades, jobs, and the respect of our *La Firar*, Almusakat. He was both a teacher and a father figure, since he was the one to discover me near dead in the sand. He took me in, and I apprenticed beneath him alongside Jabez."

Morfran hung his head, the memories trickling back. "But I couldn't stay. There was too much anger in my heart and the Sharir, though assassins, must have clear sight unmuddied by personal grievances. Almusakat gave me leave to go, though I believe he had hoped I would succeed him as *La Firar*. Now, Jabez holds that title instead."

"Morfran..."

"Please do not be concerned, Your Majesty. I knew when I wrote the letter that it would dredge up unpleasant events in my past. Jabez is an honorable man. He will not betray you nor go back on his word."

"And you?" Caro pressed, still having not received a satisfactory answer.

"Jabez and I will look past our differences to work together, and I will serve you as I always have, my queen."

Caro was heading back to Uyria's to pass on the news to Ezekiel, when she noticed a dark figure at the side of the road. It was one of the Sharir, who pulled back their hood. Caro was surprised. The formless garb and face scarf had disguised the fact that the warrior was a woman.

The Sharir noticed Caro and bowed. "*La Firar* has instructed us to obey you, Your Majesty. How may I be of service?"

"I wasn't expecting to find a woman in the company of the Sharir."

The woman smiled. Her face was gentle for an assassin, with dusky skin, tousled dark hair, and a distinct purplish tinge to her lips. "My name is Sakin. The Sharir do not differentiate between gender; I am as much a warrior as the men."

"For a queen such as myself, learning to fight has been necessary—even more so, given the circumstances—but I am unique in that regard," Caro admitted.

"If *La Firar* grants me permission, I would be pleased to practice with you," Sakin offered. "It may be beneficial to have a woman to spar with."

Caro was delighted by the idea. "I would like that, Sakin."

A Woman Scorned

Malcolm hadn't attended any of Lobelia's secret meetings since the first, but after his reprimand from Arvind, he felt it was his duty to try and dissuade her and her followers before there was no turning back.

The room was dark, the curtains drawn, lit only by the sconces on the walls, giving everything an almost eerie quality.

"Earl Dahl, welcome," Lobelia greeted, and all eyes turned to him.

His gaze scoured the ghostly faces of the half-dozen attendees, and he sighed inwardly with relief to see Arcus and Radella were not among them. Radella had been adamant in her opposition; Arcus had seemed less sure, but it appeared he had also seen the error of his ways.

Diascia stood at her sister's side, while Sejic leaned against the wall by the door, his arms crossed over his armored chest.

Lobelia's hips swayed as she made her way across the room toward Malcolm. "Have you come to give us another speech about how hopeless this action is?"

In contrast to her usual seductive dresses, she was wearing a black leather pantsuit with a jacket trailing to the floor, her long hair bound up with black roses.

She stopped, gazing up at him with a sinister smile, and for the first time, he realized that everything she had done before now was merely a ploy. This had been her endgame all along.

"I'm going to give you one last chance to join me," Lobelia said.

"You have to stop this. Nothing good can come of it."

"Strange that they disagree with you," she jeered, sweeping her hand across the room.

"There's no chance you'll succeed," Malcolm said loudly, meeting the gaze of each in turn, "but it isn't too late. If you leave now, this never needs to be mentioned again."

A few of the faces looked uncertain; others were resolute.

"You saw what he did to Nefion!" Rudo spat. "How can you follow such a monster?"

Malcolm shook his head regretfully. "What happened was a tragedy. I only want to prevent a greater one."

"He's right. I—I can't go along with this anymore, Lebby," Diascia stammered.

"My baby sister, turning on me?" Lobelia sounded both disappointed and betrayed. Her expression darkened. "I was afraid you'd been tainted by the king's attentions. If you're not with me, then you're *against* me."

Malcolm heard a dangerous undercurrent in her voice and moved to stand between them. "Lady Lobelia, this isn't necessary—"

"Sister, please stop this," Diascia pleaded desperately. "You can't win!"

"This isn't a game!" Lobelia hissed back, and smacked her sister across the cheek.

Malcolm held Diascia protectively. "Is it worth risking all our lives?" he asked, attempting to reason with Lobelia, but the fervent look in her eyes suggested it was futile.

"Major, the king has returned!" a soldier cried from the hall.

"Good," Lobelia said with a sneer, and Sejic handed her a sword. "It's time to take down that usurper once and for all."

She snapped her fingers, and soldiers grabbed Malcolm and Diascia, shackling their wrists with heavy chains.

"You will witness the triumph you could have shared, and then I will decide what's to be done with a couple of faithless cowards."

She leaned close, and Malcolm inhaled the heady scent of her perfume. "I see you've finally made your choice, Earl. Little good it will do you."

Lobelia strode ahead of the group, her sword glinting unsheathed at her side. Sejic's soldiers opened the throne room doors at her approach.

Zhelyas was standing at the center of the chamber. He turned to her, his gaze glittering with menace. "What is the meaning of this?"

Sejic's soldiers pushed Malcolm and Diascia into the room and to their knees.

"Guards!" Zhelyas bellowed.

"You're wasting your breath. We've replaced the security forces with Sejic's own men," Lobelia stated, sounding confident of her success despite his unexpected arrival.

"Sejic, you cur!" Luther spat, but Zhelyas held up a hand.

"You dare stand against me?" he seethed.

"We're not afraid of you!" Lobelia spat back.

"Is that so?" Zhelyas smiled, an expression so at odds with the situation, it gave Malcolm chills. "Then I'll have to take care of this little insurrection myself."

Zhelyas's coldly amused sneer turned to a glower of rage, mirroring the fire which burst to life in his hands. "Why don't I give you a *personal* demonstration?"

Sinister red flames gleamed off the polished white marble, and it almost seemed as if they were standing in the swirling inferno of Zhelyas's fury.

Lobelia took an involuntary step backward, her gaze flitting to Sejic at her side. His face was gray, but he tightened his grasp on his sword.

Zhelyas waved his hand sharply, and the blade grew red, the metal heated as if by a forge. Sejic cried out as the hilt seared his hands, and it fell clattering to the floor.

The rest of the conspirators backed away as Zhelyas approached. "I'm going to enjoy teaching you a lesson."

Helpless, Malcolm watched in horror as Zhelyas swept his hand through the air with a lazy affectation, and fire leaped forth from his fingers. Flames arced toward Lobelia, but she dodged, the hem of her coat set alight. She stamped on the fabric and scowled.

Lobelia was a better swordswoman than Malcolm had been aware of. Effrenian women must have some military training, and Sejic had obviously been giving her some pointers as well.

"You think you can stop me?" Zhelyas challenged.

"I can try," Lobelia replied brazenly, and took a defensive stance.

Zhelyas summoned a long, gleaming red chain and ricocheted it against the ground, sending it snaking in her direction. She rolled nimbly out of the way. Lobelia was holding her own against Zhelyas, but Malcolm had the sinking feeling the king was toying with her.

"You should give up while you still have the chance," he taunted, advancing upon her, swinging the chain back and forth. "Nobody here will save you."

"I don't need anyone to save me."

"You should show me more deference, woman," Zhelyas warned. The eerie red glow of the chain matched the fire which glinted in his eyes.

"I am Effrenian. I grew up in the midst of anarchy," she countered, again dodging his strike. "I don't fear you. I don't even fear death."

The chain hurtled toward her, but there was no time to evade it, so she batted it away with her sword.

He lifted an eyebrow. "You have spirit. I like that. Perhaps I'll keep you for myself."

Zhelyas again lashed out with the chain, but this time it wrapped itself around her sword, and he flung it away.

She balled her fist and lunged as he drew close, but he seized her wrist in a vise-like grip.

"I tire of these games. Those who followed you will be punished, but no such reprieve awaits you. You will suffer dearly for your insolence."

Lobelia clawed at his arm as he gripped her throat.

By now, Luther's own security forces had rounded up the rest of the nobles to witness the punishment for defying their king.

"Goodbye, Lady Lobelia Anthusa."

Malcolm cowered on the ground, striving vainly to block out her bloodcurdling screams as Zhelyas immolated her alive. Sejic soon followed, and the putrid smell of charred flesh choked the air.

Zhelyas turned to Malcolm, who was trying hard not to retch. A soldier pulled him to his feet.

"Prince Arvind tells me you are faultless in this matter, Earl Dahl."

"Y-yes, sire," he stammered, eyes wide, and paralyzed with fear. The manacles upon his wrists stood as testimony to his innocence.

Unnoticed until now, Arvind stood in the corner, arms crossed. It seemed he hadn't been convinced by Malcolm's assurances, and had taken the matter into his own hands.

"Good. I would hate for my trust in you to be misplaced."

Zhelyas's gaze slid to Diascia, who knelt on the floor nearby, similarly bound and numb with shock as she stared at her beloved sister Lobelia, murdered before her very eyes.

"A pity," Zhelyas murmured, and traced the contour of her jaw before turning away.

He stepped over the smoldering bodies and made his way back to the throne. "I trust you have all learned your lesson this time, my good nobles. The instigators are dead; their accomplices will be flogged and remain as guests of my dungeon for the foreseeable future." His gaze raked the crowd. "The rest of you shall return to your quarters and contemplate what has transpired here."

Diascia and the others were led away by armed guard, and Malcolm felt a pang of regret.

"Please, Your Majesty, spare Lady Diascia. She didn't know what her sister was doing."

Zhelyas turned his eyes upon Malcolm once more. "That is an impertinent request, Earl," he said curtly, then paused. "Yet it is one I shall grant."

Malcolm sighed with relief as Diascia was released.

"However, I do not wish to see her face again."

"I'll take care of her," Takaria said quietly, guiding her out of the hall.

Malcolm waited until they were gone, then turned back to the king and gave a deep bow to convey his gratitude.

"Court will resume its usual session tomorrow," Zhelyas declared with a dismissive wave. "Take care not to test my temper further."

Blind Spot

"Where were you?" Zhelyas demanded as Veena casually strolled into the palace.

She shrugged and lowered the hood of her cloak, shaking her hair free of sand.

"I was merely pursuing another avenue of opportunity, sire," she purred. "Unfortunately, it didn't pan out." Veena wasn't quite unable to keep the vexation out of her voice.

"What avenue?" he pressed, clearly incensed at her evasion.

"You know I hail from the Esaphis. I was seeking to recruit some members of a clan of assassins who are infamous there. However, they couldn't see past their shallow little desert."

It wasn't quite the truth, but it should satisfy the turbulent king.

"Well, I seemed to have managed quite well without your help," he said snidely, and Veena's lip curled.

"Of course, sire. I expected nothing less."

Veena glared at the conjuration of Khalil and the desert warriors. After she had been humiliated by the Sharir who accompanied them and forced to retreat in shame, she had decided to keep tabs on the prince. Apparently, the wayward queen had recruited more than just the Omaira clan heir on her journey through the Esaphis, and they were now camped out alongside the rest of her army.

Veena hadn't anticipated this development, and she narrowed her gaze as one clanswoman in particular caught her eye, titian hair clearly visible amongst her dark-haired kin.

Fatima was Hadiya's ward, taken in after her own parents had died, and she was fiercely protective of her chieftess. They had nearly come to blows when Veena had returned to the desert, brimming with power and seeking Hadiya's favor.

"No," Hadiya had said gravely. "We cannot turn to magic to solve our problems. It would do more harm than good."

"You just aren't seeing the potential. Imagine it!" Veena protested, and she lifted her hand, sorcerous light filling the tent.

Fatima stood at the entrance as Veena pleaded her case. She darted between them, a dagger drawn.

"*Sayyida* Hadiya has heard your argument, and there is nothing more to say," she said, facing down Veena, who bristled.

"You have some nerve to stand against me."

"You don't scare me, Veena," she retorted tartly.

"That's enough, both of you," Hadiya remonstrated. "Stand down, Fatima."

Fatima obeyed, but kept a wary eye upon their unruly guest.

"I have made my decision, Veena," Hadiya said firmly. "There is nothing more to say."

Veena pursed her lips, then swept out of the tent without a backward glance, her blood boiling at the indignity of being summarily rejected.

Khalil was waiting outside, and he shifted nervously as she stormed past. It seemed he had overheard the argument.

"Wait, Veena!" he called, and placed his hand on her shoulder.

She spun away, glaring at him. "And you? Do you agree with your mother? Would you turn away the gifts magic can bring because you're too cowardly?"

He shook his head. "The only thing I'm scared of is what it's doing to you. I hate seeing you like this," he said sincerely, and Veena's heart rebelled against his kind words.

"What do you want from me?" she demanded, voicing the question burning on her tongue.

"Ever since we were children, I have wanted you to be happy."

Fatima stepped outside the tent, giving her a disapproving frown, and Veena glared at them both.

"Don't worry," she spat. "I will be."

Seeing them now awoke conflicting emotions she had thought buried in her past. It was like her heart was a swirling miasma, and she hated feeling weak. She was above all this. She had manipulated a coward into seizing the throne; she would have everything she desired, and more.

And no pampered desert brat was going to get in her way.

Against the Grain

After the successful campaign at Ockbridge, Caro and her company—which now included Alenard's men, the desert warriors, and the few but lethal Sharir—made their way south. Ezekiel had opted to wait in comfort at Uyria's estate with a small contingent to oversee the security of the canal and the prison camp which had been established at Oswin's manor.

Khalil's arrival had been timely, saving Alenard's forces from being utterly defeated, but they were still at a disadvantage. Even with the added men, there was no way they could compete against the full might of the royal army. Still, Caro wasn't going to back down now. Ezalia had given her life for the cause, and she was going to see it through to the end. Her one hope now remained with Vittorius and the mercenaries he had promised to hire.

When Caro had left the capital in the beginning, she had veered west toward Oswin's manor. This time, she crossed the bridge and traveled down the east road instead toward Arborlisle, an area of dense, impenetrable forest, and the location of one of Vittorius's estates.

It was now mid-spring, and Caro couldn't believe that half a year had already passed since that fateful day. Wildflowers bloomed along the road, pretty yellow buttercups and bright orange poppies, papery blue cornflowers and spears of violet betony. The sun shone high overhead, not yet as oppressively hot as in the summer, but still enough to cause beads of sweat to dot Caro's forehead.

The desert dwellers seemed most comfortable since heat was a normal fixture in their lives, although the unfamiliarity of the greenlands was of evident fascination to them in contrast to the sandy dunes of their home. Sakin, despite being a fearsome assassin, queried Caro as to the names of every flower they passed, and she collected a sample of each one, pressing them within a small book.

Caro sent the bulk of her forces around the edge of the woodlands, where it would be easier for a large number of people to maneuver. The Omaira, accustomed to endless stretches of desert, had particular difficulty navigating through the trees, while the Sharir seemed to adapt quickly to their surroundings.

Vittorius was waiting at the entrance of a small villa nestled in a clearing. It was a tidy two-story building with a mauve exterior and white trim, and a porch supported by a colonnade of four slender columns. He descended the steps at their approach, bowing.

"Your Majesty," he said, then gave her a warm smile. "Dear niece, I'm relieved to see you arrive safely, and having completed your mission."

He surveyed her entourage. "You seem to have collected a number of allies. Will you introduce us?"

Caro nodded and presented Lottie, Ines, Khalil, and Jabez. When it was Morfran's turn, he bowed low—perhaps seeking to avoid an unpleasant confrontation like the one with Ezekiel.

"Despite what you may have heard, Duke Vittorius, I am loyal to the queen and serve her interests alone."

Vittorius lifted an eyebrow. "I am not a suspicious man by nature, yet I must admit this turn of events is unexpected. Tell me more. The grand duke was brief in his communications, and I am eager to learn what has transpired since your departure."

His eyes glanced over Ines, and he tipped his head. "Pleased to make your acquaintance as well, miss."

She nodded back, seeming a little surprised at being addressed.

"That woman, what do you know of her?" Vittorius asked Caro quietly.

"Ines? She was Morfran's companion. He met her in Effrenia, I believe. Why?"

He smiled, shaking his head. "It's nothing. She just seems familiar somehow."

Morfran twitched his head, and Caro followed his gaze to twin pairs of bright blue eyes staring at her from behind the door.

"Maeli, Aldin!" Caro sank to her knees and embraced the two small children who came running out of the house, barreling into her at full speed.

"Auntie Caro!" they both cried in unison as she nuzzled their gold hair.

"Caro, dear."

She rose and embraced the young woman who had spoken. "Andrine. It's wonderful to see you."

Caro turned to Morfran. "This is my cousin, Countess Andrine Iduna, Vittorius's daughter. And these little munchkins are her twins, Aldin and Maeli."

"Sir," the boy, Aldin, said, while his sister gave a little curtsy. It melted Caro's heart.

A cloud passed across Andrine's face. "What about Malcolm?"

Caro shook her head. "I'm afraid there has been no word."

"Pardon me, Lady Andrine," Morfran said politely. "I cannot say for certain, but I believe Earl Malcolm Dahl was still alive the last time I was at the palace. He took care to stay out of Zhelyas's way and calmed the other nobles after the initial attack."

Andrine sniffled and blinked back tears. "That sounds like my Malcolm."

Caro hugged her cousin again and sent Morfran an approving look. Even if it could not be verified, his words had been just what Andrine needed to hear to set her heart at peace.

"Maeli, Aldin. We should leave your auntie alone for a while, she's very tired."

"Aww," they both whined. "Play with us later, okay?"

She nodded, and they laughed and ran off, each holding tight to their mother's hands as she attempted to rein in her exuberant offspring.

They all filtered off to get settled, and Caro watched from the veranda as Maeli and Aldin played tag on the lawn while Andrine stood on the sidelines, looking exhausted but content. Aldin had stolen his sister's hair ribbon, and they were chasing each other and giggling.

"Can I tell you a secret?"

Morfran cocked his head. "I'm quite good at keeping them," he replied wryly, and Caro smiled.

"Andrine is older than me by five years. We grew up together in the palace, and I adored her. She was my dearest friend. When she met and married Malcolm, I was overjoyed for her. They were so in love."

Her smile grew sad. "But her pregnancy with the twins was a difficult one, and she almost didn't make it. She was in the delivery chamber for hours, and Gaius and the nursing staff were brought in to help, even Aunt Ez. I was only thirteen years old, concerned and hovering outside in the hall, when Ezalia dragged me into the room. They needed all the hands they could get, and mine were available.

"Ezalia pulled a white robe over my head and tied a cloth mask around my face. Andrine was sweating. The babies were causing a strain on her body, and they were going to have to induce. I held her hand, willing her to be okay.

"Ezalia urged Andrine to push, and she let out a wail, punctuated by another small cry. In Gaius's hand was a small, wrinkled baby boy. He handed the infant to me, and I dried him off with a soft towel. A second followed, this time a girl, and she cried with her brother in my arms. I soothed them, my heart overflowing with affection, so much I felt like I was going to burst. I promised they would always be loved and cared for."

Caro glanced at Morfran. "You can laugh if you want. Imagine, a princess acting as a midwife." She shrugged as he shook his head. "I would have loved them anyway, but I helped bring them into this world. I held them as they took their first breaths." Her voice stuck as she watched them play, so pure and innocent, and she blinked back tears. "It's for them I'm fighting. To save the kingdom they live in, so they grow up happy and without fear."

Caro's hand trembled on the railing, and Morfran covered it with his own. She could feel his warmth even through the glove.

"And I will fight by your side, Your Majesty. For the future you wish to protect."

Stitch in Time

Caro found Vittorius in the foyer.

"It's about time I introduced you to the mercenaries your hard-won earnings have paid for," he said, setting aside his paper and rising. His tone was not flippant—he knew what trials she'd faced.

He glanced at Morfran and seemed like he wanted to say something, then thought better of it. "Follow me."

The Veggur Mountains were a peculiar mountain range. They butted up against the sea, massive cliffs from which there was no possibility of attack, while a smaller range called the Ferilla Slopes curved around either side of the capital city, protecting it like an inlet on land.

"It's a short walk, but worth the effort," Vittorius said as he led them up a steep incline. "Please take care, Your Majesty."

Caro nodded. As she did so, her foot shifted upon the loose rock, and Morfran reached out to steady her.

"Just a little farther."

At the top of the elevation was a flattened area where a small copse of trees had sprung up. Caro's eyes widened. Fierce warriors from the North milled about, tall and hefty, wearing heavy armor over sleek furs. They were all taller than Morfran, even the women.

"Your Majesty, I present to you the Braxley clan, hailing from Salissard."

Roughly thirty mercenaries were camped out in the mountains with all their military trappings and belongings.

"Holger," Vittorius said, as three of the warriors approached. "May I introduce Her Majesty, Queen Caro, on whose behalf you have been employed."

Holger was a bear of a man with massive muscles that strained against his tunic. He had steel-gray eyes, a mane of russet hair, and a thick but well-groomed beard. He gazed down dubiously at Caro, who was little more than half his height.

"This pipsqueak is the queen we've heard so much about?" He prodded her in the shoulder, apparently unimpressed.

Morfran bristled, but Caro smiled. "Touch me again, Holger, and I will cut off that hand," she said charmingly. "Actually, only your little finger. I'm paying you handsomely for your services, after all."

Holger blinked at her cheek, then let out a great booming laugh. "My humblest apologies, Your Majesty. These are my lieutenants, Viggo and Berit. They are each in charge of a squadron of riders."

Berit had thick blond hair braided along her temples and fierce but kind green eyes. Viggo had short, thinning black hair and a shadow of a beard, his brown gaze thoughtful and patient.

Caro opened her mouth to greet them, but then she heard it—a low sound between a growl and a roar.

Morfran's entire body tensed with alarm.

"Don't you worry your pretty head," Holger said. "The lindwurms won't hurt you."

Caro gaped as a large, scaly beast lumbered into view and butted Berit in the shoulder. "They're drakes," she whispered, astonished. "So that's what you meant by riders."

Caro glanced at Vittorius, who looked pleased with himself.

"Even if Zhelyas has hired mercenaries of his own, he won't have drake mounts."

"Indeed not," Morfran murmured.

"Forgive me, Holger. I have never seen their kind in person before, only in books," Caro said, regaining her composure.

"Why don't you come closer?" Viggo suggested. "They won't bite."

Caro hesitated, then took a step forward.

"Please open your hand, Majesty."

She did as asked, and he placed a small block of seasoning in her palm.

"Lindwurms like spicy foods," Viggo explained.

Caro held out her hand and a large, dry, slightly viscid tongue scooped it up, munching with evident pleasure. The drake then sniffed her and rubbed its nose against her clothes.

"He's looking for more," Berit said with a chuckle, and produced another cube from beneath her vest for him to nibble. "His name is Grun."

"He's adorable," Caro cooed. The interaction had put her at ease with the creature.

Dragons, from what Caro had read, were many times the size of a human and fiercely intelligent, with complex societies and relationships. Drakes were smaller and closer to horses or dogs in comparison. They were covered head to toe in thick scales, longer-limbed than their stocky cousins, with a sweeping tail. They also lacked the dragon's dorsal ridges, which made them perfectly suited as mounts as long as the riders used specialized saddles designed not to impede their large, leathery wings.

Berit appeared pleased by Caro's reaction. "The wurms seem to like you, Your Majesty. They are excellent judges of character, and though docile, are not so friendly with everyone. By winning their trust, you have won ours."

"That was interesting," Morfran whispered to Caro once they'd returned to the villa. "Your uncle is quite the resourceful man."

"The wurm riders have a few additional requests, besides their stipend," Vittorius said, and showed her the balance of the account.

"Such as?"

"Decreased price of grain and wine, welfare to be dispensed to the families of those fallen in battle, and a tax dispensation for their country for a term of five years."

The first two were expected since the mercenaries had to feed themselves and their beasts during this campaign, as well as provide for their dependents back home. The third was more tricky.

"I unequivocally agree to the first two terms. The last will have to wait until I regain my throne. However, if they can help me accomplish that, I can't see anyone objecting to an amendment of the trade agreement between Artemisia and Salissard."

Sakin was practicing outside in the glade, and Caro watched with fascination as she swung the curved scimitar in a dance both deadly and beautiful. She finished her kata, then turned to Caro.

"*La Firar* has given me permission to spar with you if you would like, Your Majesty."

"That would be wonderful," Caro said, and grabbed her sword.

"You can try the scimitar if you like, but it's difficult to master." Sakin came around Caro's back and curled her fingers around the handle. "It's a close-quarters weapon. You have to slash to utilize it effectively, but it can do more damage than a straight sword. The cutting edge runs along the entire length of the blade and can slice through tendon and bone."

Caro swished the sword. It was very heavy, and she marveled at the woman's prowess.

Sakin took her scimitar back and moved to face Caro. "We Sharir utilize specialized techniques, some of which could serve you well in battle, especially as a woman."

"How so?"

"For instance, if you attack me, I do not try to counter your sword with the cutting edge of my blade. I could push away your attack, but that would take a great deal of strength on my part."

She gestured, and Caro lunged. "But if I sweep your sword away from my body, like this, then with minimal effort I can lock your blade and use my forward momentum to strike you instead, expending less energy."

Caro nodded, fascinated.

"Shall we try?"

Caro could tell at once their fighting styles were radically different. The sword's purpose was to strike a fatal blow while at a safe distance, while the scimitar's was to get close, slashing with deadly speed. She focused on diverting the blows away from her body, as Sakin had done.

"Good," Sakin declared.

Caro bent over her knees to catch her breath, exhausted and exhilarated.

"One other thing," Sakin said, and retrieved a knife from her belt. "This is called a *janbia*, but any small dagger will do. We Sharir use it both as a secondary blade and as a shield to block weaker attacks before following up with our sword. As women, we are smaller and more nimble than many of our opponents. Rather than a weakness, we can use that to our advantage, slipping through their defenses before they react."

Caro recalled the time she had fought with Morfran at the enemy garrison, when she had used a similar move. Sakin smiled at Caro's nod of understanding and handed her the *janbia* to practice with. They sparred, Caro using the dagger to reinforce her strikes.

"Excellent. Now I want to demonstrate how to fend off multiple opponents. May I ask Mukhif to participate?"

It took Caro a moment to realize she was referring to Morfran. "Please do."

Morfran was sitting on the veranda, observing with what appeared to be both wariness and interest. Sakin waved for him to join them.

"Stand here," she instructed once he strolled over. "Your Majesty, if you find yourself in this situation, you may not know who to attack first. If you keep the blade of your sword parallel to the ground, you can use the tip to gauge distance. I am closer as I approach from your left, which makes me the more immediate threat."

Caro did as instructed and feigned disabling her.

"Mukhif is next—remember to stay light on your feet," Sakin added above the clash of blades.

Caro stepped nimbly out of the way, ducking his sword as it came down in a long arc, and brought her own across the back of his neck.

Morfran knelt on the ground as the blade rested above the collar of his tunic. He stared up at Caro, his gaze reflecting amazement and admiration, as Sakin declared the sparring session a success.

"Sakin, isn't it?"

Morfran leaned against a tree, polishing his small dagger as she passed on her way back to the Sharir camp.

"So you're Mukhif. I admit, you're not what I expected."

"Just what are your intentions with the queen?"

"My intentions?" Sakin repeated. "None at all. I want to help her become a better warrior, with the blessing of *La Firar*, of course."

"Naturally," Morfran replied impassively.

"I'm more interested to find one of the Sharir acting as a guard dog—"

The words were barely out of her mouth when the dagger whizzed by her ear, embedding in the tree trunk behind her.

"I would not speak so carelessly," Morfran warned. "The Sharir were the means by which I attained my revenge, but Queen Caro is who I live for. Never compare the two."

Sakin stared at him, purplish lips agape. "My apologies, Mukhif. I had thought to goad you, to determine whether your skills had dulled since your time away from our clan, but I see now they have not."

Morfran strode past her and retrieved the blade. "To what end?" he asked skeptically.

"I cannot claim to know what has transpired between you and the queen, nor the identity of the man behind the mask. If both the names 'Morfran' and 'Mukhif' are false, does that mean you too are an illusion?"

"Is this an interrogation from Jabez? If so, then I grow tired of these games."

"Perhaps I am asking to satisfy my own curiosity."

Her answer intrigued Morfran.

"Still, I meant no offense, Mukhif. I have trained Her Majesty in our ways to some small extent. I hope it will serve her well."

"Morfran."

"Pardon?"

"Jabez will not understand, but I discarded that name when I left the Sharir. My name is Morfran now, and whether just as false, it is the name by which my queen addresses me and the one I prefer."

Sakin cocked her head. "Then I shall also call you 'Morfran,' since that is your wish. But I hope you have not forgotten your true name, and can someday make peace with your past."

The intonation in her voice was peculiar, and he had the sense she was reading into the subject, not from his vantage point—but her own.

Pinch of Salt

Caro woke early the next morning and stretched. Her muscles didn't hurt as much as she had expected from sparring with Sakin.

"Where are you off to today?" Vittorius inquired.

"To visit the mercenaries. I'd like to learn more about them and their mounts."

Vittorius nodded. "You should know their capabilities, and forging a relationship with them will benefit you in the long run."

The drakes made chirping, grunting sounds as Caro and Morfran approached, and Viggo bowed his head in greeting.

"Your Majesty."

"I have a little time, and I wanted to learn about the drakes and their riders, if I'm not an inconvenience."

"Of course not, my queen. The drakes have already had their exercise. I was about to feed them."

Caro peered into the bucket he was filling. "What do they eat?"

"Back in Salissard, we have a species of large winged insect, similar to your dragonflies but many times their size. They will also graze for worms in fields or chase crickets, but we feed them mostly vegetables, with the occasional cube of seasoning as a treat."

Viggo poured the mixture into a trough, and the drakes eagerly began to devour it.

"You mentioned they had been exercising. Do you mean flying?" Caro inquired.

"There's no need for concern. We take them to the edge of the cliffs by the sea and fly behind the mountains where they are neither visible from the ground, nor from your castle's tall towers."

Caro sighed, relieved. She had been alarmed by the prospect of Zhelyas discovering the drakes' presence before she revealed them.

"Queen Caro," Viggo ventured, interrupting her musings.

"Yes?"

"We have recently become aware we are not the only people living in these mountains."

This was surprising. "Who else is here?"

"An eccentric old man. He sometimes comes to the camp, spouting some doom and gloom prophecy or other, and we send him away with bread and wine to leave us alone." Viggo shrugged. "But since your arrival, he seems to have become even more agitated and keeps muttering he needs to see you."

Caro lifted an eyebrow. "Take me to him."

Viggo led Caro and Morfran up a steep path which graduated into rock, cut into dizzyingly narrow steps.

"Oy, old man Cortin!" Viggo called into a dark cave at the top.

"Whaddya want?" a crusty voice replied.

"I brought Her Majesty, Queen Caro, whom you've been asking to see."

A spark sprang to life in the cave, and a feeble old man doddered out with a lantern clutched in his wizened hands. His head was bald, and he had a long, matted beard which hung to his knees over his brown robes. His bushy eyebrows were furrowed in irritation, beady gray eyes squinting from beneath them.

"My name is *Cortinarius*," he corrected snappishly.

He seemed to notice Caro for the first time, and his eyebrows arched nearly to the top of his forehead.

"Ah, come in, come in." He grinned, displaying his missing teeth like rows of gravestones.

She glanced at Morfran as Cortin herded her inside, and he glared back over his shoulder.

"Only her!"

Morfran hesitated, but Caro nodded.

"I'll only be a moment."

Cortin escorted Caro deep into his cave, where he set the lantern on a table covered by a threadbare red cloth. He then gestured for her to sit, and she seated herself awkwardly on a chair which felt like it might collapse under the slightest weight.

"I understand you have been wanting to see me, Cortinarius?" Caro began politely.

"Yes, very much. I can tell you your destiny."

Caro blinked back at the old man. "My destiny?"

"Yes!" he exclaimed with rabid excitement. "Don't you want to know if you will win back your throne or be utterly defeated?"

Caro had to admit it was a tantalizing offer, but in her heart she also knew it would do more harm than good. To learn your future was to trap yourself in a prison of your own making—

either accepting your fate or fighting against it when the same would have come to pass regardless.

"It's tempting, but no thank you," Caro said, rising out of the rickety chair.

Cortin seized her wrist, his grip surprisingly strong. "Are you sure?"

"I have no wish to know my future. I will live out my life as I see fit and decide my own fate." She twisted her wrist out of his grasp.

"You'll be entirely alone at the end!" he croaked. "No one will be by your side."

Caro could see the triumph in Cortin's eyes, thinking he had broken her spirit, and her heart wavered at his words. Could it be true? Would her companions all desert her?

She bit back the doubt his prediction engendered, remembering Lottie's reassurance after the ball. She smiled to herself. "I refuse to believe that."

The self-satisfaction faded from his smug expression. "You think they are loyal to you? They only stay because they want something!"

"I would expect no less."

She said it so evenly his eyes bugged out of his skull, and Caro laughed shortly at his disbelief.

"Everybody wants something, Cortin: acclaim, validation, or to be treated with kindness and seen for who they are." She shrugged. "Of course, the nature of my position lends itself to those who seek more tangible rewards. Even so, I would be more suspicious of someone who claimed to want nothing."

"You would dismiss my words so easily?" Cortin asked, a hiss of warning in his voice.

Caro turned a cold glance upon the old man. "Not at all. I simply do not care. If I am to be alone in the end, then so be it, but do not think to frighten me with your tales of calamity."

She turned to leave, then paused, reached into her pocket, and placed three bronze chandras upon the table.

"Payment for your services, although I wonder if it is not reward enough," she said wryly. "In that case, I am sorry to disappoint you. Good day, Cortinarius."

Bell the Cat

"Khalil..." Caro ventured. "Hadiya warned us to be wary of a woman named Veena in our travels. Does that mean you know her? You recognized her at the ball."

Khalil tucked his knees up against his chest as they sat around the fire, which cast twisted shadows over the company.

"Veena is an old friend, but I guess I never knew her at all," he said morosely. "She's from another tribe, the Sufra. Veena was the daughter of the chief's vizier, and I first met her during a congress of tribal leaders where she was serving as an attendant. Unlike me, she had no rank or title of her own, and her fate had been decided for her.

"Time passed, and we chanced upon each other occasionally, but by then she had become obsessed with the notion of power. It started small, using her natural charms to extract information and favors out of men, practicing her skills of manipulation. But she soon left her tribe and traveled to the farthest reaches in search of someone who would teach her."

"Magic, you mean?"

Khalil nodded. "The use of magic in our world is rare, but not unheard of. The Sharir practice a little, which is part of the reason they are so feared. It was many years before I saw her again, and she had changed. Veena tried to convince my mother we could be as powerful and feared as the Sharir if we too employed magic, but she refused."

"Why?" Caro asked.

"Magic is unnatural," Khalil said with a shiver.

"The prince is right," Morfran elaborated. "Even the ones we call Creatures of Magic, like dragons, exist as part of our world, in harmony with it. Magic is a primal force, one that exists in all things, but we are manipulating it by bending it to our will. That thunderstorm, for instance. It was not meant to exist, but Veena brought it into being against the laws of nature. If one uses magic to turn water into wine, they have changed the innate structure of the water.

"The Sharir use it to become one with the shadows, to summon dust storms and enchant animals, but they also treat it with the utmost reverence. There is a witch named Amanita who lives in the swamp. The Sharir have had dealings with her before, but she is also known to be deeply connected to nature, and uses magic sparingly to infuse her tinctures and potions. Veena saw it only as a tool for her own benefit, and therein lays the danger. Her actions may spell her downfall."

Khalil rested his chin upon his knees, evidently unnerved by Morfran's blunt assessment.

Caro palmed her neck, digesting this information. "I'm going to ask you a question, Khalil, and I want your honest answer."

He raised his chin and nodded.

"Do you think she can be saved from herself?"

"Yes," he replied without hesitation. "I do."

Caro gathered her military leaders in the library for a strategy session.

Khalil was there as the de facto head of the desert warriors, and Alenard to represent his private army. Holger attended as the leader of the drake riders, and Jabez at Caro's personal invitation for the few but deadly Sharir. Stelian and Morfran also attended, as well as Gaius and Vittorius, her loyal advisers.

They sat in chairs which were placed out for their use or paced around the edge of a mural depicting the battleground. Upon the wooden floor had been painted a map of the capital region, including the castle and major city streets, the ridge surrounding the periphery, and the outlying areas beyond.

"This is where our troops stand," Caro began, gesturing to four markers already positioned upon the map.

"Castle, horse, pointy hat... Those are chess pieces!" Khalil exclaimed.

"I thought them fitting," Vittorius said with a shrug, looking amused by the childish descriptors.

Caro smiled, recalling the night when she had unsuccessfully tried to teach him how to play. "The white rook represents Alenard's troops; the knight, Khalil's warriors; the bishop, the Sharir; and the dragon—thank you, Uncle, for that addition—the drake riders."

Vittorius smirked. The winged beast was not a standard playing piece.

"On the other side," Caro continued, "the black knight is Luther and the royal army; the rook, the sorceress Veena." She paused, standing between the final two pieces, which required no introduction.

Those gathered nodded at the grim sight of the tall black king in the center of the palace and the white queen who challenged him. Rather than the usual game of chess, this was a very different battle.

"Place us where you will," Alenard said, speaking for the rest.

"First, I wish to lure Luther out into the open. The best way to do this would be to stage our troops at the entrance of the city, forcing him to come and meet us. I will take a third of my men and half of Khalil's."

"You?" Vittorius said, catching the pronoun. "Personally?"

"I must be in front to draw Zhelyas's attention," Caro explained, "but also in clear view of any whose loyalty might be swayed."

Vittorius frowned at the notion of a queen going into battle at all, never mind on the front lines, but nodded reluctantly.

"Morfran and Stelian will be at my side as my protectors. The rest will serve as our rear guard."

"I'll fight by your side, too!" Khalil blurted, but Caro shook her head.

"I have another plan for you. Wouldn't you agree, Jabez?"

Everyone turned to face the desert assassin, who appeared mildly surprised.

"To what are you referring, Your Majesty?"

"As you can see, my advisers favor a direct attack, but I wondered if you might suggest a more *subtle* approach?"

Jabez stared at Khalil, who seemed a little uncomfortable at the attention focused upon him. "Having traveled together in the desert, I believe he is a valiant warrior with a heart of steel."

"Why me?" Khalil inquired, baffled, and Caro smiled.

"Because you are both the bravest and most honest man I have met. You speak to assassins with no trace of fear in your voice, and I do not believe you would quail—even in the presence of Zhelyas himself."

Khalil opened and closed his mouth a few times, flushing at her praise. "I will do what I can."

"And us?" Holger asked, speaking up for the first time.

"Your drakes will be the most invaluable asset of all, because they will give us an advantage I never anticipated. They will enter the city, flying over the ridge, and block the army's path of retreat." Caro sighed. "I understand that like dragons, drakes can breathe flame. I don't want to see my beautiful city razed to the ground, so please take care in that regard. Are there any objections?"

She waited but received no answer. "Lord Vittorius?"

"I confess it is a good strategy," he said finally.

"I agree. It is well thought out," Holger added, nodding.

Caro turned to Jabez. "I want updated intelligence on Zhelyas and Luther's movements. Can you arrange that for me?"

"I shall send Husam."

"In that case, we are adjourned."

Alenard's army stood at attention as Caro walked by. She gave them a regal nod and an approving smile, and it seemed their efforts doubled.

Caro skimmed over the sheets once more. "Make sure they receive an extra ration of spirits tonight to reward them for their efficiency—and yours as well."

"Thank you, Your Majesty!" Lance exclaimed.

Caro briefly stopped by the camp of the desert warriors, observing from afar as they went about their duties. She wondered what Hadiya had told them when they were making ready to depart, and worried she had promised Caro to be

Khalil's bride. She would rather not have to confirm or deny such a supposition this close to battle, and so kept her distance.

Jabez gave Caro a polite nod as she observed Husam and Sakin sparring, while Nibal conveyed last minute instructions to Khalil, who listened intently.

"Will Khalil be ready in time?" she inquired.

"The prince already has many of the skills required for such a task, and he is an attentive student," Jabez replied. "He passed a trial much more intensive than this in the desert to prove his worth. He would have made an admirable Sharir."

Gaius and Lottie were laying out medical salves and bandages for when the soldiers returned from the front lines with the inevitable minor injuries, though they also prepared for major surgeries. Lottie had traded in her maid's garb for a proper nurse's outfit, pale gray with a starched apron and a silver chatelaine with medical tools suspended from her belt. Her blond curls were pinned back, making her look somehow mature and at ease.

The last were the drake riders, and Caro made a point to visit them personally. Unlike Alenard's men, they owed her no loyalty beyond their contractual obligations.

"Your Majesty," Berit greeted, tightening the reins of one of the drakes.

Viggo heaved a huge sack over his shoulders and set it down with a grunt. "If you wish to speak to Holger, I will take you to him."

The drakes chirped at Caro as she followed Viggo, and she paused to pet them, giggling as they crowded around her.

"My queen." Holger bowed his head. "What can I do for you?"

"I wanted to ensure you had everything you needed before we head into battle."

"About that... I must admit I am just as surprised as your uncle that you are coming with us."

"Is that so unusual?" she inquired.

"I would say so, yes," he replied bluntly. "Don't get me wrong. I'm impressed with your mettle, and as Berit said—by winning the trust of our mounts, you have won ours as well. But why have you chosen to involve yourself personally? It will be very dangerous."

"It's precisely because of the danger."

Holger's eyebrows creased. "I don't quite understand."

"So far, I have been playing the long game. I have traveled up and down this fair country, recruiting allies to my cause and benefactors to provide the donations with which my uncle hired you. But the time for that is over." Caro faced Holger, her expression both serene and determined. "If I am going to take back my throne, I will do so with my own hands. If I am not willing to risk my own survival, how can I ask others to do the same?"

"Because without you, there will *be* no country," Holger said, "and Zhelyas will win."

"If we lose, I will still die, hunted down like a dog and executed for daring to stand against him. I want to protect my kingdom and fight alongside my companions, who have stood by me."

Holger stroked his bearded chin, considering her response. "We shall be honored to fight with you, Your Majesty. Or above you, as the case may be," he added with a jaunty grin.

Mend Fences

Ines was sitting in Vittorius's library, listening to the soft music playing on the phonograph. It was a concerto of some sort, and Vittorius watched from the doorway as her chin bobbed to the melody. He wondered how a blind woman perceived music. Did she merely hear it? Or was there some deeper meaning ascribed to the dulcet strains?

She became aware of his presence and looked up.

"Pardon me, I came to retrieve a book." He perused the shelves for a moment, then pulled one out, flipping through the contents.

"I know who you are," Vittorius said out of the blue.

Ines turned her head to face him. Pale eyelashes fluttered over her cheeks, eyes the color of honey.

Just like hers.

"Pardon?"

Vittorius snapped the book shut. "You are her mirror image. Sarravia, I mean."

"I'm not certain what you are referring to, Your Grace," Ines replied carefully.

"I was only sixteen years old, but Lady Sarravia Valeska was a noblewoman of court at the palace, and she had a hauteur which drew men to her, like moths to a flame."

Ines had risen, and her hand froze as she lifted the phonograph stylus.

"My brother Roland, the crown prince at the time, was besotted with her, but she spurned his affections, much to the displeasure of our father, the king. Later, it came to light that she had married Earl Bodin Bertrand, a rather shy and unassuming man. Because they had lost favor at court, they left the palace for Effrenia, settling on one of Bodin's properties there, a winery."

Vittorius had been merely a youth, but he vividly recalled the beguiling woman. With sculpted features, full lips, and heavily lidded eyes, Sarravia had been beautiful and clever, with a razor wit. She was an unattainable jewel, striding through the palace in a dress that fluttered in her wake like the wings of an azure butterfly. Ines's face was softer, with a gentle smile; her eyes, though sightless, wide and sincere. He supposed Sarravia might have smiled like that as well, if only for the man she loved.

"There were rumors, however, that Sarravia was pregnant when she left, and the marriage to Bodin was a cover," Vittorius added. "If that were true..."

"It's not," Ines said, shaking her head. "I have no claim to the throne, Your Grace. You may put your mind at ease."

"Are you certain? You may resemble Sarravia, but I recognize my brother in you as well."

Ines hesitated. "Even if it were true, I would never desire it. Caro is fighting for what she believes in, and I respect her too much to deny her that."

"Then what *is* the truth, if I may ask?" Vittorius inquired.

Ines made her way to the window, staring out into a distance which only she could see. "My parents were deeply in love. They were seeing each other secretly, even while Roland was courting Sarravia. Everyone assumed she would marry the future king—even her. But she only had eyes for Bodin, which was why, when she discovered she might be carrying Roland's child, they married against her family's wishes. The king was furious at the insult to his son, and the two fled the palace to escape his wrath."

She paused, tracing her finger along the glass, seemingly lost in her recollections. "They used to tell me their story, you see, disguised as a child's fairy tale. They were very happy together, and my childhood was full of love. But there was a drought, and a blight infected the grapes. Faced with ruin and poverty, they made the difficult decision to send me away for the chance at a better life. I never heard from them again."

Her voice cracked slightly, and Vittorius felt a swell of guilt.

"Forgive me, I didn't mean to awaken such painful memories."

Ines shook her head. "I've made peace with my past, Lord Vittorius, and it has led me here. I have no regrets."

He nodded, then cleared his throat to draw her attention. "Thank you for confiding in me, Ines. I admit it has troubled me all these years. I was merely a youth, but Sarravia always seemed sad to me somehow. I'm relieved to hear she was happy, at least for a short while." He paused. "Do the others know?"

"I haven't told anyone," she admitted.

"Then I will respect your wishes. However, it may be worth considering, should you wish to remain in the palace once Queen Caro retakes her throne."

Ines bowed low, honey-blond hair drifting over her shoulders. "I will bear that in mind, Your Grace."

Courage under Fire

The day of the battle arrived. Caro rose and ate breakfast before the rest of Vittorius's villa was awake—save Morfran. She swore that man never slept a wink.

He handed her a steaming cup that smelled somewhat bitter. "Ginger tea. It always helps settle my stomach before a difficult mission."

It was astringent, yet somehow refreshing.

The armor she had worn during the battle of Ockbridge had been a suit from Alenard's army, meant for the smaller of the recruits. Today was different. Caro held up her arms as Stelian fastened the straps of the breastplate, fit for a royal prince.

"I wore this myself as a boy during pageants, and kept it as a memento," Vittorius mused. "Never did I imagine it would be used for such a lofty purpose."

"Thank you, Uncle," Caro replied gratefully. "It's just what I need."

Beneath the pale gold breastplate was a jade jacket woven with gilded thread; under that, a tunic and shirt of chain mail, while around her shoulders draped a long cloak. Leggings and knee-high boots completed the look. Her sword belt hung around her waist, with a small dagger tucked away within easy reach.

"You truly convey the dignity of a queen," Morfran said, bowing low.

"And you, the part of a warrior." Caro had rarely seen him without his customary black armor, but somehow he seemed even more imposing today. "But you are *my* warrior now," she added, then took a loop of gold cord and pinned it to his cloak along with a green rose. The effect was striking, a flash of color against his otherwise austere figure.

Morfran stroked the rose with his gloved fingers, then knelt at her feet and kissed her hand.

Luther's army met her at the ingress of the city, as she had planned. He brought two battalions of infantry and one of cavalry—numbering nine hundred men total. Her forces numbered a third of that, but they were seasoned warriors. Luther would not find them so easy to defeat.

"So you have come, Queen Caro," Luther said, holding up his hand to halt the advance of his forces.

Alenard did likewise.

"Are you sure Zhelyas would approve of you addressing me by that title?" she replied.

He frowned at her goading. "And I see the traitor rides beside you."

"I would be careful where you hurl insults, General. The only traitor I see here is you."

He snapped his mouth shut at her cutting remark.

"Hear me now," Caro said loudly, her voice carrying across the silent morning air. "Any of you who turn from this path shall be rewarded and welcomed as loyal subjects of the Crown. Zhelyas is a false king, and he shall be defeated."

A murmur ran through the army at Luther's back.

"I know the conflict raging in your hearts. You serve the general who was so loyal to the throne, but who now serves a pretender—and I pity you. But if you stand in my way, I have no choice but to consider you my enemy." Her final words rang across the battlefield like funeral bells tolling their fates.

"My queen!" a soldier cried, racing forward.

Luther growled at the desertion and moved to strike him down, but an arrow shot by Jabez whizzed past his ear, freezing him in his tracks.

"You shall be protected from Luther's wrath, I swear it," Caro pledged, and more men abandoned their posts, joining her ranks.

A few were cut down by their fellows, but at least ninety made it to her side.

"Will you fight with me, your rightful queen?"

"Yes!" they cried, thrusting their swords in the air.

Luther retreated to the back as his remaining men drove forward into Caro's, bellowing orders from his position of relative safety. Even he knew it was cowardly, but Zhelyas's command had been clear—he was not to involve himself in the battle, even if all his men were slain.

He gritted his teeth, recalling her cold rebuke. "I *am* a traitor," he muttered. "But what else could I do?"

After what he'd discovered that night, he could see no other recourse. Zhelyas might not be the ruler the kingdom needed, but at least there would still *be* a kingdom after all this bloodshed was over.

As he gave the order for the next wave to advance, Luther noticed a critical flaw. He had seen Caro's men proceeding toward the city, and had thought to dominate her in numbers.

He recognized the Margrave of Biding and concluded she had rallied him and his private army for her cause, but the others were unfamiliar. Their dusky coloring, like Veena's, suggested they hailed from the desert, and he had assumed them to be unskilled ruffians—but he was gravely mistaken. All fought with a ferocity bred from a life where one day led to the next in an unending struggle to survive. There were also four figures in black garb, like the riders of Death himself.

Luther's forces didn't stand a chance.

"We must issue orders to withdraw!" his captain begged.

Luther gritted his teeth, loath to admit defeat. "Press forward!" he cried, ignoring his subordinate's desperate plea. But his forces—what was left of them—were being pushed back deep into the city.

He was about to open his mouth to issue another command when he heard a horn. Luther spotted Alenard with the instrument to his lips.

"Have they called for retreat?" he wondered aloud, but then a second horn blew, this one much closer.

His gaze scoured the battlefield when he heard his captain's scream, mingling with those of his men. Luther looked to the sky, and his breath caught in his throat.

Winged beasts soared above his head, unearthly howls piercing the air. Their riders were armed with crossbows that rained arrows down upon the unsuspecting soldiers, scattering them from their formation.

A small group turned to run down an alley, but a beast swooped down low and issued forth a stream of flame, blocking their path of escape.

"Stand firm!" Luther commanded, but his shrill order could not be heard above the tumult.

He was done for. They had lost.

Luther cast one last rueful glance at Caro and Morfran before fleeing back to the castle.

Caro sighed at the carnage which had been wrought. Luther's army was defeated, but the general himself was nowhere to be seen.

Her frown at his unrelenting cowardice turned to one of sorrow as she gazed upon the bodies which littered the streets, dyeing them crimson. She would never forget that color as long as she lived.

"Are you all right?" Morfran inquired.

"I'm fine," she replied wearily. "Stelian, see that the injured are taken back to camp and attended to, by stretcher if they cannot walk. And give everyone a double ration of spirits. They have earned it today."

Stelian bowed, and those who could cheered, hobbling back to camp supported upon the shoulders of their fellows.

"Lord Alenard, secure the area. I will relocate the command center to City Hall, where we will reconvene in twelve hours."

"At once, Your Majesty," Alenard replied.

Jabez gave Caro a nod. "Don't worry, I will see to the clansmen. In their prince's absence, they will heed my authority."

"Thank you, Jabez."

"You should rest too," Sakin added. "You fought well today."

"I will see to your injuries," Morfran said, and Caro looked down at her blistered hands.

Jabez's words came back to her, and she thought of Khalil. They had done their part—now it was up to him.

Forlorn Hope

Husam went with Khalil part of the way, wearing dark clothing and using the shadows to conceal their approach. Once they infiltrated the palace grounds, he returned to fight at his master's side.

Khalil took a deep breath as he scaled the castle ramparts. Climbing was not new to him, though the walls with their fitted stone blocks differed from the desert cliffs where the young people often tested their grit. Hand- and footholds were easy to find if you knew where to look.

He reached the top and leaped from the tall stone battlements to the roof. Again, this was a new sensation, and he struggled to keep his balance as a tile shifted beneath his feet, but it did not come loose. Khalil held his breath, then released it slowly. He began to place one foot in front of the other, gauging their fixedness—just as he would the stability of a windswept dune where dry quicksand could form.

Khalil jumped down to the balcony of an empty room. He peered inside to confirm there was nobody about. He saw pale green and gold furnishings, a modest yet royal taste in decor. A pillow had been slashed; white feathers drifted haphazardly, disturbed by his footsteps.

Stelian had told him of the night they had fled the palace. Without realizing it, Khalil had found himself in Caro's quarters. He lifted a feather from the bed, feeling its fragile softness in his hand.

A mellow voice interrupted his musings. "Fancy meeting *you* here."

Storm in a Teacup

"They. Have. *Dragons*...?" Luther faltered, flopping into a chair.

He had fled with whatever men he could salvage and raced back to the palace to inform the king.

"Drakes," Zhelyas corrected in an icy voice. "I saw it all from the tower. Tell me you have something that can fight this, Veena."

"I thought you said you didn't need my help," she said smugly.

Zhelyas gave her a dark look at her gloating, and she dipped her head. "I will see what I can conjure up, sire."

"Perhaps I can be of assistance?"

Zhelyas turned to see a strange intruder at the door. "Who are you?"

The old man grinned wolfishly. "The rebel queen snubbed me and dismissed my advice. Perhaps you will not be so foolish, oh magnanimous, perspicacious king."

Zhelyas's eye twitched at the man's contemptuous flattery, so much like Oswin's. "What do you want?"

"Oh, nothing, sire. Just to see the downfall of one who would disdain my guidance."

Veena was staring at him in a rather suspicious way.

"Well, Veena? Can we trust him?"

"Trust? Hardly," she scoffed. "Cortin is a wise—if shifty—character. I would accept his word with caution."

"You know him?"

"He preys on people's weaknesses, twisting their words to suit his own purpose. He tried to pull his cute little trick on me when I first arrived at the capital, pretending to be a doddering old man at the carnival, but I saw right through him. However, he does have insight which might prove useful."

"My name is *Cortinarius,*" he said through clenched teeth.

"My apologies, Cortinarius," Zhelyas replied silkily. "Bring this man some wine, Luther. I would hear what he has to say."

"And perhaps some sausages?" Cortin asked innocently. "I have not eaten any in so long, just nasty roots and berries."

"Food and quarters as well," Zhelyas commanded, his charm faltering slightly.

Luther groused under his breath at being relegated to the position of servant but did as he was bidden.

Zhelyas stared as Cortin devoured a third plate piled high with food. He seemed determined to eat all of the castle's provisions and drink half the wine.

"You heard the queen has drakes. I could use some of those myself."

Cortin cackled, his rows of gravestone teeth spread into a wide grin. "Alas, not even I can wrangle the scaly beasts, sire. But I have something to offer that's even more valuable."

"Such as?" Zhelyas lifted an eyebrow, and Cortin waggled a finger.

"All in good time! For now, more wine!"

Cortin banged his goblet on the table, and Zhelyas sighed inwardly. He desperately wanted to know more about this valuable insight Cortin promised, but it seemed his troublesome guest needed to be indulged before he would reveal anything more.

Veena left Zhelyas and Luther to deal with the infuriating old man and descended the steps to visit the new guest who resided in the dungeon. She cloaked his presence with magic and ensured she wasn't followed before opening the door to his place of confinement.

"Hello, Khalil."

His wrists were shackled to the wall by heavy chains, but he rose at her approach, straining against them.

Veena never could understand Khalil. Morfran was immune to her influence because of the barriers he had built around his heart, a darkness so deep she could not penetrate it, and Luther resisted due to his own all-consuming guilt. But Khalil... He was different.

He was perhaps the only person to ever show her true kindness. Everyone else saw her as someone they could use; she had wielded control over both men and women with her sultry charms—but Khalil never wanted anything from her. And somehow, that was even more irritating.

"I must admit I'm impressed. I had not taken you for the stealthy type. I almost had you out in the desert, but you slipped through my fingers. Now, what are you and the little queen up to?" She made a purring sound at the base of her throat, reinforcing her query as she stroked his cheek.

Khalil stared back, his eyes sad. "What happened to you, Veena? Why are you doing this?"

"You know why," she murmured, a long fingernail tracing a crescent shape down his jaw.

"Do you desire power that much?"

Her hand trembled, then she flicked her finger, lightly scratching his tanned skin. "You wouldn't understand. You're a prince. You haven't had your life planned out for you since the day you were born."

Khalil shook his head. "You'd be surprised."

His quiet admission annoyed Veena more than comforted her. "I just want the power to control my own destiny!"

She lifted her hand to slap him—then clenched her fist and stormed out of the cell.

Luther waited upstairs, seemingly on another errand for Zhelyas.

"I'm surprised you put up with his whims," Veena purred.

He gave her a sideways look. "I've made my choice. I couldn't serve the king and queen anymore—not after what I saw that night..."

He trailed off, and Veena sidled up to him, stroking his arm. She could feel Luther's shell cracking. "I see your suffering. What you witnessed must have been truly terrible."

"That night, in the garden past the wisteria, I saw— No," he said, and shook his head, resisting her influence. "I shall never speak of it again as long as I live."

He stormed off, and Veena sighed with disappointment. The immense guilt he harbored was too strong for even her persuasion. Still—it might be just the clue she needed.

"The garden..." Veena muttered, repeating the cryptic clue Luther had provided. *"Where* in the garden, you clod?"

She cast her gaze about. There was an untold number of flowers in the garden, but only one arbor draped with wisteria.

A mural was carved on the wall, and she drew closer, surprised she had not registered its significance before. To one side was Aryama, crowned with laurel and welcomed into the home of the gods; on the other, nymphs danced joyfully; between them, a mandala that looked like an intricately carved flower—or perhaps the sun.

In the ancient text, it was written, "Between adulation and song, the solar gate will be revealed. The crystal will light your way."

Veena smiled. She had finally found what she was looking for.

Spill the Beans

Luther's guilt consumed him. Even when he managed to sleep, it followed him into his dreams. Only alcohol dulled the memories of what he had seen that night.

Drawn by sounds in the garden, he came upon the king and queen whom he served with all loyalty and devotion, sharing a glass of wine beneath the wisteria arbor.

Unable to restrain his curiosity, Luther crept forward to listen. Normally, he would never give in to the impulse—his honor wouldn't allow such an invasion of privacy—but they were laughing and celebrating. Lately, the queen had been spiritless and moody, while the king was decidedly snappish. He wondered what could have changed their attitudes so drastically. Perhaps the queen was expecting? That would be joyous news indeed! With these buoyant thoughts bolstering his courage, Luther drew closer.

"We've only the final hurdle left," Cecilia was saying, swishing wine in her goblet, "and then all our wishes will be made real."

"Are you certain?" Roland replied. "Surely there is another way."

507

"Oh, darling, you know it must be done. There will be others. Besides, this is our chance to build a new world."

Roland nodded and drained his glass.

Luther frowned, unsure of their meaning, and continued to eavesdrop on the conversation. What he heard made his blood run cold.

Before that night, Luther had never taken a sip of wine except during a toast. As he downed his third flagon of ale in the seedy tavern, his gaze met that of a woman lingering on the opposite side of the room.

She was beautiful, with dusky skin and pale hair that shimmered in the lamplight, and his eyes searched hers as she approached his table.

"You look like you have a problem, good sir," she said in an enticing voice, sitting beside him. "Luckily, solving problems is my specialty."

Luther wasn't quite ready to add debauchery to his list of sins that night, though his inhibitions had been dulled by the spirits. A heavy wool cloak was draped over his customary uniform, but she seemed to know who he was regardless.

"Unusual to see a renowned general away from the palace at this time of night."

"I can't go back, not after..." He shook his head, draining his fourth ale, and waved for a fifth.

She covered his hand with her own. "I have a better idea. There's someone you should meet."

She introduced him to Zhelyas, who invited Luther into his scheme to seize the throne.

A new king.

Luther didn't care what kind of king he was, only that he would replace the current corrupt monarchy.

He hadn't wanted them dead, however, and had almost faltered when delivering the news to the young heiress herself. But Zhelyas's plans were complete, and Luther threw himself into his role. All other regrets were stripped from his mind.

Strangely, Luther had felt comfortable with Morfran, the fourth of the malefactors. His expression was always hidden behind the silver mask, but Luther felt a kinship with the imposing, black-clad man. One evening, after being newly inducted into the conspiracy, he confessed the terrible events of that night. He had sworn Morfran to secrecy, confident of the man's discretion—he was an assassin, after all.

But even Morfran was gone.

Luther would continue to serve Zhelyas as his lapdog, come when called, fetch when ordered. After all—better a dog than a sheep to slaughter.

"I've had my fill, and I think I will be leaving you, sire," Cortin declared, licking sausage grease from his lips and washing it down with a generous gulp of wine.

"And what of the advice you promised me?" Zhelyas lifted an eyebrow. "Your revenge, isn't that right?"

Cortin's gap-toothed sneer wavered, and Zhelyas knew he'd hit a nerve.

"Yes, that. What was it now?" Cortin said, making a great show of cogitating. "Oh yes, that man who used to work for you. The one all in black."

"Morfran? What of him?"

"He accompanies the little queen everywhere, even to the cave where we had our little chat. It may be through him you can break her spirit."

Zhelyas's last nerve was straining at his deliberate vagueness. "How's that?" he asked.

"She may very well love him—and not realize it herself."

The notion was an intriguing one, yet it sounded too simple.

"With that, I bid you farewell, languorous king."

Half of the words Cortin spewed, Zhelyas was unsure of the meaning, but this one did not sound like a compliment. He opened his mouth to retort, but Cortin was already gone.

Head over Heels

Gaius found Ines standing outside on the balcony, wearing a blue silk nightdress that was slightly translucent in the light of the moon.

"What are you doing out here?" he asked softly, so as not to startle her.

"The night is calm, and the fragrance of moon blossoms fills the air. There is a mild breeze, and the stone feels cool against my feet. It relaxes me."

"Are you worried about Morfran?" he asked. "It's only natural. Everybody wants to do what they can to protect those they love."

"Love?" Ines repeated. "No, I don't love Morfran, not in that way. He and I are merely comrades who found ourselves on the same road in life."

Gaius cocked his head. "I must admit I've wondered how you two met."

Ines's sightless eyes stared at the starry sky. "I was born blind. My parents were farmers, and they were kind, but they had few resources, so I was released to a facility where children like me were raised. It was hard. We had to clean, cook, grow food, and mend our own clothes, but we made do. I suppose that's why I am so independent: I've always had to take care of myself. Ezalia was the first person who ever really understood that and let me be."

Ines smiled sadly and shook her head. "However, the country of Effrenia was unstable, ruled by criminal overlords who were always at odds with each other. There was a dispute, and my village was caught in the middle. I tried to flee, but I was captured. The thugs tormented me, tossing me back and forth between them. I was terrified, unable to see to defend myself, and they kept jeering about all the things they would do to me. They threw me to the ground and I froze, fearing what was going to happen next, but suddenly the raucous laughter was stilled into silence."

Gaius listened with rapt attention.

"I sensed him as he approached, a dark presence, but oddly I was not afraid. He held out his hand and asked me to come with him. We've been together ever since. I know what's in his heart. Perhaps I am the only one who does." She shrugged, the smile returning to her face. "I realize that must seem strange."

"I don't think so," Gaius said, shaking his head. "From what I understand of the man, which I admit is little, he found himself on a precipice—one more step into the darkness, and he would have been lost. Perhaps it was you who brought him back from it. If so, then it was fate, and not mere chance, that led you to each other."

"I never thought of it that way before," Ines mused. "So tell me, how did a physician end up becoming the tutor to a queen?"

Gaius chuckled. "The truth is, Caro was a precocious child, and she was always getting into trouble. She could never sit still, and when her mother the queen wasn't looking, she'd be outside, her beleaguered handmaidens chasing her as she

512

dirtied her clothes and made a mess. She couldn't understand why other children got to run and play and she didn't."

"I never realized how hard it must be, growing up as a princess."

"Nor did I," Gaius agreed. "But she was so full of spirit, and all of her instructors were at their wits' end trying to teach her mathematics and history. As court physician, I tended the princess each time she got scrapes from her adventures, but I never thought much of it.

"One day, she came to the library where I was reading. I was mildly annoyed at the interruption, but she didn't notice me, so I decided to observe her. She was five or six at the time, and had brought a small box of toys. She set each one out on the table, then proceeded to act out the events of her last history lecture.

"I was speechless. It wasn't that she didn't care about the material, she was simply bored. I approached her father the king, offering to become her tutor, and he accepted gladly. I realized she longed for more than old books and a dusty classroom. She needed practical education in order to really learn and appreciate her lessons. And so, between myself and Ezalia"—his voice stuck a little at her name—"we managed to wrangle a rebellious princess and guide her into becoming a wonderful queen."

Ines smiled. "You have much to be proud of. When I met her at the garrison, she was so frustrated by all the things she couldn't do, but she didn't let that stop her. And now, facing an uncertain future, she keeps going, even when it would be easier to give up. I admire that."

Ines's hair swayed in the gentle breeze, and a strand strayed across her face. Without thinking, Gaius reached out to sweep it away.

"Sorry," he murmured, realizing what he'd done.

Ines reached up to take his hand in hers. "I'm not a fragile doll, Gaius. You don't need to be afraid of breaking me."

Gaius closed his eyes, trying to imagine perceiving the world as she did. He twined their fingers together, feeling her supple skin beneath his fingertips. He listened to the quiet sound of her breathing, smelled the sweet scent of her hair. Somehow, she seemed even more beautiful.

"Gaius," Ines said softly.

He opened his eyes again, staring down at her, and her pale gaze turned toward his own.

"None of us knows what the future will bring, but for this moment, I would spend it with you."

Dead to Rights

"What is the situation in the city?" Caro asked in conference after their first successful foray.

They were now assembled comfortably in their new headquarters at City Hall, where various ministers and judicial officials would see to common business beneath the notice of the nobility at the palace. The building was empty except for Caro's council because the administration had fled along with the rest of the citizens they served.

"The capital is under our control," Vittorius replied, "excepting the palace grounds and the areas immediately surrounding it: the merchant quarter, barracks, and the industries which furnish provisions for the army."

"And the people?"

"There are members of a resistance force who are stubbornly refusing to leave. However, their leader was arrested some time ago and has only just been released, so they have been lying low. A majority of the rest departed once your forces removed the barriers at the gates."

Caro nodded and turned to Jabez. "I saw Nibal making something earlier. What was it?"

He lifted an eyebrow. "Explosives, Your Majesty."

"And how would you go about using them?"

"I had no specific plans," he said, sidestepping the question.

Caro smiled at his reticence. He was a slippery character. "Indulge me. This last battle was fought on my terms and that of my military. How would the Sharir wage war upon a more powerful opponent?"

"Power is relative," Jabez replied. "Often it relies on all of one's available might gathered in a single space. If it is divided, it is more easily dealt with."

"Hence the explosives," Caro mused. "So if we placed them at strategic locations within the city, causing chaos, Zhelyas would have no choice but to divide his forces."

"Just so, Your Majesty."

"Are you sure?" Vittorius cautioned. "To destroy parts of your city..."

"As long as the people survive, it can be rebuilt," Caro said, shaking her head at her uncle's concerns. "We've dealt them a blow, but once Luther reports the details of today's battle, you can bet Zhelyas will be thinking of ways to undermine us—and he won't fight fair. We have to strike first."

Vittorius gave a reluctant nod.

"Jabez, what targets do you recommend?" Caro asked. "Please keep in mind I want as few casualties as possible. Much of the city has been evacuated, but there are still those who remain."

Jabez stroked his chin, pondering. "The most obvious targets are the military facilities Duke Vittorius mentioned, and those which supply them goods and services. Cutting them off would be a significant blow to Zhelyas. He would essentially be under siege."

"Go on."

"They may be well defended, however, so they should be combined with non-military locations to sow confusion. Striking in the middle of the night would be best. Darkness is our ally," Jabez added, and Caro had the feeling that was the mantra of the Sharir.

She nodded at his concise explanation. "Please work with Duke Vittorius to compile a list of potential targets, as he is most familiar with the city's layout. I will approve it when you are done."

Vittorius stared at the elusive man as the others trickled out of the room.

"My office is this way," he said, gesturing for Jabez to follow.

Caro had been deliberately vague as to his purpose, but Vittorius had gathered from the way the desert tribesmen treated him and his clan that they were both feared and respected. Vittorius was hardly queasy about these things, but still, recruiting paid killers was outside of his usual expertise.

"You seem to have something to say, Duke," Jabez said, lifting an eyebrow, dark eyes intense.

"Frankly, I don't understand why you would be interested in our affairs, nor what your role is. You Sharir are assassins, are you not?"

Jabez crossed his arms. "Fair enough. I am here because Prince Khalil proved himself worthy as the proxy for Her Majesty. Mukhif, the man you call Morfran, and I were comrades as youths, and I was curious to meet the queen to whom he had professed his devotion."

Jabez shrugged, casually examining a painted tapestry on the wall. "As to your second question, life in the Esaphis is different than here in the greenlands. We have no king, merely a scattering of tribes and guilds who are in constant conflict with each other. My clan are assassins, yes, but we also maintain the balance. Your people are kept in line by laws and the fear of doing something to defy the monarchy. So too in the desert, although the Sharir are the ones who keep order amid the chaos."

Vittorius stroked his chin and nodded. "I think I understand. Apologies if I caused offense."

A small smile traced Jabez's lips. "None taken. Shall we? I am unfamiliar with your city, yet I will do my best to serve you and the queen."

They decided on five locations. Four were military: a textile store room, a granary, a manufactory which supplied armor and weapons, and a distillery. Each of these struck at the heart of Zhelyas's campaign.

The fifth target was Town Square. Caro was saddened at the thought of destroying the beautiful flowers and fountain which stood at its center, but the people hadn't been able to enjoy them under Zhelyas's strict regime, when even the smallest infraction was punishable by arrest and incarceration.

There were an additional six targets, abandoned buildings in the merchant quarter, owned by Vittorius and currently unoccupied.

"But why are *you* going?" Vittorius demanded. "The battle, I could understand—especially after hearing of the stirring recruitment speech you made and the soldiers who came over to our side—but this is madness!"

"I have to go, Uncle Vito. I need to be there to make sure there isn't any collateral damage, and to control the situation if something goes wrong. This is *my* city. If anyone is going to destroy it, the blame will fall squarely on me."

"But—"

Caro looked to Jabez for help.

"I believe what Her Majesty is saying is this: sometimes we who rule must make the hard decisions, and it is up to us to see them carried out. It is our duty."

Vittorius sighed. "I'm not pleased about this, but I will not argue the point further. Your mind is made up, and it is *my* duty to obey."

Caro smiled to ease her uncle's fears. "I won't be going alone, you can be sure of that."

She selected three teams to carry out their plan. One was led by Morfran, one by Jabez, and the third by Stelian. Each had an additional six men, including one of the stealthy Sharir who had devised the explosive devices.

Caro acquiesced to Vittorius's request and elected to go with Stelian's group. They would target the empty warehouses and square instead of the military objectives, where she might be recognized by personnel stationed there.

Morfran bowed his head and frowned in a way that suggested he was not happy Caro had allotted him a different team. He and Jabez would have the best chance of carrying out the most dangerous tasks, dealing with any opposition they were likely to meet along the way, and she knew he would follow her wishes despite his reluctance.

They confirmed their orders before departing in different directions.

Caro's group reached their initial target first, and Stelian readied an explosive. It was constructed of a piece of cloth soaked in oil and stuffed in a clay pot filled with flammable liquid: a secret formula of the Sharir.

He created a spark with flint and steel and lit the swatch on fire, then lobbed it toward the building. It sailed through the air, and the brittle pot smashed upon impact, setting the wooden structure alight. It was a crude weapon—but an effective one.

Half a city away, the granary exploded, courtesy of Jabez. Moments later, Morfran struck the textile warehouse across town, and the fabrics fueled the blaze.

"What is going on?" Zhelyas bellowed, teeth clenched with frustration as he stormed into the command center.

Reports had come in of a granary and a warehouse up in flames in the middle of the night. The explosion of the grain had woken him from a dead sleep, and he was both livid and cranky.

"W-we're still trying to figure that out," Luther stammered, quailing beneath the king's vicious glare. "Someone sighted a man in black at the warehouse—"

"Morfran?"

"—and another at the granary. Even Morfran can't be two places at once."

Zhelyas slammed his fist against the wall. "This is that damn Caro's doing, I know it!"

Stelian sent a pot hurtling at another of Vittorius's properties. Next was City Square.

They crouched behind a stone planter, peering around the corner. Stelian bashed the flint and steel together to spark the oil-soaked cloth.

"Throw it now!" he yelled, and Caro hurled it with all her might at the gazebo, one of four, the largest standing structures in the square.

Her throw fell short, but the liquid spilled onto the grass and flames licked up the carved wooden banister. Soon the columns were alight, the fragile building threatening to topple as the beams creaked and groaned.

"You did well. Let's go," Stelian urged, and they crept back the way they had come.

"What in Aryama's name is Caro thinking?" Zhelyas grumbled acidly.

Luther had stuck pins in a map, marking the reported fires. The granary, a textile storeroom, the city square, a manufactory.

"The distillery!" Luther cried from the door as he received a messenger's newest report.

Zhelyas groaned. He hoped the palace had a substantial wine cellar so he could get drunk after this. He moodily stabbed a pin into the paper.

"It makes little sense," Luther said, staring at the map. "These I get, they're typical targets for insurgents."

"Then why weren't they protected?"

"They were, sire, but there was no way to anticipate such an attack, never mind prepare for it."

Zhelyas scowled. "If they were natural targets, what about these?" he inquired, pointing at the errant pins on the other side of the map.

"That's what I can't figure," Luther replied, scratching his stubble. "They're nothing special, just abandoned buildings, former offices or packing facilities."

"Like ones that might be used for commerce?"

They turned to see a smug face with silvery eyes.

"Arvind," Zhelyas greeted coldly. "How nice of you to join us."

Other than the incident with Lobelia, he'd mostly stayed in his rooms since the trauma of being revived by Veena and her "healing hands." Even now, Zhelyas vividly recalled the agonized screaming. He didn't particularly like the man, but Arvind had been equally as instrumental to the success of the coup as any of the other conspirators.

"I was drawn by the commotion. Is my dear niece causing you trouble again, my liege?"

Zhelyas pursed his lips, irked. "Why did you mention 'commerce'?"

"My brother Vittorius built up quite a nice little side business during his stint as Minister of Trade. None of the items are illegal, of course, since that would tarnish his lily-white morals, but the goods are of a quality lesser folk can afford, castoffs that would otherwise be discarded. It's a clever little racket."

"Your point?"

"Vito acquired dozens of properties in the merchant quarter, but many have been vacant for some time, and with the recent economic uncertainty, he hasn't found new tenants. If he was suggesting places for my niece to set ablaze, they wouldn't cause too much damage."

"There have been four outliers so far," Zhelyas said, considering this long-winded explanation. "Do you know where they will strike next?"

Arvind traced an arc with his finger. "I think I might have an idea. Leave it to me, sire." He bowed, then glanced up, a cruel glint in his eyes. "And remember what you promised."

Zhelyas gave a curt nod, and the sycophantic prince slithered off.

Leaving the impotent military to their duties, Zhelyas summoned an emergency meeting of court. The nobles arrived looking bleary-eyed and still in their nightclothes. Like him, many of them had been awakened by the chaos outside, and were frazzled and uneasy.

"I apologize for wresting you from your beds at this time of night," Zhelyas began. "However, we have some urgent matters to discuss. Earl Dahl."

"Your Majesty?" Malcolm replied, stifling a yawn.

"Take a catalog of the provisions in the castle and deliver the list to me. If we are to be under siege, then I would know where we stand."

"Yes, sire."

Zhelyas thought back to Cortin and his gluttonous consumption of food and wine, and wondered if the obnoxious old man had done so deliberately, knowing this was going to happen.

"Viscount Casus," he continued, and the newly-minted royal treasurer stepped forward, having had the forethought to at least remember his keys. "I want the funds in the treasury counted at once."

Arcus bowed.

"Countess Alvara."

Radella nodded her head, her usually perfectly coiffed hair rumpled.

"As Minister of Trade, you will review your predecessors' notes and present me with any options we have in this situation." His gaze raked the crowd. "I will not be made a fool of by these rebels, do I make myself clear?"

"Yes, Your Majesty," they all murmured, and shuffled off to do his bidding.

Caro and Stelian's group were coming to the last of Vittorius's abandoned properties when there was a skirmish down the street. They ducked into an alley as torchlight illuminated the shadows of patrolling soldiers.

"Husam and I will see if there's another way around," Stelian suggested, and she nodded. The remaining three men—two Alenard's, one Khalil's—huddled with her in the dark.

"Hurry, this way," a voice said urgently, and Caro turned to see a familiar face.

"Uncle Arvind?" she whispered. "What are you doing here?"

"I was spying on Zhelyas and realized what you were doing. I knew the guards were being deployed in this area, so I wanted to warn you."

She and her three companions trickled into the building at his insistence. The door slammed shut behind them, plunging them into pitch-black darkness.

Caro knew immediately something was wrong. "Arvind?"

One of the men let out a strangled cry, then there was a thump. A sickening splurch was followed by a grunt and two more thumps. Caro's heart pounded in her chest as she grabbed the dagger and lashed out at her invisible opponent.

A strong hand seized her wrist from behind, forcing the knife from her grasp, and it clattered to the floor at her feet. Another held her still and pressed a foul-smelling cloth against her mouth.

She clawed at the face of her captor with her free hand and heard him yelp in pain, then her body gave in to the drug and she slipped into unconsciousness.

Stelian leaned against the wall of the building, holding his breath as he gripped the hilt of his sword. Husam was beside him, but what could the two of them do against so many? Caro could be injured in the scuffle.

Husam touched Stelian's arm, as if reading his mind, and shook his head. "Where are they going?" he whispered.

"Back to the palace, I think."

They followed Caro and the soldiers as far as they could go. The leader turned, issuing orders, and Stelian recognized his face.

"It's not possible..." he murmured, taking an involuntary step forward.

"Are you trying to get yourself killed?" a voice snapped, and a hand shot out from the shadows.

Stelian blinked at the man who held him against the wall, and a low growl issued from Husam's throat as he tensed, scimitar instantly in his hand.

A flash of red caught Stelian's eye—the royal crest upon a sea of black. "Wait, Husam," he said quietly. "These men are part of the resistance."

Husam frowned suspiciously but sheathed his sword.

"My name is Gerrin, and this is Yanric," the man said, indicating his younger associate, who wore a handkerchief tied around his right hand. "I didn't mean to startle you, but Luther has the castle and the surrounding area battened down tight. There's no way you're getting in. I assume you're both servants of the queen," he added, casting a wary glance at Husam's foreign attire and coloring.

"We are. I'm Lieutenant Stelian, and my friend is Husam of the Esaphis."

Surely Gerrin would have heard of the desert warriors who had joined Caro in the battle against Luther, and indeed his expression turned to one of admiration.

"A companion of yours was taken?"

Stelian nodded. He was wary of revealing Caro's identity, even to her would-be supporters. "We have to hurry back to our people and inform them of what happened."

Gerrin clapped him on the shoulder. "Aryama be with you. You did good work tonight with those detonations. We'll take over and continue to sow dissent in your absence."

Stelian had an idea, and gestured to Husam, who handed him the sack of remaining explosives. "The queen doesn't wish to have her city destroyed, but perhaps you will know how to make good use of these."

Gerrin took the bag, and Yanric peered inside curiously. "Thank you, Lieutenant. We'll do our best for Her Majesty."

He nodded before the two rebels slunk once more into the shadows.

"We should go," Husam urged.

Stelian glanced back once more at the place where his queen had disappeared, then, with a heavy heart, he and Husam crept back to the camp.

Morfran and his group had returned first from completing their mission, and he took a long swig of spirits.

Sakin filled a mug and joined him. "I haven't been on such a hazardous mission for a while."

She sounded both exhausted and exhilarated, and Morfran glanced sideways at her.

"You enjoy this life, don't you, Sakin?"

She shrugged. "You told me once to call you by your chosen name, Morfran. I want to return the favor. My name is Semira."

"I remember that name," he mused. "You were the daughter of the Khadra chief."

Sakin nodded, sliding down the trunk of a tree. "I was to be used as collateral, married off to a powerful merchant to pay my father's debts, but I ran away. Not unlike the heroine of that racy book," she said with a chuckle. "I wandered across the desert, earning what money I could by dancing. I was in a tavern, minding my business, when a rather intoxicated fellow decided to come over and harass me. He put his hand on my arm, and I pinned the other into the table with a knife."

Morfran whistled.

"Husam happened to be there and invited me to join the Sharir. I agreed, and he introduced me to *La Firar*." She sipped her drink. "As you know, we abandon our names when we devote ourselves to the clan. I chose the name 'Sakin,' but I want you to call me 'Semira.' By meeting the queen who has endured far worse than I, yet heads forward without fear, I have come to accept that part of myself as well."

She rose, and Morfran held out his hand to pull her up. She caught her foot on a root and tumbled into his arms.

"Th-thank you," she stammered, righting herself.

He smiled, holding out the pitcher. "Another while we wait for the others, Semira?"

"Please."

Grave Intentions

Caro fought her way to consciousness as if swimming through quicksand. The more she struggled, the farther she seemed to sink, but at last she broke the surface. Searing light shone from behind her eyelids and her head throbbed from the effort, but she cracked open her eyes.

Three figures came into view, fuzzy and insubstantial, with droning voices attached to them.

"Finally awake, are we?" the dark-headed shape said with a lilt of savage amusement.

She blinked to clear her vision and sweep away the cobwebs that were muddling her thoughts. "Zhelyas..."

"Yes, indeed." He laughed, and the hands holding her twitched. Large hands, with a scar across one thumb.

"Luther?"

Zhelyas sneered. "She remembers you, too. How sweet."

Luther didn't reply.

"Clever disguise." Zhelyas indicated her shorn curls. "I suppose that's how you eluded my forces. Now that I finally have you in my grasp, what should I do with you, I wonder?"

Caro felt fury rise up within her. "You took away the people who meant the most to me in the entire world. I will *never* forgive you!"

If she gave in, every loss, every sacrifice would be in vain. And Ezalia would have died for nothing. She clenched her fists and narrowed her gaze. "I won't let you win."

"We'll see about that."

Zhelyas drew back his hand to strike. Caro flinched, but Luther lifted his arm protectively.

"Sire, please..."

His voice was soft and hesitant, and Caro glanced up at him. He seemed tired and worn. A mark that looked like it had been inflicted by a cruel blow marred his cheek, partially healed.

Zhelyas curled his lip, then lowered his hand. "What are you planning next?" he demanded.

"Nothing," Caro said dully. She didn't want to answer, but something forced her against her will, a bitter taste at the back of her tongue.

Zhelyas gave her an incredulous look and bent his face close to hers. "Nothing?" he repeated. "After all the fires tonight?"

Somehow, the way the question was phrased allowed Caro to keep quiet about Khalil. "They were the second phase of a strategy which had yet to be determined." The voice which replied sounded strange to Caro, as if it wasn't hers.

Zhelyas growled with frustration.

A woman with dusky skin and ivory-blond hair stood nearby, who Caro vaguely realized was Veena. In her hand was a ball of blue flame that matched the surface before her. Caro had initially thought it was a mirror. The figures depicted in it moved, but they were not the reflections of herself or the people in the room.

Caro shook her head; she felt as if it were full of soup.

Zhelyas leered at the not-mirror. "Look, the traitor. And who is that with him?"

Caro turned her gaze and saw Morfran in the swirling fire. He must have just returned from his mission.

"She's pretty. His lover perhaps?"

Sakin? Lover?

"Surely you can see it, Your Majesty," Zhelyas jeered. "The heat in that glance."

She had tripped, falling into his arms.

"The wiles of women are something to behold. You are still so young. What would Morfran want with a girl like you?"

Caro thought she saw Veena tense at the misogynistic words, and the sorceress banished the vision.

"No, th-that's not..." Caro protested weakly, her head spinning. What was she thinking? Why did it even matter? Morfran could spend time with whoever he liked... So why did it make her heart ache?

"Of course it is!" Zhelyas gave a triumphant laugh at her denial. "Even the one who most devoutly professed his loyalty has turned on you." He ran a finger along her jaw. "There is nothing left for you now, poor sweet Caro."

A tear slipped down her cheek, and Zhelyas grinned. "Take her to the dungeon. I may get more out of her later, when she's accepted the full weight of her predicament."

Luther hauled her out of the room, and Caro struggled to keep pace with his brisk stride.

"Why...?" she pleaded.

"I never meant for this to happen," he admitted without slowing his pace or loosening his grip on her arm. "But it was better than the alternative."

"What alternative?" She gazed up at him desperately, but Luther didn't say anything further.

Caro stumbled into the prison cell as the door clanged shut after her. She was still dizzy and could barely stand on her own two feet.

What had she seen? Nothing. Just two comrades sharing a drink... right? Caro screwed her eyes shut. Thinking about it made her head hurt.

She couldn't help the niggling feeling that something else was going on. Zhelyas must have left her alive for a reason. The notion of torture floated across her brain, and she was strangely unafraid. From what she'd heard of the goings-on at the palace in her absence, Zhelyas had been unusually restrained. Then there was Luther.

She banished the matter from her mind, glancing about the cell for any means she could use to escape. Options were few. Across from the cot was an old overturned crate to use as a chair or table, with a rather unsanitary-looking latrine in the back corner.

She sighed and flopped onto the moth-eaten mattress, wondering how she was going to get out of this mess.

Luther buried his head in his hands, crushed by regret. He had managed to spare the queen from Zhelyas's wrath for a moment, but what fate awaited her now?

"Luther?" A gentle hand touched his trembling shoulder.

He looked up to see Radella's worried gaze. She was as lovely as ever, and his heart felt a little less heavy.

"Won't you tell me what's wrong? There isn't anything I wouldn't forgive you for."

"I know," he said with a weak smile. "But I can never forgive myself. I thought I was doing the right thing. I never realized it would go this far."

Luther desperately wanted to hold her right then, to feel the warmth of her heartbeat against his own. He had been so obsessed with his duty, he had neglected the one person who had always stayed by his side. Yet now, consumed by guilt, how could he expect her to soothe his pain?

He pushed her away gently. "I can't allow myself to feel anything right now, Radella. If I do..." Luther clenched his fists. "Then surely I will drown."

Caro had just drifted off to sleep when a shadow fell across the cell door. A key rattled in the lock, and she sat up.

Had Luther come to fetch her again so soon? But it wasn't the general's face she saw in the dim light.

"Arvind?"

"Thank goodness you're alive," he exclaimed.

"Wh-what happened?" Caro asked, struggling to piece her memories together. "The last I saw you, we were in that old warehouse, and then—"

He entered the cell and locked the door behind him, then turned to her.

The glow of the moon through the small window illuminated his features, and she saw fresh scratches upon his face.

Scratches made by her fingernails.

Jabez arrived back at headquarters after Morfran.

"Is there no sign of the queen?" he asked, and Morfran shook his head, a pit settling in his stomach. He never should have let her go alone.

An hour later, Stelian and Husam appeared, looking haggard.

"What happened? Where's Caro?" Vittorius demanded.

"We were ambushed," Husam said miserably. "Some nobleman lured the others into a building, then Zhelyas's soldiers cut them down."

"And the queen?" Jabez inquired.

Husam shook his head. "Captured."

By this time, Stelian had regained his ability to breathe. "It was Your Grace's brother—Prince Arvind!"

"Arvind?" Vittorius repeated, and all the color drained from Morfran's face.

"He's *alive?*"

Vittorius turned to Morfran, visibly alarmed at the sudden change in his manner. "What?"

Morfran gritted his teeth until they hurt. "I killed him. Veena must have revived him with her magic."

Vittorius shook his head, bewildered. "You—what do you mean, you killed him?"

"There is no time," Morfran declared, spinning on his heel.

"While Caro is absent, I am in command—and I demand an explanation!" Vittorius was breathing heavily, his hands shaking, and Morfran slowed to a halt.

"Then I shall be *brief,* Your Highness."

He gave a curt nod, and they disappeared into the privacy of an office.

"Explain yourself," Vittorius hissed. "You say you killed my brother? Why?"

"Because he is the one who sentenced me to this fate," Morfran replied bitterly, his anger and desperation held back by a tenuous thread. "He is a monster. The crimes he's committed are uncountable—but what he has in store for your niece is far worse."

Vittorius furrowed his brow. "What do you mean by that?"

"Your brother is a beast in human form. Arvind has *specific* desires, ones an adult woman cannot satisfy."

The duke gaped in horror as comprehension dawned.

"Now, if you will excuse me, Your Highness." Morfran bowed stiffly, then departed, leaving Vittorius in stunned silence.

"You're going to rescue the queen?"

Not slowing his stride, Morfran glanced over his shoulder at Viggo, who had called out to him. "I am."

"Then come with me. It'll be quicker this way."

Several minutes later, Morfran looked down from the back of Viggo's drake to see Veena waiting upon the parapet below, evidently expecting him.

"That woman..." Viggo murmured as his mount circled overhead.

"It's all right," he said, and Viggo descended. "Just don't let down your guard while I'm gone."

Veena faced him as he jumped from the back of the drake.

"You'll find the queen in the dungeon," she said without preamble. "I would hurry, if I were you."

"Why should I trust you?"

"Do you have another choice?" she shot back.

She was a crafty witch—but he believed her.

"And Khalil?"

Veena sighed. "Don't worry, he'll be joining you soon enough."

Morfran gave her a brief nod, then sprinted into the castle as fast as his legs could carry him.

Caro took a hurried step backward as Arvind approached. There was a hunger in his eyes, and the hackles stood up on the back of her neck. He was like a wolf, and she was his prey.

"D-don't you dare come any closer!"

"I have waited so long for this, my sweet," he purred, and a shudder ran up her spine at his honeyed words. "Don't be afraid, I won't let Zhelyas harm you. You are my prize, my reward for pacifying the nobles during his silly coup."

She stared at him, aghast. "You helped Zhelyas?"

"That fool could hardly have subdued the castle's denizens without my help," he scoffed. "A few of the more unruly ones had to die, but I can't be blamed for that."

Arvind smirked and tossed the jail key on the pillow of the bed beside her.

Her attention momentarily distracted, he crossed the space between them, pinning her against the wall. She tried to push him away, but she was still weakened by the drug in her system.

"Let go of me, Arvind!"

"I will make you mine, and you will stay with me forever," he murmured, sniffing her hair.

She shivered with revulsion and fury.

"That fool Morfran. If only he hadn't been so keen to uncover the darkness in his past." Caro blinked up at Arvind, and he gave her an oily smile. "Would you still love him, I wonder, if you knew who he was and what he had done?"

Arvind leaned close. Caro could feel his hot breath on her neck. "Shall I tell you?"

Caro fumbled for the key upon the pillow, wrapping her fingers around its reassuring cool brass shaft. She gripped it tightly, then thrust the sharp teeth into his throat, yanking sideways to sever the artery.

"Be silent, cur!" she seethed as he staggered, holding his profusely bleeding neck.

She darted to the side, and a bloody hand reached out for her. Caro grabbed the crate and smashed it into his jaw, hearing a satisfying crunch.

Arvind collapsed to his knees, making unintelligible gurgling sounds, then fell flat on his face. Blood pooled about him on the floor, his jawbone at an unnatural, crooked angle.

She dropped the crate, panting, then peered through the cell bars at the sound of hurried footsteps. "Morfran!" she gasped.

He skidded to a halt and took stock of the situation, then wrenched the door off its hinges with a brusque gesture.

Caro knew the Sharir used magic sparingly, but to see it was something else altogether. She wondered what other secrets he held, and Arvind's taunting words rattled in her brain.

"Is he dead?" Morfran asked, noting the key embedded in Arvind's neck and the rapidly growing blood pool.

She nodded, forcing her thoughts to return to the present. "Pretty sure."

"Good."

Caro perceived a mix of emotions in his voice. "Arvind was the target of your vengeance, wasn't he?"

Morfran cocked his head at her. "He told you who I am?"

"He intended to," Caro said flatly. "But I have your promise. He didn't deserve to speak those words."

Morfran sighed, relief written on his features. "I killed him the first time, but you finished the job for me. I have no complaints."

He held out his hand. "Let's get you out of here, Your Majesty. Our ride is waiting."

Caro's knees were shaking. She took Morfran's hand, stepping over the twisted metal of the cell door.

Veena cocked her head at the tall drake rider whose shoulders tensed, apparently wary. He was of no use to her, so she swept off toward the dungeon and her own hapless prisoner, who looked up as she entered. He appeared a little gaunt but otherwise fine.

"Veena?"

Khalil was the one crimp in her otherwise flawless plan. Since that humiliating day when she had been expelled from Hadiya's camp, she hadn't given him a single thought, but when she sent the tracking storm after Caro and her company, she saw him again, and old feelings began to bubble to the surface.

Conflicted, she had resolved to seize him upon his return to the desert, and her chance had come when he was captured by Anwar, the brutish leader of the Zarqa tribe. Unfortunately, the Sharir had foiled her scheme, using their graceless magic against her and forcing her to retreat.

What had she hoped to accomplish by capturing Khalil? Did she intend to use him as collateral to win Hadiya's favor, which had been denied her before? Or was it something deeper? Was she merely obsessed with corrupting him, someone so faultless, like a diamond free of inclusions? Proving that his kindness had always been a lie?

But if it wasn't that... what then? She didn't have a good answer.

Veena waved her hand, and the shackles unlocked themselves, tumbling to the floor.

"Go. Morfran has come to rescue your queen, and a drake rider is waiting on the roof. You should join them." She motioned again, and the door at the far end of the prison swung open. "You'll encounter no resistance."

"Come with me," Khalil pleaded, and she shook her head.

"I came to this castle looking for something, and now I've found it. It's time for me to claim my reward."

She paused, then tugged on the star-like crystal pendant around her neck, snapping the chain. "Take this to Queen Caro. She may also find the answers she is seeking."

When Caro and Morfran reached the top of the tower, Berit had joined Viggo, and it was a good thing she had, because Khalil had also made his escape.

"Hey, Caro," he said, and gave her a crooked grin.

"Did it work?" she asked, relieved to see him.

"We should talk later," Morfran interrupted, though he also offered Khalil a small nod.

"I'll take him," Berit said, and Caro looked at Viggo's drake.

"Are you sure Morfran and I won't be too heavy?"

"You are no burden," Viggo assured her, and Morfran cleared his throat, seemingly amused.

At a low whistle from their riders, the drakes beat their powerful wings, lifting into the air.

"I have a request, if I may," Caro said over her shoulder, then told Viggo her idea.

He let out an interested hum. "I think I can accommodate that. Hold tight!"

The drake swooped and soared lazily in the sky above the army barracks, and the soldiers waking early for the morning stared at the sky in wonder.

"Zhelyas thought to defeat me!" Caro cried. "I was his prisoner, yet he could not hold me! He tried to shatter my will, yet he could not break me!"

She lifted her fist into the air, triumphant upon her flying mount, and to those below she surely seemed a goddess of battle, the fiery light of dawn wrapped around her like a mantle. "I have prevailed—and I will be victorious!"

Zhelyas was drawn to the balcony by her rallying cry. He growled and thrust out his hand, crackling with energy. A stream of red burst forth, streaking across the sky toward Caro and the drake.

Morfran snatched Viggo's crossbow and aimed at the magic lightning. The bolt, fueled by his violet light, struck Zhelyas's and exploded in a shower of sparks like fireworks.

Caro smiled as the light show was reflected upon the awed faces of those below. "Lay down your weapons, good men, and be welcomed in the encampment of the true Queen of Artemisia!"

His face burning with humiliation, unable to meet the expectant stares of the soldiers, Zhelyas clenched the fabric of his cloak and spun away.

With one more exultant swoop, the drake sailed above their heads and out of sight.

Caro, who had gotten little sleep that wasn't drug-induced, put up little resistance as Morfran ushered her to bed upon her return.

Vittorius's face was pale and wan, obviously still shaken by the revelation of his brother's depravity. "Did Arvind...?" he inquired in a hushed voice, and Morfran shook his head.

"No, I was in time. But the point was moot—she took care of him herself."

"You mean Caro killed him?"

"Yes, Your Grace, and quite methodically as well," Morfran replied, rather impressed by the feat. He had reverted to

Vittorius's title as duke, since he was no longer heir apparent as the chain of command dictated.

"That is not what I would have hoped," Vittorius sighed. "Killing her uncle couldn't have been easy, but Caro is a fighter. I'm relieved you saved her, in any case."

"Always," he replied simply, and the words rang true.

Vittorius studied him thoughtfully for a moment. "Commander."

"Your Grace?"

"What did my brother do to you? Who are you, really?"

Morfran shifted uncomfortably. "I can't tell you that, not until I tell her."

Vittorius appeared confused. "Caro doesn't know?"

"No," Morfran replied, avoiding his gaze. "She will know at the end—I gave her my word. And then I will find out if she can forgive me."

"I don't understand," Vittorius said, frowning. "I don't understand any of this. How could I have not seen it? My own *brother*?" He slumped in the chair across from Morfran.

"Forgive me for saying so, but I believe sometimes we have trouble seeing what is closest to us specifically because it *is* so close."

"All this time I wondered why he and Roland fell out... I wonder if this was the reason."

"Parents are very perceptive. Even if they weren't sure why, they must have sensed something was not right about the way Arvind treated their daughter and took extra steps to protect her. You're not the only one who was fooled. He was very discreet," Morfran added, trying to be reassuring. "Zhelyas discovered it by chance, and Arvind revealed it was the reason why he had caused my suffering."

Vittorius apparently didn't have a suitable response, and stayed silent.

"Now, if you will pardon me, Your Grace, I should return to Her Majesty's side."

Grist for the Mill

The next morning, Lottie went to wake Caro since she hadn't risen for breakfast, then raced down the stairs, eyes wide with panic.

Morfran watched from the door as Gaius felt Caro's forehead and took her pulse.

"Perhaps the strain of the past few days was too much for her." He dunked a cloth into the bowl of water and placed it upon Caro's brow. "We should let her sleep a while."

Stelian paced in the corridor. "Is Caro sick?"

"I don't know," Gaius replied, crossing his arms and shaking his head. "She has a fever and her heartbeat's elevated, but her breathing is irregular and slow. Her skin is clammy and she's flushed, and the tips of her fingers are blue."

Morfran's head snapped up. "What did you say?"

He strode heedless past Gaius, who scooted his slippered feet away lest they be trod on. Morfran paused by the edge of the bed, then removed his glove and took Caro's hand, placing two fingers beneath her wrist.

"I've already done that, you know," Gaius muttered.

Morfran ignored him. He placed his palms on both sides of Caro's pillow and leaned over, sniffing the breath coming in

542

ragged puffs from her parted lips. It smelled overly sweet, like rotting fruit.

"She's been poisoned," he replied grimly, straightening.

"How do you know?"

"When I found Her Majesty, she appeared to be suffering exhaustion and delirium from a drug, but I now believe a particular slow-acting poison was administered. It is called *alzilu*, and it has now rooted itself in her body, destroying it from within."

Stelian went white, and Gaius swallowed at this frank explanation.

"What can we do?" the physician asked.

"Keep her comfortable and try to bring her fever down. That will slow its progress. This particular poison has no antidote, but I have an idea where I can procure an elixir."

Arborlisle stretched on for miles, and within the forest nestled a forbidding swamp. Its true name long forgotten, it was colloquially known as the Murk, which suited the place well enough.

Berit had taken Morfran part of the way before letting him off, and he now trudged through the oppressive morass. The air was different here, quiet but stifling. It was protected by sorcery; he could feel it prickling on his skin.

Morfran's boot slipped and he stumbled, the unstable ground making it difficult to keep his footing. Despite his haste, he deliberately slowed his pace, picking his path with more care.

The swamp seemed innocuous at first glance, but Morfran was keenly aware of its dangers. The Murk was known to be home to a dangerous array of creatures, and few who ventured into their midst ever returned.

He had also heard rumors of the fearsome witch who dwelled within its borders, Amanita; if anyone could save Caro, she could. But would he make it in time? Or would he even come out alive?

Still, he had to try. Caro had been suffering the effects of the *alzilu* poison for more than a day. Time was running short.

A vine hung in his way. He pushed it aside, then jumped as it let out an agitated hiss. It wasn't a vine at all, but an annoyed snake who bared its venomous fangs. Morfran quickly sidestepped the creeper. More vines draped across his path, and he drew his sword warily. Some were just that, but others were the cleverly disguised vipers, and light glistened off their green scales as he passed beneath.

He emerged from the corridor of vines into a clearing. At the center of a wide lake blanketed by green algae sat an island with a cottage perched upon it. Slimy stones formed a path to the door of the hut, which looked like it had been constructed from tree beams and branches. An uneven railing led to the rickety porch.

The lake rippled ominously, and he thought he saw a shape in the water, suggesting something might be living in its noxious depths.

As he drew closer, delicate pink butterflies fluttered around his head, and he shooed them away impatiently. A cloud of sweet-scented mist trailed from their wings and filled the air. He breathed it in and sneezed.

Morfran felt lightheaded and swayed, lumbering into a patch of fungi. The tops glowed eerie purple, casting a faint light in the gloom. He fell to one knee and leaned forward on his hands, smushing one of the mushrooms.

His fingers began to tingle, covered with the purple goop that oozed out. He peeled off his glove to see a black rash spreading from his palm up his arm.

His vision swam; he was rapidly losing consciousness. He collapsed to the ground, and the butterflies gathered around him, alighting upon the seeping mushrooms.

"Well now, what do we have here?"

Morfran barely registered the voice and a weathered face peering into his, then everything went black.

"Morfran's not back yet?" Gaius inquired as Stelian came upstairs to check on Caro. Vittorius had been apprised, and requested frequent updates on her condition.

"Not yet," Stelian replied glumly, shaking his head. "Any change?"

Caro moaned in her sleep, and Gaius dabbed her face with water.

"None. She's getting worse, as the commander predicted." He hunched over in the chair. "I looked through some of my old notes and found only a brief mention of this *alzilu*. It's a plant that hails from the desert, and like he said, there is no known cure."

Stelian squeezed the doctor's shoulder.

"I have no idea what Morfran thinks he can do to save her," Gaius said, "but I hope he does it soon. She doesn't have much time left."

Morfran woke, staring at the exposed beams of a rustic ceiling, and took a moment to gather his bearings. He must be in the cabin he had seen from across the lake. He sat up quickly, then regretted it, cradling his pounding head.

"Awake, are we?"

An old woman busied herself about a small stove. Puffs of steam issued from a pot in which she seemed to be boiling something. The hut was even tinier than he'd thought, with barely enough space for a kitchen nook, a rocking chair beneath a small window, and the bed he lay in. The frame consisted of entwined branches with a patchwork quilt, his long legs sticking out the end.

The woman tossed a few roots into the pot. They looked like ginger except for their disconcerting magenta hue. She smiled at him, stirring the strange concoction.

"Amanita?" he ventured.

"Just so," she replied with a chuckle. "You fell afoul of some of the more charming ways for the unsuspecting to die in the Murk. First the creepers, then sporewings, and even the glowshrooms. You do know how to make an entrance."

Amanita was an old, crooked woman, her face and hands so wrinkled she looked to be a hundred years old. Long white hair was piled on top of her head like a bundle of wool, and she leaned upon a gnarled cane as crooked as she was.

Morfran stood, fighting a wave of nausea, and hobbled to the window.

"I wouldn't do that if I were you," the old woman cautioned in her merry voice. "Nibbles doesn't much like visitors."

"Is Nibbles a rabbit?" Morfran grunted.

"No, he's a jormungand."

Morfran blinked at her, then staggered backward, sinking onto the bed. "A—a *jormungand*?" he repeated in a hoarse whisper.

"I call him Nibbles, but he'd most likely devour you in a single bite," Amanita said matter-of-factly.

Not even Morfran's formidable skills could defeat a jormungand. It was a monster from the old world which had apparently made a comfortable home in this swamp, a convenient gatekeeper for its lone denizen.

He stared at the old woman, who had finished her stirring and was now tipping the mixture into a wooden bowl. It was the unappetizing color of boiled beets, but he was fairly certain there were no beets in it.

"Who—*What* are you?" he asked breathlessly.

Amanita cocked her head at him. "The powers of a Sharir are mighty indeed. You have guessed in moments what few would ever suspect."

"Someone who could command a serpent of lore is no ordinary mortal."

She shrugged. "What I am does not matter. Suffice it to say, my kind are as old as the sun, as old as time. However, having such a handsome young man faint on my doorstep is not a usual occurrence," she added cheerfully.

She tottered over with the repulsive soup. It smelled as rancid as it looked; he couldn't even guess at the taste. "This will clear up the last of your lingering symptoms," Amanita said, offering him the steaming bowl. "Go on."

Not wishing to test his host's unpredictable patience, Morfran took a hesitant sip and coughed. The taste was far more vile than its look or smell.

"That's a good boy," Amanita cooed.

Her condescension irked Morfran, but he decided it would be best to do as he was told. He braced himself and took another sip, finding to his relief it was mildly less revolting now, and in fact almost tolerable.

A smile spread across her craggy features, her skin like wrinkled parchment, and she sat in the moth-eaten upholstered chair.

He began to feel distinctly uncomfortable in her small hut, but he swallowed his unease. "You know why I have come, then?" he asked.

"Of course," she chided with a hoarse cackle, picking up her knitting, a scarf made out of what looked like nettles. "I know you better than you know yourself, my boy."

Morfran fought to keep calm, despite the crone being privy to all his most dangerous secrets. "I have heard you are a powerful apothecary. The poison is ravaging Caro's body, and she will be beyond hope before long."

"The poor little queen," Amanita sighed. "How long must her suffering continue?"

The question seemed rhetorical, so Morfran chose not to comment.

Amanita leaned back and sized Morfran up as if she were trying to decide whether he could be trusted. Any other man or woman would meet a quick end for daring to look at him in such a way, but Amanita was neither human, nor to be underestimated. Beneath her "dotty old lady" façade, she was a creature as ancient and dangerous as the serpent slithering in the acrid waters outside her door.

"You stand at the crux of a destiny you can barely comprehend," she said, her voice low and clear, and he felt the weight behind her words. The pit in his stomach deepened. "You will confront your past and face your deepest fears. Knowing this, are you willing to risk everything to remain by her side?"

He gave a curt nod, unable to give voice to the feelings welling up inside him.

Amanita's fierce gaze bore into his, and she was no longer amused. There was a splash outside, and it seemed to Morfran that the gatekeeper was agitated at his mistress's potent displeasure.

"I am," he managed.

She smiled again and relaxed in her chair. "Now where did I put that...?" Amanita rummaged through the knitting basket. "Ah, here it is."

She triumphantly withdrew a small object wrapped in a handkerchief. He reached for it, and she jerked it back, waggling her finger. "Tsk, tsk. Nothing ever comes for free."

Morfran frowned. "What do you want?"

"If I refused, you'd probably try to kill me for it, wouldn't you? Still as ruthless as ever, yet you say you've changed."

Her ability to see straight into his heart unnerved him, and he felt as helpless as a small child. "Please, Amanita. I have nobody else to turn to."

She seemed placated by his desperate plea. "Very well. You will face a choice in the near future, and you'll be commanded to do the one thing you do not wish to—and you will obey without question."

"By whom?" Morfran asked, puzzled by the vague ultimatum.

"You'll know when the time comes. I want your word."

Morfran's heart was conflicted by the possibilities, but Caro's life mattered more. "You have it."

"For now, I require something a little more tangible. That dagger will do."

Morfran's hand strayed to the small blade he always wore at his waist, the one thing that connected him to his past. It was part of who he was, indelibly tied to his identity. The blade was almost like a security blanket, always within arm's reach, and he was loath to part with it.

"Take care of it, old woman," he said, handing over the dagger and sheath. "You know what this means to me. I'll be needing it back."

"And you'll have it, don't you worry," she replied.

Morfran nodded as she dropped the wrapped object in his hand, and he tucked it safely inside his tunic.

"Amanita," he said, rising and bowing to her.

Her eyes twinkled at his false humility. "Now, assassin, you do not fool me," Amanita tutted, and gestured to a basket on the table. "Take one ere you go. They are quite tasty."

Morfran peered beneath the cloth to see biscuits with some sort of vibrant orange berry baked in. He picked the safest-looking one and held it lightly in his gloved hand.

"Come again, Morfran dear," she cackled, retrieving her knitting and setting the nettle scarf once more in her lap. "You know where to find me, should you need me."

With that, Morfran shuffled out the door, which snapped shut behind him, leaving him once more alone in the muggy, eerie swamp.

He glanced at the biscuit, certain none of her baking would be palatable to human digestion, and tossed it into the lake. It teetered upon the surface of the water for a moment before sinking into the murky depths. Perhaps the jormungand would be more appreciative of her efforts. Upon second thought, that was likely her intention all along.

"Dratted old biddy," Morfran muttered.

His gaze swept across the lake, but he didn't see any telltale ripples. Taking a steadying breath, he stalked with deliberate care across the mossy stones, mindful not to disturb the water. He had, perhaps, placated the serpent with a mid-evening snack, but he still didn't want to become dessert.

The sporewing butterflies fluttered close, and he waved them off, careful not to breathe in the mist which trailed in their wake. He stepped gingerly over a patch of purple glowshrooms and made his way back through the hazardous trail of creepers draping from the trees. He stooped under another vine/snake and continued undaunted to the place where the drake rider waited.

"Did you find what you were looking for?" Berit inquired as he emerged.

"Yes. We should hurry back."

Morfran shivered in an unnatural breeze as he mounted the drake. The wind whistled through the leaves, sounding like sinister laughter. He urged Berit to take off as quickly as possible and leave the swamp behind.

Despite his misgivings, their journey was swift and uneventful. Once more at Caro's side, Morfran produced the cloth which Amanita had given him and unwrapped it before his comrades' expectant gazes.

Gaius peered at it, adjusting his spectacles. "A rock?"

"It's a bezoar," Morfran corrected with a sharp sigh. "This poison has no antidote, but the bezoar will serve as a panacea."

Gaius took the odd stone between his fingers. "Haven't seen one of these in ages—an authentic one anyway." He glanced up as if to question its provenance, and Morfran gave a short nod.

"I guarantee it's genuine."

Apparently satisfied, Gaius began to crush it up with his pestle and mortar. "Bring me some thin broth. If we mix this in, she should be able to drink it."

He carefully spoon-fed Caro, who swallowed the soup even in her half-conscious state.

"That should do it," Gaius sighed. "Now we wait."

"How long?" Stelian inquired.

"We should know by morning."

Caro's dreams were strange and mystifying, obscure and disturbing. She was wandering through a misty wood, lost and alone.

"Stelian? Morfran? Anyone?" she called, but the only sound she heard was the hollow echo of her own voice.

Her throat felt sticky, and she tasted something sickeningly sweet at the back of her tongue. She licked her lips to suppress the nausea, wishing she had some of Gaius's peppermint tea. The last time she'd had some was before the Accession ceremony.

Caro looked down and realized she was wearing the same dress, dark teal with gold lace, and Ezalia's heavy pearl diadem. The skirt caught on the brambles as she tried to make her way through the wood, branches tearing at her sleeves and hair.

She was running, but she didn't know what from. Shadows crept toward her, pulling her in. Arms thrust out from the darkness, fingers grasping and clawing. She recoiled from their icy touch. But there was nobody there to save her, and as the shadows drew closer, she felt despair consume her heart.

Then a bright light pierced the woods, making the darkness recede, and she felt a spark of hope. With every last fragment of her being, she reached out for the light, and it enveloped her.

Caro's eyes opened to see sunlight streaming through the windows. Lottie was about to draw the curtains.

"Leave them open," she said, her voice hoarse, and Lottie spun in her direction.

"Caro, you're awake!" She flung herself onto the bed, hugging Caro tightly. "We were all so worried," she said, hiccuping between sobs.

Caro stroked her soft gold curls. "I'm okay now."

The men had gathered in the kitchen, leaving Lottie on shift to watch by her bedside, and they looked up at a soft pitter-patter upon the stairs.

"Caro!" Gaius exclaimed, leaping up and scattering cards upon the table.

"I'm starving," Caro said sheepishly. "Got anything to eat?"

Gaius laughed. "That's my girl. Baked eggs?"

"That sounds fantastic."

Clean Slate

Everything was falling apart at the seams.

The king was obsessed with his recent mastery over magic, experimenting with all manner of unnerving things, while Veena was off doing something mysterious, flitting about the palace, heedless of Zhelyas's wishes.

And now the prince had been murdered, found slain in the queen's former cell. Luther had been tasked with going through his office, and so he bit back his discomfort as he rifled through the papers in Arvind's desk.

He slouched in the chair, rubbing his temples. What was he even supposed to be looking for?

It was then he noticed a slight depression in the wood. Luther thumbed it, and a secret drawer popped open. In it was a small book and some hastily scrawled notes.

"*Reminiscence* by Mallory Blanc," Luther read aloud. "Poetry?"

He flipped to the bookmarked page.

We met once
Beneath the bending bows
of a weeping willow tree

It wept with tears of flowers
Now I weep with tears of sorrow
For we can never be

Though it struck a poignant chord for Luther, it seemed a rather odd thing for the pretentious prince to have in his possession. Perhaps it was a gift from an admirer? There were some passages circled in red ink, and Luther frowned, reading them. They didn't seem to have any particular significance.

He turned his attention to the sheaf of papers. Arvind had rather tiny handwriting, and it was tidy as per royal instruction, but these documents seemed to have been written hurriedly. They referenced a clandestine plan to offer aid to the citizens still within the capital, especially those who had been previously imprisoned, and then assist in their escape from the city. It was very risky.

The meaning of the poems became clear as he saw that the circled passages referenced the particular details of their missions. Luther flipped through the pages, skimming the contents, and he came to a list of those involved in the conspiracy. Malcolm and the rest he couldn't care less about, but two names in particular caught his notice, and all the color drained from his face.

"What were you thinking?" Luther raged.

He threw the papers and book to the floor, the pages strewn across the ground, proof of their transgression.

Radella cringed, but Takaria stared back stone-faced. "Cease your whining, General. This was my doing, not hers."

"If the king finds out, you're done for. You know that!"

"Will *you* tell him?" Takaria retorted.

Luther furrowed his brow, conflicted. "No."

"Then it seems you aren't as loyal as he makes you out to be," she scoffed.

"Lady Takaria," Radella murmured at her scathing words.

"And perhaps that means you're a better man than I thought you were."

Luther stared at her.

"There's something eating at you, and it led you to abandon your principles and ally yourself with a usurper. I never approved of your choice to enter the military. I felt you were casting aside your responsibilities to go play soldier, but I was wrong. You believed so strongly in your fealty—whatever shattered your faith left you a shell of a man." Takaria's voice wavered at this somber admission. "I misjudged you."

"Mother..." He hadn't called her that in years, but the look in her sorrowful eyes made him question himself. "Is there any way for you to get out of the castle? I don't want to see either of you get hurt."

Takaria gave a slow nod. "That shouldn't be a problem."

"Luther, what will you do?" Radella inquired softly.

"The only thing I can," he replied, shaking his head. "Whatever the cost."

"Your Majesty, we have a couple of visitors I think you will want to see," Vittorius said. "They were sequestered upon their arrival and brought to me at their request."

"Who?" Caro was intrigued, but she had no idea what to expect.

"Your Majesty," they both said, rising as she entered the foyer of the villa.

One was in her late fifties with an imperious presence, dark hair, and smoky gold eyes; the other had blond curls, brown eyes, and a bright countenance.

"Duchess Takaria Ruxa, Countess Radella Alvara?" Caro blinked at them as they bowed deeply. "What—how are you here?"

They shared an anxious glance.

"My son warned us to get out of the palace. We were able to slip out unnoticed and came to find you," Takaria said, speaking of Luther with an affection Caro had never heard before. It was well known the two were estranged, yet somehow their relationship had been mended—surprising, given recent events.

A young woman with ash brown hair stood in the corner unobtrusively: Takaria's maid Senna, as Caro recalled.

"There are some things you need to know," Radella added.

"Such as?" Caro gestured, and they retook their seats.

"In your absence, a few of us nobles formed a coalition of sorts. We communicated through coded messages and snuck out into the city, helping the remaining citizens escape via bribes and falsified papers," Radella explained.

Caro remembered Vittorius mentioning something of the sort.

"In the process, a noblewoman named Lady Lobelia Anthusa became involved as well, convincing us to trust her with our plans. What we didn't realize at the time was that she was using us, or rather the other nobles we had recruited to our cause, to stage an insurrection of her own."

"What did she hope to gain?" Caro asked.

"Unfortunately, we may never know," Takaria replied. "Zhelyas returned to the castle after having been away for some time, and he put a stop to it."

The grim way she said it made Caro's palms sweat. "How?"

"Magic," Radella whispered in a hushed voice. "He... he burned her alive. It was horrible."

Takaria stroked the younger woman's hand as she trembled. "Not only her, but her lover Major Sejic too," Takaria added. "The rest of the nobles she had under her sway were imprisoned."

Caro cast a glance at Morfran, who gave a small shrug. Apparently, this was news to him as well.

"Thank you, ladies. I realize it must have been dangerous to come all this way," she said, rising. "Please make yourselves comfortable. The duke will provide anything you require."

"You're still planning to confront him?" Takaria asked, furrowing her brow.

Caro nodded. "I have no other choice. If I am to retake my kingdom, I must face the usurper who stole it from me. However, I am not alone. I have many friends and companions, and I know they won't let me down."

Takaria looked unconvinced.

"Thank you for the warning, both of you," Caro said. "I now feel as if I can better prepare for the days to come. I am in your debt."

Both women rose and bowed again as their queen swept off.

Caro made her way to her room and slumped against the wall. She had put on a brave face for their benefit, but the news filled her with fear. She closed her eyes, and she imagined Zhelyas killing Lobelia, heard her anguished screams. How could she defeat such a monster?

"Your Majesty?" Morfran's soft voice filtered in from the hall.

Caro straightened. "Come."

"Are you all right?"

"I'll be fine," she replied, forcing a smile. "I was just a little shaken."

"You're not alone. You said so yourself," he pointed out, and Cortin's dire prediction drifted across her brain.

"I said that to reassure them, but I'm not so sure," she admitted. "What if I fail, Morfran? What happens to all these people? Am I sentencing them to death? Maybe I should give myself up to Zhelyas and beg for their lives to be spared."

She clenched her fists. "I swore on my parents' grave I would get revenge on their killer, but is it worth it in the face of certain defeat? I have no magic of my own with which to fight him."

"It's your choice," Morfran said gravely. "I would go with you, no hesitation, no judgment. That is the oath I have made, and I will live by it. But can you? Could you live with yourself if you surrendered now?"

"No." Caro hung her head, a great swell of shame washing over her. "I've come this far, I have to see it through to the end. Even though... I don't know if I have the strength."

"You're the strongest person I know. You faced me, your enemy, unflinchingly in the garrison. Zhelyas is no more than I was—in fact, he is less because he relies on threats and coercion but has no real courage. He is a coward, and that is why you will defeat him, magic or no magic."

Morfran's unwavering faith made some of the dark clouds disappear. They were still there, but she could glimpse the sun through them.

Caro took a walk to clear her head and came upon Takaria in the library, staring out the window. She bowed hurriedly upon noticing Caro's presence. For a moment, it seemed as if the stoic woman had a tear in her eye, but in a blink it was gone.

"Duchess, I didn't mean to disturb you," Caro said kindly. "What were you thinking about?" Takaria looked uncomfortable, and she smiled to reassure her. "You needn't tell me. I don't mean to pry."

"I was thinking of my son, and all the time wasted," Takaria replied with a somber sigh. "I was cruel to him, and for so many years I couldn't bridge the distance between us. He discovered the coalition, you see, but instead of reporting it to the king, he confronted Radella and I. His only fear was he wouldn't be able to protect us."

She shook her head. "You have every reason to condemn him. He is a traitor to both you and the throne, and now the country is seized within a grip of fear by the military under the vile king's orders. I didn't believe Radella when she said Luther was haunted by his choices, and now I can't do anything to save him from himself."

Takaria fell silent, and Caro's heart went out to the woman who had always seemed so proud and strong, but now showed such vulnerability.

"I confess, I despised Luther," Caro said, voicing her own conflicted feelings. "I couldn't comprehend why someone so loyal to my father would betray me, even covering up my parents' murder. With every step I took, he was right there, forcing me to flee. But he didn't hurt my friend when he had the chance, and when I met him on the battlefield, I saw no hatred in his eyes, only a deep, consuming emptiness.

"I can't let him stand in my way, Lady Takaria. If he does I will have no choice—but I need to know the truth. Only then can he answer for his crimes."

Takaria stared at her a moment, then bowed low, her hands shaking. "Thank you, Your Majesty. That's all I can hope for."

In a Nutshell

"Oh, Morfran. Are you finished with the inspection?" Caro inquired, glancing up at him from the desk where she was reviewing documents.

A steady stream of supporters had been pouring into the encampment as more of the Crown's soldiers abandoned their posts under the command of the false king, and Morfran dutifully inspected the queue for any who might be spies for Zhelyas.

"Nearly. I thought there was someone you would like to see first."

He stepped aside. A hooded figure stood there, slim, with dark tendrils drifting over their shoulders, and they tugged off their cowl. Sapphire eyes stared out of a familiar face, radiating love and kindness.

"Ezalia?" Caro gasped, numb with disbelief and the realization of a fragile hope she had tucked away deep inside. She knocked over her chair, stumbling as she ran into her aunt's open arms.

"My dear girl," Ezalia murmured, stroking her hair.

"I—I don't understand. How are you here?" she stammered, the words thick with sobs. Caro wanted to laugh and cry at the same time, smiling with delirious joy while her eyes pooled with tears that poured uncontrollably down her cheeks.

"Why didn't you send a message? We all thought—" The words stuck in her throat, unable to voice the pain which had choked her heart.

"I wish I could have sent word to let you know I was all right, but I couldn't risk it." Ezalia shook her head. "After the fire, Zhelyas ordered his agents to scour the area for me. I bided my time until I could safely emerge from hiding, then followed you to this place."

"I didn't know if I could go on without you," Caro said in a small voice.

"I'm here now, dearest," Ezalia replied gently, holding her close. "And I promise I'll never leave you again."

Alenard entered with the day's reports, and the papers slipped from his shaking hands as he laid eyes on her. "Ezzy...?"

"Hi, Allen," she said with a smile that conveyed more than words ever could.

Alenard reached out a tentative hand, as if to prove she wasn't an apparition. "Am I dreaming?"

Ezalia entwined her fingers in his. "I assure you, I'm very real."

"But how?"

"It doesn't matter anymore, love."

She embraced him, an eternity of grief and longing coalesced in a single kiss.

"Excuse me, Grand Duke?" a messenger ventured, looking as if he'd ridden all day without stopping.

"Yes?" Ezekiel said curtly.

"I have a letter for you from the queen."

He nodded and took the missive. Caro had fled the palace without the royal signet ring, so Vittorius's ministerial seal was imprinted upon the wax: a set of balance scales symbolizing equivalent exchange.

Ezekiel cracked it open, his hands shaking as he registered the contents.

Confusion. Shock. Relief. His heart was ready to burst out of his chest, hardly believing it could be true. Finally, a sense of calm swept over him and he sank into a chair, letting the plush upholstery swallow him like a cocoon.

"Your Grace, what is it?" Uyria inquired worriedly. "Is it bad news?"

He shook his head, unable to answer, and silently held up the paper. Her gaze flitted across the words, her transformed expression mirroring his own.

"Oh, dear Ezalia!" she exclaimed joyfully, hugging the letter to her bosom.

Uyria admitted the haggard messenger with an insistent wave. "This calls for a celebration! We must have wine and cake at once!"

Ezekiel was oblivious to the flurry of excitement. He stared at the ceiling as though looking up from the bottom of a glassy lake, perfectly still and serene. He felt poured out like water, despair, grief, and sorrow ebbing out of him with the revelation that his daughter was still alive.

Ezalia was alive.

After dispatching a letter to Ezalia's father with the joyous news, Caro gathered the others to hear her tale. Ezalia related how she had escaped from Zhelyas's clutches through a panel in the wall, and had gone into hiding after the fire, waiting for her chance.

Everyone expressed delight and amazement at her return, and she gazed fondly at Alenard. He hadn't left her side since their reunion.

"I hear you did a wonderful job, both at Ock and during the battle with Luther," she said, and Caro beamed with pride. "But that's not why I'm here. There's something you need to know."

Caro cocked her head. "Does it have anything to do with what you were trying to tell me at the ball?"

"Yes," Ezalia replied, and explained what she had learned about Zhelyas's troubling family history.

"So, Zhelyas Ralston's ancestor was Tarthan Ralston, who killed King Guillam and fled," Gaius mused. "Had he married Guinevre, Tarthan might indeed have become king, and his descendants after him. It's a stretch, but I can see how such a notion could take root."

Caro chewed her lip, disturbed. "That history lesson and my curiosity about the scratched-out name was the cause of all this...?"

Ezalia shook her head and squeezed Caro's hands. "You can't blame yourself. It was sheer coincidence he was walking by and overheard you. A spark was lit within him, and when he discovered the truth, his delusion grew and festered in his mind until it mutated into something distorted and deformed."

"I overheard him once, muttering to himself when he thought he was alone," Morfran added. "He is obsessed with keeping the power he has claimed, terrified it will be taken from him."

Caro sighed. "Okay... that makes some twisted sense. But I still don't understand why Luther fell in with him. And why did my parents have to die?"

"Maybe you can find out," Khalil said, speaking up. "Veena told me to give this to you. She said she had found what she was looking for, and you might find your answers there, too."

He handed over a glittering crystal, and Caro rolled it around in her palm, marveling at the points of silver and viridian light it cast upon the wall.

"But what does it mean?" Ezalia asked.

Caro pondered. "Whatever it may be, it seems I have to return to the palace. Not only to confront Zhelyas once and for all, but to bring to light the secrets hidden there and expose the lies in my past."

Bird in the Hand

Ines hummed to herself as the kettle whistled upon the stove top.

"If you wanted tea, you should have asked." Vittorius's voice held a trace of reproof.

Though once it would have irked Ines, it no longer bothered her. "I'm perfectly capable of making tea," she replied.

Vittorius cleared his throat. "I didn't mean to offend. I've never had a blind woman in my house before."

"Think of me as any other woman," she said with a wry smile. "If I need help, I'll ask for it."

She heard Vittorius chuckle at her clever rebuke. "Fair enough."

"Would you like some tea?"

"Please."

Ines used her the tips of her fingers to gauge how far to fill the cups with hot water, then walked to the table. She had memorized the layout of the villa shortly after her arrival, and was now able to navigate with relative ease. Vittorius waited until she was seated, then sat across from her, his chair scraping the floor.

"What kind is it?" Ines inquired, sniffing it. "It smelled lovely in the tin."

"Salissardian tea with rose petals, cinnamon, and cloves," he replied, and gave a wistful sigh. "It was my wife's favorite."

Ines took a sip. The aromatic spices melded together perfectly, and it was both invigorating and refreshing.

"Your wife was from Salissard?"

"That's right. I hold the post of Minister of Trade, you see."

"Hence why you are a duke instead of a prince," Ines mused. "I wondered, when you mentioned that the late King Roland was your brother."

"Yes, the title of duke is traditionally conferred upon royal ministers, regardless of their rank. I met Iduna during a business trip to renegotiate a trade agreement between our countries. She was beautiful, with a spirit like the wind, untameable and wild. I loved her the instant I met her." He chuckled. "Of course, she made it difficult for me to woo her, but she eventually accepted my proposal and agreed to accompany me back to Artemisia. We had one child, Andrine, who you may have met."

Ines recalled the sweet, soft-spoken lady with the rambunctious twins.

"Iduna had a fragile constitution, however, and fell ill when Andrine was very young. My duties often called me away, and I wasn't around as often as I should have been," he said, his voice suffused with regret. "I wish I could go back in time and spend every moment with Iduna, but those days are gone, and I have to hold on to what I have."

There was a moment of long silence, and Ines circled the rim of the cup with the tip of her finger.

"Ines..."

"I know what you're going to say," she interrupted, shaking her head. "It changes nothing. Caro is the queen. I am her servant and, I hope, her friend. I have no need for anything else."

Vittorius sighed. "Even if you refuse the royal privileges of your birth, can you really keep that from Caro?"

"I... I don't know." Ines clutched the cup, conflicting emotions welling up within her heart. "I keep asking myself, is she better off not knowing?"

"You and Caro have been given a rare chance. You lost your family, and hers was taken from her—yet you found each other." He let out a small hum, and Ines could tell he was smiling. "Now I have two nieces, I can't help but feel you both deserve to be happy."

It was strange, thinking of the stodgy duke as her uncle, of all things, but it was reassuring, too. Maybe she had been afraid, not wanting to risk revealing the truth and losing everything.

It was early morning. Caro was sitting alone in the foyer, taking some time to herself before the day ahead. She set aside her tea and made to rise.

"Wait, Caro," Ines said, standing at the door. She rested her hand against the frame, and seemed to be struggling with something. Caro had never seen the self-assured woman so troubled before.

"What is it?" she asked, concerned.

"There's something I need to tell you." Ines stepped away from the door and came to sit beside her on the settee. Trembling, she took Caro's hands.

"Ines?"

"I—I don't know how to say this..." She faltered.

"Would it be easier if I told her?"

569

Caro glanced up, and Ines turned her head in the direction from which Vittorius had spoken.

"Uncle Vito?"

Ines bit her lip and nodded. "If you would, Your Grace. I can't bring myself to."

Vittorius tipped his head, then moved to stand beside them. "Caro—Ines is your half-sister."

For a moment, Caro wasn't sure what he'd said. "What?" She stared at Ines. "Is that true?"

"Yes," Ines whispered. "When Roland was not yet king, he pursued my mother Sarravia, an Artemisian noblewoman. Discovering she was with child, she left the palace for Effrenia, where I grew up and eventually met Morfran."

"It would be years before my brother fell in love again and married your mother, Cecilia," Vittorius added.

Ines hung her head, her shoulders shaking. "I didn't want to tell you. I'm sorry."

Caro remembered all the times Ines had comforted her back at the garrison, then after the tragedy at the opera house. She'd felt an intangible bond with the gentle woman, a close friendship. Now it was revealed to be kinship.

She embraced Ines, who drew in a soft breath at the unexpected gesture.

"It's okay," Caro soothed. "I must admit to being surprised, but somehow I don't mind if it's you."

She pulled back and swept away a tear from Ines's cheek. "Take care of my sister while I'm gone, Uncle Vito. I'm leaving her in your hands."

"I will see it done, Your Majesty."

"Caro..." Ines murmured.

"I'm coming back," Caro assured her fondly. She leaned forward until their foreheads touched. "I've always wanted a sister, and now I have one. I'm not giving that up."

Burning Bridges

"Where do you think you're going?"

Veena strode past Luther, heedless to his protests as he followed her out the back entrance to the garden.

"You can stay with that simpering fool of a king. I've found what I want and I'm taking it."

He grabbed her arm, spinning her to face him. "You can't!" Panic seized his heart. If Veena left now...

She growled and swished her hand in the air, blue flames leaping from her fingertips, and he staggered backward into the bushes as fire scorched the stone at his feet.

"I'm not a coward like you, Luther," she snapped, her cold voice laced with disdain. "I didn't ally myself with Zhelyas to escape the pain of my weakness; I intend to seize the power to change my fate. Don't try to stop me, or you'll find out just how far I'm willing to go to get what I want."

Luther stared at the sorceress as she swept off down the path into the depths of the garden, then picked himself up and made his way to the throne room.

"Veena's gone, isn't she?" Zhelyas said, even as he opened his mouth to deliver the news.

Luther nodded. "It seems so, sire."

"It matters not. I have no further need of her." Zhelyas's voice was like a great chasm, devoid of life or feeling, and Luther shivered.

"And me?" he asked tentatively, fearing the answer.

Zhelyas glanced over his shoulder, his gaze searing into Luther's very soul. "You have been loyal, I will grant you that, albeit a devotion born out of cowardice." He gestured dismissively. "Do as you will. I shall gather my power and await the rebel queen here. The symbol of her authority will be the place of her downfall."

"Sire..." Luther murmured.

"*Go.*"

The word cut like a knife, and he bowed, shuffling out of the room. What was he to do now? Zhelyas was his king, but with no command to follow...

The chips would fall where they may. Until then, Luther would guard the gate with his paltry remaining force.

Zhelyas was awaiting the queen. Luther would grant her entry, and wait for the outcome of their final confrontation.

Malcolm trudged into the throne room. Court was not set to convene, and he'd been in the middle of reviewing some lengthy documents.

There had been a palpable unease in the castle since the siege and the queen's triumphant escape from captivity. Prince Arvind had been discovered murdered rather gruesomely, and it was clear what Zhelyas had promised him in exchange for his support. The thought made Malcolm ill. However, he had been left to assume most of the prince's duties, a task which was made all the more difficult since Takaria and Radella had mysteriously vanished from the castle.

Now, the king had gathered all of the nobles in the throne room. He looked around, noting a number of surprising faces. Diascia, whom Zhelyas had commanded never to see again, had been summoned, and she hovered nervously in the shadow of her protector Arcus, whose quarters she was now sharing. Even Baron Oswin Odric, who had been thrown into the deepest pit, had been dragged from his gloomy little cell. Among the others were also Lobelia's former conspirators, who had been sentenced to the dungeon for their part in her insurrection.

"Perhaps the king intends to pardon us?" Rudo murmured.

Malcolm didn't know what Zhelyas was planning, but it certainly wasn't anything so benign. He was reminded of that first night after the coup, and had an unsettling feeling.

"Good nobles, you have all served me well, some more so than others," Zhelyas began, holding out his hands to them. He wore a benevolent smile, though his eyes were cold as ice. "It's time to reward you for your loyalty and faithfulness."

Malcolm's lungs felt heavy. His throat was sticky as he struggled to breathe, and he bent over, choking as his life dripped from his body.

There were gasps and muffled screams as everyone in the room collapsed, as though they had all been struck by an unseen enemy.

Zhelyas unsheathed his sword and began cutting down people at random, their blood flowing and pooling at his feet. His eyes glowed red with power and malevolence.

The last thought which crossed Malcolm's mind as his vision dissolved into blackness was that the queen would have no hope of defeating such a demon.

They were all lost.

Topsy-turvy

Morfran was talking with Stelian on the lawn, the amber light of the setting sun glinting off his mask.

Caro leaned her chin on her hand. Her heart was in turmoil. Did she really love Morfran? Zhelyas, and even Arvind, seemed to think so.

And if she did, what then? When she reclaimed her throne, she would be expected to marry a nobleman or a foreign prince. She was a queen—she couldn't just give her heart to anyone. Like Gisela and Darim, she would have to give up love for the good of her kingdom.

"You seem troubled."

Caro glanced at the door to see Ezalia standing there. It was still surreal having her aunt back, the one person she'd needed to talk to the most but couldn't. Now, with the chance to say everything in her heart, she wasn't sure how to phrase the words.

Ezalia came over and stroked her back in rhythmic circles. "You don't need to say anything. I know. Your heart is so full, it's like you're drowning, but you feel light as air. One moment you're elated, the next you want to cry, with no rhyme or reason to it."

Alenard had joined the other two men in their discussion.
"That's what it's like to be in love."

Caro sighed heavily, and Ezalia chuckled.

"Just like that."

"I'm so confused. I'm happy when I'm with him, but it hurts somehow. And knowing we can't be together... It's like when I thought you were gone, Aunt Ez. I feel empty inside."

Ezalia wrapped her arms around Caro's shoulders, staring out the window with her. "Nothing is certain, dear. I've learned that much." She turned Caro's chin gently. "Don't look so far ahead, simply focus on what today brings. If you're happy, *be* happy, and don't feel shame for it. The future will come, and you'll face some hard choices, but for now, hold onto what you have. And maybe, just maybe, fate still has a surprise left in store."

Carry the Day

Caro wasn't sure what to expect at the castle, so she sent Jabez ahead to investigate.

"Apparently Zhelyas has barricaded himself in the throne room," the Sharir leader said when he returned. "The sorceress is nowhere to be found, and Luther... Well, he doesn't seem to be putting up much of a fight."

"Oh?" Morfran asked.

"He and a few soldiers who are still loyal to him are stationed at the front gate, but they don't appear to be doing much other than standing guard."

It seemed as if most of Luther's dwindling forces had allied with Caro now, leaving a few strays to follow their disillusioned general.

"Thank you, Jabez. From what Veena told Khalil, the answers to the questions we have all been asking can be found at the palace. I would suggest first searching the grounds. Since her words were intentionally vague, I suspect the answer is obvious."

"We'll all go with you," Alenard said.

"No, I think a smaller party is better. I will leave some of you outside the castle to keep an eye on Luther and ensure

Zhelyas doesn't escape. Once this matter is dealt with—I will come for him next."

She took a deep breath, twirling the crystal in her fingers. It still had a piece of the broken chain left, and she pinned it to her lapel, where it dangled, refracting the light.

"Alenard and Jabez, along with Khalil's men, will stand guard at the entrance and monitor the perimeter. The rest will remain here. Vittorius, I'm leaving you in command."

He bowed, Ines at his side, and her calm serenity renewed Caro's resolve.

Caro relished the rush of wind as she and her companions lifted off with the aid of the drake riders, and she touched the crystal to ensure it hadn't been blown loose.

Morfran was unruffled as always, but it seemed to Caro he was rather enjoying the flight. Stelian let out a whoop of joy as they soared above the forest, while Gaius appeared to be trying not to lose his lunch. Khalil was at ease, and Ezalia was visibly delighted by the experience.

It was a short flight, and Caro saw the banners of Alenard's army as he advanced upon the castle, Jabez and the Omaira at his side. Luther took a defensive stance, readying his troops to respond, but seeing Alenard had no intention of attacking, he backed down.

Caro met his gaze as she soared overhead—and she thought she saw pity in his eyes.

The drakes landed in the garden, the largest space available on the grounds. It was immediately apparent the place had been disturbed. A patch of shrubbery had been trampled, and a line of what appeared to be scorch marks marred the stone.

"Looks like Veena got here first," Ezalia said, nodding politely to Berit before elegantly hopping off.

"At least we know we're in the right place," Stelian replied, patting the beast.

Khalil slid off his mount, catching his foot in the reins, and shrugged to Viggo sheepishly. Morfran gave him a disapproving look as he dismounted with more refinement.

"We will await your return, Your Majesty," Holger said, and bent his head.

"So what are we looking for?" Gaius asked, his green complexion returning to normal.

Caro was intimately familiar with the garden and had every inch memorized. She stared thoughtfully at their surroundings, then closed her eyes, visualizing the space. What was different?

She stood upon the central promenade, pale ivory paving beneath her feet. A fountain bubbled merrily, plumes of cool water spraying upon her skin. Clear pools were recessed into the ground with lotus blossoms floating upon the surface, around which paths diverged, framing plots of grass with flowers of every hue. Sweetpeas filled the air with heavenly fragrance, while the showy blooms of peonies lured the attention of visitors. Even the azalea bush which had concealed Caro and Stelian from the watchman's eyes was now bedecked with vibrant pink blossoms. The garden had become a little less pristine since Zhelyas had neglected to tend to it, but it was still as beautiful as always.

Before Caro was an arbor draped with vines of wisteria, purple and lavender blossoms cascading from the wooden frame. The area was bathed in mottled luminescence, and a bench sat by the path in the welcoming shade. The polished white limestone wall lent an impression of light and warmth to the ambiance, and on the surface was carved various attractive bas reliefs.

At the center of the courtyard beyond stood a statue: a warrior goddess holding a sword and shield, one hand opened invitingly. On either side were two winged lions sitting upon tall pedestals. One had its left front paw raised; the other, both lowered.

Odd. Caro didn't remember them that way.

"What is it?" Ezalia inquired, having watched in silence with the others while Caro was deep in thought.

"That statue, it looks different. Like part of it's been moved."

"Moved?" Gaius repeated, coming to take a closer look.

He inspected the base of the statue, locating a small raised triangle pointing up. He twisted it downward, and the lion's paw lowered. He repeated the motion, and the paw raised again.

"Well, I'll be. That's some fancy engineering. There are hidden joints in the stone."

"But nothing else is happening," Ezalia noted. Perhaps that's the clue Veena left you?"

"Maybe we have to do the same on this side," Stelian guessed.

Khalil fumbled around for the switch. "Got it!" he exclaimed, mirroring Gaius's actions, and the second lion's paw raised. A shaft of stark white light poured out from the lions' eyes, converging upon the beckoning hand of the statue.

Stelian peered around the lions, scratching his head. "Is it done by mirrors?"

Gaius shrugged, equally perplexed.

"So what next, Caro?" Khalil inquired.

"I would guess that's where this comes in." Caro unpinned the crystal and placed it in the goddess's hand.

The light from the lions' eyes refracted through the gem, splitting it into three distinct colored beams, each leading to a different point on the wall.

Stelian followed the path of the purple light, which illuminated a handful of grapes held by nymphs as they danced in the left bas relief. He pressed the grapes, and a clanking sound was heard, like tumblers in a lock turning.

Green light refracted near the top of the right bas relief, where a wreath was being placed upon Aryama's head. Ezalia reached up, but Gaius was taller and he pressed it first. Another set of tumblers clunked into place.

The final beam of yellow light splayed from the crystal, alighting off-center of the middle mandala, bathing it in gold like the blazing sun.

Caro pressed the spot where the light fell. There was a heavy thud, then grinding as the final key activated. The stone upon which the mandala was carved slowly shifted, revealing a hidden entrance.

"You should take the crystal with you, just in case," Ezalia suggested, "and turn things back to the way Veena left them. We don't want to be followed."

Caro snatched the crystal from the statue's hand while Stelian turned the lever controlling the lion's paw. The gears could be heard grinding slowly as they reverted to their original formation, and the group slipped through the door as it thudded closed behind them.

"It's dark," Khalil said, stating the obvious.

"I still have the flint," Stelian offered. "We could make a torch—"

No sooner were the words out of his mouth than the floor illuminated beneath their feet, forming a path.

They emerged at the end of the corridor, and for a moment, Caro thought she was dreaming. They appeared to be in the sitting room of a small house, though there were no windows or adjoining doors. Even the way they had come vanished behind them, as if an illusion.

Caro glanced around the room. Against one wall stood a bookcase, while in the corner was an unlit fireplace. Upon the mantle was a vase of flowers and a small wooden box.

Ezalia seemed to be drawn to the box and opened it reverently. It was an orgel, and it began playing a delicate tune.

"What is that?" Caro inquired. "It sounds somehow familiar."

Ezalia hummed a few bars along with the tinny music. "It's a song from the opera *Aryama and Mahira*. Though forbidden to be together, eventually Aryama's heroic deeds win him a place among the gods, and the lovers are reunited in a joyous duet."

Caro spied a sketchbook resting against the fireplace. It was filled with chalk rubbings, the drawings all depicting the same beautiful woman from different angles and varying expressions. Though her entire face was outlined with red chalk, white had been used to lighten her skin tone, while her hair had been done with so many layers it looked like flame upon the page.

"Legend says that Mahira had stunning red hair, like the most vibrant sunset," Ezalia said, gazing over Caro's shoulder with admiration.

"The winged lions at the entrance—they're Aryama's symbol, aren't they?"

Ezalia nodded. "The lions are also found on the royal crest of Artemisia, and are a common design element within the palace."

"The music box, the sketchbook... I think we're in his home," Caro mused. "The one he lived in when he was human, at least."

Gaius had found a strange assortment of paraphernalia upon a table and was staring at the items intently, perplexed. "Well, this is odd."

"How's that?" Caro asked, setting down the sketchbook where she'd found it.

"These things all appear to be ingredients for a concoction, but I have no idea what to do with them."

"Will this help?" Stelian inquired. "I found it sticking out of a book."

Gaius took the slip of paper, and furrowed his brow at the seemingly childish illustration. "Speckled powder plus water... equals white. That's cryptic."

"What about salt and pepper?" Stelian suggested.

"No, that's not it..." Gaius mused, staring at the assortment of things on the table with new eyes. "I've got it! They're ingredients to make lye."

"Lye?" Caro inquired.

"It can be used for soap and washing clothes, but I bet there's another purpose. Ezalia, is there anything in that music box?"

She nodded, holding up a block of metal which had initially looked like part of the mechanism. It was no longer than her finger and dull silver. "Just this."

Gaius scooped some wood ash left over from the fireplace, speckled powder like the drawing. He then placed it in a metal cup suspended above a candle which he lit with Stelian's flint and steel, covering it with a lid and boiling it with water poured from the vase of flowers. The ashes settled to the bottom while the clear liquid rose to the top.

He carefully poured the lye over the metal bar, and the lightweight shell began to dissolve. Inside was a small gold key.

"Anybody see a keyhole?" he inquired, lifting it with tongs and wiping it clean.

"Over here!" Khalil exclaimed, gesturing to the top of the bookcase.

Gaius tried the key. There was a click, and the bookcase swung away from the wall.

They found themselves in a large, black stone chamber flanked by columns which supported the massive ceiling. There was a giant door at the far end with two pennants: one red with a stylized yellow sun, the other gold with a green circle of interlocking shapes resembling leaves.

"We must be in the mountains," Gaius said. "There's no other explanation."

"You mean this place has been here all this time, and nobody knew about it?" Stelian asked, dumbfounded.

Caro shrugged. "I'm not sure. Ezalia?"

But Ezalia wasn't paying attention to the conversation; she was staring at a pillar. She stepped back and walked to a nearby pillar and did the same.

"I think it's safe to say we're being tested," she said.

"Tested?" Caro repeated.

"Each of the pillars has a symbol carved on it, see? As well as a pictograph."

"This kind of thing makes my head ache," Stelian muttered.

Caro couldn't blame him; he and Khalil were warriors bred for skill, not puzzle solving, while Ezalia and Gaius were in their element, nattering between themselves.

"This one is first, obviously," Ezalia said.

"What's obvious about it?" Gaius retorted.

Ezalia let out a labored sigh. "Look here. The way these diamonds interlock creates more diamonds. So this one isn't two, it's three. And this isn't four, it's nine."

Gaius scratched his head, counting shapes under his breath. "So this is, uh... eight."

"Right."

"And this is seven," Caro said, following her aunt's train of thought.

"But pressing them doesn't do anything," Khalil said, prodding the figures.

"Could it have something to do with these designs?" Stelian inquired, pointing at the odd pictographs carved beneath the figures.

The symbol beneath the number three looked like a leaf. There was also a tomato under the one, a crescent moon under the seven, and a rose under the eight.

"What in the world...?" Gaius muttered.

Caro's head was calculating, and she shared a glance with Ezalia.

"Substitution!" they exclaimed at the same time.

"Substi—what now?" Gaius said, blinking in confusion.

"There's only one thing these items have in common. They're either terrestrial or celestial." To make her point, Ezalia indicated the trio of small stars under the nine and a stylized lily under the four. "Just like the banners over there," she added, gesturing to the sun and leaves.

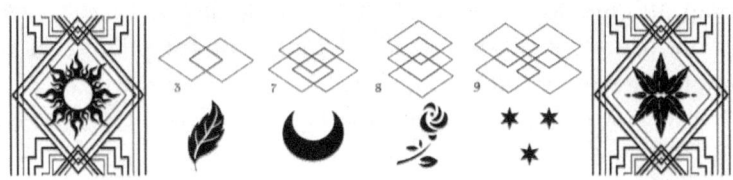

"Okay, following you there," Gaius admitted. "But what do they mean?"

"Somewhere in this room must be another piece of the puzzle."

The group scoured the chamber, searching for something with which to input the clues they'd discovered.

"Knowledge and ingenuity," Caro murmured.

Come again?" Stelian said, searching nearby.

"As Ezalia surmised, these are most likely tests. The puzzle in the garden outside was obvious when you knew where to look. Then the room we just passed through required scientific skill. This is more challenging, since it requires both resourcefulness and imagination."

"But why?" he asked. "Not everybody is a scientific genius like Gaius, or excels at deductions like Ezalia."

"I can't be certain, but I suspect each person's test would be different. If we had come in here alone, it would have played to our particular strengths and weaknesses." She shrugged. "I believe we have to prove ourselves worthy of whatever lies at the end."

"Whatever that *is*," Stelian said. "More importantly, what other tests lie in our path? They can't all be clever like this one."

"True," Caro admitted. "And that makes me nervous."

"What about this here?" Khalil said.

A closer examination of the door revealed what appeared to be a clock, but it had no hands. Instead, six random numbers in an antiquated script were etched in a ring upon the face, theoretically corresponding to the figures on the pillars. On an inner ring were small black gems.

Caro pressed one, and it turned green. Again, yellow. Then back to black.

"Yellow and green—like the pennants!" Gaius exclaimed.

"Green for plants, yellow for celestials. Makes sense," Stelian agreed.

"Let's try this. One, plant; three, plant; four, plant; seven, sky; eight, plant; nine, sky."

With Ezalia's prompting, Caro dialed in the code. There was a satisfying click, and the door opened.

"Two down?" Gaius quipped.

The next room appeared to be a very different sort, as if they had stepped into the hollow of a cave. The rock was roughly hewn, the walls unscalable to all appearances. In the distance was the statue of a man with a proud bearing, a giant mace held at his side. There was an odd sense of unease in the air, and Khalil and Stelian drew their weapons, gazes sweeping the chamber.

"What do you think? More puzzles?" Stelian asked.

As if in answer, the cave erupted around them with a bloodcurdling shriek, a monstrous figure leaping down from the walls.

It was a giant three-headed dragon. Each head had massive jaws and long curved fangs, and it gnashed its teeth, sharp claws raking the air.

"Guess not!" Khalil yelled above the creature's hideous cries. "This looks like a monster from the desert. Was it intended to be Veena's challenge?"

"If so, she failed the test!" Stelian scoffed.

"Don't talk so glibly, boy."

Veena crouched in a corner, holding her arm, which was bleeding from what looked like a rather deep wound.

"We'll take care of this, Khalil," Caro said. "Go to her."

Veena frowned as Khalil rushed to her side. "But I tried to kill you."

"You spied for Zhelyas but never raised a hand, not even when Khalil was your captive."

"I don't need your help," Veena grumbled through gritted teeth.

"Naturally," Caro replied dryly. "But we need yours. This beast was intended for you; how do we defeat it?"

Stelian was busy fending off the monster.

"That is the Azhi Dahaka," Veena replied as Gaius tended to her wound. "Be careful, it bleeds venom!"

Caro turned to ask Morfran if he'd ever heard of it before—then froze. Where was he?

"Stelian, did you see Morfran?"

"Not since we entered the mountain, now that you mention it."

She turned to her other companions, but they all shrugged.

"This temple is tricky. It may have taken him," Veena said.

"But why?"

"Watch out!" Stelian dove into Caro as a dragon head snapped in her direction.

"Even if we take out a head, there's no guarantee it'll kill the rest," he said. He covered his mouth as his blade sliced open one of the necks, releasing greenish-yellow venom that dissolved into poisonous gas.

"Told you."

"Now is not the time to be snarky, Veena! Isn't there anything we can do?" Caro admonished, reiterating her question.

Khalil gave Veena a pleading look, and she sighed.

"You're wrong. This beast wasn't *my* fight. Facing it is the penultimate test for whoever makes it this far. Legend says that Aryama defeated the Azhi Dahaka, trapping him within this mountain."

Gaius slapped his forehead. "Of course! The Azhi Dahaka was going to destroy the world, and defeating him was the feat that won Aryama inclusion among the gods."

"So how did he beat this thing?" Ezalia asked, growing restless.

"It is said with his great mace and the Divine Spirit of Fire."

Caro glanced at Veena, who held up her uninjured hand.

"Don't look at me. I may wield magic fire, but it's hardly divine."

"Besides, that wouldn't make sense," Ezalia added. "If this beast is here to be fought by whomever should enter this temple, they couldn't be certain to have a magic user around."

"True," Caro mused. "So there needs to be something here that can produce holy fire."

There was a pool of greenish water near where Veena was sitting.

"Gaius, why is that water green?"

He placed his hand in it experimentally. Slimy goo stuck to his fingers. "Looks like algae."

"The previous puzzle had four parts plants to two parts celestials. I bet the plants are the algae water," Caro said.

Veena looked reluctantly convinced. Her tests might have been different, but it seemed the resulting code was the same. "And the celestials?"

Caro thought about that. "They must be metaphorical. What else looks like a star and gives off the same heavenly glow?"

Veena stared back at her. "Crystals. One was needed to enter the cave, but where would there be a second?"

"We both have one," Caro said, but Veena shook her head.

"Yours is a piece of mine. It contains enough power on its own to open the door, but I would wager it still counts as one."

"I wonder..." Ezalia stared at the Azhi Dahaka. Its eyes were glowing red and it was difficult to tell, but one on the center head appeared to be missing.

"That's it!" she exclaimed. "Try to get one of its eyes. That's the key to defeating it!"

"You have got to be kidding," Stelian groaned as Khalil jumped up to help. He braced himself. "This is gonna hurt."

He aimed for the leftmost head while Khalil kept the other two occupied. The dragon snapped its monstrous jaws, and he rolled out of the way. While it was close to the ground, he leaped up onto its neck and clung on for dear life as its head jerked back and forth, trying to shake him off.

Locking his elbow around the beast's neck, he swung down and kicked it under the jaw. Then, while it was stunned, he jabbed his sword into its eye socket, prying the crystal out.

Stelian leaped out of the way as it writhed furiously, snapping in every direction, but he wasn't quick enough. Venomous blood spewed onto his leg. "Arrrgh!"

"Damn!" Gaius cursed as Stelian limped to safety. "Now I have two patients with poisoned wounds. This had better be worth it."

Caro dove, retrieving the crystal while Khalil covered her back.

"So what do we use for a vessel?" Stelian inquired, biting down on his tongue as Gaius applied a tourniquet.

"Again, it has to be something we either have with us, or can be found in this room."

Ezalia glanced about, then pointed to a natural depression in the ground. "That could serve as a bowl."

Veena nodded, shifting to look. "But how do we carry the water?"

Caro gazed around helplessly, not seeing anything useful. "By hand. That's got to be it."

She scooped up a handful of the algae water and carried it to the depression, careful not to spill any. She could hear Khalil fighting desperately, but she had to focus. She drained her hands into the bowl. Twice more she repeated the action.

"Then a crystal, if we're following the recipe," Veena said, plucking hers from the top of her magic staff.

Caro placed it in the water along with her own fragment for good measure, then brought another handful of water. Lastly, she took the crystal Stelian had won and added it to the potion.

Nothing happened.

"Well, that's a dud," Gaius said with a sigh.

The water began to glow faintly.

"We need a spark!" Caro cried.

Stelian tossed her the flint and steel, and she bashed them together. Searing white fire erupted across the surface of the water, but it gave off no heat. Fascinated, Caro ran her fingers through the flame; it didn't burn.

"The Divine Spirit of Fire," Veena murmured. "It worked."

Caro knew what she had to do. She had no mace, but her sword would suffice. She needed a torch, so her body would carry the fire.

She rose and dipped the tip of her sword into the water. The white fire licked up the blade and along her arm until half her body was aflame.

Khalil froze, stepping aside as she approached.

The Azhi Dahaka focused all its furor upon her, but she didn't flinch. It lunged, but recoiled from the flame as she held up her sword. It tried again with a different head from another angle, and she again repelled it.

Caro braced her feet and held the hilt with both hands—then drove her sword into the Azhi Dahaka's chest. Venom spewed forth, but the flames vaporized the blood.

The beast trembled and howled, its heads swaying back and forth in agony. Then it retreated, climbing the walls back into the darkness to heal.

"It's not dead?" Stelian sighed, exasperated.

Veena shook her head. "No. Even Aryama himself couldn't kill the Azhi Dahaka. He could only defeat and imprison it."

"Will it come back?" This from Khalil.

"I think we're safe for now," Gaius said. "It's injured severely, and even an immortal creature will need time to heal."

"Speaking of mending... Do you think the fire-water will diffuse the poison in their wounds, too?" Ezalia asked.

"Worth a try." Gaius nodded, and Khalil hurried to fetch some of the still-smoldering water.

Now that the beast was gone, Caro slowly approached the statue as if compelled.

"Caro?" she heard Ezalia say, but she couldn't stop herself. "Caro!"

Still Waters Run Deep

The world dissolved around her. Gone was the damp, claustrophobic cave. Caro found herself upon a platform, but there was nothing beneath it except a starry abyss, a giant well with no bottom. She let out a breath, backing away from the edge.

A familiar face with pale hair and eyes the color of honey appeared before her.

"Ines?" Caro ventured. "No, you're not Ines. Who are you?"

"I am Aryama," Ines replied in a voice which was hers, yet unearthly. "I can no longer appear on this mortal plane without a vessel. The blind are blessed—I can see through their eyes."

"Have you been watching all this time?"

Ines-Aryama shrugged. "Occasionally. You intrigue me."

Caro frowned, unsure of how to respond without offending him. "Is Ines all right?" she asked instead.

"I promise, no harm will come to your sister. I merely needed to speak with you."

Caro nodded nervously. It was rather intimidating—chatting in the void with a god.

"You have passed the tests," he began. "First, you found the entrance to this place and solved the puzzle of the lye, then deciphered the code sequence. Lastly, you defeated my age-old foe using what you had learned."

"I had help," she said, a little overwhelmed.

He shook his head. "This is your final test, Queen Caro."

"That being?"

"You must face your greatest fear and sacrifice what is most precious to you—that which gives your life meaning."

Caro pondered the significance of those words. Ines-Aryama smiled, and it seemed the god was amused.

"And if I pass this test? What then?"

"You receive your reward: the answers you are searching for," Ines-Aryama replied, "and that which you desire most."

Even Caro didn't know her own heart. How could a god?

"Do you accept?"

She couldn't turn back now, not after coming so far. "Yes."

"Then I shall be your guide. Come." Ines-Aryama waved a hand, and a stone arch materialized, blazing with swirling energy.

Caro steeled herself and followed the god through the portal.

They appeared in what looked like an arena, but one which had been obliterated by some previous battle. Columns lay in pieces, fragments scattered upon the ground. At the center was a stone throne and a figure with its head held in its hands, as if crushed by sorrow.

"This is your final test. None can complete it but you," Ines-Aryama said, and Caro was reminded of the disconcerting words old man Cortin had said to her.

In the end, you will be entirely alone.

Caro stared at the figure, then a whisper escaped her lips. "Morfran?"

The figure stirred, and the face of the masked commander looked up from his grieving pose.

"What are you doing here? Where were you?"

Morfran rose and descended the steps in his black armor, his expression as impenetrable as ever.

Caro shot a sideways glance at Ines-Aryama. "You—you're my final task?" she said, knowing it to be true even as she spoke the words. He held more than just his own secrets—he held hers as well. Only through him could she find the truth.

"I won't fight you," she said, shaking her head.

"Are you sure?" Morfran countered. "Back at the garrison, what did you tell me you would do when you found Zhelyas?"

"That I would give him the same mercy he gave my parents..."

Morfran slid his sword from its sheath. "You seem to laboring under a delusion, Your Majesty. It wasn't Zhelyas who killed your parents—it was *me*."

All the color drained from Caro's face. "What?"

The feelings she had been repressing bubbled to the surface, the pain spilling free and fueling an anger that erupted in her heart.

The corners of Morfran's lips turned up, goading her, and she raced at him, her previous denials forgotten. He batted her sword aside, but she was undaunted and came back with twice the fury.

Her greatest unspoken fear: his inevitable betrayal.

"I trusted you!"

"That was your mistake."

Caro lashed out wildly and growled, her sword slashing as he backed up. She jabbed, but he stepped out of the way. She knew she was forgetting Sakin's teachings in the heat of the moment and fought to regain control of her emotions.

She struck again, but this time Morfran used his momentum to knock her off balance. Caro rolled to a crouch, turning her upper body and slashing behind her. As he evaded, it gave her enough time to rise and recover her stance. Caro's heart was pounding as they circled each other, the tips of their blades barely touching.

They tapped swords. Then he slashed, and she ducked again, aiming a couple of low blows followed by high ones. Their blades met with a flurry of motion—the only sound their labored breathing and the clanging of metal.

Morfran made a wild strike, and she danced out of the way as Sakin had taught her, forcing him to swing his sword behind his back to counter. He spun, and their swords met at the hilt, their faces close enough Caro could see the icy blue of his eyes through the mask.

He pulled back, trying to tip her off balance, but she hooked his arm, then struck his jaw with the back of her fist. Morfran staggered, mild surprise reflected on his thin lips.

Caro pressed her advantage, and when he stabbed at her, she held up her sword so his ran along the length of her own, trapping it; then she ripped it out of his grasp and flung it away.

The sword clattered upon the broken stones, and she placed the tip of her blade at his throat. Disarmed, Morfran sank to his knees.

"Will you not hear his reason?" Ines-Aryama asked from the sidelines.

"Tell me," Caro commanded, her hand trembling with fury.

Morfran stared up at her. "I am, and have always been, your servant. That has never changed," he said, repeating his oath. "I did it to save your life."

"I don't understand."

"Your parents discovered this temple," he explained softly, "and the power it could bestow. They had passed all the challenges, save for the Azhi Dahaka. Following the final test, they would have to sacrifice what was most precious to them—and that was you, their only child."

Caro shook her head. "Th-that's not possible."

"Luther witnessed them in the garden, discussing your fate and their plans to remake the world. He was so horrified he lost all faith in the monarchy, so when Zhelyas offered him a chance for an alliance, he took it rather than face his conflicting feelings. He confessed to me one night what he had heard, and I knew I had to act quickly. I killed them before they had the chance to kill you."

Caro looked desperately at Ines-Aryama, and the blond woman nodded. She gestured, and an image flickered in the air. In it, Caro saw her father's final moments, and Morfran standing above him.

"I won't let her become the sacrifice."

"Everything he said is true," Ines-Aryama confirmed. "The question remains—will *you* sacrifice what is most precious?"

Caro backed up and held her hand to her mouth, denial bubbling up like bile in her throat.

Morfran rose and reached out to comfort her, but his hand stilled in midair and fell to his side. "Take your revenge. Your parents' murderer stands before you now."

"You said you would tell me who you were!" she accused, tears stinging her eyes. "You would dare break your word to me?"

Morfran blinked at her vehement words.

"I won't kill you," she said hoarsely, her heart warring with feelings of love and devotion, duty and betrayal. "I can't change that they're dead, and if I kill you for saving me, then my own life will have no meaning."

She let the sword fall from her shaking hands. "I suppose this means I've failed."

Caro turned her head, and was surprised to see Ines-Aryama smiling.

"On the contrary. What has been driving you all this time is vengeance, and you have cast it aside for the sake of friendship and honor."

The auditorium dissolved around them, and they appeared in a grand hall of amber and jade, the domed ceiling painted with stars and all the constellations. Against the wall sat a gilded throne, while high above a golden sculpture shone with dazzling luminescence like the sun, a thousand rays of light bursting forth. Winged lions yawned, sitting at the base of the throne, awaiting their master's return.

The true Temple of Aryama.

"Now comes your reward," Ines-Aryama said. "Whatever you wish is yours, to the limits of the universe. Veena desired power; your parents, immortality. You can save the world or destroy it with a single thought. It is your choice."

"My... choice?" Caro repeated, her head spinning. "Nobody should have that right."

"Is that your wish?" Ines-Aryama asked, lifting an eyebrow.

The rest of Caro's companions had also been transported to the temple, and she looked at Morfran, whom she had spared; Stelian, Ezalia, and Gaius, with whom she had started this journey; Khalil, who had fought by her side along the way; and Veena, who had proven herself an ally rather than an adversary.

"I want the ability to protect my people, something that will help me defeat Zhelyas and bring peace to my kingdom. A symbol to stand for that peace for generations to come."

The god in the vessel of her sister nodded sagely.

Ines fainted, and Gaius rushed to catch her. The spirit of a man stood in her place. He was the very image of the statue in the Azhi Dahaka's cave: dark-skinned, with eyes of fire, braided hair, and gold armor like the pelt of a lion.

"Aryama?" Caro ventured.

"I am," he replied in a sonorous voice unlike Ines's mild timbre. "You are the victor, and so I may appear to you in this guise, just once. Is it truly your desire that none other be given the chance to change the fate of the world?"

Caro nodded. "Even if it's selfish of me. If Zhelyas, Veena, or even my parents had achieved this power, they could have laid waste to everything."

"Then I shall do as you ask." He waved his hand, and the space around them began to fade. "As for the other, your wish is granted. You could have asked me to destroy the usurper for you, but you chose to face him yourself. I respect that valor. Farewell, Queen of Artemisia."

There was a flash, and the group found themselves back in the courtyard. The lion statues were now facing away from the mural, as was the warrior goddess.

Caro stared at the magnificent statue in disbelief. Where once the shield and sword she held were formless and stone, they had been transformed. The shield was as tall as Caro, shining gold with green enamel, intricate designs engraved upon its surface: scrollwork leaves, the night sky, and curling flames—symbolic of her triumph over the trials she had endured. The sword was long with delicate etching along the blade, a gem resembling a dragon's eye upon its hilt. The weapons seemed to glow with inner radiance, and she was astonished to find they were amazingly light.

"Veena," Caro said, "I understand Zhelyas can use magic now."

"He insisted," she confirmed. "His dark personality and hatred have mutated the power, and it is truly destructive."

"With these, I think I can face him. Will you test them for me?"

Veena nodded, then lifted a hand, twitching her fingers. She let loose a stream of blue fire, which struck the shield and fizzled out into sparks. Another was cleaved in two by the sword, nullifying it.

"Why did you leave me the crystal?" Caro asked curiously.

Veena gave a slight shrug. "Perhaps I saw myself in you, a young girl like I once was, forced into this by a cruel twist of fate. I thought you at least deserved answers. I never imagined you would overcome all the tasks where I could not, but maybe I found what I was really searching for all along—a way to change my own destiny, but not through magic or some power bestowed by the gods."

She smiled up at Khalil, and Caro could see the affection mirrored in her eyes. All Veena had needed was to feel truly loved and wanted.

"Are you sure about this?" Gaius inquired, and Caro turned her determined gaze upon him.

"Yes. I no longer have any doubts."

The goddess's hand was still open, and sitting in her palm was the small crystal. Caro lifted it reverently. The burden was hers now.

She glanced up at Morfran. "I'm sorry for striking you," she said, and he massaged his jaw.

"It was a good hit. Sakin will be pleased."

Caro smiled. He had confessed his sin, knowing she might reject or even kill him to attain the vengeance she had vowed. All during their long journey together—from the garrison, to his oath of allegiance, the tragedy of the ball, and even her battle with Luther—he must have been tormented by the truth, but he had never let her down, not once. She had trusted him without knowing why, perhaps because she had sensed the pain in his heart, which he had been unable to give voice to except through his devotion.

"Will you come with me? I need you by my side."

He nodded, bowing bow. "I am with you until the end."

"Then let us face Zhelyas and finish this once and for all."

Luther started upon seeing Caro with her newly-acquired sword and shield.

"I will not harm you, General," she said, as Morfran tensed beside her. "I now understand what you saw, and the paralyzing doubt that seized your heart and led you to turn on my family. I will dispatch Zhelyas and retake my throne. When I do, you may return as my general, or leave Artemisia if that is your choice. However, if you face me now, I will cut you down where you stand."

Luther blinked at her unyielding resolve, then hung his head and stood aside. "When the throne is yours once more, I will surrender myself to your judgment."

Caro nodded. "Morfran."

"I'm here."

"The rest of you, please stay behind. I can't allow anyone else to accompany me."

"But Mukhif gets to go?" Khalil asked glumly.

"Morfran has his own score to settle with Zhelyas, but he will not defeat the usurper. That duty is mine. Besides, I promised your mother I would return you safely, and I will not renege on that vow."

Khalil gave a reluctant nod. Stelian looked unconvinced and set his jaw stiffly.

"You have stayed by my side all this time, but I need to fight my own battles," Caro said with a smile for her faithful bodyguard.

The injury to his leg was no longer poisoned, but it still caused him evident pain as he limped with Ezalia's aid. Veena's magic would be useful, but she was also injured and appeared to be drained from her fight with the Azhi Dahaka. The magic with which she had tested the god's weapons had used the last of her strength, and she sagged against Khalil.

Caro briefly wondered why Aryama had not healed her companions as part of her reward, but perhaps he too recognized that facing Zhelyas alone was her destiny.

Ines stirred in Gaius's arms, and he set her on her feet.

"Are you all right?" Caro inquired.

Ines nodded. "It was an odd sensation speaking, yet not with my own words; seeing, yet not with my own eyes." She stroked Caro's cheek. "Aryama has been watching. I could feel his mind inside my own, but he didn't wish me to tell you."

"I don't blame you. It seems somehow as if this was all meant to be."

Ines smiled sadly. "You and Morfran are both set upon this, then?"

"We are," Morfran replied.

"Then I wish you well and hope for you to return soon."

Ezalia nodded, her eyes brimming with tears. "We'll be waiting."

Caro turned to the castle. There was no more that needed to be said.

Empty Vessels

Caro gripped the sword and shield as she mounted the steps and entered the castle. Morfran's reassuring presence was at her shoulder, and she drew comfort from that—as if by having him near, she could banish the fear that fluttered in her stomach.

The fury she had felt when she fought him in the duel no longer consumed her. Her mind was clear and at peace. She knew what she had to do; she could not allow herself to fail.

The castle was so quiet, it was haunting, as if no other living souls dwelled in it other than the two of them and their adversary. As they drew close to the throne room, Caro could feel the oppressive atmosphere grow thicker until it was crushing in its intensity.

"Has Zhelyas grown so powerful in such a short time?" she wondered aloud.

"Magic is a strange thing," Morfran replied in a low voice. "It preys upon the weakness in your soul. You either bend it to your will—or it bends you to its own. He has been corrupted."

Caro shook her head. "I remember little of Zhelyas from before, but he always seemed so polite, shy even."

"That was all an act, Your Majesty. As a member of the nobility, he was bound by certain rules and expectations of behavior. His reticence was because he had to hide his true self from the world."

"What does that say for the rest, then?" Caro mused, troubled by the notion, and Morfran sighed.

"Zhelyas may not have been cruel in the beginning, but once he was no longer bound by regulations, he could act as he pleased. There is a saying in the desert: 'Riches have disclosed in thy character the bad qualities formerly hidden by thy poverty.'"

Caro nodded. "So the sinister magic could worm its way into his blackened heart. Then what about you and Veena?"

Morfran cocked his head at the query. "An interesting question. I believe Veena saw her magic from a purely logical standpoint; like a chef mixing ingredients for a soufflé, it was a tool and nothing more."

"And you?" Caro asked.

"The Sharir wield magic for their own ends, but they respect it and understand the price. I have used it sparingly, as you have seen. Zhelyas has neither reverence nor caution for the magic he wields."

Caro stopped as the hall darkened in the distance, an unnatural mist seeping across the floor and up the walls. The hackles on the back of her neck stood on end.

"On your guard," Morfran advised.

Crooked figures lumbered out of the fog, their heads rocking back and forth on their necks as they walked, as if they were puppets on a string.

"Caraaughhh."

She recoiled upon seeing Arvind among them, reaching out for her. The brass key was still embedded in his neck, and he

605

rattled her name through his jaw, which was barely held on with sinew.

"What are they?" she asked with revulsion.

"Ghouls," Morfran replied, wrinkling his nose in disgust. "Zhelyas has even raised the dead."

There were roughly a dozen of the abhorrent creatures. One had a gaping wound in his chest, while another's neck had been severed, and he was carrying his head like a bag of potatoes.

"That's the first noble Zhelyas killed, the night you fled," Morfran whispered, answering her querying look. "The other was a soldier who was too afraid to hinder my escape."

"And the rest?"

"As Zhelyas's rage grew more potent, so did his patience decline. They are the victims of his tyranny and an ill-placed word or deed. No doubt I would have been among them eventually, Luther and Veena as well."

He spoke so blandly Caro couldn't help but look up to see if he was jesting. He wasn't.

"So how do we defeat something already dead?" she asked.

"Magic."

"I was afraid you would say that."

"Luckily, you and I have that in spades. You with your fancy new toys, me with my spellfire."

"Used sparingly, of course," she quipped.

Morfran smirked as she parroted his words.

The corridor was a cramped space, which was both an advantage and a hindrance. The narrow area meant the ghouls could not move as freely, but they were densely packed.

Caro soon learned that dodging was the best way to avoid an encounter. If she rolled, she was too far away to strike them, since their reflexes were much slower than when they were alive.

She held up her shield as ghoul-Arvind lurched toward her, then lashed out with her sword. The blade sizzled as it met the undead flesh, and Arvind's arm fell to the ground with a thump. If she couldn't defeat them with a single blow, she would cut them to pieces.

Morfran was dealing a certain amount of damage with his fire, but it only stunned the ghouls, singeing them at most.

Caro backed up, glancing about the hall for something they could use to turn the tide. "Morfran, stay here. And be ready to use your fire when I say."

He wavered, but nodded. "What are you planning?"

"You'll see."

Caro held the shield and sword close to her body, darting through the writhing mass, but she didn't attack them.

There, that was what she was looking for. Upon the wall in elaborate sconces hung oil lamps whose glow did little to pierce the murky gloom. She lifted her sword and cut one down, spilling oil over the ghouls, then did the same with the next, a few feet away. The ghouls rocked back and forth, groaning as the slick substance covered their hands and faces.

"Now!" Caro cried, and grabbed hold of a tapestry, shimmying to the bar at the top, praying it would hold her weight.

Morfran's fists erupted with violet flame, and he unleashed it at the mob of undead. Where before his magic could only singe them, upon contact with the oil, it set them alight. They staggered as their rotting flesh disintegrated. Caro's eyes burned from the rancid smoke, but she gripped her perch as they were consumed beneath her.

Once the last of the ghouls was left twitching upon the floor, Morfran held up his hands to help Caro down.

"That was clever, Your Majesty."

She shrugged with a small smile. "I have my moments."

Zhelyas's guard dogs had been dealt with—it was time to meet the master himself.

She took a deep breath, then pushed open the door.

Caro retched as she stepped into a scene even more putrid than the charred corpses, the air filled with the cloying stench of death and decay. The dead and dying bodies of nobles littered the room, the surrounding floor stained with their blood.

Amidst it all, Zhelyas sat languidly upon the throne, one leg hooked over the arm, an elbow resting upon the hilt of his menacing black sword. Lank hair hung about his face, his once-handsome features twisted and unrecognizable. His eyes burned like embers in the dark.

"So. You made it." He almost sounded bored. "It was dull waiting, but now you and my former commander have come to entertain me." His lips curled into a vicious leer. "Excellent."

Zhelyas wrapped his hand around the sword's hilt and rose, savoring the moment. His armor resembled that of a royal king, but it had been blackened as if by soot, with gleaming blood-red rubies and a crimson cloak. Heavy boots thudded as he stepped down from the dais, narrowly avoiding the bodies lying at his feet.

Caro widened her stance, readying the sword and shield as he strode toward her. She recalled Sakin's lessons. Deflect his strikes, be aware of how close he is at all times, avoid being backed into a corner, use a smaller weapon to her advantage.

Caro resisted the urge to brush her hand against the concealed dagger. She was certain it was still there, awaiting its time of need.

Zhelyas swung his sword in lazy circles, then pointed it at Caro. She poised defensively, keeping her distance, and they circled each other. Unlike her battle with Morfran, Caro kept her cool and waited for Zhelyas to strike first.

She didn't have to wait long. She lifted her shield to parry his downward strike, then slashed toward his stomach.

He arched his back to evade the sword and gave her a patronizing smile. "Ah, ah."

His triumph was short-lived as he realized the tip of the blade had carved a small nick in his armor. He conjured a fireball and thrust it at her, but she placed her shield in its path, and the magic bounced harmlessly off.

"Weapons won through valor, false king," Caro taunted. "Sorcery enough to match against yours."

Zhelyas growled, and his eyes glowed. Upon the ground, one of the nobles moaned, and the tear in the metal was mended. Caro realized the victim was Malcolm, his life force being drained to feed the monster, and fury pulsed through her veins.

"An endless supply of energy." Zhelyas sighed, as if high from a drug. "The easiest way to deprive me would be to kill all of them first." He sneered, and Caro scowled back at him.

"Never! Not even if it means defeating you a hundred times."

"Your choice." He shrugged, then lifted his sword once more.

Their blades met in a furious dance. Zhelyas spun, slicing her upper arm, then kicked her clear across the room.

"Your Majesty!"

Zhelyas gestured, and Morfran was engulfed by red energy. "You keep out of this," he snarled. "The fugitive queen and I are having a private discussion. It's not polite to *interrupt*."

The magic forced Morfran to his knees, ankles and wrists bound by glowing red chains. Zhelyas gripped his hair, jerking his head back, then punched him in the gut.

Morfran doubled over, wheezing, his armor providing little protection against the magically enhanced blow.

"Now, where were we?"

Caro rose gingerly, pushing the pain and anger to the back of her mind, and turned her attention back to Zhelyas. "This is far from over."

Despite Caro's recent training, her stamina was no match for his, fueled by his hatred and the energy he drained from his living victims. She was tiring fast.

She glanced at Morfran, who stared back helplessly, straining against the fetters which bound him to no avail. Even his own magic could not cancel Zhelyas's.

But her sword could.

"Don't worry about me," Morfran said, reading her intent. "This is your battle, not mine."

"What did I tell you about speaking out of turn?" Zhelyas admonished with the air of one lecturing a small child. "You need to be taught some manners."

He grinned and held up his hand, clenching his fingers into a fist as Morfran screamed in agony. "I could have used an assassin of your talents. Pity you wish to join your wretched queen in the afterlife."

While his attention was diverted, Caro saw her chance. She dashed forward, pressing the shield to her shoulder and used it as a battering ram.

Zhelyas skidded backward, surprised by the impact. "Someone else needs a lesson in manners! I'm going to take my time with you, little queen!"

He leaped in the air, his sword raised high to deliver the killing strike.

"Don't—call—me—that!"

Caro braced herself, lifting the shield above her head as it met the shattering blow; then she dropped her sword.

In the blink of an eye, she retrieved the concealed dagger and thrust the blade beneath Zhelyas's chin.

He staggered, stunned.

Caro picked up the sword. With her last ounce of strength, she swung the blade down as hard as she could. It severed his pauldron and carved straight through his heart.

Zhelyas teetered a moment, his dead hand twitching by his side as he tried to drain strength from the nobles, but no amount of ill-begotten magic could heal such a fatal wound.

"No sin goes unpunished, Zhelyas."

His gaze registered brief confusion, then the ruby glow in his eyes faded, leaving only steel-gray, empty and lifeless. His mouth fell open but no sound came out, and his knees buckled beneath him as he fell upon the marble, his blood mixing with that of those he had slain.

The full weight of what she had done finally struck Caro, and she stumbled backward, shaking with the effort of wielding the sword. A hand steadied her shoulder, and she looked up to see Morfran, free of the binding chains.

"Though you have always been my queen, you are now once more the kingdom's sovereign ruler." He wrested the blade from Zhelyas's body and cleaned off the blood before sinking to one knee before her, the sword held in his outstretched palms.

She held it up to the light, which now streamed through the windows, dispelling the darkness. Was it really over? Or was she dreaming? It was as if a burden had been lifted, one she hadn't even realized was crushing her. In its place, a new feeling suffused her heart, one that had been buried for so long: hope for the future.

"What are your orders?" Morfran ventured, gesturing around the throne room, and Caro grimaced.

"This place will need a lot of cleaning before I set foot in it again. We should let the others inside so they can see to these poor people."

"And Zhelyas?"

Caro glanced disdainfully at his body. "Give him a traitor's burial."

Though it was called that, it was less a burial than a desecration. Denied funerary rights and the release of the soul to the heavens, the body would be chopped up into pieces and fed to ravenous beasts—doomed to dwell upon the earth in eternal suffering.

It was no less than he deserved.

Caro emerged from the castle with Morfran by her side. She was battered and bruised, but they could see the triumph in her eyes.

Luther gaped at her. "My queen," he said, kneeling and hanging his head in shame.

"General."

"You would still call me that? Even after all I've done?"

"To be afraid is not cowardice. I have learned that much. You ran rather than confront your fear, and even threw in with a man who became more of a tyrant than those you betrayed."

Caro softened her voice. "You have the rest of my reign to make amends and regain your honor."

"Yes, Your Majesty," Luther whispered.

"See to the nobles in the throne room. Gaius, go with him. They will be weak and may be injured. I'm returning to the villa, and I'm not setting foot in this castle until every vestige of Zhelyas's evil deeds is scrubbed clean."

Gaius nodded as he finished tying a loose bandage around her arm.

"Oh, and don't mind the ghouls in the hall," Caro added. "They're all quite dead."

Blue Moon

Upon their return, Caro gathered everyone in the foyer of Vittorius's villa.

"Are you sure...?" Ines murmured.

"We've only just begun to know each other," she whispered back, her voice soft with affection. "Please stay with me."

Ines gave a gentle smile. "I would wish for nothing more."

Caro took a deep breath, then led Ines to the center of the room. "Everyone, may I introduce Princess Ines—my half-sister."

Gaius's jaw dropped, and there was a chorus of disbelieving looks and whispers. Vittorius, who had uncovered this fact, bowed low, and the others followed suit. Ines shifted her feet, visibly flustered by the attention.

"Sister?" Morfran blinked, glancing between Caro and Ines.

"I'm sorry I kept it from you. I didn't want to face my past until recently," Ines admitted. "I guess in that, we were more alike than we thought."

She shrugged, and Caro squeezed her hand. "I hope you don't hate me."

"I could never hate you, Ines," Morfran reassured her. "You were my trusted companion and confidante, but you always seemed so lonely. I couldn't be happier, Your Highness."

He kissed her hand, and she smiled, tears sparkling in her eyes.

Bury the Dead

Her heart melancholy with the truth she had been seeking for so long, Caro slowly mounted the steps to her parents' mausoleum.

The last time she had been here, she had recited the eulogy to those gathered, attempting to keep her composure and hide her grief. It seemed so long ago.

Caro entered the building and made her way to the sepulcher. She stood there a moment staring at the marble coffin, frozen in time like her recollection of them, then lifted her hand and placed a flower—a single violet promethia, the symbol of pledges and promises kept.

"Forgive me. I could not fulfill my vow and deliver vengeance upon your murderer, but I do not feel as if I have failed you, for I now know it was done for my sake, to stay your own hands."

A silent tear splashed upon the marble floor. "Even so, I can't reconcile the memories of my loving parents with the people who would have sacrificed me to gain the power of Aryama's temple, but I suppose it doesn't matter anymore. The past cannot be undone. I can only look to the future, and I promise I will make you proud."

She closed her eyes in prayer. "Let this circle of death be ended, and may your souls rest in peace."

Once Caro had reclaimed her throne, King Farangis of Drusus was eager to support her, and assisted with the return of her citizens from the refugee camps. Now, the majority were once more settled in the capital, looking to her for guidance.

Gerrin and Yanric had been awarded with medals of bravery for their part in the resistance, as well as those involved in establishing the coalition on behalf of the oppressed.

Of the thirty-two nobles she had discovered in the throne room that day, three had died from their wounds and the energy which had been drained from them. The remaining twelve dead included four servants, seven guards, and the first unfortunate nobleman to feel Zhelyas's wrath. Caro had sent handwritten letters of condolence to each of their families. The rest had survived, but her heart ached for the loss. Now, it was time to commemorate that loss.

"For all those I was unable to save, may this memorial serve as a testament to their bravery and courage," Caro began. "May we never forget the lessons these events have taught us. We must strive to be open and transparent, and not let the fear of the past fester in our hearts. Tell your children what has passed, and your children's children, so it is never forgotten. Then look forward to the future and know it is peaceful and free."

She inclined her head, and Luther pulled the cord, unveiling the statue which was to be the new centerpiece of Town Square.

There were murmurs of awe as the citizens gazed upon the magnificent sculpture. A giant winged lion, as seen on the royal crest, stood with its wings outstretched, symbolizing freedom. Beside it was an eagle to symbolize valor and a scorpion to symbolize fidelity, as in the ancient tale, yet not in conflict but brotherhood.

Caro descended from the rostrum and reverently laid a wreath of promethia upon the monument before rising and turning once more to her subjects. "In the wake of this tragedy, let us also remember the power of kindness and charity. So much evil was wrought here, but in my quest to defeat it, I found comrades from all walks of life in every corner of this fair country. They stood by my side despite insurmountable odds, and I could never have done this without them. I encourage all of you to look at your neighbors and see them not as strangers—but as companions, kinsmen, and fellow Artemisians."

A joyous cry rose up, and a shower of rose petals blanketed the square. Gazing at the adoring faces of her beloved people, Caro's heart was finally at peace.

Weather the Storm

Eight months. That was how long Caro's mission had taken her, from fleeing her castle under the cover of darkness, to emerging triumphant having reclaimed her throne.

The coronation followed a mere month after the battle's end, but the majority of it had been coordinated before the coup, so there was little else to do but perform the ceremony itself.

The resident nobles, most of whom had recovered from their own ordeals, were in attendance, and Radella beamed proudly to finally see all her planning come to fruition. Luther stood at her side along with his stoic mother Takaria, who had finally reconciled their differences. He had worked diligently to cleanse the palace of Zhelyas's taint—as if doing so could purge the guilt from his soul—and once more, the throne room was white and pristine, the polished marble gleaming.

Caro sat upon her throne in a resplendent gown of pale green and gold. A fur-trimmed cloak draped from her shoulders and a heavy chain of office hung around her neck. The sides of her still-short hair were braided, while the rest was pulled back and pinned with a net of pearls.

She had chosen to discard the ruby crown which Zhelyas had soiled, and so she had commissioned a new one to be made. It now rested upon her head, decorated with emeralds and moonstones matching the shield and sword mounted upon the wall behind the dais, with the small viridian crystal set at its center.

The nobles and military had reaffirmed their pledges of allegiance, with the notable exception of Oswin, who had been stripped of his rank for his cowardice. Those soldiers who had been cruel to Caro during her stint at the garrison had been demoted, and Luther was keeping a stern eye on them as he paid penance to his wronged queen. Stelian, newly promoted to commander, looked resplendent in his uniform, and Caro couldn't have been prouder of her former bodyguard.

After the ceremony, the lesser aristocrats were dismissed from court. Now only the higher nobles remained, Ezalia, Vittorius, Ezekiel, and Alenard among them. In attendance were also the rest of her traveling companions.

"Commander Morfran," Caro said regally.

He stepped forward, kneeling at the foot of her throne.

"You swore once that when this was all over, you would tell me the truth which has been hidden and reveal your identity. If you serve me, I charge you to do so now."

He bowed his head and nodded.

"You are my dearest and most trusted friend," she added kindly. "Let there be no more secrets between us."

"Yes, Your Majesty." With shaking hands, he reached up and unfastened the strap of his mask, letting it slip to the floor.

He met her gaze and bright blue eyes stared back, genuine and clear, unshadowed for the first time. The scar from an old burn marred his right cheek. It must have been agonizing when it was fresh. Even so, his face was still handsome, and a twinge of recognition flashed in Caro's mind.

"Who are you?" she asked.

Morfran took a deep breath before saying the name which, by his own admission, he had not spoken for ages. "I am Prince Francis of Drusus."

"Prince Francis?" Gaius repeated. "But he hasn't been seen for years, not since—"

"It was the celebration of my ninth birthday." Caro mused. "A boy a little older than I spoke to me in the garden. I was so lonely. Even though it was my party, nobody wanted to play with me. He cheered me up with a warm smile and a dance beneath the stars that sparkled like his blue eyes."

Morfran's face was lined with sorrow. "After the festivities, I returned home, but my carriage was accosted along the way and I was captured by brigands. I discovered only recently it was your uncle who engineered my kidnapping. He didn't like the attention I paid to the princess—whom he wanted for himself."

He spoke the last part in a low voice, since Arvind's depravity was not widely known. "For four years I was enslaved, and this wound came from my captors during that time. I escaped and found refuge with the Sharir, who took me in and trained me."

"Is there any proof of this?" Ezalia inquired.

"Here are his credentials."

"Amanita?" Morfran murmured.

They turned to see an old woman, who seemed to materialize out of nowhere.

"Credentials?" Caro repeated, and gestured for her to approach.

Amanita hobbled forward on her cane, a sly grin upon her craggy face. She handed a dagger to Morfran, and Caro recognized it instantly.

Morfran held it reverently, then slid his nail beneath the leather binding and snapped it. He unwound the wrapping, revealing jewels and gold beneath. Diamonds and sapphires studded the handle in a pattern resembling the dignified head of a unicorn. Caro could hardly mistake an heirloom from the royal house of Drusus.

"Is it true?" she whispered.

Morfran nodded. "From that moment we met as children, I have wanted nothing more than to serve you and see you become a great queen. I regret that fate forced my hand and led me to take away something you cherished. I will always bear that guilt, but now you know the truth."

He hung his head as if fearing her answer.

Caro rose, reaching out her hand, and Morfran kissed her ring. She stroked his cheek gently with the other, the scarred skin rough and uneven beneath her fingertips. "I have grown to care for you deeply during this journey and the trials we shared." She smiled, her heart swelling with emotion. "It delights me that destiny has seen fit to grant me the chance to make my feelings known—for as a prince, you are a suitable consort for a queen."

He gazed up at her, eyes wide with wonder.

"However, I do not want to hear your answer from Prince Francis who is dead, but Commander Morfran who is before me now."

He blinked away unshed tears and pressed his cheek to her palm, then rose and held her hands in his own. "I, Morfran, by the status bestowed upon me by my lifelong rank as Prince of Drusus, consent to marry you, Queen Caro of Artemisia." He smiled, softening the stiff formality of his words. "I am now free to admit my feelings as well... Caro."

Caro beamed as he used her name for the first time.

She turned to Khalil. "I am afraid I will be unable to fulfill your mother's wish, as it seems I am otherwise engaged."

She winked up at Morfran, who grinned at her pun.

Khalil shrugged and glanced at Veena, who stood nearby wearing a shy smile of her own. "I will pass along your regrets, Your Majesty, but I think she will accept it with grace."

"Well, I never imagined," Ezalia said, tears of joy brimming in her eyes, "that fate would bring you two together."

"It brought us together," Alenard pointed out fondly.

Caro squeezed Morfran's hand, conveying her unspoken emotions through the simple caress.

Ezalia and Alenard were reunited; Stelian had confessed his affections for Lottie; and Khalil had saved Veena in more ways than one. As an earl, Gaius was of high enough birth to be wedded to the newly-revealed Princess Ines, in whom he had found a fitting partner. Caro couldn't be happier that all her friends had found love—and now she had as well.

Following the revelation and Caro's proposal, which had been witnessed by all gathered, an official announcement of their engagement was released, bearing the official royal seals of Artemisia and Drusus, granted by the bewildered king of that country when he received the news. In emerald wax was the sigil of twin winged lions bearing a crown; in blue, the proud head of a unicorn.

I, Queen Caro Amarynth, make known my intent to ally myself in marriage with Prince Francis Belliphor of Drusus, known hereafter as Prince Morfran Francis Belliphor, of his own will.

We are therefore engaged and shall be married one year hence, to restore the peace of this fair country and to cross the threshold of my eighteenth birthday, upon which I will be of age to wed.

I dearly hope all my loving subjects will join me in this moment of joy, promising the happiness of myself and the shared fortune of both realms.

Queen Caro Amarynth
Prince Morfran Francis Belliphor

"I—I can't believe it," Farangis said. "My little brother, I never thought I would see you again." As King of Drusus, he had been invited to the coronation, and was stunned at the revelation of their engagement. "Why did you never let us know you were still alive?"

Morfran shook his head. "I'm sorry, brother, but I couldn't bring myself to. I was no longer the innocent boy you remembered, and I was ashamed."

"I can't say I quite understand, but you evidently suffered much. I'm just relieved to find you safe." His voice cracked with emotion and he embraced Morfran tightly, who hugged him back after a brief moment. Two brothers reunited after a lifetime of sorrow.

Farangis seemed to recover his stoicism and nodded respectfully. "Queen Caro, I believe our parents would have been overjoyed at the union of our two kingdoms."

"I am grateful for the aid you provided my people during these uncertain times," she replied, "and I look forward to a prosperous future for both Drusus and Artemisia."

"As do I."

Caro smiled at her soon-to-be brother-in-law. Upon his robe, he wore a silver brooch depicting a unicorn inset by diamonds and sapphires—unmistakably one of the Drusian crown jewels, matching Morfran's dagger, which he now wore proudly. With dark hair prematurely streaked with silver, he bore little resemblance to his brother, except for his eyes, which were the same vibrant, gentle blue.

Under Gaius's strict observation, Malcolm had been permitted to attend the ceremony despite his injuries, and Andrine crooked her arm in his as they bowed to the new royal couple.

"Your Majesty. I hope you find peace and joy together."

"Thank you, Earl," Caro said. "I heard how you sought to protect everyone from the usurper's rage, and even helped the citizens escape the capital. I am in your debt."

Malcolm appeared overcome by her praise. "I did my duty, my queen. I had faith you would come for us, and it was rewarded."

"I am thankful nonetheless. Now, you should sit down before Gaius comes over to give you a scolding," Caro teased, and Malcolm smiled.

"Take care of my cousin, Your Highness," Andrine added to Morfran. "She is precious to me and this country."

Morfran nodded at the use of his former lofty title, once more reinstated. "You have my sincere promise, Countess."

The royal couple moved on to exchange a few words with the other nobles. Caro paused before Diascia and Arcus.

"Lady Diascia, I heard what happened to your sister, Lady Lobelia. Please accept my condolences."

Diascia nodded numbly. "Thank you, Your Majesty. Lebby was disillusioned, but I loved her."

"I want you to know you are always welcome in Artemisia, and in my court. I never want you to feel like you're a stranger."

Diascia's cheeks blushed, and her pinky entwined Arcus's. "I've finally found a happy life for myself, and I'm pleased to be allowed to remain here in your beautiful country."

Arcus gazed affectionately at Diascia as she curtsied. "When you find the one you love, you know right away, don't you?" he mused, and Caro smiled up at her betrothed.

"I like to think so, though sometimes it takes a while to arrive at that conclusion."

She and Morfran approached several of Malcolm's co-conspirators next to express appreciation for their efforts on behalf of the Crown. Rudo had escaped Zhelyas's scourge, as had the tragically blinded Nefion. He stood before Caro, a blue silk scarf wrapped around his eyes, a sleek cane in his hand.

"Lord Nefion," she began, her voice suffused with remorse. "I am deeply sorry for what transpired during my absence."

"Please don't be, Your Majesty," he replied, shaking his head, and the ends of the scarf swayed with the motion. "It was my own stubborn pride. I lost my sight and nearly lost my friend, which I would have regretted more." He smiled at Rudo, who stood by his side.

"After meeting your serene sister, the princess, I no longer feel that being blind is such a bad thing. Perhaps I see more clearly now than I did before." He shrugged. "Besides, I am still able to fulfill my duties. Now that Earl Dahl has taken over the former prince's responsibilities, he has nominated me as Royal Officer in his stead." He bowed low, one hand resting upon his cane for support, the other tracing the blue enamel crest pinned to his collar.

"I will be relying on you, Lord Nefion," Caro said gently, touched by his solemn words.

Looking around, she spied a lone black-clad figure in the corner, and he tipped his head as they drew near.

"My queen," Jabez said politely. Though still dressed entirely in black, he appeared to have made an attempt to be less austere, with limited success.

"I'm glad you could come, Jabez."

"It is strange how destiny has its quirks. I am pleased for you both."

"And what of you?" Caro inquired.

"Alas, I am a wretched old bachelor," Jabez quipped, though his eye strayed to Fatima, a warrior of the Omaira clan with titian hair.

Caro smiled knowingly. "Well, I hope your journey was worthwhile."

"Have no fear of that," Jabez assured her. "I am honored to be counted among your acquaintances, and to have been of assistance in reclaiming your rightful crown."

She tipped her head in acknowledgement, then spotted her sister across the room.

Ines was radiant, wearing a gown of deep violet silk, a gold and amethyst diadem sparkling in her honey-blond hair. Gaius, her escort, was dapper as always—although he kept getting distracted, one eye twitching as his patients casually milled about.

"You look lovely," Caro said fondly when she reached them.

"Thank you, sister. And now you and Morfran, I'm absolutely delighted. I would never have imagined—back at the garrison, you two were so contentious." She gave a puckish grin. "But perhaps that was indicative of your feelings all along."

Morfran chuckled. "I can't deny that."

"How are you finding it at the palace?" Caro asked.

"It's a bit of an adjustment, being waited on hand and foot," Ines admitted. She squeezed Caro's hands. "But there's nowhere else I would rather be."

Ebb and Flow

A year passed in the blink of an eye, and the wedding was held on the first day of summer, a lavish affair with delegates from all the realms. It was like a dream, and Caro's heart fluttered in her chest as she and Morfran stepped to the altar.

Caro wore an ivory dress with tiers of lace ruffles, adorned with white roses and purple promethia blossoms for her fidelity to her country and groom. A lace veil cascaded to the floor, where it pooled elegantly at her feet. Upon her head sat the emerald and opal crown, the viridian crystal glinting in the candles' glow and the light streaming through the tall windows.

Morfran's black suit was buttoned up to the neck, with a deep blue velvet cloak emblazoned with the crest of Drusus and an embroidered sash draped over one shoulder, and a golden alstroemeria bloom upon his breast, symbolizing devotion and the friendship of their two countries. The jeweled heirloom dagger hung from a silver belt, matching his ever-present mask.

"Queen Caro Amarynth, Regnant Queen of Artemisia, and Morfran Francis Belliphor, Prince of Drusus, you come here today to pledge yourselves to the sanctity of marriage. All those gathered shall witness your exchange of vows to serve as a testament to this commitment," the officiant began formally. "Know now that since your paths have crossed in this life, you have formed eternal bonds. As you seek to enter this state of matrimony, you shall declare your intent before these witnesses. The vows made today are ties that shall bind and strengthen your union. Do you seek to commit to this ceremony?"

"Yes," Caro said clearly.

"Yes," Morfran said likewise.

"Take each other's hands."

Caro and Morfran joined hands, crossed over in the space between them.

"These are the hands that will love and cherish through the years, for a lifetime."

Ezalia stepped forward with a blue ribbon and draped it over their hands.

"These are the hands that will wipe tears from your eyes, both tears of sorrow and tears of joy."

Gaius stepped forward with a yellow ribbon and draped it over their hands.

"These are the hands that will comfort you in illness and hold you as you struggle through difficult times."

Vittorius stepped forward with a green ribbon and draped it over their hands.

"These are the hands that will give you support and encourage you to chase your dreams. Together, everything you wish for can be realized."

Khalil stepped forward with a red ribbon and draped it over their hands.

"Queen Caro, will you be Prince Morfran's faithful partner and constant companion? Will you share in his laughter and his burdens? Will you share in his pain and seek to alleviate it? Will you seek to cherish him and dream together to create new prospects and hopes for this marriage?"

"I will."

"Prince Morfran, will you be Queen Caro's faithful partner and constant companion? Will you share in her laughter and her burdens? Will you share in her pain and seek to alleviate it? Will you seek to cherish her and dream together to create new prospects and hopes for this marriage?"

The vows were the same for any wedded couple, be they peasant or noble, but the burdens and strife were all the more real as the husband of a queen. The microseconds seemed an eternity as Caro waited for Morfran's answer.

"I will," he said without hesitation.

The officiant took the four ribbons and tied them together. "And so the bindings are made."

He stepped back, and Morfran and Caro looked into each other's eyes. Morfran still wore the silver mask, and she would not ask him to do otherwise—but she could see the love reflected in its shadowed depths.

"When you love someone, you do not love them all the time in exactly the same way, from moment to moment, for that were impossible," Caro began softly. "It is a lie to even pretend to, and yet we have so little faith in the ebb and flow of life and of love. We leap at the flow of the tide and resist the ebb, as if it will never return.

"Yet we must accept these tides of life and hold on to what is most dear, for the only continuity in life, as in love, is fluidity and motion. I cannot say that life will never change, but with you by my side, I can face whatever comes, no matter what it might be." Her words hinted at the strange complexity and uncertainty of their journey, and the feelings that had blossomed when fate led them to be together again.

Morfran's eyes glistened. "Love is never looking back to what was, in nostalgia or regret, nor forward to what might be in dread or anticipation, but by living in the present and accepting it as it is now. Though the future may not be certain, neither expectation nor hope shall distract me from the peace which I have found in the safe harbor of your love."

Caro swallowed back her emotion, as he was clearly referring to the pain he had suffered as a child and the tragedy which connected their fates. That he found solace in her presence, enough to fill the hole in his heart, was more than she could ever hope for.

The vows complete, the officiant stepped forward once again. "Queen Caro and Prince Morfran, as your hands are bound together, so your lives and spirits are joined in a union of love and trust. The bond of marriage is not formed by these cords, but by the vows you have made. Above you are stars, and below you is earth. Like the stars, your love should be a constant source of light; and like the earth, a firm foundation from which to grow.

"May these hands be blessed this day. May they always hold each other. May they have the endurance to remain strong during the storms of stress and the dark of disillusionment. May they remain tender and gentle as they nurture each other, and be healer, protector, carer, and guide."

The officiant then presented the rings, two bands of silver and gold entwined. "The circle of the ring symbolizes eternity. It came from the raw elements and was transformed. Love is like that, for it comes from humble beginnings. Like these rings, it is purified, shaped, and polished into something which can never be torn asunder. These rings seal the vows you have made, an eternal and binding promise."

Morfran slipped the ring upon Caro's finger, careful not to dislodge the ribbons, and Caro did the same, her hand trembling.

"Queen Caro Amarynth and Prince Morfran Francis Belliphor, on behalf of all those present, I pronounce you married," the officiant declared. He removed the cords as Caro and Morfran unclasped their hands so as to leave the knot intact. "You may seal your vows with a kiss."

Caro smiled shyly up at Morfran and entwined her fingers in his. Due to her rank, she could not express her elation with as much fervor as she wished, but he leaned over so she wouldn't have to stand on tiptoe—hardly a queenly posture— and kissed her demurely. She could feel the heat of his kiss and looked forward to when they might further explore their affections for one another.

They turned to the audience, who rose from their seats and all bowed low, then erupted in thunderous applause.

Caro and Morfran took their honeymoon in Agassey. Surrounded by the beautiful landscape of the rolling green hills and the highlands beyond, it filled her with a sense of peace and tranquility. Despite the tragedy which had occurred there, Caro's memories were of dancing with Morfran at the ball, safe in his arms, her heart filled with delight. It was the first time, perhaps, she had realized she was falling in love with him.

Morfran squeezed her hand as the carriage pulled up to Ezekiel's estate, and she knew he was sharing the same fond recollection.

"Grandfather," Caro said warmly as she stepped out of the carriage, and he genuflected before embracing her, the walls of propriety crumbling at their shared joys and sorrows.

Morfran, now his superior as prince consort, nonetheless bowed respectfully to the grand duke. "Your Grace. Thank you for welcoming us once more to your lovely home."

"It is an honor, Prince Morfran." Ezekiel bowed in equal respect and smiled, his former enmity for his new grandson-in-law—forgotten.

One of Caro's first acts after restoring stability to her country was to commission the restoration of the opera house. It would take many years before it would be returned to its former glory, but enough had been reconstructed to hold a special performance at her request: *Gisela and Darim*.

Caro passed by a portrait of Mavella in the hall, much like she had before. The original, of course, had been lost to the flames, but Ezekiel had donated another from his private collection. In this one, the grand duchess wore a gown of shining jade, her dark brown hair upswept with a few loose curls escaping to frame her radiant face. Her sapphire eyes stared out from the painting, and she seemed to be gazing benevolently down at them.

"This was your grandmother?" Morfran inquired, coming to stand beside her as they waited for the performers to take the stage. "I see the resemblance."

"She died when I was little, but I feel as if she has guided me here. Is that strange?"

"Not at all, since both Lady Ezalia and the grand duke have been such strong influences in your life."

Somehow Morfran understood her, even those things she had difficulty putting into words. "I'm reminded of why I married you," Caro quipped.

"Is that all?" he replied glibly. He still wore the mask, but she saw only his sincere blue eyes and kind smile. Illusions no longer stood between them.

"Pardon me, Your Majesties, but the opera is about to begin," Ezekiel said with a small chuckle at their newlywed flirting.

Morfran offered his hand. "May I, my queen?"

Caro had seen the opera many times, but never had it resonated so strongly. A tale of forbidden romance, passion, and duty—she could now truly empathize with the characters.

Gisela sang the final aria as Darim stood beneath her balcony, reminiscing upon their nights spent together, and the lyrics thronged in Caro's heart.

The love we shared was like the petals of a desert flower, never to wilt away,

Yet it was a dream, one which we held but for a short time, like sand slipping through our fingers.

As the sleep of night gives way to day, so too must we wake from our dreaming,

But we'll always remember when we lay in love's embrace, beneath the starry sky.

She closed her eyes, the strains of the haunting melody echoing through the silent halls.

Epilogue

Caro lay upon the bed, her back propped up by pillows as she read.

Morfran entered, peeling off his cloak and jacket. Instead of black, he now wore only white, and Caro thought he looked even more dashing.

"What are you reading?" he inquired as he sat on the bed and slipped off his boots.

"*The Desert Prince*," Caro replied sheepishly. "It really is quite a *naughty* book."

"Don't you be getting any ideas," Morfran teased, and Caro giggled at his mock reproach.

"Not a chance, love."

Morfran snatched the book from her hands and sent it sailing across the room.

"Hey, I was reading that," Caro protested with a laugh as he tugged the pillows out from beneath her head and bent over for a kiss.

She raised her hands to his face. "Won't you take it off, even when we're alone?"

"Are you sure you want me to? It's not pretty."

Caro reached up and lifted the mask aside, stroking his scarred cheek. "*I'm* not pretty. Your face bears the proof of your heart, and that makes you captivating in my eyes."

Morfran leaned close until their noses were almost touching. "You're right, Caro. You're not pretty—you're beautiful. Your courage and conviction shine like a radiant beacon. And I love you."

They were husband and wife, prince consort and queen, and she couldn't wait to begin their new life together, with the peace they had forged side by side.

She pulled him into a kiss, his lips soft and yielding, and all the events that had transpired, the pain and suffering, the guilt, sorrow, and regret—dissolved, as a shadow vanishes upon the dawn.

~ The End ~

Acknowledgements

Amy Elmore, without whom this book would not be so beautiful and polished.

And all the people who encouraged me on my writing journey.

Yvonne M Thompson

Computer programmer by day, author by night, Yvonne papers her cubicle with sketches of her characters. She writes fantasy with dashes of intrigue, mystery, and romance, and her dreams are often a source of inspiration for her stories. She lives in Canada with two mischievous cats who are constantly vying for her attention. Dauntless is her debut novel.

You can find her on social media as @ladytevish.